THE MACINNESS LEGACY

TO
TOUCH
THE SKY

JULIE MOFFETT

ZEBRA BOOKS
Kensington Publishing Corp.
http://www.kensingtonbooks.com

To my grandmother,
Winifred B. Braden,
for always being there
and loving me no matter what.

And to my grandfather,
Don D. Braden,
for letting me sit on your lap,
for the wonderful smell of your pipe,
for singing to me of spearmint on the bedpost.
I miss you so much.

PROLOGUE

Salem, Massachusetts
All Hallows' Eve
October 31, 1752

Against the stifling gray of the sky, a thick shawl of mist descended on the small wooden cottage. A heavy chill hung in the air, weighing down the gnarled trees and nearly impenetrable brush that surrounded the structure like a fortress. No wonder only an adventurous few in Salem dared traverse the path to its door.

This evening the fog made the journey even more treacherous. The swirling mist was an unexpected and unwelcome guest, stirring eerie shadows past the young girl who stood trembling on the doorstep. She'd been here many times before, but tonight would be different.

Drawing the dense air into her lungs, she summoned her courage and pushed open the door. She stepped across the threshold and paused, letting her eyes adjust to the dim light. After a moment, she saw the old woman sitting in a rocking chair in front of the blazing hearth, her back to the door. The chair creaked as it moved back and forth, the sound creating a strong and compelling rhythm that pulsed like a heartbeat. A warm fringed blanket had been wrapped around the woman's thin shoulders, and a pale ribbon of moonlight threaded across her silver hair, making it shimmer. Although the sight seemed innocent enough, the girl felt a cold chill race down her spine.

"Come in, my child," the woman said suddenly. " 'Tis time for me to tell you a tale of witches, magic, and power gone astray. It's not a story for the fainthearted or weak, but those who are pure should not be afraid. Dare you to enter?"

She hesitated only a moment before stepping farther into the room, her heart pounding and her palms damp. There were no candles ablaze, no light except that provided by the flickering fire. Reverently she approached the rocking chair and stood directly in front of the old woman.

She managed not to flinch when the woman reached out a gnarled hand and grasped the hood of her cloak, pushing it off her head. Her copper-colored hair spilled onto the woman's hand, the reflection of the fire dancing off the heavy mass of curls. The woman fingered a few of the strands and then lifted her gaze.

"Remove your cloak and sit, Hannah," she instructed quietly. "The day of reckoning cometh with your passage into womanhood."

Hannah nodded, although she did not fully understand. For all her three and ten years, she'd been preparing for this moment. But now that it had come, she feared she hadn't prepared enough. Carefully she removed her cloak and knelt by the rough skirts of the seated matriarch.

"Do you understand why you have been summoned?" she asked.

"Aye, Grandmama. 'Tis the day of my birth."

"And 'tis also Samhain, a time of reflection and a time to honor the ancient ones who came before us. We must all contemplate the wheel of the year and recognize our part in the eternal cycle of life. Tonight you shall learn of your destiny."

Hannah felt her pulse quicken but kept her expression

calm. Gently she rested her head on her grandmother's bony knee. The old woman stroked her hair quietly for a moment.

"Have you fear of what you will hear, Hannah?" she finally asked.

Hannah studied her grandmother's face. Though her skin was translucent and wrinkled, the cheekbones were delicately carved and proud. Remarkable emerald eyes, both mysterious and intelligent, peered at her, sharp and assessing.

"Aye, I'm afraid," Hannah freely admitted, linking fingers with her grandmother and marveling at the strength she felt there. "But I shall not let it command me."

As soon as she'd crossed the threshold of the cottage, she had a feeling that she'd already lived through this night. It unsettled her because much of what had already been said and done this evening, she'd relived many times over in her dreams.

In one such dream, she sat in front of a blazing hearth at the feet of her grandmother, just as now. Except then, the fire was a malevolent force, hissing and issuing a thick, writhing smoke. As she watched, paralyzed in horror, the flames would swell into a grotesque beast that opened its fiery, gaping jaws, intending to devour her whole. She would awaken screaming, her bed gown soaked and her entire body shaking. Even now, the thought of it caused her to tremble.

"Fear is natural," her grandmother replied, nodding in approval. "Become acquainted with it and then use it to sharpen your skills."

Hannah raised her chin. "I shall try. I am ready."

"Aye, I know, my child. I would not have called you here if I were not confident of that." She leaned back in the chair and began rocking again. "Tonight I shall tell you the tale of our people. At last you will understand who you are."

Hannah's heart began to beat faster. "I . . . I want to know. I must know."

"Aye, you must," the grandmother agreed, exhaling a deep breath and closing her eyes. She was silent for so long, Hannah feared she had fallen asleep. Still, she dared not speak.

After several minutes had passed, Hannah suddenly heard a strange hissing sound behind her. Startled, she turned her head to see the flames in the hearth rising higher, leaping and dancing crazily. Her breath caught as images of her dream flooded back. She opened her mouth to speak, but no words came forth.

"Face your fear," her grandmother murmured, reaching out to grip her hand so that Hannah could not move away.

Terror cloaked her as the flames shot out of the hearth, singeing the corner of her gown and licking at her with what seemed to be a long, fiery tongue.

"I do not know what to do," Hannah cried out in trepidation. "Help me, Grandmama."

"You must face your fears alone. See your destiny."

"I don't know how."

"You must concentrate."

The fire licked out again, this time catching the hem of her gown. Swallowing a scream, Hannah beat it out with her hand. "I don't understand."

"You will. Now, close your eyes."

Hannah looked fearfully at the fire as the flames leaped higher and more menacing than ever. "But the fire will c-consume me," she stammered.

"You must trust me, child."

Hannah swallowed her fear, took a deep breath, and closed her eyes. The fire roared in her ears, but she held still, and after a moment her dread subsided. Doing as her grandmother requested, she concentrated on the blackness of her own eyelids.

Suddenly, the darkness began to twist and heave with

shadowy images. She saw the dim outline of a hooded body swaying from the gallows, and a red-haired woman nearby, sobbing. The threatening fire was temporarily forgotten.

"I see a body," Hannah whispered, her voice catching with horror. "Someone has been hanged. There is a woman nearby, watching and weeping. What has happened?"

"That is John Gardener," her grandmother answered softly. "John was convicted of witchcraft and sentenced to death. Priscilla, the woman watching, was his wife."

Hannah shuddered in revulsion. "How dreadful. I heard about the witchcraft trials from Mother."

"Aye, 'twas a shameful period in the history of our town and an affront to us personally. John and Priscilla Gardener are your ancestors."

Hannah snapped her eyes open in surprise. "My ancestors?"

"Aye. And now you must help them."

"Help them?" she repeated in astonishment. "But they are long dead, are they not?"

"But they do not yet rest in peace."

"What would you have me do?" Hannah whispered. "I am just a girl."

Her grandmother shook her silvered head. "You have never been *just* a girl, Hannah." And as if to confirm her words, the fire roared up again in the hearth, seeming to reach right out for Hannah. Swallowing a scream, she threw an arm across her face to shield herself from the heat.

"Quiet the fire," her grandmother commanded.

"I—I do not know how."

"Yes, you do. Concentrate. Feel the fire and bring it under your control. Use your mind."

Hannah breathed deeply, clenching her hands together in her lap. Slowly, tentatively, she reached out with her mind. "Ow!" she exclaimed, drawing back. "It burned me."

"Concentrate. This time deeply."

Hannah closed her eyes with fierce determination. This time the fire flared high and then settled down quietly in the fireplace. She opened her eyes in wonder.

"I did it!" she cried triumphantly.

"Aye, Hannah, for you have the power. As do I."

Hannah was silent for a moment. "Does this mean I am a witch, Grandmama?"

Amusement flickered in the eyes that met hers. "It means that you possess some very unusual powers, Hannah, as is so with all the women in our family. 'Tis naught to fear, but you must always use your power for good. And soon you must use it to set our family free."

"Free?" Hannah exclaimed.

Her grandmother focused her gaze on a spot above the fireplace and stared at it, a pensive shimmer in her eyes. "You must hone your craft, understand your inner power, and trust your instincts. You must never lose faith in yourself or your abilities. *Magica tua anima tua est.*"

"What does that mean?" Hannah asked, puzzled. Somehow the phrase was familiar to her, although she was quite certain she'd never heard it before.

"It means thy magic is thy will."

"My will," she murmured in response. "I shall endeavor never to lose faith, Grandmama."

"You will be sorely tested."

"I will be strong."

"I know, child. You are of Clan MacInness."

"Clan MacInness?" Hannah repeated in surprise.

"Aye, your Scottish heritage has given you great powers. But 'tis not without a dark side. You must have courage. Tonight I shall tell you a tale of two clans who were once united by a special and powerful gift before being ripped apart by lies, treachery, betrayal, and murder. Your destiny, my child, is the culmination of a long chain of events that began more than three centuries ago. You and your children will be the ones to face the Clan MacGow."

Hannah stirred uneasily, trying to absorb all that she had been told. "How do you know this?" she finally asked. "How can you know my future?"

The old woman smiled, the wrinkles on her face fading. For a brief moment, Hannah thought she could see the pretty young girl her grandmother must have once been.

"It is my gift, Hannah, and my curse. As it is yours and that of the children you shall bear."

A thrill of frightened anticipation touched Hannah's spine. "Tell me, I beg of you. Will I be successful in the tasks my destiny shall place before me?"

Her grandmother sighed deeply. "You will succeed and you will fail. I do not understand how, but that is what has been written."

"Written? By whom?"

"Destiny. Fate. Call it as you wish."

"I do not understand," Hannah whispered.

"You will, my child," the old woman replied, placing her hands over her granddaughter's and giving them a reassuring squeeze. "I promise, you will. Now, close your eyes and listen carefully to my tale. . . ."

ONE

Forty Years Later
Salem, Massachusetts
October 1792

The sea lured Spencer Reeves like a siren calling to her lover.

He smiled in response as his small vessel, a skiff named the *Rosemary*, swept atop the glossy waves, leaving Salem Harbor behind. A strong, whipping breeze blew across the water, carrying faint scents of sea salt and cod while a brilliant orange sky encompassed the New England coast in a spectacular sunset. He took a deep breath of air, lifting his face to the wind and embracing the stinging October chill.

"There's nothing like a sail on a brisk autumn eve, is there, Spence?"

Spencer turned to his friend Charles Harrington, who sat lounging back against the gunwale, his legs stretched out in front of him. "Nothing," he agreed. "It's the perfect end to an otherwise long day. All too soon we'll have to dock the skiff for the winter. But not yet."

Grinning mischievously, Charles pulled a small flask out of his breast pocket, popped it open, and took a long drink. He handed it to Jonathan Duttridge, the third member of their small crew, who took a deep pull and passed it to Spencer.

Spencer declined. "No. Someone has to remain in full control of his faculties in order to sail us back home and not on into Gloucester."

"Always the physician," Charles grumbled. "Must you be incessantly wed to your profession?"

"Only when I sail . . . and perform surgery, of course," Spencer said dryly. "I have no intention of going as far as Gloucester this eve."

Jonathan snorted in disapproval. "What would be wrong with a trip to Gloucester? I met a pleasant young lady there once."

"Pleasant, indeed," Charles said chortling. "Need I remind you she lives at a house of ill repute? I'm sure she'll remember you if you come calling again with coin."

Jonathan pursed his lips, and Charles snatched the flask from him, taking another swallow. "Come on, Spence, if you refuse to partake in the spirits, then let's see how fast this lady can go."

Rising to the challenge, Spencer adjusted the sail and angled it nearly into the wind. The skiff picked up speed, gliding deftly across the water.

As Salem became a dot on the horizon, Spencer felt the tension of the day release. He also had had a long, though productive day. His father had personally commended him on the excellent sutures he had made on the tiny hand of three-year-old Mary Brewer, and he had correctly diagnosed and treated old Sam Forsythe for a mild case of gout. His own confidence as a physician was growing daily, as was the trust of the patients he treated while apprenticing with his father. But as his patient list and the number of people depending on him grew, Spencer found that he recently spent more time worrying about his work and less time visiting with friends and reinvigorating his body and mind. Today he had decided to ignore those needs no more. He'd sought out his friends, and now they were all reaping the rewards of a revitalizing sail.

They chatted companionably until dusk deepened. Spencer slowed the skiff and lit the small lantern that sat wedged between two wooden planks at the front of the bow. The light cast ghostly shadows over the men.

"Take a look at that, would you?" Jonathan exclaimed, pointing toward land, where a few scattered lights blinked along the shoreline.

"It looks like a cottage," Charles commented with interest, coming to stand beside Jonathan. "How far are we from Gloucester?"

"A good distance yet," Spencer replied, squinting. "It's rather peculiar, but the structure seems to be neither in Salem nor in Gloucester, but somewhere in between."

"How odd," Jonathan murmured. "I didn't know anyone lived out this far."

They were silent for a moment before Charles said in a dramatic whisper, "That's because it doesn't house *human* inhabitants."

Jonathan sniggered. "Then just what does it house?"

"Oh, a small but malevolent coven of witches," Charles said. "Beautiful, alluring witches, but evil just the same. Spence, what do you think?"

Spencer watched the dim lights wink and glow in a fascinating pattern. Someone had placed candles in the windows, as if beckoning to strangers. For some unknown reason, a strange chill skittered up his spine, raising the hairs on his arms and the back of his neck.

"Frankly, I think we should beach Charles here," he said lightly. "Let him visit the cottage. Maybe the witches can cure him of his unremitting obsession with women."

"Ha!" Charles snorted, "That's one obsession I prefer not to be cured of, thank you. I rather think we should leave *you* there, Spence, so you can have a life outside your respectable but utterly tedious practice."

Spencer tipped his head. "Tedious or not, I assure you, my life is quite full. Besides, am I not partaking of some leisurely activity at this very moment? Although some might question if being with you two truly counts as leisure."

"Oh, it's leisure, all right," Charles answered, thudding back against the hull as the skiff picked up speed from a sudden gust of wind. "Is not our company much sought after in Salem? And are we not fortunate to have a lady such as the *Rosemary* at our disposal?"

Spencer grinned. "On the last point I shall not disagree."

"Speaking of ladies, Charles," Jonathan interjected while skillfully swiping the flask from Charles's grasp, "What's this I hear about you being caught with your hands up Anna Wendall's skirts?"

"It was an accident, I swear," Charles said, lifting his hands innocently. "We were taking a stroll when she tripped and toppled into my arms. Her considerable weight caught me off balance and we both fell to the ground. In my haste to help her up, I became entangled in her skirts. It's not my fault her derriere was exposed to several passersby. I've been told it was quite a spectacle."

"Her derriere, or your hands extracting themselves from her considerable flesh?" Spencer asked dryly.

"Very amusing," Charles said, pressing his hand in an exaggerated fashion against his chest. "You wound me by disparaging my intentions toward Mistress Wendall."

Jonathan chuckled. "That's a damn fine accounting of what happened, Charles, and I'd stand by it if I were you. Especially when word of the unfortunate incident reaches her father. After all, most of Salem knows that you are constantly on the lookout for dastardly ways to take a quick peek beneath the skirts of any young lady."

They all laughed and further debated the finer points of Anna Wendall's derriere until an abrupt gust of wind caused the boat to lurch to one side. Concerned, Spencer stood, gripping the mast.

"A storm seems to be brewing," he said as the wind began to whip furiously. "We'd better head back to Salem. Where in the hell did it come from?" He staggered toward the tiller as the vessel began to roll drunkenly from side to side.

"Would it not be more prudent to go on to Gloucester?" Charles yelled over the howl of the wind.

"If my calculations are correct, we are still about half-way between the two towns," Spencer shouted back. "And the storm seems to be coming more or less out of the north from Gloucester. If we head back for Salem, perhaps we can outrun it."

As Spencer reached the tiller, a jagged flash of lightning lit up the sky, leaving a trail of crackling sparks in its wake. Thunder boomed around them as the sky seemed to open up and rain poured down in untamed fury. His view of the shore and horizon rapidly diminished.

Spencer clung to the rail, his skin tingling, his breath coming in shallow, fast gasps. "I've got to put her into the waves or she'll break apart," he shouted. "Help me get her hard aport. Now."

Charles and Jonathan scrambled to aid him, but a wave crashed into the craft, slamming Charles's head into the mast. He nearly slid overboard, but Spencer dragged him back by the collar of his shirt and dumped him on the deck. Charles sat up, rubbing his skull. Thunder boomed again, this time so violently that even the skiff shuddered.

"Hell and damnation!" Spencer shouted as he fought with the tiller. His fingers slipped on the wood, and he narrowed his eyes against the onslaught of blinding rain.

Spencer knew at once they would never make Salem and were in imminent danger of capsizing.

"Look out!" Jonathan screamed.

Spencer glanced over his shoulder, his eyes widening at the enormous wall of water coming toward them. Before he could move, the wave slammed into them, crushing the boat like a toy. The skiff disintegrated beneath his feet, and the water reached up and yanked him violently under the white foam.

With barely a gulp of air in his lungs, Spencer flailed about, kicking hard against the undertow that threatened to drag him to his death. His right leg tangled in a rope, twisting his ankle and slamming it against something hard. Hot pain shot up from his foot along the right side of his body. In a moment of startling clarity, Spencer realized he was on the brink of death.

His last thought before blackness enveloped him was not one of despair, but of hope that at least his friends had made it to safety.

Gillian Saunders sat in front of the fire, reading one of her father's beloved medical journals. It was her favorite pastime and one she permitted herself at the end of every day when all the chores were done and everything was peaceful and comfortable in the cottage. Tonight the cottage seemed even cozier because of the storm raging outside. The rain was angry and thick, slashing fiercely against the walls and the roof. But her father had built the large structure with the finest woods and sturdiest beams. For twenty years, it had kept Gillian warm, dry, and safe within its sturdy, loving walls.

She glanced over to where her younger brother, Lemuel, sat on a thick woven throw rug near the hearth, whittling away on one of his carvings. He would agonize over every stroke, but his hand was deft and his finished product would no doubt be breathtaking. Gillian was fiercely proud of her brother's talent and would tell him so at every opportunity. But Lemuel was so modest that even the lightest praise made him uncomfortable.

Already nineteen, he was far more man than boy, with the shadow of a beard and the roughened and steady hands of a master craftsman. But she knew she would always be fiercely protective of him, considering him her responsibility, her charge.

Perhaps it was because he was so painfully insecure, Gillian thought sadly. Though how could he not be? His mind, so quick and lively, was trapped within a body barely larger than a child's and cruelly misshapened. Yet, as if to soften the blow, God had blessed him with the face of an angel: sky blue eyes, high cheekbones, a wide mouth, and a head topped with thick golden hair that curled softly about his ears. He was both astoundingly handsome and frightfully deformed. A study of opposites, some said, while others more cruel simply called him grotesque.

He must have sensed her gaze on him now, for he paused and met her eyes with a shy smile. "A penny for your thoughts, Gillian."

She smiled back. "I was just listening to the storm outside. The sea is raging tonight." She could hear the waves crashing against the beach. The cottage was but a short walk up from the water, and Gillian had long ago learned to recognize the moods of the sea. Now, she could imagine the waves dashing themselves mindlessly against the rocks, shooting up a column of white foam, mingling with the rain and drenching the rocky beach in a glorious and furious spray.

Lemuel took a sip of the hot, spicy cider from a pewter mug near him on the floor and observed his sister. "What are you reading?"

"An essay called 'Covington's Smythe's Common and

Uncommon Uses of Comfrey and the Native Ginger Root.' It was one of Father's."

Lemuel shuddered. "Not again. I thought you'd already read that one."

"Only once."

"Isn't that enough? Even Father couldn't bear to read it more than once. He said it was dreadful and tedious."

Gillian stretched out her legs. "It's not dreadful by any means. Tedious at times, yes. Mostly it's fascinating and rather complex. Botany is an important part of medicine. 'Twill take some time for me to fully understand it."

"I don't know why you bother with such now that Father is gone."

Gillian felt a stab of sorrow at the thought of their beloved father, dead three years now, and their mother, just six months gone. The grief was still too fresh, the pain of missing them not quite healed.

"It's a part of our livelihood now," Gillian quietly reminded him. "It's my herbs and medicines, as much as your carvings, that give us something to barter with in town."

Lemuel sighed. "I know. I wasn't criticizing. 'Tis just that you already know so much that it seems odd to me that you still quest for more knowledge in Father's books."

"Oh, there is so much I don't know, Lemuel. I'll never know as much as Father did. He knew more of herbs and medicines than anyone in all of Massachusetts."

Lemuel nodded. "Perhaps, but it seems a rather lonely pastime for a young woman. You should spend more time in Gloucester. You could make some friends and mayhap even meet a young man who would one day take care of you."

Gillian's mouth tightened. "I don't need to be taken care of."

"That's not what I meant."

"I know what you mean. I don't need a man," she replied firmly. "I have you."

Lemuel sighed deeply. "I know what you're doing, Gillian. You can stop trying to protect me. I am what I am, and I've accepted that. You shouldn't waste your life out here with me. Just because Father and Mother lived in isolation doesn't mean you must."

"I don't consider this isolation," she snapped. "It's my choice to stay here. Besides, why should I look for warmth and companionship among those who were so unkind to Mother and Father? What makes you think I'd even want to move to town?"

Lemuel tapped his chest. "Because I know it here in my heart. You're yearning to see the world beyond this cottage. You have an intellect and a curiosity just like Father. You were meant to be with people, Gillian. Not trapped in a cottage with a hideous creature like me."

"You are not hideous!" Gillian exclaimed, glaring fiercely at her brother. "That's truly an awful thing to say about yourself."

He reddened but lifted his chin determinedly. "You don't need to hide the truth from me any longer. I'm not a child. I know what the townsfolk think of me. I also know what it cost Father and Mother to take me in when they already had enough trouble of their own. I am a lot stronger than you think. I don't need you to coddle me anymore. I'm not afraid to be alone."

"You're not going to be alone, because I'm not leaving."

"Coward."

"On the contrary. I'm being practical."

Lemuel looked at her sadly and returned to his whittling.

Gillian sighed, resting the open book against her chest, and thought about what her brother had just said. It pained her to know that much of it had been the truth.

While she loved her brother deeply, he had been right—she was lonely. She had no friends in Gloucester. They were not welcome there and were barely tolerated during their brief visits to barter their goods. Those times were particularly painful for Lemuel, who was often the object of ridicule and contempt. Still, he refused to allow her to go into town alone, and as selfish as it was, Gillian was glad for his company.

The last time they were in town, she had noticed a young man staring at her. He was young and handsome in a reckless sort of way. He had caught her eye and winked at her, his gaze slowly traveling down her body. She had been shocked to feel her body respond with unexpected warmth in her stomach and a tingling in her breasts. She had looked away quickly, a deep blush staining her cheeks.

Her body's response both embarrassed and intrigued her. Scientifically, she knew what happened between men and women and understood the human body well enough to realize these were natural urges. Nonetheless, that she could not control hers was unsettling. Even worse, of late, the urges had manifested themselves in her dreams, where she imagined herself wrapped tightly in the arms of a faceless stranger. The dreams left her breathless, discomfited, and, if she were to be honest with herself, aching for human touch.

Exhaling a frustrated breath, she wiggled deeper into the worn armchair that had belonged to her father. She would do better not to think such thoughts. She would never depart the safety of the cottage, nor would she dream of leaving Lemuel alone. The cottage was their sanctuary. It was large and roomy, now even more so with just the two of them. Father had once been wealthy and had managed to maintain enough of his fortune to build the cottage using the best materials money could buy. There were four rooms in all—two rooms for sleeping and dressing, a large common room with a giant hearth, and a pantry area.

In the common room where they now sat, a kettle bubbled merrily above the fire, filled with the leftovers of their dinner of rabbit stew. The aroma wafted pleasantly throughout the cottage, soothing and familiar. A variety of dried flowers, plants, and herbs hung from the rafters, and a collection of pewter pots, plates, and cooking utensils had been arranged atop the mantle.

A handsome table of maple sat in one corner with four wooden chairs. She now sat in one of two large armchairs that were positioned near the hearth, a luxury her parents had relished. Since they had passed on, Lemuel refused to sit in them. A large armoire stood in another corner near one of the windows, containing linens, candles, and wicks.

She closed her eyes, permitting herself to doze comfortably. Life was comfortable and safe in their cottage. These were the kind of evenings she loved best.

TWO

Cold water pounded against Spencer's face, awakening him to the disorienting sound of crashing surf. He blinked, fighting off the vestiges of pain and confusion that clung to him. When his head was clear enough to think, he took mental note of his situation. He determined it was raining and that he lay flat on his back on a rocky and uncomfortable surface. His entire body was in agony. A deep, wet chill permeated his skin, and he shuddered uncontrollably. Grimacing, he tried to sit up, but his muscles were exhausted and would not obey.

Breathing deeply, he turned his head, trying to look around. He presumed he had miraculously made it ashore, but he had no idea whether Charles and Jonathan had also survived.

Peering up through the curtain of rain, Spencer thought he saw a dark shape hopping back and forth as if trying to keep warm.

"Charles?" he called out.

The shape knelt beside him, picking up his hand and squeezing it. "Thank God you're alive, Spence," Charles said. "We feared you'd expired on us."

Spencer grimaced. "Not yet, anyway. Is Jonathan all right?"

"Right here," Jonathan said, kneeling down as well. "You gave us quite a scare. I think you hit your head.

Charles pulled you the last few feet out of the water. You've been out for some time."

Spencer reached up to touch his forehead. It was tender and his vision was blurred. He wasn't sure whether it was from a head injury or the rain. "I seem to be in full control of my faculties, thank God, at least for the time being."

Gripping Jonathan's hand, he tried to sit up but felt his head spin. He tried moving his legs, but a vicious pain ripped through his right ankle. He swore furiously and then fell back to the beach.

"What is it, Spence?" Charles asked worriedly.

Spencer closed his eyes for a moment and flexed his leg, letting his years of physician's training take over. "I think I've broken—or, at the very least—badly hurt my ankle." There were possibly other injuries, perhaps internal, but he'd not go into that now. "Are you and Jonathan harmed?"

"We're a bit shaken," Charles said, wiping the rain from his nose. "My head hurts like hell, I've got a nasty lump on my forehead, and my left shoulder is throbbing, but I can walk, at least. Jonathan seems mostly unscathed. We are lucky we were rather close to shore when we capsized. What should we do, Spence?"

Spencer heard the desperation in Charles's voice and knew that without an imminent plan, hysteria, fear, and a deadly chill would unite to finish them off.

He had no idea where they were or what he could do to get them out of this predicament, but he'd be damned if he'd try to muster a plan while lying flat on his back in this undignified position.

Grinding his teeth and grasping Jonathan's hand, he struggled into a sitting position. The effort made him dizzy and nauseated. Turning his head slowly to the side, he retched up seawater several times. After he finished, he wiped his mouth with the back of his hand and tried to sound calm.

"First, we need to find some shelter. If we don't get out of this rain soon, the elements will finish what the sea did not."

"Shelter?" Jonathan said, his voice rising. "Where? We are stranded on a stretch of godforsaken shore."

Spencer peered up the dark, rocky beach, thankful that the rain seemed to be easing a bit. "How far from Salem do you suppose we are?"

Charles followed his gaze into the murky darkness. "Too far to walk in our condition, I fear."

Spencer rubbed his chin thoughtfully. "Well, if we came ashore close to where we were positioned when the storm hit, we may not be all that far from those mysterious lights we saw earlier."

"The mysterious lights!" Charles exclaimed. "I forgot all about them."

"But we don't know in which direction to head," Jonathan protested.

"South," Spencer said firmly. "Even if we don't find the source of those lights, eventually we'll run into Salem's wharves."

"We'd never make it to the wharves, and you're in no condition for a stroll down the beach," he protested. "None of us are."

"We don't have any choice," Spencer replied firmly. "We'll die if we stay out here in the open. Shelter is our primary concern now."

Charles nodded. "He's right, Jonathan. What should we do next?"

Spencer thought for a moment. He was a tall man, and his body weight would be a considerable drag on their progress, especially on Charles if he was nursing an injured shoulder. He made a quick decision.

"You two go for help and I'll wait here," he said calmly. "Pull me up under the shelter of those trees over there.

The rain should let up soon, and you'll be able to send someone back for me."

Charles frowned. "Like hell we will. We're not going to split up."

"He's right. I don't need to be a doctor to know that you'd die out here in no time," Jonathan interjected. "Charles is right. We must stay together. We're not leaving you, Spence."

"Don't be foolish," Spencer snapped impatiently. "I'm a good head taller than either one of you. I'll do naught but slow you down. You might not make it at all if you have to drag me along."

Charles grabbed Spencer's hand and squeezed it hard. "We're not going without you. If you want to waste time arguing about it, that's fine. But we're not changing our minds."

Jonathan nodded vigorously, rain dripping off his hair and cheeks.

Spencer blew out a deep breath between his teeth, annoyed by their stubborn refusal to listen to good sense, yet touched by their loyalty.

"All right, we go together, then," he said. "But you'll have to half carry, half drag me between the two of you. It won't be easy."

"We'll make it," Charles said firmly.

"You'll need to make a splint for my leg first," Spencer said. "See if you can find two sturdy pieces of driftwood."

Jonathan and Charles left him on the beach and scoured around the trees before returning with two pieces of wood. Jonathan ripped the sleeves off his shirt and used the material to help Spencer secure the splint to his leg.

"That should do it," Spencer said with a final tug.

Jonathan grabbed Spencer firmly beneath one arm, while Charles lifted him up under the other. Spencer gritted his teeth in pain as the two men shifted his weight between them.

"You all right there, Spence?" Charles asked, breathing heavily. "I'd offer you a swig from the flask, but unfortunately I no longer have it."

"I'm . . . fine," Spencer replied between clenched teeth, although at this moment, a swig from the flask would have been heaven. "Let's go."

As they staggered forward, Spencer forced his mind to ignore the pain and instead think of other more pleasant things like a glass of expensive brandy, a blazing fire in the hearth, and a thick wool blanket.

"Are you certain you're not that badly injured?" Charles asked him again worriedly. "I can't even tell if you're breathing or not, you're so quiet."

"I'm all right," Spencer lied, his teeth starting to chatter. "I'm just thinking."

"Of what?" Jonathan asked.

"Of things to keep a body warm."

"Like a soft and willing woman?" Charles offered.

"That would work."

Charles sighed. "Right now, the generously endowed body of Anna Wendall has a particularly strong appeal."

"God, yes," Jonathan piped up wistfully. "One could truthfully say her body is as full and welcoming as a warm summer evening."

"Make that a sweltering summer's eve, would you?" Spencer added.

Charles grinned, getting into the spirit. "Let us not forget her ample bosom and wonderfully round derriere."

"Christ, how long must we endure your debauched obsession with derrieres?" Jonathan snorted as they slogged along the rocky beach. "I much more prefer a slender waist and a wide, generous mouth."

Charles snickered and then gave Spencer a sidelong glance. "What's your preference in a woman, Spence?"

Spencer exhaled sharply, the pain starting to cloud his

thinking. He was barely hanging on to the last vestiges of consciousness as it was.

"Frankly, I don't care a whit about the shape of her derriere. Right now I'd give my soul to any woman with a warm blanket and a hot cup of broth."

A sudden pounding on the door sent Gillian springing to her feet, and her precious medical book tumbling to the floor. Lemuel rose as well, quickly reaching for the only weapon they had, an old sword that stood by the door—a far more ornamental piece than a useful one.

"Who goes there?" Lemuel called out in a deep voice without opening the door. His voice sounded steady, but Gillian noticed that his sword hand trembled slightly. She understood why; they rarely had visitors, and certainly never any at this late hour.

"We're in dire need of help," a male voice replied faintly, the sound not carrying well through the stout door and the howl of the wind outside. "We shipwrecked down the beach and are badly injured. We saw the light in your window and came. Please, we need your help."

Gillian moved to open the door, but Lemuel shook his head warningly. "Your voice is not familiar to me. Who are you?" he asked.

There was a shuffling near the door. "My name is Jonathan Duttridge. My two companions are Charles Harrington and Spencer Reeves. We are from Salem. Please, we can go no farther and will expire on your doorstep if you do not let us in."

Gillian moved closer to her brother. "Open it, Lemuel," she whispered. "They are injured."

"It might be a trick," he argued. "They may have come to harm us."

"For what purpose?" Gillian hissed back. "And on a night like this? It makes no sense."

"Anyone in Gloucester knows you'd open the door to help anything wounded, be it man or beast."

"Now you're being ridiculous."

"You are too trusting, Gillian."

"And you are too suspicious. Open the door, Lemuel. I'll not have three deaths on my conscience."

He stared at her fiercely for a long moment, but she did not back down. Finally, he drew the bolt and threw open the door. Stepping back, he held out the sword warily in front of him.

"Take care," he warned. "I am armed."

For a minute, Gillian could see nothing. The wind and rain rushed into the cottage with a fierce blast. Then, as it settled, she saw three men, wet and bedraggled, standing on the doorstep. Two of the men held a third propped between them. With a quick glance, Gillian saw the tall one in the middle was nearly unconscious and had a splint on his leg.

"God's mercy," she cried, lifting her skirts and rushing past Lemuel. Quickly she ushered them inside.

"Lay him down here," she ordered, moving Lemuel's carving tools aside and pointing to the thick rug by the fire. The two men gladly dropped their burden, and Gillian knelt beside the tall man, feeling his neck for a pulse.

In the moment her fingers touched his skin, she felt a hot jolt shoot through her that streaked clear to the bottom of her feet, causing her toes to tingle. Gasping in surprised shock, she released him.

"Is he dead?" one of the men asked fearfully.

She shook her head, shaken by the powerful sensations she had just experienced. "He's alive, but his pulse is faint. Make haste and help me get him out of these wet clothes."

When the men didn't answer, she glanced in dismay at them over her shoulder. They were not looking at her but were staring openmouthed at Lemuel, revulsion and pity evident in their expressions.

"He's a . . . dwarf!" one of the men exclaimed.

Like a wolf protecting her cub, Gillian barked, "I need your help, *now!*" Both men immediately jumped in surprise at the authoritative tone of her voice. The darkhaired man knelt down beside Gillian. He pulled off one of the man's boots with his right hand, wincing as he moved his shoulder. Gillian reminded herself to check on it later.

"I'm Charles," he told Gillian as he worked. "I'm sorry to inconvenience you this evening."

"Inconvenience us?" Gillian exclaimed in amazement. "Why, you are all near death. And you've injured your shoulder," she observed. Cautiously she touched his arm and he flinched in pain. This time there was no strange jolt of heat racing through her fingertips. She breathed in relief.

"I consider myself lucky," he answered. "Spence here is in much worse shape. He had to splint his own leg before he lost consciousness. Thank God he knew exactly what to do."

"He did?"

"Spence is a physician."

"A physician," Gillian murmured, looking down at her pale charge. He looked about five and twenty years of age. A jagged gash marred his left temple, but the cut was shallow and long ago had stopped bleeding. However, his pulse was faint. She was still hesitant to touch him after her initial jolt, but she steeled herself and reached out to touch him again. Another rush of heat surged through her, but this time it was soothing and strangely familiar.

"I know you somehow," she murmured without thinking.

"What did you say?" Charles said.

Blushing, she shook her head. " 'Twas naught but a foolish musing. Could you please lift him up? I'll remove his coat."

Charles obliged and she tugged off his wet coat, struggling with his soaking shirt.

"We'll need to remove the splint and cut off the other boot," she determined. "Lemuel, bring me one of your carving knives."

Lemuel handed her the knife and she quickly gave it to Charles. "If you would, please."

Charles nodded and sliced through the material holding the splint. Together they carefully removed the linen strips and the wood pieces. Charles then cut into Spencer's boot, ripping it up one side. He had nearly finished when he swayed, nearly toppling headfirst onto his unconscious friend.

Gillian reached out and caught him by his uninjured arm. "Please, Mister . . ."

"Harrington," he rasped. "But given our current circumstances, I insist you call me Charles."

"Well then, Charles, you and your friend need to get out of those wet clothes immediately and have something warm to drink. I'll tend to your friend here. Go on, now." She cast a glance over her shoulder at her brother. "Lemuel, show them where they can change out of their garments, and fetch some warm blankets."

Her brother didn't move and instead stood glaring mistrustfully at the two men. Gillian stood up, placing her hands on her hips.

"Lemuel, I assure you that they are in no condition to harm us. Please let them change and find some blankets. They will chill to death standing here in their damp clothes."

Lemuel scowled but reluctantly turned to do her bidding. "Follow me," he snapped, heading back to the bedroom.

Gillian sighed as the three disappeared. Returning to her patient, she set her lips determinedly and pulled the remaining boot from his foot. Next, she unfastened his drawstring trousers and, straddling his thick thighs, began tugging them down slowly and gently. Her cheeks burned as she pushed and pulled at them, careful not to look directly at his private area. But to her dismay, the material would not budge past his hips.

She readjusted her grip and yanked harder, mortified when her hand slipped and accidentally brushed his thigh. He shifted slightly and her cheeks flushed hotter.

"Sorry," she whispered even though she knew he could not hear her.

Taking a deep breath, she tried to calm herself. She watched as his mouth tightened and then relaxed in a fevered delirium. She had removed Lemuel's trousers a dozen times or more when he was ill or injured, and had done it quickly and efficiently. So, if it was such an easy task, why was she having so much trouble now?

It was *him*.

There was something about her patient that both unsettled and compelled her. He was somehow familiar even though she was certain she'd never met him. Puzzled, she stared at him as if he could solve the mystery. Although not breathtaking, he was ruggedly handsome, his cheekbones finely chiseled, his chin jutting and firm. His shoulders and chest were corded muscles, his stomach flat and tight. Unable to stop herself, she let her gaze travel down to where his pants were untied and crooked, still stuck on his hips. For a fleeting moment, the image of him standing in front of her completely naked flashed through her mind.

She gasped, appalled by her thinking. For God's sake, she was here to help him, not engage in sinful thinking. Gritting her teeth, she reached for his trousers again, but her fingers were suddenly clumsy.

"God help me," she whispered, gripping the trousers

as tightly as she could and giving the material another hard yank.

To both her relief and discomfiture, the trousers finally slid off his hips and down to his knees. Gillian quickly averted her eyes, her cheeks so hot she thought they might burst into flames. She pulled some more until the trousers slipped down to his knees and finally off his legs.

She rolled another blanket and placed it under his right leg, elevating the injured limb. A quick glance told her he'd badly hurt or perhaps even broken his right ankle. The entire area was badly swollen with red, purplish, and blue bruises. Averting her eyes from his private area, she draped a heavy blanket over him.

She looked up guiltily just as the man named Charles came back into the room, wrapped in a blanket.

"What did you say his name is?" she asked, looking down at the unconscious man.

"Spence . . . Spencer Reeves," he answered.

"Spencer Reeves," Gillian murmured softly. "A physician." Standing, she went into the pantry and gathered handfuls of dried herbs from a variety of small pouches and carefully placed them in a wooden bowl.

Charles followed her to the pantry and stood in the doorway watching. "What are you doing?" he asked as Gillian drew a cupful of hot water and added it to the mixture.

"I'm preparing a potion for you to drink," she said, stirring briskly. "It will ward off the chill."

"A potion?" he inquired, raising an eyebrow and exchanging a quick glance with Jonathan, who now stood slightly behind him. "Are you certain you know what you are doing?"

"Gillian has a way with healing," Lemuel said defensively. He followed watchfully behind the men, the sword resting by his side. " 'Tis only because of her that I allowed you in here in the first place."

"It is much appreciated, sir," Charles replied, gripping the blanket tighter around his neck. "I'm afraid we haven't all been properly introduced."

"I'm Gillian Saunders and this is my brother, Lemuel. Our father was a physician and I'm familiar with many of his prescriptions. I'm afraid you'll just have to trust us. Please, go warm yourselves by the fire."

The two men returned to the hearth as ordered. Gillian followed, carrying two cups of steaming liquid.

"We do thank you for coming to our rescue," Jonathan said, sinking into one of the armchairs and cupping his fingers around the mug. "It's our great fortune that you live out here so close to the beach. How far are you from Gloucester?"

"About a three-hour walk, if the pace is brisk."

"Three hours!" Charles exclaimed. "Why in God's name do you live so far from town?"

"Yes, why would a physician live so far from town?" Jonathan added curiously.

" 'Tis none of your concern," Lemuel growled protectively, causing Gillian to flush a deep red.

Jonathan quickly apologized. "I'm sorry. I didn't mean to pry. I'm afraid my manners are quite lacking this evening."

" 'Tis naught," Gillian murmured. "No harm done."

Tension silenced the room, broken only by the sound of the men sipping their brew.

"Do you think Spence will be all right?" Jonathan asked.

Gillian glanced down at her semiconscious charge. "I promise to do my best," she said.

Jonathan took another sip and then coughed. "By God, this is truly bitter."

"I assure you, it is not harmful, but you must finish it all."

Jonathan lifted his mug to Charles in a silent toast and

then drained the contents. Sighing, he leaned back in the chair and closed his eyes. Charles did the same.

Gillian took the mugs and then approached Charles. "Let me examine your shoulder, please."

Shrugging, Charles slid down the blanket, wincing when she probed his muscles. "Thankfully, 'tis not separated from the bone. I'll bind the shoulder to keep it still. That should ease some of the pain."

She went to the wooden armoire and removed several long strips of linen. Returning to Charles, she wound the strips carefully around his shoulder and arm.

"Thank you," Charles said when she was done, flexing his arm slightly. "I can see you are indeed skilled."

Once the two men were comfortably relaxing in front of the hearth, Gillian knelt beside her more seriously injured patient.

Now that he was dry, she could see that the flush on his cheeks had deepened. Quickly she dipped a cloth into the hot drink she had prepared for the two men and wrung it out against his lips, pressing the liquid inside. Then she began to bathe his forehead with a cool cloth, murmuring to him gently.

As she patted the cloth against his temple, his hand slid to one side. Gillian gently picked it up, feeling the same jolt of awareness she seemed destined to experience whenever she touched him. However, now that she was familiar with the sensation, she welcomed it. Curiously, she turned his hand over and studied his palm. He had an intriguing number of lifelines crisscrossing the skin. Yet to her dismay, the most pronounced line was abruptly cut short. For some reason, a chill snaked down her spine. Unsettled, she put the hand back on his stomach.

He moaned and she gently smoothed his hair back from his forehead. Now that his thick hair was dry, she realized it was rich golden-brown in color and long enough to touch his shoulders. She combed her fingers through the strands stiff with salt, working out the tangles. Brushing her hand over his cheeks, she felt the rough rasp of his whiskers against her fingers, and a strange thrill shot through her. The feel of him intrigued and mesmerized her. Although she'd nursed Lemuel a hundred times before, never had she felt such a deep and familiar connection to a man.

Gillian heard a snore and glanced over her shoulder to see that both men had fallen asleep in the chairs where they sat.

"Lemuel," she said softly. "You can set the sword down. They do not mean to harm us. You should try to get some sleep. I need to stay with this one until his fever breaks."

"Then I'll stay awake with you."

" 'Tis not necessary. After the potion I just gave them, they will sleep well through the night and into the morn." She smiled wearily at her brother. "Don't you trust me?"

He stared at her thoughtfully with his magnificent blue eyes. "I have all my life, Gillian. 'Tis they who are strangers."

"Injured strangers who could not do us harm even if they wanted to. You've seen that for yourself. Sleep, so at least one of us will be clear-headed in the morning. Please."

He hesitated and then reluctantly nodded. "But I'll sleep out here. And I'll stay fully clothed with the sword beside me. If they stir at all, you must promise to waken me."

"I promise."

He dragged out a straw mattress from the bedroom and lay down, placing the sword beside him. After a few minutes, Gillian heard his breathing deepen. Rising, she draped a blanket over him and returned to her patient.

"Spencer Reeves," she whispered, dipping the cloth in

cool water and applying it to his forehead. "Can you hear me?"

She touched his cheek, the skin still hot beneath her fingertips. She could not seem to keep from touching him and maintaining some kind of physical contact. Perhaps it was because he needed her so. Somehow, this fact alone created a special bond between them.

Her gaze swept over his mouth. His lips seemed firm and sensual, moving ever so slightly in delirium. An intense curiosity swept over her. Without thinking, she bent over and brushed her lips against his. The feel of his mouth against hers was a deliciously forbidden sensation, and pleasurable warmth swept through her body. She gasped in surprise when she felt his tongue, raspy and hot, sweep across her lips as if in response.

She pulled away, her stomach quivering, her thoughts scattered. For a long moment she stared at him, relieved when she realized it had only been an involuntary reaction on his part and not intentional. He was still quite fevered, his arms stirring and his legs twitching slightly.

"You are going to be fine Dr. Reeves," she whispered. "I give you my word."

He moaned, his brow furrowing. Then abruptly, the dark lashes fluttered opened and a pair of stunning blue eyes gazed at her. He gave her a look so clear and intense, every fiber of her body seemed to melt.

Her first mortified thought was that he knew about the kiss. Heat raced to her cheeks as his gaze narrowed and he struggled to sit up. The blanket fell to his waist, and Gillian gently pushed him back to the floor with both hands on his bare chest.

"Wh-who . . ." he started, but the sound came out as a weak croak.

"Shhh," she comforted him, pulling the blanket up to his chin and tucking it around him. "You're going to be well."

He blinked as if uncertain that she really existed. "W-water," he whispered hoarsely.

Nodding, she left his side and poured a small cup of water for him. Gently supporting his head, she held the cup to his lips. He drank greedily, licking his lips when the water was gone.

"More," he begged.

Gillian shook her head. "Not yet. First you must drink something else."

She stood up, hurrying over to the table where she quickly mixed a new concoction for him to drink. Kneeling beside him, she held his head against her shoulder and pressed the cup to his lips. He drank a large swallow and then gagged.

"Wh-what in God's name is that?" he croaked. "Poison?"

Gillian smiled. "Boiled catmint leaves to help bring down your fever."

He blinked at her in surprise. "You know something of medicine?"

She nodded, self-conscious to be discussing medicine with a real doctor, even if he was barely conscious and fevered. "I know a little."

He looked at her suspiciously and then took the cup and swallowed the rest of the contents without further comment. Wearily he lay back on the rug and closed his eyes. Gillian thought he had fallen asleep when he suddenly reached out and grabbed her hand. His hand was warm, his grasp surprisingly firm.

"What is your name?" he asked softly.

"Gillian," she whispered back, marveling at how well her hand seemed to fit in his.

"Gillian," he murmured. "You don't look like a witch."

"A witch?" she exclaimed in surprise. "Why would you think I am a witch?"

He managed a weak smile. "Charles said only a coven of witches would live this far from town."

"I assure you, there is no coven here," she said, tucking the blanket tighter around him.

"Nay, I would have to say you look more like an angel with all that red-gold hair."

Gillian blushed in spite of herself. "You are delirious."

"I know."

He coughed, and Gillian was worried by the wet and raspy sound of it. "You must rest now," she urged.

"You're not real," he whispered, closing his eyes. "I'm just dreaming."

"You're not dreaming," she assured him, squeezing his hand. "Can you feel my hand? I am real."

She blinked in astonishment when he lifted her hand to his lips and pressed a warm and lingering kiss on her palm. Heat shot through her body all the way to her toes.

"Then you truly must be an angel, Gillian," he murmured sleepily. "For you have gentle hands, soft skin, and warm lips. And you make one damn . . . fine . . . cup of broth."

THREE

Spencer's first thought upon waking was that he lay on something infinitely more comfortable than a rocky beach. Turning his head slowly, he blinked, letting his surroundings come into focus.

To his right, leaning back against a stone hearth fast asleep, was his lovely angel of mercy. Her arms were loosely crossed against her chest, and stunning red-gold hair tumbled in a loose mass about her slender shoulders. The firelight reflected off the strands, creating a shining halo of gold about her head and body.

"If angels walked among humans . . ." he murmured softly.

Her gown was simple, almost coarse, but her skin was a soft ivory white with a charming dusting of freckles. Her cheekbones were high and delicately carved, her mouth full, and there was a dusty rose color to her cheeks. He thought her at once to be flowerlike and strong—willowy and yet somehow otherworldly. He felt a strange tug on his memory. She seemed oddly familiar to him, yet he was certain he had never met her before.

The memory of her soft, cool hands smoothing his hair and touching his skin rushed back to him. She had the hands of a physician, soothing and gentle. He remembered she'd said she was familiar with the healing arts. If true, and Jonathan and Charles had managed to bring him here, then they were all more fortunate than they could ever know.

His gaze returned to her mouth and he had a faint memory of soft lips brushing against his like a whisper. Had it been real or just a result of his fevered imagination?

Frowning, he lifted his head to see if Charles and Jonathan were about, and was relieved to see them asleep in the chairs by the dwindling fire, apparently alive and well. To his left, he saw a child lying on a bed next to a sword. His frown deepening, he turned his gaze back to the woman.

What had she said her name was?

He struggled to sit and then realized he was completely naked beneath the blanket. Before he could ponder it further, she awakened and darted to his side. Her cool hands touched his bare chest and face, sending shafts of heat directly to his groin.

"The fever has broken," she said softly, smiling at him, not even realizing her soft strokes along the curve of his jawbone were astonishingly arousing. "I feared you might have expired during the night."

"That thought has been a frequent one of late," Spencer replied wryly. "Frankly, I considered that possibility myself."

Her gentle laugh rippled through the air and she dropped her hand to her side. Spencer immediately wished she'd touch him again.

"Well, there will be no more talk of dying now," she said softly. "You are quite lucky your friends were able to bring you to me. Be still and I'll prepare something for you to drink."

He didn't want her to leave. Stopping her, he reached out and took her hand. Again he felt a strange rush of warmth, mingled with familiarity and, strangely since he had just met her, sensuality.

"Wait," he said. "What did you say your name is?"

She met his gaze. "Gillian Saunders."

"Miss Saunders, do you live here alone?" Her eyes were beautiful, a startling emerald green color that seemed to hold both a serene promise and high intelligence.

"Nay, I live here with my brother, Lemuel," she said, tipping her head toward the child on the pallet. "And you may call me Gillian," she added, amusement flashing in her magnificent eyes. "After last night, we all decided to forgo society's convention of polite behavior. Circumstances were such that we were forced into a more intimate knowledge of one another."

Spencer thought of his naked body beneath the blanket and nodded in agreement. "Yes, I can see how that would be sensible."

He reluctantly released her hand and she stood, disappearing into another room. Spencer managed to bring himself to a sitting position although his head pounded with the effort. At that moment, her brother stirred on the pallet, sitting up and immediately reaching for the sword. Drawing in a quick breath, Spencer realized that he was not a child at all, but a young man trapped in a child's body.

"What are you looking at?" he snapped irritably, rubbing his eyes. "Where's Gillian?"

Spencer nodded toward the room where Gillian had just disappeared, relieved when she stepped back in after hearing her brother's voice.

"Good morn to you, Lemuel," she said cheerfully, going over to add wood to the fire. "Have you met our patient yet?"

Spencer held out a hand to the dwarf. "Spencer Reeves, at your service."

Lemuel narrowed his eyes and didn't move. Gillian cleared her throat and finally Lemuel stood, walking across the room, muttering his name and briefly shaking Spencer's hand.

Permitted to have a closer look at the man, Spencer was astonished by the sheer beauty of his face. His features were so perfect, so symmetrical, that any more delicacy would have made him too beautiful for a man. His head was capped with a lustrous wealth of gold hair, and one lock fell a little forward onto his forehead.

It seemed a cruel trick of nature to grace such a face with the body he had been given: short, stumpy legs, a squat torso, and arms that seemed slightly uneven. Uncomfortable, Spencer looked away as the young man shoved his feet into his boots and left the cottage.

Gillian had disappeared again, but thankfully Charles and Jonathan were stirring. Spencer watched as Charles awoke, stretching his legs and rubbing the back of his neck. His left shoulder had been expertly bound. Charles grinned as he saw that Spencer was awake.

"Spence," he said coming to a stand and holding the blanket around his waist with one hand. "I'm glad to see you actually made it through the night alive."

"Thanks to the generosity of our kind hosts. How does your shoulder feel?"

Charles touched the bandage. "I don't honestly know, as I can't move it. Mistress Gillian bound it for me last night. But I must say the pain has diminished considerably, most likely thanks to whatever magical concoction I was forced to drink."

"Our hostess seems quite knowledgeable in the healing arts," Spencer observed.

"Better for you that she doesn't live in Salem and could serve as competition for your services," Charles teased. "She's a much prettier sight than you and has a gentler touch."

"I simply thank God that we are all alive," Jonathan spoke up. "Last night was the most dreadful experience of my life. It was surely a stroke of fortune that we found this place."

"Or perhaps the guiding hand of destiny," Charles offered.

"Whatever it was, we owe our lives to Gillian and Lemuel," Spencer said.

"Amen," Charles agreed.

Gillian took that moment to walk back into the room and hand Spencer a mug of steaming liquid. He sniffed at it curiously.

"Thyme, comfrey, and something else," he said, looking up at her expectantly.

"Echinacea root," she said. " 'Twill help fight off infection and a sore throat from the chill."

"Your knowledge of herbs is most impressive," Spencer said, observing her as he sipped the liquid. *She* was impressive. She'd mixed a bit of honey in it, which made it much more tolerable to drink. He catalogued that useful tidbit away for his own use.

"I'll prepare something for you all to eat," she said. "You must be famished. Lemuel will draw some fresh water from the well so you can drink and wash your hands and faces if you'd like. Your clothes should be dry now as well." She took the mug from Spencer as he drained the last of the contents. "I would suggest that you continue to rest until I've had a chance to examine your ankle a bit closer."

Spencer held out a hand to Charles, who grasped it and helped pull him to a standing position. Grimacing and clutching the blanket around his waist, he hopped to a chair. "At the very least, I'll do this in a more dignified manner than flat on my back on the floor."

"Then be certain to keep the leg raised," Gillian ordered.

"As you wish, Doctor," he quipped, and Charles and Jonathan burst out laughing.

She pursed her lips at them and disappeared back into the pantry. Charles grabbed his breeches from in front of the fire and quickly drew them on, lacing them up one-handed. Jonathan followed suit, and soon both men were dressed except for their stockings and shoes.

Charles found a small footstool and placed it under Spencer's leg.

"And where might my clothes be?" Spencer asked when they were finished.

Charles ran a hand through his dark hair and grinned. "Sorry, Spence. We had to cut through your trousers and boots to get them off. I'm afraid you're going to be confined to naught more than a shirt and a blanket until we can get some help."

He tossed Spencer his shirt. Spencer grabbed it with one hand and pulled it over his head. "Well, this will be a bit awkward."

"For a bit longer, at least," Charles said. "I'm afraid we'll once again have to impose on the kindness of our hosts. Jonathan and I will go to Gloucester. But we'll need a guide. According to Miss Gillian, we're about a good three-hour walk from town, and that's if the pace is brisk."

"Have they no mount?"

"My initial impression is that they do not."

Spencer raised an eyebrow. "That does complicate matters, although I'm not certain you're in any condition to ride with that shoulder of yours."

"Bound like this, I sincerely doubt I'll feel a thing. Hopefully we'll be able to convince someone in Gloucester with a carriage or horse that we're good for the coin and able to pay upon our arrival in Salem."

Gillian entered the room, carrying a tray of sliced bread and several bowls of what smelled like delicious hot pudding.

"I don't think 'twould be wise to try walking or riding such a distance yet," she said.

Jonathan shrugged. "We really have little choice. Our families will be quite distraught by our sudden disappearance. We need to try and return home as quickly as possible in order to alleviate their fears."

"I agree," Spencer said. "If your brother would be so kind as to show Jonathan and Charles the way to town, we would be most grateful."

"I think . . ." Gillian started when Lemuel entered the cottage, carrying a bucket of water.

"There's another bucket outside for washing," he said gruffly. "Here is the cooking water," he told Gillian, carrying the bucket past her and into the pantry.

Jonathan and Charles quickly disappeared out the door to wash, and Gillian brought Spencer a damp rag. He wiped his face and hands gratefully, then handed it back to her.

"We greatly appreciate your kindness and do not want to be an imposition any longer than we must," he said softly.

"You're not an imposition," she replied, kneeling down beside the chair. "We don't get many visitors out here and 'tis a welcome relief to our solitude. But I understand that your families must be dreadfully concerned. After breakfast, Lemuel will show your friends the way to Gloucester. We have some coin to lend them so that they may reach Salem safely."

Spencer looked at her in astonishment. "I'm at quite a loss to adequately express my thanks. I'm not certain we can ever properly thank you for all you've done. We are enormously in your debt."

She smiled, the gesture lighting up her lovely face. "If I may, I will ask for one boon. It isn't often that I have the opportunity to speak with a physician. I have many questions and would ask only that you share your knowledge with me."

God forbid, Spencer thought; did she have any idea

how beautiful and alluring she looked? Her red hair tumbled wildly about her shoulders, and her emerald eyes were innocent and yet beguiling, fringed with long, thick lashes. He was all too painfully aware of the soft curves of her body and the way her small breasts pressed against her simple gown. His body tightened and ached from an urgent desire to hold her. Yet he hesitated. There was a refreshing openness and naiveté about her, certainly borne of limited contact with other people. Nonetheless, at that moment she could have asked for the moon, and he would have damn well tried to pluck it from the sky for her.

"It would be an honor," he said sincerely, both curious and intrigued to discover just how far her knowledge extended.

Her smile brightened and widened. Spencer had the strangest sensation that he had just been warmed and comforted, as if she had reached out and physically embraced him.

He looked away from her, shifting uncomfortably on the chair and telling himself sternly that it would be better to think of things other than how lovely she looked when he sat in front of her naked from the waist down except for an old blanket.

She must have sensed his discomfort, for she rose gracefully and brought him a bowl of the pudding. As he took a bite of the delicious mixture, he found himself quite looking forward to some time alone with Miss Gillian Saunders.

After breakfast and a brief but private argument with Lemuel, Gillian finally persuaded him to take Jonathan and Charles into Gloucester and help them secure transportation to Salem. Lemuel didn't want to leave her alone with Spencer, but finally acquiesced when Gillian assured him that their guest couldn't walk, let alone pose a threat to her well-being.

After helping Charles and Jonathan find their way to Salem, Lemuel would return home to the cottage. The following day, he would go back to Gloucester and retrieve whoever would come for Spencer.

Gillian packed the men food and water for the journey. She hugged Lemuel fiercely, much to his embarrassment, and gave him a kiss on the cheek.

"Go carefully, brother," she said softly.

"I'll be home by nightfall," he promised her. "I've left the sword here for your protection."

She smiled at him. "Thank you, but I shall not need it. Godspeed to you all."

When they were gone, she took a deep breath, closed the door, and turned to look at Spencer. He sat in front of the fire, staring into the flames thoughtfully, his profile strong and handsome. His right leg was stretched out in front of him, elevated and still as she had ordered. Her insides suddenly quivered in anticipation of being alone with him, but she was not afraid. Instead, she felt something else flutter inside her, warm and anxious but not quite definable.

Shaking her head, she walked over to him. "I need to take a look at your ankle," she said softly. "I think 'twould be best to construct another splint to keep it rigid. But first, I'll prepare something to help you keep your strength up."

"I'm fine," he said shortly. "I don't need anything else."

She blinked in surprise at the curt tone of his voice. "But . . ." she started.

He reached out and took her hand, and the mere feel of his skin against hers sent a warming shiver through her.

"I know what you are doing, Gillian," he said softly,

squeezing her hand. "And I thank you for it. I know it will be painful to splint my ankle again. But I don't want anything more to ease the pain. I wish to keep a clear head right now."

She looked at him for a long moment, and then down to where he still firmly held her hand. "Are all physicians so difficult as patients?"

A smile curved across his handsome face. "I would suspect so. My father is even more fractious than I when he is unwell."

He released her hand and she felt a momentary loss of warmth. Hiding her disappointment, she walked over to the armoire, where she secured several clean strips of linen.

"Your father is a physician as well?" she asked curiously.

He nodded. "One of Salem's finest. I work in his practice."

"He must be very proud of you."

"I would like to think so. He certainly needs the assistance I give him. It seems we have more and more patients to treat every day."

"Why is that?"

"It seems that these days the fine citizens of Salem require relief from even the slightest of ills. My father's reputation is such that people believe he can cure every ailment."

"He must be a very knowledgeable man."

Spencer chuckled. "He is, but more than that, he has a way with people. They trust him."

"I think that is the finest compliment one could give to a physician," she said quietly.

"Indeed," he agreed.

Gillian retrieved the pieces of driftwood that had served as a splint for his leg the night before and knelt beside the chair, setting them out carefully.

He reached out and touched her shoulder. Again, unexpected warmth flared through her. How could it be that she so craved the touch of a man she had only just met?

"Tell me something about yourself," he said softly. "How is it that you know so much of healing?"

She sat back on her heels and looked up at him. "My father was a physician, too," she said and felt a pang of loss.

"Really?" he replied, and she could hear the skepticism in his voice. "What was his name?"

"Zachariah Saunders."

A puzzled look crossed his face. "For some unfathomable reason, that name sounds familiar," he said slowly. "Perchance was he ever in Salem?"

She rose suddenly, her heart starting to beat faster. She had no wish to discuss her past with him, especially since she barely knew him. "It was a long time ago. We should set your ankle now."

Surprise crossed his face at her abrupt change of topic, but to her relief he did not press the subject. She lifted the blanket up to his knee, folding it up on top of his upper thigh. Although careful to keep her gaze on the lower part of his leg, she blushed nonetheless as her fingertips brushed the hairs on his shin. She felt him flinch and her cheeks heated further.

His ankle was still badly discolored and swollen, and the skin around it a horrid mixture of blue, red, and purple. She probed at it gently, feeling around the bone, pulling back when he winced.

"Do you recall how the injury occurred?" she asked.

"My leg caught on a rope as I went under. I also hit it against what I think was the hull of the skiff. It's possible it might be broken, although my first inclination is to say that the injury is not that severe."

She thought for a moment and then nodded. "Either

way, 'twould be best to bind it and keep it raised. 'Twill give it time to heal."

He gave her a slow smile that sent her pulse racing. "I concur with the proposed treatment, Doctor."

She blushed and then smiled back. "Then I shall do so at once," she said, reaching for the driftwood.

"Hand them to me and I'll hold them while you bind," he instructed.

She nodded and handed him the wood. He held them steady on either side of his leg while she unraveled the linen strips and then began to wind them about the wood.

"I presume your parents are no longer living," Spencer said quietly. When she nodded, he continued. "Pray tell, then, why do you still choose to live out here so far from town?"

"Because this is our home," she said simply.

"Do you fear the townsfolk's reaction to your brother's disfigurement?"

"He's not disfigured!" Gillian shot back, pulling a strip of linen too tight and causing Spencer to wince. She loosened it quickly and then flushed. "I'm sorry."

"No, I'm sorry," he said, reaching out and touching her shoulder lightly. "I didn't intend to offend you. Lemuel's condition is not all that unusual. In fact, I've seen a case of it myself among a family in Salem. Other than an obvious physical abnormality, many people with his condition go on to leave long and fulfilling lives."

"You don't understand," she protested. "It's not so simple. Lemuel is easily hurt, and people can be so . . . cruel."

He fell silent, obviously not able to disagree with her statement.

" 'Tis just that he's a sensitive soul," she said softly, tying off another linen strip and then rising. She walked over to the mantel and picked up one of the wooden carvings Lemuel had made. "He made this," she said, handing it to Spencer. "He's able to see things like this in wood, stone, and other ordinary things. He sees the life within."

Spencer took it and turned it over, the expression on his face keen and curious. "It's magnificent," he breathed. "Truly breathtaking. His talent is astounding."

"We sell his work, along with my herbs, in town. Sometimes we barter with them. We go in every two months or so. It's painful for him to have everyone look at him so."

"And for you?"

"Sometimes. But out here, we have almost everything we need."

"Except human contact."

She lowered her eyes. "It can be lonely. But Lemuel and I . . . we have each other."

He reached out and took her hand in a curiously tender gesture. "That will not always be enough, Gillian," he said softly. "For either one of you."

She felt that strange tingle in her stomach and pulled her hand away, kneeling back at his feet and resuming the binding.

"You still haven't told me how you happen to know so much about healing," he said.

"My father taught me," she said, binding the last strip tightly and sitting back to observe her work. "I was fascinated by his knowledge."

Spencer reached down and examined her work. "It appears as though he had an apt pupil. Medicine is not typically an area of interest to most women."

"It has been an area of interest for me for as long as I can remember. I was constantly bringing home wounded birds, squirrels, and raccoons for my father to heal. Soon I was able to mend them largely by myself. But I hungered for more."

"Your father permitted this?"

"Not only permitted it, he encouraged it. He also taught

me to read, instructed me in herbal preparation, and helped by observing my surgery on animals. I think he allowed it because he knew that I would one day be left to care for Lemuel."

He rubbed his jaw, now covered with dark whiskers. "Have you lived out here long?"

"For most of my life," Gillian said, rising and going to add another piece of wood to the fire. "About a year after we moved here, my father found Lemuel. He had been left on our doorstep, not even bundled in a blanket. He was so tiny. It was the happiest day of my life."

"Your brother was fortunate to have found such a caring family. Sometimes fate can be kind."

"Such as guiding you here to us?"

"Yes, such as that." He smiled and looked down at his leg. "Your binding is excellent."

She rose. "And you didn't complain once. Mayhap your disposition as a patient is improving after all."

"Then I owe it to a lovely lady who eased my discomfort by her engaging and lively conversation."

Gillian felt a flush of warmth at his praise. "Would you care for a concoction now?"

He shook his head. "No, thank you. But I will be so bold as to request a cup of water and a prescription for much more of your fascinating company."

"Granted," she agreed with a smile.

FOUR

Gillian helped Spencer wash up, rubbing the salt out of his hair with a coarse bar of soap and, because of his insistence, dumping a bowl of water on his head. Good-naturedly, he shook his hair, spraying her with droplets as she laughed. She found a comb for him and he slicked back his hair, causing him to look even more handsome, if not a bit devilish.

After some time had passed, Gillian noticed Spencer scratching his chin uncomfortably. "Is your beard bothering you?" she asked.

He nodded. "I'd like to shave it. You wouldn't happen to have a blade about, would you?"

"You can use Lemuel's," Gillian said, going to retrieve it. She then drew some water from the well and brought him a thick linen cloth, a lump of soap, and a small chipped mirror.

" 'Twill be easier to do this at the table," she said, holding out a hand.

He grasped it and hopped over to the table, lowering himself carefully into a chair.

"I'll hold the looking glass," she said, pushing the water basin across the table toward him. "That is, if you'd like me to help."

"I'd appreciate it. But I'll need to remove my shirt, and I don't want to offend your sensibilities any further than

I already have. So if you'd rather retire to another room . . ." He fingered the material on his shirt, and Gillian shook her head, trying not to blush.

"I'm not . . . I mean . . ." she stammered.

He lifted an eyebrow. "I don't want to make you uncomfortable. I can do this alone, Gillian."

She lifted her chin determinedly. "I am not offended. Besides, 'tis not as if I haven't seen you without a shirt."

"And a lot less, indeed," he murmured looking down at the blanket wrapped around his waist, mindful that he had nothing else on underneath it. Shrugging, he pulled his shirt off over his head. Gillian took it from him, trying to keep her eyes averted from his magnificent chest. Folding his shirt, she placed it over the back of a chair and returned to the table, holding up the mirror. She kept her eyes fixed firmly on his face, determined not to act like a silly girl scandalized by the sight of a naked chest.

Grinning at her, he splashed some water on his face and rubbed the soap between his hands. He spread the lather on his cheeks and beard and then lifted the blade, scraping it downward on his face. As if of its own volition, her gaze strayed to the muscles in his arms. He looked so lean and sinewy. She wondered what physical exercises a doctor undertook to become so fit. More than that, he was comfortable with himself. He didn't seem embarrassed in the least to be sitting in front of her clad in naught more than a blanket around his waist.

"A little to the right," he suddenly said.

"What?" she said, flushing guiltily.

"Move the mirror a little to the right."

She did as he asked. "May I ask you something?" she suddenly blurted out.

He dipped the blade into the water, rinsing and lifting it to his face again. "Of course you may."

"Why did you become a physician?"

He seemed surprised by the question, and for a moment

stared at her as if assessing the reason for her inquiry. "When I was a child, I used to observe my father at his practice," he finally said. "People came to him sick, distraught, sometimes near death. They all had faith that my father could aid them. Most of the time, he did. He made a difference in their lives; he helped them. I suppose I wanted to provide people with that kind of hope. I never considered doing anything else, even though my father didn't insist on my studying medicine. In fact, I do believe he rather hoped I'd be more interested in our family's shipping business."

"Shipping business?"

"Physicians don't make much money," Spencer said wryly. "Thankfully, my father also has a rather profitable shipping business. To his dismay, however, it takes up much of his time. But now that he has me working in the clinic, it does help ease the burden. However, I'm certain he'd rather be spending his time treating patients."

Gillian took a minute to ponder the information. "Did you study outside of Salem?"

"I did. I attended Philadelphia University for two years. Then I apprenticed for three months at the new hospital there."

She leaned forward, fascinated by their discussion. "What sort of studies did you engage in?"

He chuckled, pausing in midscrape. "I must say that I've never been so thoroughly questioned about my profession."

"I'm sorry. I don't mean to pry."

He dipped the blade in the water and shook his head. "I'm not offended, just intrigued. Frankly, I find it a refreshing change from the mundane topics I typically discuss with most women. I quite enjoy talking about my profession, as well as finding someone who is truly interested and not just making a show of it."

He nudged her hand with the mirror, urging her to hold

it higher, and began to scrape beneath his chin. "To answer your question, I took classes in botanics, childbirth, and the physiology of man. In later years, I studied herbology and physical remedies."

"It must have been wonderful," she said enviously.

His grin widened. "I assure you, wonderful is not how I would describe it. It was an insufferable amount of work, including surviving the instruction of old, doddering Herbert Walkin. It's nothing shy of a miracle the man hasn't yet disemboweled anyone in his one hundred years of practice."

Gillian laughed. "Oh, how dreadful."

"Thank God that in his later years he has had plenty of younger hands to steady him."

Gillian's eyes widened. "As a student, were you permitted to practice on real patients?"

"Of course," he answered, and then his eyes twinkled. "But I gleaned more useful practice elsewhere."

"Where?"

He shook his head. "I'm not certain you want to know. I have no wish to shock you."

"Oh, please," she pleaded. "You can trust me."

He lowered his voice to a dramatic whisper. "Cadavers."

She gasped in horror and he chuckled. "It sounds shocking, but it is the only way to work your way properly through a body."

"But . . . but dissection is forbidden by the church."

"By a group of sanctimonious men who have no understanding of science."

"Did you . . . have to steal the bodies, then?" she said, half appalled and half intrigued by his confession.

"Personally, no. But there were some among us brave enough to procure what we needed."

"And no one minded?"

"Certainly not the cadavers," he said lightly. "I know

it sounds ghoulish, but this was not a task lightly undertaken. I assure you, the information we gleaned from the dissection of their bodies was quite useful. As it was, our group only stole the bodies of prisoners that had been discarded by a nearby prison. In death, they likely contributed more to society than in life. During my last month there, the hospital made arrangements with the prison to purchase a few of the bodies. The church approved of the sale, although that fact was not made public. It was all quite legal."

Gillian leaned forward. "Forgive me for asking, but what was it like the first time you were able to examine the innards of a body?"

"The first time is rather disconcerting," he admitted. "But after that, you get used to it. The smell, though, is more difficult to overcome." He wrinkled his nose and promptly nicked his chin.

Gillian picked up the towel and dabbed it at his chin. He caught her hand, holding it against his face, and Gillian realized how intimate a gesture it had been. His eyes blazed hot, and Gillian had the strangest feeling that he intended to kiss her. She held her breath, not daring to move until he released her hand, dipping the blade back into the bowl.

"I learned a lot from my studies," he continued evenly as though nothing had occurred. "But I assure you there is much more to be learned in the actual treatment of patients themselves. That is an entire study of its own, and perhaps the most difficult."

" 'Tis surely so," she agreed earnestly.

She fell silent, watching him methodically remove the facial hair from his jaw and cheeks. She could not tear her gaze away from his hands: long-fingered, graceful, and strong—the able hands of a physician.

"And you, Gillian?" he asked. "Why does healing fascinate you so much?"

His question intrigued her and she considered it, trying to pinpoint a moment in time when she realized that healing was something she'd always wanted to do. It seemed to have been a need she was born with—or born *to,* perhaps.

"I believe my father stimulated my interest or fed it," she replied slowly. "I've wanted to heal people for as long as I could remember."

Spencer nodded, and for the briefest of moments, something powerful flared between them. It happened so quickly that Gillian wondered if she had imagined it.

"I understand what you mean," Spencer said, and his gaze lingered on her face for a bit longer than was proper. Perhaps he had felt it, too.

Gillian swallowed hard, her pulse skittering alarmingly. Every moment she spent in his presence, her attraction to him grew stronger. Her instinctive response to him was powerful, his nearness overwhelming. She wondered if he had similar feelings, because he leaned toward her with a look so hot that she felt tied to the chair.

Then his mouth curved into a smile and he held up the blade.

"All done," he said, wiping it off on the linen towel and placing it on the table. He splashed a bit of cool water on his cheeks and jaw and patted them dry.

She exhaled, her heart still thumping uncomfortably. Nonetheless, she was able to marvel at how different he looked clean-shaven. If it were possible, he was even more handsome. He had a firm, square jaw, and the thrust of his chin suggested a stubborn, headstrong streak. His mouth, freed from the shadow of his beard, seemed even more sensual and mischievous. *He's a good man,* she thought, *kind and intelligent. A man I could easily fall in love with.*

To her disappointment, he reached behind him on the chair and pulled his shirt over his head. Gillian felt a twinge of regret that the action obstructed her magnificent view—one she had tried so hard not to enjoy. He stood, leaning on the table to keep the weight off his ankle. She rose quickly as well, going over to help him. He slid an arm comfortably about her shoulders, but instead of moving, he looked longingly at the door.

"Do you think we might sit outside today?" he asked. "I think a bit of the sea air might refresh me."

"Will you not be chilled?" she asked worriedly.

His eyes glinted with amusement. "Not if you come with me."

She pursed her lips at his gentle teasing. "Well, then, I'll fetch another warm blanket for you. But first, I'll take some chairs out there for us to sit in."

She dragged two of the table chairs outside, angling them so they faced the water. He leaned heavily on her as they moved outside. Gillian exhaled, her breath emerging as a white puff.

"I forgot that winter is fast approaching," Spencer said, settling in the chair.

"Indeed," Gillian agreed. "November, and likely the first snowfall, is but weeks away."

He leaned back, looking out at the sea. "The cottage is certainly located in a beautiful spot. In some ways, isolation has its advantages."

Gillian followed his gaze to the sea. "I do love it here, having the sounds of the sea so close. The rhythm of the waves has eased my mind more times than I can count."

"There is something soothing about the water," Spencer agreed, the wind tousling his hair. "A good sail on my skiff is usually enough to clear my mind." He sighed. "Except now the *Rosemary* is gone for good."

"The *Rosemary*?" Gillian asked, feeling a twinge of jealousy. "Why did you name it such?"

He smiled at her and she felt her heart turn over in response. "I named the skiff after my mother," he said.

"She's the finest woman I know. Especially since she so valiantly tolerates the harried lifestyle of a physician."

"She sounds wonderful," she said, feeling a surprising rush of relief that the craft was not named after a wife or another beloved.

"She is. Especially since people come to the clinic at all hours. Yet she never protests and does everything she can to make them feel comfortable."

Gillian nodded, thinking of her own mother. "My mother was the same. I miss her very much. She always knew just what to say to make someone feel less anxious. I think it takes a special kind of woman to abide such an occupation."

Spencer rubbed the back of his neck. "Unfortunately, my mother is also overly anxious about my welfare. This means she'll be quite frantic. I do hope Charles and Jonathan have reached Salem safely and were able to convey to her that I'm safe and in good hands."

"I'm certain they have. In no time you'll be able to alleviate her concerns yourself," she reassured him.

He grinned. "You have a soothing way with words yourself."

She smiled. "Have you any brothers or sisters in your family?"

"One younger sister, Juliet. She's ten years old and a shy little thing, although she has a wicked stubborn streak. A fault of all Reeveses, I'm afraid. She doesn't have many friends, but she harbors every stray animal in Salem she can find."

Gillian chuckled. "She sounds quite like me. Father constantly complained at how crowded it was at times in the cottage, but he never turned a single one of them away. After a while, he built me a small pen behind the cottage, where we could house them."

Spencer laughed. "We did the same for Juliet, much to Mother's relief and dread. She doesn't approve at all of Juliet's preoccupation with the strays, and Father and I are constantly berated for encouraging her in such endeavors." He looked over his shoulder. "Have you any animals in the pen now?"

"Only one sandhill crane, and he'll be healthy enough to fly away any day. But any injured animal—or person, for that matter—is welcome here."

"I am personally thankful for your generosity."

They shared a smile and her heart took a perilous leap. How could one look from him fill her with such longing? She wanted every moment with him to last forever.

They sat in contented silence for a few minutes before Gillian glanced down at his leg. "How does your ankle feel?" she asked. "I should have brought something out to keep it up."

She started to rise, but he put a hand on her shoulder. "Sit down, Gillian. I'm fine. In fact, if the truth be known, I feel remarkably better, thanks to you. Either you have magic in your fingertips or I didn't injure it as badly as I thought."

"Certainly the latter."

"I'm not so convinced." He cocked his head and stared at her thoughtfully for such a long time, she felt the heat rise to her cheeks.

"Why do you look at me like that?" she asked.

He suddenly snapped his fingers. "Bridget Goodwell."

"Excuse me?"

"Bridget Goodwell," he repeated, this time more certain. "Ever since I met you, you reminded me of someone. Now, today with your hair bound back like that, I realize that you look remarkably like an acquaintance of mine. She lives in Salem and is the daughter of the Reverend Goodwell and his wife, Abigail."

An unexpected shiver raced up her spine at his mention of the woman's name, raising her gooseflesh. "I cannot say that I've ever met her."

"No, I can't imagine you would. She just wedded, if I'm not mistaken. She's quite sharp-witted and one of the few women I know who is not afraid to speak her mind. I suppose, in a way, that's also another manner in which you resemble her."

"Oh, I'm certain she is far more interesting than I."

"I wouldn't be so certain about that. I hope you don't consider me too forward in saying this, but I will truly miss your company, Gillian. In such a short time, I feel as though we have become quite good friends."

"I feel that way, too," she said shyly. "Perhaps you can come visit again some time."

"Perhaps," he said, but the manner in which he spoke led her to believe that, for some reason, he would not.

"I owe you the debt of my life," he continued. "If you ever need anything, I want you to know that you know you can come to me in Salem."

She looked down at her hands, already thinking of him gone and of how empty the cottage would be without him. "You do not owe me anything," she said, tucking a stray strand of hair behind her ear. " 'Twas simply the godly thing to do."

"Gillian," he said, and she lifted her gaze to look at him. "You may not see it as such, but you saved my life, as well as the lives of my friends. I do not so easily dismiss such a momentous favor."

He reached out and took her hand, bringing it slowly to his mouth. Keeping his gaze on her face, he pressed his lips to her knuckles, letting them linger a bit longer than was proper. Gillian felt a warm tingle start in the pit of her stomach and spread outward, a bittersweet longing filling her body.

"You have amply repaid any debt you may think you have," she said, her heart beating rapidly in her chest. "You've generously shared your knowledge of medicine with me. That alone means a great deal."

He slowly lowered her hand; the smoldering flames she saw in his eyes both startled and thrilled her. "Nonetheless, I am not a man who so carelessly dismisses a boon, nor shall I so easily forget you, Gillian."

"You are far too generous. I really have no wish for a favor."

"There may come a time when you do," he replied firmly. "And if so, I will be waiting."

FIVE

Spencer couldn't remember the last time a day had passed so quickly and pleasantly. Gillian Saunders intrigued him, fascinated him, and even more unsettling, attracted him. It was as if by a twist of fate, he'd met his soulmate. Bloody rotten luck that the timing was so wrong. Better that he simply enjoy the time they had together.

The afternoon was filled with fast and furious conversations about medical therapies, herbs, and even hunting. For dinner, she fixed him the most delicious rabbit stew he'd ever eaten. He ate three bowls, his appetite ravenous and his spirits high. Later she prepared steaming mugs of hot spiced wine and lit several candles around the cozy room. It amazed him how they were able to talk endlessly and passionately about a far-reaching number of topics without any of the awkward pauses that occur between strangers.

Drowsy and contented, Spencer took a sip of wine and regarded her over his cup from his chair in front of the hearth. Gillian looked both beautiful and serene sitting beside him, her stockinged feet tucked up beneath her. Her fiery hair tumbled loose about her shoulders, and her cheeks were flushed pink from the heat of the fire and perhaps also from the wine.

He looked down at himself, amused that he had spent

the entire day in the company of a woman while clad in naught more than a shirt and a blanket wrapped around his waist. And yet, she had made him feel so comfortable and at ease that he had barely even remembered his nakedness.

"May I ask you a personal question?" Gillian suddenly asked, leaning her head back against the chair.

"Of course," Spencer said, curious as to what she might wish to know about him. He'd already told her more about himself than any other living soul.

"Do you subscribe to the Humoral Theory?" she asked.

His jaw dropped open. "Wh-what?"

"The Humoral Theory," she repeated slowly. "Do you subscribe to it?"

He snapped his mouth shut. Of all the things he might have expected her to ask, this wasn't among them.

"I don't know what to say. I'm simply astonished that you are familiar with it."

She looked at him, baffled. "Why wouldn't I be?"

Spencer shook his head. "Gillian, the Humoral Theory is quite an advanced topic. I never expected you to know of it, especially since you've had no formal training. But to answer your question, yes, I happen to subscribe to the Humoral Theory, as do all decent physicians." He studied her expression. "But for some unfathomable reason, I have a feeling you are going to tell me that you do not."

She shrugged and took a sip of wine. "Would that shock you? After all, to admit to disbelieving the theory would be heresy, since it is church doctrine."

Intrigued, he set his cup aside. "Doctrine or not, it is a sound theory. It is reasonable to assume that cures can best be found by restoring the balance of the body's natural humors."

"Yes, but one must believe that these humors are the four most important ones in the human body in order to believe in the cure," she replied softly.

She had his full attention now. Intrigued, he leaned forward in his chair, clasping his hands together. "What other theory might you believe?"

She cradled her cup in her lap. "Well, in the Humoral Theory, the body is thought to be comprised of four humors—blood, black bile, yellow bile, and phlegm. If you subscribe to this circle of four, then you must believe sickness is the result of an extreme imbalance between the humors. Treatment must be based on restoring the four humors to an equal amount. Am I correct?"

"Very much so."

"Then, in order to restore balance, the most popular elements of the theory support removing bodily fluids by lancing veins, leeching, blistering, and bloodletting as the best methods of treatment."

Spencer sat back in his chair, steepling his fingers together and wondering what she was getting at. "Not only," he amended. "The theory also supports the use of herbal and psychic treatments."

"In combination with the removal of body fluids," she reminded him.

"True."

"Personally, I believe that excessive bloodletting hampers the body's natural defenses."

He stared at her, flabbergasted. "Surely you don't really believe that."

"Why not?" she said a bit defensively. "In many cases, the body simply needs time and rest to heal itself. In order to do so, the proper herbal concoctions can be made and administered either orally or directly to the skin in order to quicken the process. I believe that removing the body's much needed fluids by leeching or bloodletting will counteract the effects of the potions given to calm and heal a patient."

Spencer's mouth dropped open for a second time before he closed it firmly. "Did your father teach you this?"

"Not entirely. Like most physicians, he was instructed in the Humoral Theory. But I think in the later years of his life, his mind slowly began to change. Part of it, I think, was due to the fact that I strongly supported a more natural process of recovery."

"And on what do you base your faith in this natural recovery?" Spencer countered, narrowing his eyes.

She lowered her gaze. "My work with injured animals."

He scoffed at that. "Animals are hardly representative of the human physique."

"True. But they are more like us than you know. And they responded well to a natural recovery."

He was not convinced. "Explain what you mean by a natural recovery."

"Rest, fluids, a varied diet, and herbs." She pushed her hair off her shoulders. "I'm not saying bodily fluids should never be drained. Only that it should be done far more rarely than is currently practiced."

He shook his head, unsettled by what she espoused. Her thoughts were astounding and so radically opposed to anything he'd ever heard before, he needed a few minutes to consider the implications of what she had said. And yet he couldn't deny that a part of him was stimulated and challenged in a way he'd never been in all his years of study and practice.

"Well, Gillian," he finally managed to say, "I may not agree with your theory, but you've certainly given me quite a bit to think about. I must admit that your knowledge of healing is quite extensive and impressive, even if a bit misguided. Have you ever considered the good you could do by practicing your knowledge? As a midwife, for example?"

A small crease furrowed her brow. " 'Tis a noble thought, but 'twould mean moving into town to be closer to my patients. I can't do that. This is my home and I will not leave it."

He shrugged. "You wouldn't necessarily have to leave the cottage. You could go into town as you were needed."

"That is not so simple," she said, shaking her head.

He raised an eyebrow. "Because of Lemuel?"

"Yes."

Refusing to give up so easily, he leaned over and lowered his voice. "You have a gift, Gillian," he said quietly. "A healing touch, a soothing manner that any decent physician would envy. It's a waste of your remarkable gift to hide out here away from the people who would benefit most from your abilities. I don't think Lemuel would wish that of you."

She stiffened. "You don't understand."

"You can't protect him forever, Gillian. Personally, I don't think it's wise. Lemuel is a lot stronger than you think."

She bristled at his words. "I wish my circumstances could be different, but they cannot. I believe each of us is born with a destiny, and it is mine to live here and use my abilities to aid my brother."

"I won't deny that aiding your brother is an honorable cause," he argued. "But why confine your talents to just one person when so many more could benefit? If it's destiny you follow, then take charge of your own. Do what you know to be right."

Color burned high in her cheeks. "Staying here with Lemuel *is* right. This is my destiny. I have no desire to go beyond that."

Spencer felt a rush of frustration. "Explain to me why you insist on isolation. Are the circumstances of your life so painful that you'd not even consider trying to live a normal life in town? Have you not thought that it might turn out well for Lemuel?" He paused for a moment and then, on impulse, said, "Come to Salem. My family will help you and Lemuel get settled."

He saw the panic in her eyes. "Nay, I cannot."

"Why not?" he pressed.

"Because there are things about me . . . about my family, my father, that you don't know."

"Things that force you to live out here alone?" he said quietly. "Gillian, no one in their right mind is going to hold you or Lemuel accountable for the sins of your father."

"My father had no sins," she countered hotly.

Spencer took her hand. "Then tell me why you bristle so when I mention his name?"

She paused and then exhaled a deep breath. "He was accused of something he didn't do."

"Such as?"

She withdrew her hand, abruptly rising. "Please, I don't wish to speak of it."

He ran his fingers through his hair. He'd pushed too hard. "Gillian, I apologize. I didn't mean to pry."

"I know." Her voice trembled.

"I had no right to broach such a personal subject. I typically don't behave in such an abominable manner. It's just that in this short time, I've grown fond of you. I worry about you living here so far from town."

"Lemuel and I have lived here almost all of our lives without incident. We are safe here."

"Of course you are," he said with a sigh. "I'm not familiar with your circumstances and it was rude of me to presume."

She shook her head but still did not meet his gaze. " 'Twas only natural for you to be curious. I know our circumstances are likely to raise questions. The fault is not yours." She rose and approached his chair, reaching for his cup. "Shall I fill it again?"

He nodded, but when she leaned forward to take the

cup, he gently pushed her hand away and stood up. "I'll fetch it myself," he said, taking a cautious step forward. "I'm weary of sitting here like an invalid."

To his surprise, his ankle didn't buckle beneath him. Instead, it felt remarkably better, even holding a bit of his weight. He hobbled toward the hearth, where the wine simmered in a small black kettle hanging from the turnspit.

"Spencer!" she exclaimed in surprise. "Your ankle. Why, it seems to be much better."

"It does," he observed, dropping the wooden ladle into the wine and pouring some into his cup. "That's rather remarkable."

He turned around to head back to his chair when he stumbled. Gillian rushed to his side, throwing an arm around his waist and steadying him. A bit of wine sloshed out of his cup and onto his hand.

"Sorry," he said, looking at her ruefully.

"You mustn't rush the healing," she chided him.

"Are you saying I must follow the advice of my physician?" he said in amusement.

"Unconditionally."

He laughed and at that moment, became acutely aware that she was pressed firmly against him, her breasts just inches from his fingers. Her chin touched his chest, and several silky strands of her strawberry-colored hair splayed out against his shirt, a few tickling his chin and jaw. He felt his body stir as he realized how perfectly they seemed to fit together. Fighting for control, he took a breath, attempting to steady himself. It was a mistake. He drew the scent of her deep into his lungs—an earthy mix of cinnamon, lavender, and woman. It made him weak with pleasure.

I want to kiss her.

He struggled against the thought, a cold sweat breaking out on his forehead. She didn't deserve or ask for this.

Instead, she had aided him when he needed it most. Was this how he would repay his debt?

"Spencer?" she said, looking at him, her green eyes clouding with concern, her lips parting as she said his name.

There was a soft color in her curled lips, and her skin glowed with pale gold undertones. She looked ethereal, almost waiflike in the dim light. He felt unwell, fevered. He had a burning desire to taste her, to yank her toward him, crushing his mouth to hers.

I'm going to kiss her.

It wouldn't be proper; it wouldn't be right. And still, he would do it. He *had* to do it. He felt any resistance crumbling.

Slowly he lowered his mouth to hers, intending to have a quick taste. He felt her stiffen in surprise, but instead of pulling away, her lips stirred to life beneath his. Her reaction caused him to deepen the kiss, taste the wine on her lips and feel the heat of her mouth. Need, desire and warmth unexpectedly exploded within him. Forgetting all else but a burning need to hold her, he yanked her closer, the cup falling from his hand and shattering on the floor.

The noise jolted Spencer to his senses and caused Gillian to take an abrupt step away from him. Spencer toppled unsteadily but managed to right himself without placing too much weight on his injured ankle. He was shaking from the experience.

"Gillian," he said, his heart thundering and his breathing coming in tortured gasps. What had he done? "I shouldn't have taken such liberties. I'm sorry."

Color rushed to her cheeks, and he hated himself for the stricken expression he saw on her face. "It's just . . . I . . . I need a moment outside," she stammered.

She fled to the door, snatching her cloak and disappearing outside, closing the door behind her.

A gust of cold air rushed through the cottage and Spencer shuddered. Swearing a string of curses, he hobbled to the chair and lowered himself into it. Well, now he'd gone and made a fine mess of things. She'd saved his life, and in return he'd nearly ravished her. Fine bargain for him, not so good for her. Frustrated, he drummed his fingers on the arm of the chair, waiting impatiently for her to return, so he could properly apologize.

She took a damnably long time. He had just decided to go and find her and to hell with his ankle, when the door opened again.

"Gillian," he said, turning in the chair. "I . . ."

His sentence trailed off as Lemuel entered, bringing with him a burst of frosty wind. He held a plucked chicken in his right hand that he dropped on the table as he entered. He removed his hat and then tipped his head at Spencer.

"Where is Gillian?" he asked gruffly.

"She stepped out for a moment."

As if hearing her name, Gillian appeared in the doorway. She pushed the hood of her cloak off her head, and her magnificent red hair spilled wildly about her shoulders. In spite of himself, Spencer felt another jolt of desire.

"Were you able to get the men to Gloucester safely?" she asked Lemuel anxiously, removing her cloak and hanging it on the peg.

He nodded, coming forward and handing her the chicken. "Supper for tomorrow," he said simply, handing it to her.

She took it and disappeared into the pantry. Returning moments later, she drew Lemuel some wine and handed the cup to him. He took a long drink, wiping his mouth with the back of his hand when he finished.

"So, tell us what happened," Gillian said, taking his cloak as he shrugged out of it.

"We had to wait a long bit, but they were fortunate to

finally secure seats on a carriage to Salem," he said, looking at Spencer. "We arranged that tomorrow I'll wait in front of the Anchor Inn for whoever will come to take you home. They will bring a mount for you to ride. Do you think you'll be fit enough? I'm afraid no carriage would get through to us."

Spencer nodded. "I'll manage. Thank you for your efforts."

Lemuel shrugged. " 'Twas easy enough."

Gillian ushered her brother to the table. "Sit down, Lemuel, and I'll bring your supper. We've already eaten."

Lemuel grunted and took his place at the table, eating quickly and quietly. When he finished, he rose, stretching his legs. Spencer wished the young man would go outside so he could apologize to Gillian. But instead, Lemuel removed his boots and sat down on the floor, picking up his carving knife and starting to whittle. After clearing the table, Gillian disappeared into the pantry, presumably to prepare the chicken for tomorrow's soup.

With nothing else to do, Spencer watched as Lemuel methodically and expertly carved the wood.

"How do you do that?" he asked curiously. "Do you have an idea of what you intend to carve before you start?"

Lemuel shrugged. "Nay, the carving is already here, deep within the wood. 'Tis my work but to free it."

Gillian came out, setting a cup on the table. " 'Tis time for all of us to get a bit of rest. Lemuel, if you would help me get Spencer back to his bed, I would greatly appreciate it."

Spencer stood by himself on one leg and hopped over to the blankets on the floor that served as his bed. "No need," he said calmly. "I can manage by myself."

Lemuel blinked in surprise, and Spencer realized that even he was shocked by how quickly the recuperation was proceeding.

Once he had seated himself on his pallet, Gillian pressed the cup into his hands. "One more potion to drink before you go to sleep," she said softly, avoiding looking at him directly.

He caught a whiff of the warm liquid and nodded approvingly. "Chamomile."

" 'Twill help you sleep, and hopefully keep the swelling down."

Spencer took the cup, willing her to look at him. Instead, she kept her gaze averted the entire time he drank. When he finished, she took the cup from him and withdrew to her room, closing the door behind her.

Disappointed that he would not have the opportunity to apologize this night, Spencer bit back a sigh. Resigning himself to his fate, he rolled up a blanket and put it beneath the injured ankle to elevate it. Then he lay back with hands linked beneath his head, thinking.

After a few minutes, Lemuel set aside his carving. After bidding Spencer a good night, he retired to his room, leaving the door open.

Spencer felt hours from sleep despite the mild sedative Gillian had given him. His mind and body were too restless. He tried to distract himself with a few mental exercises, but to no avail. His thoughts were firmly fixed on his kiss with Gillian. He had no idea what had possessed him to kiss her. He'd never taken such liberties with anyone in such a way before. His behavior had been forward, ungentlemanly, and bold. She'd received an advance she certainly hadn't asked for or deserved.

He exhaled heavily. He needed to apologize for his behavior and set things right between them before he left. If all went well, tomorrow he'd be gone from the cottage and her life forever. He expected to be cheered by the thought of going home, but he felt uncharacteristically gloomy.

It seemed like hours later before he finally fell asleep.

Yet his dreams were not filled with comforting thoughts of home. Instead, he dreamed of a willowy red-haired witch with a soft mouth and magical, healing hands.

SIX

Gillian woke early. She'd tossed and turned through most of the night, reliving every moment of Spencer's kiss, both mortified and intrigued by her body's eager response to him. They had been the most wonderful, magical moments of her life. It had hurt her deeply to see the regret in his eyes when he had pulled away. He clearly believed it to be a horrible mistake. Or perhaps he'd sensed her desire and had been rightfully appalled that she hadn't made a move to deny him.

Eventually, she gave up trying to sleep and rose, washing her hands and face in the cool October air. She shook out her gown, mending a small tear in her sleeve and smoothing out the wrinkles. Then she spent a good half hour brushing out her hair and carefully securing it in one long, thick braid down her back. She gazed at herself for a long time in the tiny mirror, wishing she were not so plain-looking. Certainly she must seem that way to Spencer compared to the more sophisticated and worldly ladies of Salem.

Melancholy, she set the mirror aside and opened the door. She stepped out into the common room, the morning light already filtering gently into the cottage. Hearing a noise, she peeked into Lemuel's room, observing that he had slept with his door open. He lay on his stomach, snoring softly, and for a moment she permitted her gaze to rest affectionately on her brother. She then quietly walked toward Spencer, looking down. She saw that he'd remembered to elevate his ankle before falling asleep, and felt a rush of guilt that she'd been too distracted by their kiss to remind him.

This morning he looked strikingly handsome, his agile, capable hands splayed across his stomach. Hands that had held her, cupped the back of her neck while his lips had moved across hers in a sensual fervor. His eyes were closed, and long, dark eyelashes rested against his cheeks. Despite his shave yesterday, he already had a fresh growth of dark whiskers. Her gaze lingered on his mouth, the wondrous mouth that had created such a stir of sensations within her. Even now her pulse quickened at just the thought of it.

His eyes suddenly opened and she started. He didn't appear at all surprised to see her. Horrified, she realized he hadn't been asleep at all, but had permitted her to stand there and leisurely peruse him. Flushing hotly, she started to move away, but his hand abruptly shot out and grabbed her by the ankle. Heat from his hand streaked through her stocking and up to her face.

"You'll not run from me this time," he said softly, sitting up while carefully keeping a hold on her ankle. "Sit down," he ordered, patting the floor beside him.

She bit her lower lip uncertainly. "I'm not certain 'tis a good idea," she whispered, looking pointedly at Lemuel's room.

"Gillian," he said in a low voice, "I need to speak with you, and it is blasted awkward for me to do so while you stand up there. But I'll shout if I must." He tugged again on her ankle until she finally knelt down beside him.

"Better," he said softly. "Now, I want to properly apologize for last night. For being so forward. You've been nothing but kind and generous, and that is not how I wished to repay you."

Gillian felt her throat tighten. She only wished he didn't look so wretchedly sorry for giving her the most thrilling moments she'd ever had.

She cast her eyes down. "I . . . I accept your apology. But only if you'll accept mine." She dared a glance up and saw he was surprised.

"You're apologizing to me? For what?"

"For wanting it to happen."

His mouth opened and he started to say something when they both heard Lemuel stir. Gillian rose, quickly busying herself at the hearth as Spencer pushed himself to a sitting position. As she stirred the fire to life and added kindling, she heard Lemuel step into the room.

"Good morn to you, Gillian," he said. "And to you as well," he said to Spencer.

"Good morning," Spencer replied. "It appears I'm fortunate that all in this household are early risers like me."

"Fortunate also, I suppose, that you'll soon be heading home," Lemuel said, straightening his shirt.

Gillian noted that her brother seemed quite cheered by the thought. But she felt a jolt to her heart, realizing just how much she would miss Spencer. Somehow, she knew that their banter, their unusual closeness, and the nature of their conversations would never be the same, even if he did come back and visit some time.

Holding back the tears that suddenly threatened to fall, she added a few more logs to the fire and went to prepare breakfast. The three of them ate in relative silence. After they had finished and Gillian cleared away the dishes, Lemuel took his hat and bade them all a good day, heading out to Gloucester again. Gillian stood at the window and watched her brother leave, a part of her foolishly wishing that no one would ever come for Spencer so that he could stay with her forever.

* * *

As Gillian had feared, the morning and early afternoon passed quickly. Spencer kept up a lighthearted banter, not mentioning the kiss again. She felt the tension between them ease. In fact, they were inside having a late lunch at the table and arguing over the best remedy to cure a backache when she heard the thud of horses' hooves outside the cottage. Surprised she leaped to her feet and ran to the door, throwing it open. To her amazement, she saw Lemuel on a horse, and behind him, a broad-shouldered gentleman with a shock of white hair. They had made excellent time in their journey.

The gentleman slid off his horse and walked forward eagerly, holding out his hand.

"You must be Miss Saunders," he said, enfolding her hand in his big, strong one. His blue eyes were kind, yet tinged with anxiousness. "I'm Dr. Phineas Reeves. I understand you have my son here."

She nodded, suddenly speechless in front of Spencer's father. Wordlessly, she stepped aside, motioning for him to enter the cottage. He did so and in two large strides was at Spencer's side, enveloping him in a big hug.

"Thank God you're all right, son," he said, holding him tight, and Gillian felt a lump in her throat at the obvious affection between the two men. "We feared the worst."

"I must say it's damn good to see you, too."

Phineas knelt at Spencer's side, inspecting the splint with a professional eye. "How badly are you injured?"

"Actually, I've been quite fortunate. I have a twisted ankle at most, as well as a small bump on the head. Overall, I feel surprisingly well."

"Well enough to travel home?"

"Tomorrow," Gillian interjected quickly. "My brother and I respectfully offer our hospitality for another evening to permit you both to properly rest before returning."

She held her breath as Phineas looked at Spencer for

confirmation. When Spencer nodded, Phineas looked at her gratefully. "We would be much obliged, then."

Gillian released her breath as Phineas bent over to inspect Spencer's ankle more closely. "You did a damn fine job on the splint, son."

Spencer grinned at her over his shoulder, and Gillian's heart leaped wildly at the pride that flashed there. "I didn't do it," he said. "Gillian did. She's quite proficient in the ways of doctoring."

A white eyebrow shot up in surprise as Phineas turned his head to study her. She blushed profusely under his scrutiny and yet couldn't help but feel a glow of happiness at Spencer's praise.

Phineas stood, a smile widening across his face. "It seems I owe you and your brother an enormous debt."

Gillian shook her head. " 'Tis just what anyone would have done."

"Not everyone is so skillful."

"You are too kind," she said, nonetheless pleased by his comment. She quickly insisted everyone sit for some refreshment as Phineas looked curiously about the room. "You have a beautiful home," he said. "Even if it is rather isolated."

"My father built it," she said, sitting. We don't mind the isolation. Lemuel and I have lived here almost all of our lives."

A shadow crossed Phineas's eyes as he lowered himself into a chair. "What did you say your father's name was?"

Gillian tensed. What if he knew of her father? "Zachariah Saunders," she said slowly.

Phineas's brows knitted together, but to her great relief, he did not say anything further. Instead, the conversation turned to medicine, art, and literature.

Phineas was especially impressed by Lemuel's work. It took only a few minutes for the doctor to win her brother over completely by insisting on seeing more of his work and commenting on the various artistic techniques Lemuel used.

All too soon, Gillian realized that both Phineas and Spencer were tired, so she reluctantly suggested that they retire for the evening.

Gillian insisted Spencer and his father stay in the bedrooms while she and Lemuel slept in the common room by the hearth. Despite strenuous arguments from Spencer and his father, Lemuel and Gillian stood firm, and the two men finally relented.

After everyone was settled, Gillian lay on her pallet, certain she'd never fall asleep. It had been a terribly exciting day filled with stimulating conversation and wonderful company. Somehow, it made her feel closer to Spencer to have met his father and heard stories about life in Salem. It seemed so grand a life, something so unattainable to someone like herself. Yet while a part of her was saddened, she also felt grateful to be afforded a glimpse into a life she could only dream about—a glimpse that would have to last her a lifetime.

Although she thought she'd never fall asleep, Gillian was surprised when she opened her eyes and realized it was morning. Hearing Spencer already stirring in her room, she rose quickly and dressed. She hastily tied her hair back at the nape of her neck and then stirred the fire at the hearth to life, adding wood. When the fire was burning cheerily, she went into the pantry to prepare breakfast. Upon her return to the common room, she saw the door to her bedroom ajar, with no one inside. Puzzled, she slipped outside and saw that Spencer had left the cottage and now stood alone down by the rocky shore, staring at the sunrise coming up over the water. She felt something stir deep within her, a bonding of her heart to his and a sense that she had somehow known him for a lot longer than just the past few days.

Streaks of orange and pink filled the sky. Early morning seagulls swooped down across the waves, searching for their breakfast. It was a glorious sight, one she'd seen hundreds of times before. But it was not the sunrise that enthralled her this morning. Her gaze returned to Spencer and his long, lean form. She could see the clean-cut lines of his profile as the morning light illuminated his handsome face.

"Good morning, Gillian," he called out without turning his head.

She blushed, wondering how long he'd known she was standing there watching him. Smoothing down her skirts, she walked over to join him. As she moved alongside him, he surprised her by casually reaching out and lacing his fingers with hers. The gesture was startling in its simplicity, but the heat that streaked between them, skin to skin, flesh to flesh, was exhilarating. She dared a sideways glance at him, wondering if he felt it, too, but his gaze remained on the sea, pensive and calm.

It suddenly occurred to her that he stood unaided on both feet.

"You've removed the splint!" she gasped in surprise. "How does your ankle feel?"

He shrugged. "It's sore, but it appears able to hold my weight, at least for a short period of time. I walked down here without the aid of a cane or crutch. I don't know how it's possible, but you seem to have performed some kind of magic on my injuries."

"Apparently, you hadn't injured it as badly as you thought."

"Apparently not," he murmured thoughtfully.

He continued to look out at the sea, his fingers still wrapped tightly around hers. She thought he seemed unusually thoughtful, almost melancholy this morning, his brows drawn together as if he were thinking of something weighty. Unsure what to say, Gillian kept silent, allowing her hand to remain in his. The breeze ruffled her hair and she shivered.

"You're chilled," he said, glancing at her in concern. "Let's go inside."

"Nay," she said quickly, not wishing to end what were most likely their last moments alone. "I'm fine. Please, let's watch the sunrise a while longer."

"Are you certain?" he asked, his cheeks ruddy from the fresh air and wind. She nodded and he put an arm around her, drawing her into to his warmth.

"I want you to know I'm saddened that my time here is ending," he said after a moment. "It's odd, but I feel as though I've known you for years."

Gillian nodded. "Yes, I feel that way as well."

He looked down at her, his blue eyes serious and somber. "You've been good to me and for me, Gillian. I feel refreshed and rejuvenated, but in more ways than just my physical condition. I feel it spiritually as well. You are a remarkable woman, and I shall greatly miss our conversations."

Gillian felt her heart twist at the thought of him leaving. She willed herself to be strong. "Whether it was fate or circumstance that brought you to me, I am deeply thankful," she said softly.

He reached out and lightly fingered a loose tendril of hair on her cheek. "If you or Lemuel ever need anything, I want you to know that you can come to me in Salem. You do understand that, don't you?"

She felt ridiculously close to tears, but held them back. *What would I ever need there except you?* she thought, her heart aching. *Because in these few days I've known you, I've fallen in love with you.*

"We thank you for your generous offer, but I don't think that would ever happen."

He took her by the shoulders, turning her until she faced him. The warmth of his fingers seeped through the sleeves of her gown and spread outward. Slowly he lifted a hand and touched her lips with his finger. Then he rested his mouth against her cheek, holding her tight, his breath warm against her skin. The strength of his embrace was so comforting, she wished to stay like this forever.

"This doesn't have to be good-bye, Gillian," he said softly, but she could hear the sadness in his voice and knew that for some reason it was.

Swallowing a sob, she removed herself from his embrace. Lifting her skirts, she hastened back to the cottage. She removed her cloak and walked past Lemuel, who had just awakened. Blinking back tears, she fumbled with her apron.

Lemuel followed, still groggy with sleep, but puzzled enough to eye her curiously.

"Is there something amiss?" he asked, running a hand through his hair to smooth it down.

She tied the strings on the apron at the small of her back and shook her head, firmly suppressing her emotions. "Nay, I just need to prepare our morning meal."

She walked over to the small trundle table and pulled out a bowl and wooden spoon. She could feel Lemuel's eyes still on her, but was relieved when he turned and left.

Spencer entered the cottage a few minutes later. Gillian busied herself making porridge, refusing to let herself dwell on the fact that she'd never see Spencer again. When she felt sufficiently in control of herself, she took the steaming bowls to the table and called everyone to breakfast. She avoided Spencer's gaze and spoke very little. Despite Phineas's best efforts at cheery conversation, the mood at the table was decidedly somber.

When breakfast was over, Gillian cleared the table while Phineas checked Spencer's ankle. After some discussion, they decided to bind it tight with linen strips to keep it immobile during the ride to Gloucester, where Phineas would arrange a carriage to take them to Salem.

"There is one more matter to be attended to," Phineas said as he finished wrapping Spencer's ankle. "After we reach Gloucester, I would like to leave the two horses with you as a gift for saving my son."

Lemuel's mouth dropped open, and Gillian blinked in shock.

"Th-that's not possible," she stammered. "We can't possibly accept so generous a gift."

"I insist," Phineas said, taking her hand and pressing a kiss on the top of it. "I can't begin to tell you how grateful Spencer's mother and I are that you and your brother were here to help our son. Please, do not offend me. Take our small gift as well as our sincere and deepest gratitude."

"I should warn you, my father is not a man easily swayed," Spencer added. "Take the horses. It will make your trips into town significantly less arduous."

"We had a horse until six months ago when it died," Gillian explained. "So things are not as bleak as they may seem."

"Then it appears my timing is most fortunate," Phineas said firmly. "Accept the small offering, my dear."

Gillian glanced helplessly at Lemuel, who was speechless for one of the few times in his life. After a moment, he shrugged.

Gillian sighed. "I truly do not know what to say."

"Then make me a happy man and say yes."

Gillian lifted her hands in defeat. "If you insist, then we thank you kindly, sir."

"Nonsense," Phineas said dismissively, with a wave of his hand. "I'd hardly consider it a fair exchange. We'll be forever in your debt. But I will, in return, offer a word of advice to you, my dear. Your knowledge of medicine and herbs is most impressive. Certainly you should consider sharing that knowledge with people who would benefit the most from it."

He turned his gaze on Lemuel quite sternly. "And you, my boy, have a breathtaking artistic talent that cries out to be nurtured and shared with others. Perhaps the horses will give you two cause to reconsider your decision to visit the town so infrequently. I have no desire to preach, but I am a firm believer that no one should waste their God-given talents."

For a moment, Gillian and Lemuel stood there like chastised children. Then Gillian straightened. "That sounds remarkably like the advice I received from your son," she said, smiling weakly.

Phineas winked at her. "I've brought him up well, then, haven't I?"

They all laughed, releasing the tension as they walked around to the back of the cottage, where the horses were tethered. Phineas supported his son as he hobbled along.

Gillian tried to prepare herself, dreading the awkward moment when she would have to say good-bye. But before she was ready, Phineas enveloped her in a fierce bear hug and passed her on to Spencer. Spencer held her in a light embrace and then brushed a kiss against her cheek and hair.

"Thank you for everything," he said softly.

Gillian didn't trust herself to answer, so she simply nodded. He squeezed her hands and gave her a smile that melted her heart as Phineas and Lemuel helped him onto his mount. After a brief discussion, Lemuel and the elder Spencer decided to double up for the ride to Gloucester.

As they rode away, Gillian felt the tears prick behind her eyelids. She lifted a hand to wave, even though she doubted any of them would look back.

She was mistaken. Spencer looked over his shoulder, and she thought she saw a flash of wistfulness and longing cross his face. Then he raised his hand to her in a silent farewell.

The gesture completely undid her. She pressed a fist

to her mouth and made a dash for the cottage. Once inside, she leaned back against the door as the tears started to fall.

Spencer Reeves was gone for good, and she knew in her heart that he was never coming back.

SEVEN

"Well, that should do it," Spencer said, securing the last linen strip around the burned arm of the young blacksmith's apprentice, Jonah Wilder. "How do you feel?" he asked, stepping back to examine his patient.

The boy's gaunt face had gone pale, his fair brows drawn so close across his forehead, they appeared to be knitted together. His hands were shaking uncontrollably. Spencer considered mixing a mild sedative for him to go along with the concoction he'd provided for the pain, but then dismissed the thought. Jonah would return to work regardless of a recommendation to rest. Given the severity of the injury, and the boy's current anxious state, Spencer thought it better to have him as alert as possible.

Jonah flexed his arm and winced. "I feel foolish. I should 'ave known better than to rest the iron against the pole. I'd plum forgot I'd put it there. I'm lucky it burned me instead of Westin. Either way, he's going to flay my hide."

Westin Sommersfield was the blacksmith and a man Spencer intensely disliked. "You tell Westin that if I have to treat you again for another injury, I'm going to charge him directly," Spencer said sternly.

Jonah smiled, his brows finally relaxing a bit. "Thanks, Doctor."

Spencer gave the boy a pat on the back. "I want you

to come back here tomorrow afternoon so I can change the dressing," he instructed. "Do your best to rest the arm, no heavy lifting, and avoid getting the dressing wet."

Jonah stood up from the chair and retrieved his hat, placing it on his head. He smelled of smoke and sweat, and his face was streaked with grime. Nonetheless, he held out his uninjured hand and Spencer shook it.

"See you tomorrow, then."

After Jonah left, Spencer began picking up soiled rags he had used to clean the burn.

"So, what's it like to be once again involved in the regular humdrum of life after barely escaping the jaws of death?" he heard someone ask from behind him.

Turning, Spencer saw his friend Charles leaning against the doorway, his hat cocked jauntily on his head. Other than the sling around his shoulder and arm, he looked none the worse from his ordeal and, in fact, looked downright cheerful.

Spencer dumped the soiled rags into a basket. "Leave it to you to be merry. I've heard you've turned our misadventure into some kind of dashing grand adventure."

"And why not?" Charles replied, his eyes sparkling. "It *was* a grand adventure. And now the boys at the pub are most curious about our mysterious red-haired savior."

"Charles, tell me you didn't," he said with exasperation.

Charles feigned a wounded look. "Why shouldn't I talk it up a little? After all, it's the truth. She did miraculously nurse you back from certain death."

Spencer pulled up a stool and sat down on it. His ankle was still sore, and standing for a time on it made it ache.

"We were lucky we found shelter," he admitted. "And I agree that Gillian is quite skilled in the use of herbs and medicine. But it is more likely that I simply did not hurt myself as seriously as I thought."

Charles snorted. "I saw you, Spence. I don't need to

be a doctor to know you were near death. She made you well again. Hell, she made *me* well. There was something about her touch that just seemed to make me feel better."

"The touch of any woman makes you feel better," he said wryly. "But frankly, in times of distress, injuries can seem exaggerated. We were exceedingly fortunate that Gillian and her brother were able to provide warmth, food, and shelter, as well as some helpful medicinal potions. It's more miraculous that we weren't seriously injured to start with."

"I won't disagree with you on that," Charles said, shrugging. "And in any case, it is healthy to get our lives back to normal. Will you meet Jonathan and me at the Blue Shell Tavern tonight?"

Spencer ran his fingers through his hair, debating the merits of the offer. He'd been back in Salem a week now and had been working hard, almost as if driven. He had no idea why he felt so restless and impatient. Perhaps he felt as though he'd been given a second chance at life. Or perhaps it was just that he missed Gillian.

It was odd, but more than once during the day, Spencer found himself wondering what she would say about the concoction he had just prepared for Mrs. Herman's indigestion or the compress he'd prescribed to ease Tom Hartford's headache. It was astonishing for him to feel this way about a woman he'd just met, but he truly missed her company.

Sighing, he rubbed his temples. It had been a long day. Perhaps a drink, a hot meal, and some aimless chatter would ease the taut feeling he'd had in his gut ever since he returned to Salem.

"I suppose there would be no harm in sharing an ale later," he told Charles, who flashed a grin in approval and left the clinic.

Slowly Spencer got to his feet and began collecting the instruments he had used in the course of the day's treatments, dumping them in a bowl of water. In the past few months, he had almost single-handedly managed their patient load. His father had been increasingly preoccupied with troubles involving their new shipping agent and delicate negotiations to purchase another vessel for transporting their cod to Boston. They badly needed an apprentice to manage some of the more tedious tasks, such as washing the instruments, seeing that there was an ample supply of linens, and making frequent trips to the apothecary to procure the rarer herbs and potions they needed. But since there was no one except himself, he did the chores as efficiently as possible. In fact, he had just finished drying the last pair of scissors when his father stepped into the clinic.

"I'm beginning to hate cod with a passion," Phineas said, plopping down wearily in a chair.

"I'm sorry," Spencer said. "Were the negotiations a failure?" He pulled up a stool and sat down, offering a sympathetic ear.

"No, actually they were a success," Phineas said, a bit mournfully. "If fact, we are now the proud co-owners of the shipping vessel the *Steadfast*."

Spencer lifted an eyebrow. "I would consider that good news."

"Of course, it is. It's just that this infernal bickering and so-called business diplomacy wears on my nerves." He looked hopefully at Spencer. "Any problems with today's patients?"

Spencer shook his head. "Little Dusty Carmichael broke a finger, and Mrs. Herman was in again, complaining of indigestion. The most serious case was Jonah Wilder, who came in with a severe burn on the arm. I dressed and bound it. He went back to work even though he was shaking like a leaf. I wouldn't be surprised to see him in here tonight again. All in all, a rather docile day."

Phineas groaned. "The end is near. I'm not even needed

anymore in my own clinic. I wish you would at least pretend that I am useful in my own practice."

Spencer thought about bringing up the need for an assistant, but he had something else more pressing on his mind. He leaned forward. "Father, there is something I've been meaning to ask you since we left the cottage. When Gillian spoke of her father, you had this look on your face as though the name was somehow familiar. Did you happen to know Dr. Saunders?"

Phineas shook his head. "No, not personally. However, I did know of him. But I thought it polite not to speak about it in the young woman's presence."

"Why not?" Spencer asked, leaning forward with interest.

Phineas leaned back in the chair and stretched out his legs in front of him. "Some twenty years ago he was involved in a scandal here in Salem."

"A scandal?"

"I don't know many details about what happened. I do know, however, that it caused quite a uproar. I was young and had just started my practice and did not know him that well. As I remember, it was a scandal of some magnitude."

"What kind of scandal?"

Phineas lowered his voice. "It was said that Dr. Saunders caused the death of a prominent citizen."

Spencer was momentarily taken aback. "Death?"

Phineas nodded. "His name was Rutherford Soward. His demise was quite sudden, really. According to all accounts, he seemed healthy enough at the time. But that is not the reason for the scandal. Rutherford was a powerful part of Salem's politics at the time."

"What does that have to do with it?"

"Don't you know who the Sowards are?"

Spencer shrugged. "They own the East-West Tannery, right?"

"That and a half-dozen other businesses in this town. When I say powerful, I mean *powerful.*"

Something stirred in Spencer's memory. "Did he have two sons?" he asked, a frown creasing his brow.

"Yes. Their uncle now runs the tannery for them."

Spencer considered for a moment. He was slightly acquainted with Jack and Thomas Soward. They'd crossed paths once or twice, but nothing more substantial. Spencer thought the young men had more brawn than brains, but they seemed harmless enough. He'd always assumed the young men, like so many of Salem's residents, had lost their father at sea, but now realized he'd been wrong.

"What happened?"

Phineas shrugged. "I'm not certain. But I do know that after Soward died, there was some kind of official investigation. It was kept quite secret. From what I understand, Dr. Saunders was exonerated from any criminal charges. But the Sowards found other ways to punish the doctor. He soon lost his lucrative business dealing with the Wakefield Shipping Company. Shortly after that, I heard the doctor moved his family out of Salem. The rumor at the time was that the Soward family had made certain Dr. Saunders would never practice business or medicine again in Salem or elsewhere in Massachusetts."

Spencer frowned. "Was there no one to stop them?"

"The Sowards are quite an unpleasant family," Phineas said wearily. "That's why I've been careful to avoid any business dealings that involve them, and why I'm thankful they do not come to us for their medical needs."

Spencer exhaled a deep breath. "There has to be more to this story than we know. Gillian was quite reluctant to speak of it. Is there anyone else who might have more information on what happened to Dr. Saunders?"

Phineas looked at Spencer curiously. "Why does it matter, son?"

Spencer thought for a moment. Truly, he wasn't certain

why it mattered or why he should make the effort to find out. But somehow, he knew that it was important, even though he couldn't explain why.

"I suppose I'm just intrigued," he replied. "Besides, what harm can come from looking into an old scandal?"

Phineas shrugged. "Nothing, as long as you are discreet. I don't know how happy the Sowards would be if they discovered you were dragging this matter out into the light again after all these years. However, if you are intent on pursuing this further, you might have a chat with old Doc Corwin."

"Corwin?" Spencer said with affection. "Is he still alive?"

"Alive and well. I saw him the other day at the Blue Shell Tavern. He's still as crotchety as ever."

"Are his faculties still in order?"

"Were they ever?"

Spencer chuckled. "Frankly, it's hard for me to imagine that he was young once."

"It's my firm belief that he was born an old soul. If you pay the old codger a visit, give him my best, would you?"

"I suppose it couldn't hurt to stop by and see him. I'm finished here for the day, and I have some time before I'm to meet Charles and the others at the tavern."

Phineas sighed and stood up. "Ah, to be young again. Shall I tell your mother you won't be home for supper?"

Spencer nodded, reaching for his coat, which hung on a peg by the door. "I'd be obliged."

Spencer parted ways with his father and headed toward Main Street. He pulled his coat tighter around him, wishing he had remembered to retrieve his hat. The October wind was cold with just a hint of frost in the air. Passersby were understandably sparse on the cobblestone streets as Spencer made his way to Corwin's town home.

He lifted the heavy knocker and was greeted by a young

maidservant, who ushered him into the parlor and asked him to wait. The mistress of the house, town seamstress Betty Corwin, stopped by to offer some tea and inform him that her father-in-law would be down shortly. Spencer thanked her and stood in front of the hearth, warming his hands.

After a few minutes, James Corwin shuffled slowly into the parlor, leaning heavily on a wooden cane. Spencer thought him to be at least eighty years old, maybe older, with a gaunt frame and skin stretched taut over the bones in his face. His nose was long and sharp, and he had thick silver eyebrows that seemed to cross his face in one crooked line. His hair was long and white, and his beard reached down in a scraggly mass to his chest. But while the body clearly showed signs of aging, Spencer observed that his eyes were as sharp and assessing as ever.

"Well, if it isn't the young upstart doctor," James said, seating himself in a chair near the fire. "What brings you out on a frosty October evening? Come to ask my opinion on a matter that all your fancy schooling isn't able to help you solve?"

Spencer grinned. "No, sir, not exactly. It's something else."

James paused, his eyes flashing interest. "What else is there in life of interest except medicine? Surely you didn't come here to speak to me of women?"

Spencer felt a flash of amusement. "Not tonight."

James studied him. "You studied at Harvard like your father, did you not?" he finally asked.

"No, sir, in Philadelphia."

"Ah, yes, the new school. I heard Herbert Walkin is teaching there. Is he still there, the old goat?"

"The last I heard," Spencer replied. *Unless he's fallen over dead on top of one of his patients from extreme old age.*

"He is an excellent surgeon," James commented, stroking his beard. "If you were instructed under his tutelage, then you can consider yourself well taught. Perhaps that is true, because I've heard you've become quite capable yourself. How is your father doing?"

"Fine, thank you. He sends his greetings."

"That's kind of him. Well, if you aren't here to seek my wisdom on a medical matter or women, then just what does bring you here, boy?"

Spencer leaned forward on the settee. "I have a question about a physician who practiced in Salem about twenty years ago. My father said he thought you might have known him. His name was Zachariah Saunders."

James's eyes widened, a surprised expression crossing his face. "Zachariah Saunders," he murmured. "Well, that's a name I haven't heard in many years. May I ask what has prompted this sudden interest in a doctor many years gone from Salem?"

"His daughter."

The silver eyebrows shot up. "I thought you said there wasn't a woman involved."

Spencer pressed his fingers together. "Only indirectly."

"Indirectly, my arse," James snorted. "Women are the root of all evil, boy. They'll get you into a kettle-full of trouble before you know it."

Spencer leaned forward. "Zachariah Saunders," he repeated, gently nudging the man back onto the topic.

James shifted his gaze to the fire, his expression turning pensive.

"Zachariah Saunders was one of the most innovative and brilliant doctors I knew. He was also a shrewd businessman and built up a decent fortune for himself. Yet despite all that, he was not particularly well liked in town among those in positions of power."

"Why not?"

"Because Dr. Saunders considered himself a champion of the destitute. He refused to accommodate well-to-do patients at the expense of the poor ones, and he detested politics with a passion. He was a bit of an odd fellow at times, but an accomplished physician whom I greatly respected."

"What happened to him?"

Corwin sighed. "It was a rather unfortunate event. Do you know of the Sowards?"

Spencer nodded. "More than I'd like to, it seems. They own the East-West Tannery."

"Yes. That and quite a bit more. Anyway, as I remember, Rutherford Soward came to Dr. Saunders, accompanied by his brother and several servants. He complained of feeling ill and demanded to see the doctor at once. But Dr. Saunders was in surgery and could not comply. When Soward found out the doctor was tending to a mere dockworker, he and his companions stormed the room and tried to force Dr. Saunders to attend to him. When the doctor refused, Soward took a swing at him."

Spencer looked at the old man, appalled. "While he was performing surgery?"

"With the patient stretched out on the table. Needless to say, Dr. Saunders shouted at Soward to get out. Soward took two steps, and then keeled over dead."

"Jesus," Spencer breathed.

"As you can imagine, it soon became the mission of the Soward family to ruin Dr. Saunders."

"What happened could hardly have been construed as Dr. Saunders's fault."

"Of course not," Corwin said with a snort. "Not to any logical-minded folk, anyway. But this is the Soward family we are talking about. They are a mean-hearted lot and they were determined to see Saunders pay. Remember, the Sowards had, and still have, a lot of powerful friends in Salem."

Spencer shook his head in disbelief. "Surely Dr. Saunders would have been permitted to carry on with his practice. You said he wasn't charged with any crime."

"He wasn't. But the Sowards put pressure on Saunders's shipping partner. Within days of Rutherford's death, Saunders's partner withdrew from their dealings."

"Not very courageous of them."

"Unfortunate, but true. Soon afterwards, strange accidents began to befall Dr. Saunders. There was no outward evidence to implicate to the Sowards, but naturally he began to fear for his life and the welfare of his family. Within a month, he'd packed up his family and left Salem."

"Could he not have gone to the authorities?"

"Without any direct evidence linking the Sowards to the accidents, what could he do?"

Spencer pondered that for a minute. Was this why the doctor had moved his family to such a remote location? To protect them?

"Was there no one to stand for Dr. Saunders?"

Corwin folded his bony hands on one knee and sighed. "He had few friends, and none of us was in a position of power to help him."

"Nonetheless, it's simply unthinkable."

"It really was a shame, you know. Besides being such a fine doctor, Saunders had a lovely wife. They tried hard for many years to have children, as I remember, but to no avail. They adopted an adorable little girl just a few weeks before this all happened." He threw a quick and curious glance at Spencer. "Perhaps she is the young woman of whom you've spoken."

Spencer looked at him, momentarily speechless from the surprising revelation. "Adopted?" he finally uttered. "From here in Salem?"

"It's possible this is she, is it not?"

Spencer considered it, his mind racing. Of course it was possible. After all, Lemuel had been adopted; why not Gillian as well? He wasn't certain why he was so surprised to hear it, or even why it mattered. But for some reason it did. And it also caused an uneasy feeling to begin to churn in his gut.

"Well, thank you for talking with me," Spencer said, standing. He had received the information he had come for, even though it wasn't what he had expected.

Standing, he reached out and shook the old man's hand. As he left the house, Spencer hunched his shoulders against the cool air and headed to the Blue Shell Tavern for a drink, some dinner, and a bit of reflection.

Jack Soward sat drinking a mug of ale at the tavern, his mood surly. His nose hurt like hell from a brawl he'd had earlier with a fisherman who had tried to cheat him on the cost of a pound of fresh cod. Now his dinner tasted like sawdust, and the ale was watery. Scowling, he tore off a piece of bread and dipped it into the stew to soften it before he began to chew. The motion caused his nose to ache, and he threw the bread down on the table in disgust.

Leaning back in his chair, he glared at the patrons around him. The place was packed with sailors and dockworkers, many angling to get a better spot nearer the huge stone hearth. Jack hoped one of them would try to encroach on his table. Despite his injury, he was spoiling for a fight to work off a little tension.

The door to the tavern opened and a blast of air shot in. Jack's younger brother, Thomas, stepped inside, closing the door behind him. He glanced around the room and then walked over to where Jack sat, slipping into the empty chair beside him.

"What in the hell happened to you?" he asked, eyeing Jack's nose.

Jack picked up his ale and took a swig. "I had to convince someone he needed to sell his cod for considerably less than he intended."

"I hope you got what you wanted."

"Don't I always?"

Thomas grinned and shrugged out of his cloak. He waved a hand at the owner's wife and she sauntered over, bringing a mug of ale with her. As soon as she was gone, Thomas leaned closer to his brother.

"I heard a bit of noteworthy news today," he said.

Jack shrugged, not particularly interested in hearing one of his brother's boring tales. But his brother seemed intent on telling him, so he set down his ale and pretended to listen.

"Spencer Reeves and his two friends were involved in a shipwreck up the coast," he said in a conspiratorial voice. "Apparently they were nearly to Gloucester when a sudden squall came up and they capsized. Reeves lost his vessel and nearly his life."

Jack yawned. "That's old news."

"I know. But do you know how they were saved?"

"They swam to shore and walked home," Jack sneered. "Why the hell would I care? They could have died and it wouldn't have concerned me."

Thomas smiled, an annoying gleam in his eyes. "They didn't walk home. They supposedly saw the lights of a cottage near the shore and made their way there. At the cottage, a mysterious young woman and her hunchback brother nursed them back to health."

"So what?" Jack said, annoyed. He was half drunk but it wasn't helping, the pain from his nose was still excruciating, and he wanted nothing more than to throttle his brother to keep him from yammering.

"It's important."

"What's important?" he snapped irritably. "Why do you think it would interest me in the slightest to hear about the misfortunes of Spencer Reeves? Must you continue to torture me with your witless drabble?"

"I'm coming to the good part."

"You'd better make it soon."

"I'm going to tell you the name of the mysterious woman who saved them."

"Why would I care what her name is?"

"Oh, I assure you, you will."

Jack stood up, leaned across the table, and grabbed his brother by the front of his shirt. Thomas gasped in fear as Jack tightened his hold.

"Either speak your mind or shut your mouth," he growled. "I'm in no mood to be trifled with."

"Her name is Gillian Saunders," Thomas managed to squeeze out. "I think she's the bitch daughter of the man who killed Father. From what I understand, she lives alone with naught more than her crouchie brother to protect her."

Stunned by the news, Jack looked at his brother for a long moment before releasing him. Thomas massaged his throat for a minute and then sank into his chair and took a swig of his ale.

Jack sat down as well, his mind racing. "What about her father?"

Thomas shrugged. "Dead, or so I'm told."

Jack considered this while taking a drink of his ale.

"We know approximately where she lives," Thomas said after a minute, his eyes excited. "Do you know what this could mean, brother?"

Jack nodded, his mood having improved drastically. "Damn right, I do," he answered, a cruel smile crossing his face. "Revenge."

EIGHT

The days passed slowly after Spencer's departure, and Gillian wondered if her life would ever be the same. Instead of feeling better with the passage of time, she felt worse. An empty, aching loss had settled in her heart, and she didn't know whether it would heal or whether she would simply have to learn to live with it.

She wrapped herself in her cloak and donned the hood, protecting herself from the brisk October wind. In her left hand she carefully held a kerchief with some crumbs of bread for the injured sandhill crane snuggled in the pen behind the cottage. The wind blasted cold as she left the cottage and went around back to check on the crane's progress.

Unfastening the latch on the pen, she clucked softly until the bird peeked his head out. She unwrapped the crumbs and held them cradled in her fist to protect them from the wind. Hungry, he emerged farther, stretching his long, gangly legs. He eyed her suspiciously for a moment and then strode closer, trying to get a better look at the food in her hand. Finally, he nuzzled her hand and she opened her fingers and ran her other hand lightly down the back of his crimson head while he nibbled.

"You're almost ready to fly," she said softly. "And not a moment too late. Your family has long ago flown south.

Perhaps even as early as tomorrow we'll have to say good-bye. It seems I've been doing quite a bit of that lately."

She felt a pang in her heart. Spencer had been gone just a week, and yet it felt like a lifetime. As if sensing her sadness, the crane lifted his head to look at her with his small black eyes.

"I thought he was the one for me," she whispered. "How could my heart be so wrong?"

Feeling increasingly melancholy, Gillian waited until the crane had finished and then ushered him back inside the pen. She returned to the cottage, closing the door behind her. Lemuel had gone out hunting several hours earlier, and she expected him back at any time.

She stopped to kindle the fire and add a few logs before stirring the stew. The meat was soft and ready for supper as soon as he returned. She had just set aside her spoon when a knock sounded at the door. Thinking Lemuel had his hands full and could not manage, she quickly crossed the room, pulling open the door.

"Lemuel, I . . ." she started and then let her sentence trail off in shock.

Two large men she had never seen before stood on the threshold. They gazed at her with cold, empty eyes, and unbidden, the hairs on her neck and arms rose.

The bigger one pushed his way into the cottage uninvited. His arms were thick with muscle, his expression grim. He glanced around the room disdainfully and then brought his gaze back to Gillian, giving her a long and uncomfortable perusal.

"So, we meet at last," he said.

Her heart jumped to her throat and lodged there uncomfortably. "Who are you?" she asked, her voice wavering.

A faint sneer touched his lips. "What? You don't recognize me? Well, I suppose I can't blame you. You were probably naught more than a babe when you left Salem."

The contempt in his voice hit her in the face like a slap. She felt her stomach roil in fear. Why had they come here? Had they seen her and Lemuel in town and decided to cause mischief or perhaps worse?

"What do you want?" she said as calmly as she could manage.

"You, of course. You are the Saunders girl, I presume."

The mere mention of her name on his lips seemed obscene. An icy chill snaked up her back. The other man stepped inside, forcing Gillian to step back farther to avoid touching either of them. He was clearly the younger of the two, although his eyes were just as empty.

"Let me get a look at her, Jack," he said, leering at her. "It's our fortune that's she rather comely."

"Why are you here?" she whispered, not certain she wished to hear the answer.

"There's a matter of a debt to be settled between us," the one called Jack said. "And my brother and I thought we might just collect on it."

Gillian felt her blood turn to ice. Trying to maintain her composure, she inched back toward the hearth, where earlier she had set the poker.

"I think you should leave at once," she said with surprising firmness, although her heart was racing.

The younger one laughed and strolled boldly through the cottage, looking into all the rooms and then into the pantry.

"She's alone," he announced, a grin spreading across his face. "Fortune is indeed with us."

"Where is the crouchie that lives with you?" Jack asked, taking a step closer to her.

Gillian backed up against the hearth, her fingers closing around the cold iron of the poker. She gripped it tightly in her hand, pressing it against her skirts, hiding it from sight.

"I asked you a question, woman," he repeated irritably. "Where's the crouchie?"

Gillian lifted her chin defiantly, refusing to answer. An annoyed expression crossed his face and then he shrugged and jerked his head at the door.

"He's likely outside somewhere. Find him and take care of him. I'll handle matters in here."

The younger one looked disappointed but headed out the door. "Save some fun for me," he threw over his shoulder as he disappeared into the twilight.

Jack smirked at Gillian and then lurched toward her as if intending to grab her. She tensed, but instead of attacking her, he laughed and sat down in her father's chair, stretching his feet out toward the fire.

"You know, it took us a lot longer to find this place than we expected," he said conversationally. "We always wondered where your coward father had run to."

Gillian felt as if he had punched her. "My father? What do you know of my father?"

He crossed his ankles. "Are you dense, girl? This is all about your father. Didn't he ever tell you he was a murderer?"

Gillian felt a flare of anger. "My father was a physician. He healed people."

The man laughed again. "He was a spineless, pathetic excuse for a man. He killed in cold blood and then ran instead of facing the consequences like a real man would."

"You're spouting falsehoods. Who are you?"

He lifted an eyebrow. "You still don't know? The name is Jack Soward. Does *that* mean anything to you?"

Gillian swallowed hard; her worst nightmare had come to life. "What do you want from me?"

He leaned forward, his eyes hard. "So, I see you do know who I am. What do I want, you ask? I want justice, of course. An eye for an eye. Your father murdered my father."

"My father never murdered anyone."

"Oh, I assure you, he did."

Gillian gritted her teeth together, fury rising in her throat. "There was an investigation. My father was cleared of any wrongdoing."

An angry flush crossed Jack's face. "Let me tell you the real tale, girl. Your father refused to treat a respectable citizen who needed immediate attention."

"My father was performing surgery."

Jack's face flushed red. "On a stinking dockworker. Your father had the responsibility to treat an upstanding member of the community, not a man who had nothing but his smell and filth to contribute to society."

"Medicine is not about social status," Gillian retorted heatedly. "It's about helping the needy."

"It's about helping those who deserve it the most, like my father."

Gillian's anger made her reckless, but at this point she couldn't bring herself to care. "Your father could have gone to a another physician when he saw my father was occupied. You cannot blame him for your father's arrogant assumption."

At this, Jack rose from the chair, his face twisted into a furious sneer. "And just how are you going to stop me from blaming him, or by extension, his daughter? The only fitting justice for him would have been death. Your father may have escaped the brunt of my justice, but you won't."

Gillian felt terror claw at her throat, but she held tight to her composure. "The only real justice served here was that your father paid for his conceit with his life. You and your family already served your warped sense of justice by forcing my father out of Salem and taking away the most important thing in his life: his ability to reach a large number of needy people. But you should know he didn't stop practicing his medicine. He continued to treat people until his death. Despite your best efforts, your family was never able to take away his skill or compassion. And although he dearly missed his work in town, he nonetheless died a happy and contented man."

"How unfortunate that will not be the case for his daughter."

Before she could move, he lunged toward her, grabbing her by the shoulder. Gillian screamed and twisted away, bringing the poker out from behind her back and thrusting it at him. The sharp point slid into the fleshy part of his right shoulder and Jack shouted in rage.

With alarming ease, he grabbed the poker with one hand and backhanded her across the face with his other. Gillian stumbled into the wall, her head rapping hard against the stone hearth. Dazed and terrified, she staggered toward the door, but he caught a handful of her skirts and dragged her back toward him. She grabbed on to the corner of a chair and held on, causing him to try to pry her fingers loose one by one. He finally removed the last finger, and she lunged again for the discarded poker he had thrown to the floor.

More quickly than she had expected, he snaked another arm around her neck and squeezed.

"Worthless trollop," he said between gritted teeth, kicking the poker and sending it clattering across the floor.

She flailed and twisted in his grip, causing him to stagger sideways and slip on the small rug in front of the hearth. Swearing, he loosened his grip to seek a better hold. The moment she felt him relax, she freed her hands and poked at his eyes with her fingers. Surprised, he howled in pain and clutched at his face. She shoved him backward and he fell hard against the corner of the fireplace.

She gasped in horror when she saw the edge of his breeches catch fire. He hadn't yet noticed when he grabbed her again, sending them both hurling to the floor in a tangle of limbs and skirts. Moments later, she heard Jack scream in pain. He rolled off her, beating at the flames on his leg with his hands.

Gillian's heart pounded in fear when she realized her own gown was on fire. She rolled away from him, smothering the flames with her body and coming to a crouch, breathing heavily. Horrified, she saw the fire had now spread to her father's chair and was rapidly making its way across the cottage floor. She stumbled to the door to escape, but Jack grabbed her from behind, pushing them to the floor again with the sheer force of his weight.

Screaming, Gillian groped blindly on the floor for something to help her when her fingers curled around one of Lemuel's wooden statues. As Jack rolled her over onto her back, she slammed it against the side of his head with all the force she could muster.

For a fleeting moment, he looked at her in surprise before his eyes rolled back in his head and he slumped sideways. Sobbing, Gillian pushed him the rest of the way off her and crawled toward the door. Smoke now filled the cottage and she could hardly see or breathe. She cried with relief as her fingers came in contact with the wooden door. But she was shaking so badly, she could scarcely stand up. With sheer determination, she rose, wrenching the door open and stumbling outside. Coughing, she collapsed to the ground and promptly retched. She lay there sobbing until she felt a heavy hand on her shoulder. She shrieked in horror and then looked up into the concerned face of her brother.

"Good God, Gillian!" he shouted, kneeling beside her. "The cottage is on fire."

"Lemuel!" she cried, throwing her arms around him. "Two men came to the cottage. One of them tried to hurt me, but I hit him with one of your statues. There is still another man out here looking for you."

"I know," Lemuel said grimly. "I found him. I dropped a rock on his head in greeting. I had a feeling 'twasn't a friendly social visit."

She gripped her brother's arm. "Oh, God, Lemuel! The other one is still inside. He said his name was Jack Soward."

She didn't have to offer any more explanation. Her brother's face turned ashen in the flickering light of the fire behind them.

"Then let him burn," Lemuel said quietly.

Gillian pressed her hand to her mouth as smoke billowed from the open door. "I—I can't. Lemuel, I'm a healer. I can't let him die, despite what he tried to do."

"Gillian, don't start this . . ." he said, his voice trailing off with a warning note.

"He'll burn to death," she protested. "Alive."

"Good riddance to him, then," Lemuel retorted bitterly. "Do you have any idea what he was going to do to you? To us? Look what he's already done."

She raised her chin. "Lemuel, 'twill make us no better than him if we leave him there to die." Determinedly, she stepped toward the cottage.

Uttering an oath, Lemuel pushed her aside and darted in through the door. After a moment, he appeared again, dragging her attacker out of the cottage in an underarm hold. Gillian ran to help and they pulled him beneath a tree, dropping him to the ground.

"Is he dead?" Lemuel asked hopefully.

Gillian knelt beside him, hesitant to touch him. Forcing herself to overcome her revulsion, she pressed a finger to his neck and felt the steady thump of the blood pumping in his veins.

"Nay, he's still alive. And he may come to his senses any moment."

Lemuel stepped into the woods and picked up a heavy stick, handing it to her. "If he comes to, hit him with this."

Gillian held the branch in her hands and looked at her brother in surprise. "Where are you going?"

"If you have no other mercy missions for me, I'll go around back and free the crane and the horses."

Lemuel removed his cloak and draped it about her shoulders. The cottage had begun to burn in earnest now, the horrid orange light flickering in an eerie display against the night sky.

"What will we do?" she whispered, a lump sticking in her throat. "The cottage is lost. Everything is gone."

Lemuel patted her comfortingly on the shoulder and then headed around the cottage. Moments later Gillian saw a dark shape rise in the sky and watched through her tears as the sandhill crane circled once above her and flew away.

Soon Lemuel returned, leading the two horses by the reins. The beasts were visibly uneasy, snorting and shying away from the fire.

"What about the Sowards?" Gillian asked, taking one set of reins and looking down at the still unconscious man at her feet.

Lemuel shrugged. "Hopefully they'll still be here when the constable returns. We mustn't tarry any longer, Gillian. 'Tis no longer safe here."

Stricken, she looked at her brother, the dire reality of their circumstances setting in at last.

"But where will we go?" she said. "We have no coin, no food, no home." A wave of grief slammed into her like a fist in the stomach as she watched a wall of her beloved cottage collapse. Holding back the tears, she pressed her lips together in determination.

Lemuel climbed up on his horse. "We have little choice. We'll have to go to Gloucester and get help."

"But what about the fire?"

"We cannot fight the fire alone. We need help." He looked down at the unconscious man in disgust. "As far as these strangers are concerned, I hope the fire spreads and burns them to death. I did what you asked and pulled him from the fire, but I'll do no more. He jerked his head at her mount. "Come on, Gillian, we need to leave *now.*"

Torn, she took one last look at the cottage she had called home for the past twenty years. Flames licked at the roof. The east side of the wall where her bedroom had once stood now collapsed in a fiery heap. Tears slipped down her cheeks as she realized the only life she'd ever known was now lost to her forever. Thank God, at least she still had Lemuel.

Numb, she threw aside the heavy stick and climbed onto her horse. They rode slowly toward Gloucester, the fire now visible on the horizon behind them.

When they finally arrived in town, Lemuel rode directly to the constable's house to inform him of what had happened. To her dismay, the constable professed irritation at being roused from his comfortable bed and showed little concern for their plight. He offered no invitation into the house and left them waiting in the cold, huddled by the horses. With a discernible lack of enthusiasm, the constable finally gathered a small band of men to ride out and investigate the damage to the cottage.

Lemuel agreed to lead the group while Gillian was taken farther into town to occupy a seat by the hearth at the nearby Anchor Inn. Gathering her pride, she refused to give in to despair. She sat stiff and proud, despite the fact that her mouth was swollen from where Jack had hit her and that her body ached from the bruises she'd received in the struggle. She waited there for hours, alone and ignored by the owner's wife, who had been roused to stoke the fire in the hearth to provide warmth for the unexpected guest before disappearing back to her warm bed.

She was weak from hunger, and several times she nearly nodded off from sheer exhaustion. But concern for Lemuel kept her awake.

As dawn broke, Lemuel finally returned, haggard and despondent. His jaw was covered with dark stubble and his eyes were red-rimmed from the smoke. She hugged him tightly, glad for his safe return.

"What happened?" she asked worriedly, taking his cloak.

He held his hands out to the warmth, oblivious of the curious stare of the tavern owner's wife, who had risen to prepare the morning meal. "The fire is extinguished," he said wearily. "But the cottage is gone, naught more than ash."

Gillian caught the sob in her throat and swallowed it. "What about the two men?" she asked, her voice almost a whisper.

"Vanished," Lemuel said dully. "Both of them. There was not a trace of them anywhere."

"Did you tell the constable who they were?"

"I did. But when he heard the name Soward, he didn't look any too eager to investigate the charges."

"But they must," Gillian insisted heatedly.

Lemuel shrugged. "The constable promised to pass on the information to the authorities in Salem." He turned to look at her. "I'm sorry, but I doubt we will see justice, Gillian."

Tears filled her eyes. "It's not fair."

He sighed. "I know. But we are on our own now."

Gillian pressed a hand to her mouth. "My God, what are we to do?"

Lemuel returned to the table and sat in a chair, his expression grim. " 'Tis time to take charge of our futures."

"How shall we do that?"

He stroked his chin thoughtfully, his remarkable blue eyes eerily calm in the flickering light of the fire. "We go to Salem to collect on a debt. Then we will see about finding our own justice."

NINE

"I'm afraid, Mrs. Samson, that foxglove is not the correct remedy for colic," Spencer said patiently while gently pressing on the protruding stomach of two-month old Jenny Samson. Although he thought it physically impossible, the infant howled even louder, causing his ears to ring unmercifully.

"Perhaps she's just hungry," Mrs. Samson hollered.

Spencer grimaced, shaking his head. "Her stomach is in distress," he bellowed over the cries. "She's not hungry. Have you been feeding her something other than breast milk?"

Mrs. Samson stiffened. "Nothing but a bit of milk porridge. There's no harm in providing a little more proper nourishment."

Spencer frowned. "At this age, breast milk is all the nourishment she needs, Mrs. Samson. Offer her the breast more often, but keep her away from the milk porridge, as this is likely the source of her distress."

Mrs. Samson shifted her considerable weight from one foot to the other, clearly upset. Spencer quickly realized what was wrong. Ignoring the fresh wails from little Jenny, he tried a new approach.

"Having a babe can be a difficult experience. Jenny is your first, is she not?" Mrs. Samson nodded and Spencer patted her arm kindly. "Are you producing enough milk?"

Mrs. Samson shook her head shamefully, looking ready to burst into tears. Spencer motioned to a chair and urged her to sit down.

"There is no shame in this," he said gently. "I assure you, it is a far more common occurrence than you think. You need simply to get as much rest as you can and eat well. I often find that the aid of a wet nurse to supplement the feedings helps enormously in these matters. I do hope you'll consider it."

The woman seemed relieved that Spencer was not blaming her for the child's distress. "Well, I suppose I could consider a wet nurse."

"Excellent," he said, smiling. "Now, I'm going to swaddle Jenny. I want you to give her three grains of nitre with some water every four hours. In addition, she'll need to be fed from the breast every two or three hours. And remember, no milk porridge."

He handed the squalling baby back to her mother and carefully poured the nitre into a small glass container. "If her condition doesn't improve by tomorrow, bring her back in."

Mrs. Samson nodded and carefully took the container. Juggling it and the still crying infant, she left his office. When the ringing in his ears had sufficiently diminished, he wiped his hands on his breeches and headed out to the small parlor that adjoined the clinic and served as a waiting room. Two people sat there, heads down, looking disheveled and exhausted. It took him a moment to realize who it was. In the fleeting space of a moment, elation, concern, and surprise filled him.

"Gillian?" he uttered. "Lemuel? What brings you here?"

Gillian quickly looked up. Spencer was horrified to see the torn and soiled condition of her gown and the clear distress in her eyes.

"You've been injured," he said, hastily crossing the

room and taking her hand in his. A jolt of familiarity and warmth swept through him at the mere contact of his skin against hers. "My God, what has happened?"

She swallowed hard. "I'm sorry, Spencer. We had nowhere else to go."

"You were right to come here," he said firmly. He knelt in front of her, taking a quick inventory of the more obvious injuries. Her upper lip had been split and was badly swollen. An ugly bruise had formed on her right cheekbone. But the grief and anguish in her lovely emerald eyes worried him the most. He glanced over at Lemuel, who fared little better.

Spencer nudged her chin up with his index finger. "What happened, Gillian? How have you been hurt?"

She took a deep breath. "Some men came to our house. They tried to hurt us. The cottage . . . Spencer, it has been burnt to the ground."

Spencer looked at her, stunned. "Burnt to the ground? Whatever for?"

Her hands trembled. "One of the men who came . . . he said his name was Jack Soward. He's from Salem. Do you know him?"

Spencer felt as though a fist had slammed into his gut. Jack Soward had found her? Guilt, sickness, and fury swept through him in a fierce rush. Guilt because he knew just how the Sowards had found her. He, Charles, and Jonathan had led them right to her door.

"What happened?" he asked, his stomach twisting in concern.

Tears filled her eyes, and Lemuel rose and stood behind her, putting his hands protectively on her shoulders.

"I was out hunting when they came," he said quietly. "Gillian confronted the big one while the brother came after me."

Spencer clenched his hands into fists. "Those black-hearted bastards," he spit out. "How badly are you injured?"

Gillian pressed her lips together. "He . . . he hit me and pushed me to the floor. Somehow I managed to render him unconscious with one of Lemuel's heavy carvings. But during our struggle, the cottage caught fire. We couldn't save it."

The misery in her voice tore at Spencer's heart. He squeezed her hand gently.

"I took care of the other one," Lemuel said. "Dropped a rock on his head. I sensed he hadn't come for a friendly visit when I saw him slinking around the woods with a blade drawn. I rushed back to the cottage and saw Gillian out in front lying on the grass. The cottage was already on fire."

He paused for a moment, remembering. "The one who attacked Gillian was still inside. I would have left him there, but I'll be damned if she didn't make me drag him out."

"You are not a murderer, Lemuel, and neither am I," Gillian said quietly.

Spencer was fairly certain he would have left Jack Soward to die, his profession as a physician notwithstanding.

"Did you inform the constable of what happened?" he asked, anger coiling in his gut like a snake.

Lemuel nodded. "But when I brought him back to the cottage, both of the Sowards were gone. In any case, he didn't seem too eager to investigate the charges, although he promised to pass on the information to the constable here in Salem."

Spencer stood and began pacing across the room. He stopped when Gillian exclaimed, "Spencer, your ankle! You can walk on it."

"Thanks to you, it's nearly completely healed," he said. "It's nothing short of a miracle. And speaking of miracles, we will need one if we believe the constable is going to do anything about Jack Soward."

"It doesn't matter," Lemuel replied. "I have my own idea of what will constitute justice in this case."

"The Sowards are a very powerful family," he said slowly. "Be careful in what you intend."

"Oh, I intend to be very careful."

Gillian looked up worriedly at her brother. "Lemuel, we must wait to see what the constable will do. Mayhap you are wrong about them."

"Perhaps," Lemuel said lightly, but his gaze remained on Spencer.

Spencer crossed his arms casually against his chest. "You do realize you're not going to achieve anything alone."

"I don't need anyone else's help."

Spencer's eyes narrowed. "I'm afraid you don't fully understand exactly what you are up against. At the very least, you will need my help."

"This is not your fight."

"It is now."

Gillian stood up, a dismayed expression on her face as she looked from one to the other. "There's a lot you don't know, Spencer. About me, about Lemuel, about what happened to my father right here in Salem."

Spencer kept his gaze on Lemuel. "I know more than you think. Regardless of what you could possibly tell me that I didn't already know, these men committed a crime."

"While I agree, I think 'twould be best if you let Gillian and me handle this alone," Lemuel said.

Spencer had no intention of doing so, but he didn't press the matter. "You'll stay here," he announced briskly. "You both must be exhausted. I'll see that your horses are watered and fed, and the housekeeper will prepare rooms for you. We can discuss the finer points of this argument later."

Gillian clasped her hands in front of her. "There is one matter to be settled first. While your offer to stay here is both generous and welcome, we will not accept charity. We intend to work for our room and board until we determine what to do next."

Spencer threw her a scowl. "Do you think so little of me? You are my guests here."

Lemuel raised his chin stubbornly. "Gillian is right. We are not beggars. We will earn our keep while we are here in Salem."

Spencer looked between Gillian and her brother, exasperation filling him. "You've just lost everything you own and all you can think of is earning your keep with me?"

"We'll not be a burden," Lemuel repeated firmly.

Spencer's scowl deepened. "I'll be damned if I'll argue about this now. Wait here for a moment and I'll speak with the housekeeper."

He found Mrs. Doyle in the pantry and informed her about the new houseguests. She promised to prepare the rooms at once, so he returned to the parlor. In his absence, three more patients had been admitted, including the young blacksmith's apprentice, Jonah Wilder, who had come to have his dressing changed. Sighing, Spencer realized that any further discussion of what had happened at the cottage would have to wait until later.

"Mrs. Doyle will inform you when your rooms are readied," Spencer told Gillian and Lemuel. "She'll have some food prepared for you as well." He turned to Gillian. "When you feel ready, you will return to the clinic so I can give your injuries a closer look."

Gillian flushed slightly. "I feel fine. 'Tis not necessary."

Spencer narrowed his eyes. "It was not a request, Gillian. I want to make certain that your injuries are properly treated. You will come see me for an examination whether you like it or not."

She opened her mouth, presumably to argue with him, but a glance at Lemuel's face told her she would get no help there. Wearily, she nodded.

Satisfied that he'd been accommodated, Spencer told them he'd be by to speak with them later and motioned Jonah Wilder into the clinic.

Spencer perfunctorily changed the dressing on the boy's arm, his thoughts with Gillian. More than anything, anger still boiled at the thought of what Jack Soward and his brother had done to Gillian and Lemuel. It was a problem that would have to be addressed at the first opportunity. And it was a problem he intended to handle as soon and as thoroughly as possible.

Gillian stood in the middle of the room, looking around in amazement. Surely this couldn't be the chamber Spencer intended for her. It was elegant, luxurious, and surely intended for a far more important guest than she.

"Are you certain this is the room Mr. Reeves wished for me to occupy?" she asked Mrs. Doyle.

"Is it not suitable?" the kindly housekeeper asked.

"Suitable?" Gillian echoed. Her gaze swept over the huge canopied bed, beautiful mahogany lowboy with drawers, and comfortable wing-backed chair that sat in front of the warm, cozy hearth. A washstand stood in one corner with a basin and pitcher and, beneath it, a porcelain chamber pot.

"Why, 'tis magnificent," she breathed. "Fit for a princess."

Mrs. Doyle beamed. " 'Tis one of my favorite rooms in the house," she confided. "I think you'll be quite comfortable here."

With that, the housekeeper led Lemuel down the hall to his room. Gillian heard her brother inquire about the privy, and smiling, she closed the door and began exploring her new quarters.

A thick plaited rug lay near the hearth, and Gillian removed her shoes, rubbing her toes against it. A flask with water and a pewter mug sat on an elaborately carved tilt-top table within arm's reach of the wing-backed chair. Curiously, she walked over to the window and gently fingered the blue velvet drapes that framed the deep recess. Pushing aside the heavy material, she was delighted to see the leaded windowpane was hinged and could be opened.

" 'Tis quite grand," she said, sighing.

Spencer's family was far wealthier than she suspected. Still, she'd been stunned to see for herself how elegant and expansive the estate really was. The two-storied brick house with black-and-gold shutters was nothing short of a mansion. Several small buildings surrounded the main one, and Gillian had observed that the estate even had its own stable. The lawn was meticulously kept, with flowers and shrubs placed artfully around the grounds. A large black-iron gate surrounded the property, creating a sense of intimacy and privacy even though it had adjoining estates on either side of it.

Gillian had been surprised when she realized Spencer and his father had actually located their clinic inside their house. Upon further reflection, however, she understood it to be a convenient and logical arrangement. Now, she understood why Spencer had praised his mother's tolerance. Why, the clinic was a part of her home.

"Personally, I can't think of a more perfect arrangement," Gillian said, sighing and sinking onto the soft bed. She linked her hands behind her head and looked up at the ceiling. For the first time since the horrid events, she felt a spark of relief that someday all might be well again.

A knock sounded on the door and she got up to answer

it. A young maidservant with pale blond hair held a tray with bread, fruit, and cheese.

"I've brought you a bite to eat, mistress," she said shyly.

Gillian thanked her profusely, even offering to share some of the fare, but the girl hastily scuttled out of the room, her cheeks flaming. Gillian wondered if she'd somehow offended her. She'd never had anyone serve her before and wasn't quite certain how to interact properly in this situation.

Deciding to ponder this later, Gillian ate quickly, surprised by the savagery of her hunger. Feeling revitalized by the food, she smoothed down her skirts and peeked out the door, deciding to visit Lemuel and see how he was faring. She approached his door and knocked, but heard no answer from within. Timidly she opened the door and peeked in. He lay fully clothed on the bed, snoring loudly. His tray of food sat untouched on a nearby table.

Smiling, she entered, pulling off his boots and covering him with a blanket. Not feeling tired, she decided to investigate the house a bit more. She went quietly down the stairs, sitting on the bottom one near the open door to the clinic and listening to Spencer speak to a patient. The man was complaining of a headache and inability to sleep. She approved when she heard Spencer suggest aconite as a remedy, it came from the dried root of monkshood and would both reduce a fever and act as a sedative. It seemed that despite their differences on the fundamental approach to medicine, they had much in common.

The patient said something else to Spencer and then abruptly stepped out the open door, stopping in surprise when he caught Gillian sitting on the stairs, eavesdropping.

She felt her cheeks warm in horror. Stammering an apology, she started to dart up the stairs when she heard Spencer call out to her.

"Gillian, please come and meet George Lockhart," he said.

Her mortification deepening, she slowly descended the stairs, feeling like a naughty child. Spencer stood at the bottom, one boot on the bottom stair, looking more like a handsome prince than a town doctor. Dressed in a white linen shirt open at the throat, dark breeches, and black boots, his startling casual attire was at odds with the elegance of the house but completely suited to his personality. He had rolled the sleeves of his shirt up to his elbows, revealing muscular forearms, and his thick golden brown hair looked as though he had run his fingers through it several times. Nonetheless, despite catching her in the awkward position of eavesdropping, he didn't seem perturbed with her in the least.

"George, I'd like you to meet my new assistant, Gillian Saunders," he said easily, holding out a hand to her as she approached the final stair.

Gillian took his hand, looking at him dumbstruck. "Assistant?" she breathed, half afraid that she hadn't heard him right.

George looked between her and Spencer for a moment, seemingly as dumbstruck as she. "A woman?" he finally said.

Spencer smiled. "A very capable woman. Her knowledge of healing is quite impressive."

George looked doubtful, but he tipped his head in greeting to her and then left the house. Spencer turned to look at her.

"George is one of Salem's finest leather crafters. He has frequent headaches and blurry vision. Did you get something to eat?"

Gillian nodded, still stunned by his revelation that he intended to take her on as his assistant and trying to file away the information about Mr. Lockhart for future study. "Yes, thank you. Spencer, I'm sorry. I didn't intend to eavesdrop on your conversation. 'Twas just that I came down the stairs and heard you talking. 'Tis all so interesting to me and . . ."

"Gillian, you don't have to apologize," he said, waving a hand dismissively. "Honestly, I'm quite eager to hear what you have to say about our methods once you've seen them in person. That is, if you will agree to be my assistant."

Her heart thumped so hard in her chest, she thought it might explode. "Are you certain you trust me enough for such a duty? Even knowing how differently we see things?"

He looked at her steadily. "I do."

"I'm honored by your trust," she said softly. "No matter what I may think, I will do as you ask. 'Tis your clinic and I respect that."

"I know you will, Gillian. And frankly I'm interested to hear what you think of some of my treatments. Sometimes they do not work. I'd like to hear about other remedies that might."

"You are a good physician."

"In that we are not so different. We both wish to heal."

She felt perilously close to tears. "Then 'twould be like a dream come true to be your assistant. I don't know what to say."

"Say yes."

She felt like throwing her arms around him in sheer exuberance. "Yes," she said breathlessly.

"Good. But first there is another matter that must be resolved between us."

Gillian looked at him worriedly. "What might that be?"

"It seems there is a matter of a special patient I must treat."

She saw the determination in his eyes and took a step back. "If this is about me, 'tis not necessary. I assure you that other than the bruises on my face and legs, I'm quite well. Besides, there are other needier patients who require your attention."

Without a word, he took her by the elbow, steering her toward the small parlor. It was empty.

"See? No other patients but you," he said.

With a firm grip still on her elbow, her took her back to the clinic and pointed to a chair. But instead of sitting docilely like a good patient, she roamed the room.

"It's simply wonderful," she breathed, examining a neatly arranged row of small glass vials. "Why, you practically have your own apothecary right here." She ran her finger lightly over the labels. "Sassafras, comfrey, nitre, calomel, rhubarb, and jalap," she said reading some of the labels aloud. "Did you collect and prepare all of these yourself?"

"Mostly. Father insisted I do it as part of my apprenticeship. The rarer ones we purchase. But as is painfully obvious, many of the vials are nearly empty. I've been so busy of late, I haven't had time to do it. I'll have to take care of it before winter sets in completely."

"I'll help," Gillian said quickly and then blushed. "I mean, if you would trust me enough to do so."

He smiled. "I thought you'd never offer. Consider it one of your new duties as my assistant. Under typical circumstances, I'd reserve such a duty for an actual apprentice. But you've clearly got the knowledge and skill to do both."

"Why don't you have an apprentice of your own?" she asked curiously.

He began unrolling several strips of linen and setting them out. "Actually, I had someone in mind, but he was snatched away by Doctor Mahoney. So, alas, I remained in dire need of some assistance until today."

"Who is Doctor Mahoney?" she asked picking up a vial and sniffing it.

"He's a physician who lives not far away on Main Street

and serves as our primary competition." Spencer's voice dropped as he imitated a thick Irish brogue. "Ye have to watch those Irish carefully, ye know. They'll steal the garments off your yer very back if ye're not careful."

The teasing note in his voice told Gillian that despite his words, Spencer held this Doctor Mahoney in high regard. "I've never met an Irishman," she said a bit intrigued.

Spencer snorted. "If I know Doc Mahoney, it's only a matter of time until you do. He'll likely be quite curious about you for no other reason than to make certain he got the better deal. Which, of course, he did not."

Smiling, she turned her attention to a gleaming display of surgical instruments. Scissors, prongs, needles, and a cauterizing iron had been carefully arranged on a wooden tray. Nearby was a long trundle table atop which had been strapped a straw mattress covered with a sheet of linen.

"How often must you perform surgery?" she asked.

"Not often. Mostly Father handles those matters, although I do assist him on occasion."

She spread her hands wide, twirling around in a circle. "The clinic is perfect. How thrilling it must be to have all this at your fingertips."

He laughed. " 'Thrilling' is not always how I would describe it. But satisfying, yes."

"To be able to help so many people . . . I would think that in itself is a reward."

He touched her arm lightly. "It is a reward, Gillian. It is why my father and I undertake such work in the first place. And so do you, I think."

"There is still so much for me to learn," she said, feeling a bit foolish for her childlike enthusiasm. "Have you any medical books?"

Spencer chuckled. "In Father's library. I'll show them to you, if you'd like."

"Now?" she asked hopefully.

"After the examination," Spencer said firmly, pointing to a chair. "Sit down, please."

She hesitated. "Must you do this?"

"I must." He went over to a scarred lowboy and began to root around for something in one of the drawers.

She sighed and sat in the chair. "Has your father returned yet?"

Spencer paused, glancing at her over his shoulder. "Would you prefer for him to conduct the examination? I can ask him, if you would feel more comfortable."

"Nay," Gillian said quickly. " 'Tisn't necessary. I was just curious as to what he would think of me becoming the clinic's new assistant."

"I daresay he'll be enormously pleased."

"Are you certain?"

"I am."

She fiddled with her skirts. "Is he away often?"

Spencer came back with a small jar and set it down on a small table beside Gillian. "These days he is a busy man. Our investments in the shipping business have become quite lucrative, but they require a skilled and knowledgeable hand. My father would deny it, but he is a formidable opponent in matters of business."

She looked at him curiously. "And you?"

"I am not anticipating the time when I will have to assume his duties in those matters. Both my father and I are men of medicine, yet if we wish to practice in relative comfort, we must attend to both. Thankfully, as winter sets in, he'll have more time to spend in the clinic with me."

He took the top off the jar, and Gillian saw that the ointment inside was a soft, yellow salve. Likely, he intended to treat her bruises with it.

"Hold still, now," he ordered, "and let me take a look at your injuries."

He took her chin gently in his hand, turning her bruised

cheek toward the light and studying it carefully. Her flesh prickled at his touch, and a familiar shiver of awareness rippled through her. Yet a quick glance at his face indicated that he now looked at her through the eyes of a doctor concerned about his patient.

Carefully he probed her cheek with his fingertips. The spot was tender, and she winced.

"You're fortunate he didn't hit the eye," he muttered and released her. "Your cheek is badly swollen, but the bone beneath doesn't appear to be broken. I'll prepare a hot poultice that I want you to apply for as long as you can bear it. It should bring down the swelling."

"Perhaps a cold poultice would be a better," she offered. "Soaked in jalap and comfrey to . . ." She looked up at his face and let the sentence trail off. "Sorry," she said, casting her eyes down.

"It's all right," he said, a smile touching his lips. "I suppose I'll have to get used to it. Now I'll need you to lift your skirts so I can see the rest of the bruises. I noticed you were limping when you went up the stairs."

She flushed in mortification. "Just a little."

"Let me take a look, please."

Nodding, she slowly lifted her skirts and rolled down her stockings. When she finished, Spencer knelt at her feet. Gillian inhaled sharply as his fingers lightly brushed a bruise on the inner skin of her left thigh.

"Does that hurt badly?" he asked.

"Nay, not badly."

The lines around his mouth tightened with anger, but he said nothing. "I'm sorry, Gillian, but I must ask," he said gently. "Did he . . . harm you in any other way? There are salves and potions that can help if he did."

She understood what he asked and shook her head, her stomach churning with nausea at the thought. "There was no time for that."

Spencer took her chin gently in his hand, causing her to look directly into his eyes. "You are a brave woman."

She had to blink back the tears. "Thank you."

Releasing her chin, he continued with his examination. "Did you twist your knee?" he asked, probing at her left leg.

"A little when I fell."

"It's a bit swollen," he said, standing up and letting her roll her stockings back up. "Have you pain anywhere else?"

"Nay," she said. "Just a few aches. I'm most fortunate that Mr. Soward was not able to harm me further."

She saw his eyes deepen with anger before he turned away. "I'll prepare a larger poultice for your knee," he said. "I want you to rest it as much as possible."

"I shall do your bidding, Doctor," she said, trying to lighten his mood.

It didn't help. He turned to her, a lock of his brown hair falling over one eye. He still looked angry. "I want you to know that I will have a talk with the constable," he said quietly. "Jack Soward will not get away with this."

" 'Tis most kind of you. But neither Lemuel nor I wish for you to become involved in this. There is much you don't know. The Sowards hold a deep bitterness against my family."

"I know more than you think," Spencer said. "I must confess that my curiosity about your circumstances got the better of me. As soon as I returned to Salem, I inquired about your family. I know what happened between your father and Rutherford Soward."

Gillian felt somehow betrayed by his confession even though she recognized his curiosity as completely normal.

"Then you know my father was innocent," she said, twisting her hands in her lap. "There was an investigation and he was not charged."

"I know," Spencer said quietly.

The memories dredged up a misery so acute that it was a physical pain. "He was a good man, an excellent physician," she said softly. "He cared about his patients."

Spencer reached out and touched her hand. "You have no need to defend him to me, Gillian. I heard what happened, and in no way can your father be faulted."

She gave a choked, desperate laugh. "I think he . . . he held himself accountable nonetheless. It wasn't his fault, and yet he still blamed himself to a certain extent. The death of that horrid man killed his dreams and then slowly killed him. I understood how he felt. All his life he was sworn to uphold life. And yet, in some way, he had been blamed for taking one."

Spencer shook his head. "Only the Sowards blamed him, and only because they were not able to take responsibility for their own actions. I won't let it happen again. The Sowards attacked you and burned your cottage to the ground. They must be held accountable."

"Then you realize why this is something that Lemuel and I must settle ourselves," she said. "It is our responsibility alone to settle this feud between our families."

He swore under his breath. "For God's sake, Gillian, do you not understand how this is my responsibility, too? Charles, Jonathan, and I led the Soward brothers to your door. This is our fault. If we hadn't been shipwrecked, then Jack and his brother would never have found you."

Gillian crossed her arms against her chest. "You didn't encourage them to come to our house and attack us. What happened has happened. Lemuel and I only wish for them to be justly punished for their crimes. I intend to place my faith in the constable."

Spencer pulled up a chair and sat down across from her. "I will be quite forthright with you. The Sowards are a very powerful family in Salem. Simple accusations without evidence will be hard to prove."

"Are not my injuries enough evidence? What about the cottage? It's been destroyed."

"No one saw the Soward brothers at your cottage except for you and Lemuel," he countered quietly. "How will you prove they were there?"

She thought for a minute. "Someone surely will have noticed them missing for a day."

"And who will confirm that? His family? Blast it, Gillian, that just won't happen. I'm afraid your faith in the constable is entirely misplaced."

She felt as though she might be sick. "Then what shall we do?"

"I'll try to limit the damage. I'll go to speak with the Soward brothers myself. Rest assured, I'm not going to let them hurt you or Lemuel again."

"How could you stop them?"

Spencer stood up. "I can be persuasive on occasion," he said lightly, but she saw an unusually grim determination in his eyes.

"Lemuel won't like this," she said uncertainly.

"He doesn't have to know."

"You intend to do this without his knowledge?"

"Would you rather see Lemuel get hurt trying to confront the Sowards?" he said harshly. "Trust me, Gillian, I know what I'm doing. Now, I suggest you retire to your room and rest."

"But I—" she started, but stopped when he placed a finger on her lips, silencing her.

"There will be no more discussion on this matter," he said. "As your physician, I'm ordering you to rest that knee. I'll bring up the poultices when they are ready."

She hesitated, uneasy and troubled by the now shuttered expression on his face. "I still wish we could talk about this further," she said quietly.

His tone and expression softened. "There will be time for that later."

A footstep sounded in the corridor and they both turned their heads. Mrs. Doyle appeared in the doorway.

"More patients have arrived, sir," she said.

Spencer thanked her and she disappeared into the corridor. Standing, he put a gentle hand on Gillian's shoulder.

"There is no need to be disquieted," he said. "All will be well. You have only to trust me."

His touch sent a warmth seeping though her. Although she could not explain why, she felt oddly reassured.

Without another word she left the clinic and slowly climbed the stairs. Once in the privacy of her chamber, she removed her shoes and stretched out on the bed to think. But before she could fathom a suitable argument to stop him from confronting the Soward brothers alone, her eyelids closed and she drifted off to sleep.

Not for the first time, she dreamed of a handsome doctor with healing hands and a kiss as wondrous as magic.

TEN

Spencer knocked firmly on the front door of the Soward estate. Shortly, a matronly housekeeper opened the door. She politely acknowledged his request to see Jack and ushered him into the parlor to wait.

Ten minutes passed before Jack finally swaggered into the parlor, looking ravaged. His eyes were bloodshot and ringed with circles. Scratches graced both his cheeks, and a purple bruise had swollen to the size of a small apple on his right temple. Spencer felt a surge of savage anger flare within him but ruthlessly suppressed it. He knew what had to be done here, and it had to be handled right for Gillian's sake.

"What the hell do you want?" Jack asked rudely and sank into one of the large chairs that had been placed in front of the blazing hearth. "I don't ever remember you paying me a social call."

Spencer walked across the room and leaned against the stone wall of the hearth. He had not removed his cloak and had no intention of sitting.

"I assure you, this is not a social call. I've come to talk to you about a matter of mutual concern."

Jack eyed Spencer curiously. "I can't see how we'd have any concerns in common, Doctor," he said, reaching up to touch his bruised temple. "Unless you want to take a look at this."

Spencer eyed it without moving. "Not particularly. What happened to you?"

"A deranged cat attacked me. Went crazy, it did. Can you give me something to help ease the pain?"

"No."

Jack frowned. "Then state your business and be gone from here."

Spencer casually crossed his arms against his chest. "It has come to my attention that you have taken a special interest in a friend of mine."

Jack's eyes narrowed, but Spencer saw a quick flash of caution in them. "And just what friend might that be?"

"A woman by the name of Gillian Saunders."

"I don't know her."

Spencer sighed. "I'm aware of your nasty little secret, Soward. You and your brother attacked a helpless woman and her brother and then burned down their cottage."

Jack's face flushed red with anger, making his bruise look even darker and more ominous. "I told you, I don't know what you're talking about."

"You're careless, inept, and a coward," Spencer said mildly. "You confronted an unarmed woman, yet she still managed to knock you unconscious. Then, for some reason unfathomable to me, she saves your miserable life. Did you know she insisted her brother pull you from the burning cottage?"

Jack stood up. "I don't know why that Saunders bitch and her crouchie brother are accusing me of something I didn't do. I already told the constable all I know. I was here in Salem on the night she claims the attack took place. I have a roomful of people ready to swear on the Bible by it. I don't know why she accused me of anything. I've never met her before in my life."

"You will stay away from her and her brother," Spencer said evenly.

Jack laughed. "And who is going to stop me? You?

You're nothing in this town but a rotten do-gooder who makes my blood curdle."

Spencer raised a dark eyebrow. "Coming from you, I'll consider that a compliment. Especially since you are the one who believes that knocking around a woman makes you more of a man."

The smile vanished from Jack's face. "Get out," he growled, his lips baring into a sneer. "Your accusations are groundless. It's her word against mine. And in this town, we both know whose word matters. Besides, the constable just happens to be an old family friend."

"How fortunate for you," Spencer said. "And since you are such good friends, I presume it also means he knows all about your little illegal distilling operation. Didn't care to spend the money to get a permit, did you? Or perhaps you have no desire to share the profits with the taxman?"

Jack blinked in surprise and then narrowed his eyes. "I wouldn't take that path if I were you, Reeves."

"And just which path would you recommend I take?"

"One that will keep you out of my family business."

"This is *my* business now," Spencer said, permitting himself a smile, satisfied with the progress of their conversation. Jack was visibly anxious now; a trickle of sweat had started to bead at his beefy temple.

"You are wrong to think you can blackmail me," Jack said, the sweat slipping down his temple toward his jaw. "You are wasting your time. I can make the constable do whatever I want."

"Perhaps," Spencer said shrugging. "Perhaps not. But the constable is not your problem and we both know it."

Jack swore under his breath. "I'm warning you, Reeves."

"No, I'm warning you," Spencer replied coldly. "Just what do you think your uncle would do if he discovered you have been dabbling in an iniquitous, not to mention illegal, venture? Being the righteous and godly man that he is, I do believe he would be expressly disappointed. He might even go so far as to cut you out of your inheritance."

"You wouldn't dare to cross me."

"I wouldn't?" Spencer said with a raised eyebrow.

"You have no idea what I could do to you."

"Now you bore me," Spencer said, rolling his eyes. "I urge you to save your aggressive posturing for some of your weak-minded friends."

"You're a bastard," Jack spit out.

"Well, at last we are coming to a clearer understanding of each other."

Jack clenched and unclenched his fists, and Spencer could see he was weighing his options. "What the hell do you want?"

"It's rather simple, actually. Stay away from Gillian Saunders and her brother."

"No!" Jack shouted. "You've no right to interfere. This is a family matter."

"I don't give a damn about you or your family."

"Her father is a murderer who never saw justice. It's my right."

"Her father is dead," Spencer said bluntly. "Your father is dead. Let the matter lie."

"No. I will have my satisfaction, my justice."

"Harming an innocent girl and her brother is not justice."

Jack looked at him incredulously, taking a step forward. "Why the hell have you become her champion all of a sudden? She's nothing, a worthless trollop."

Spencer looked at him with an unwavering stare. "You have no idea how wrong you are."

Jack snorted uneasily. "Is this because she supposedly used some miraculous cure to heal you? Or perhaps she simply used her whoring ways to nurse you back to health."

Spencer slammed his fist into Jack's jaw so hard, it sent the man flying into the chair. The overbalanced furniture tipped over backward from the weight and force of his body, slamming him onto the floor with a hard thud. Clearly surprised by the unexpected blow, Jack looked up from the floor with renewed appreciation for Spencer as he gingerly touched his jaw where he'd been hit. Then hate crossed his features as he slowly stood.

"Now you've made this personal," Jack said, clenching his fists.

"It was personal from the moment you laid hands on her," Spencer said. Cold, hard rage still pounded in his head. He wished Jack would make a move toward him, because he had a burning, primal need to pound this piece of filth into the ground. But Jack stood where he was, touching his jaw as if he couldn't believe Spencer had hit him.

"I'll explain it to you clearly one more time," Spencer said coldly. "If you ever touch Gillian Saunders or her brother again, there will be hell to pay. And that means more than just the uncovering of your profitable moonshine operation."

"Are you threatening me now?" Jack replied, his fists clenching at his sides.

"Openly and unequivocally," Spencer said, his own eyes narrowing into tiny slits. "Think hard before you act. I'm only giving you this one warning."

Jack's face became alarmingly red, and for a moment Spencer had hope that he might actually throw a punch of his own. But instead, Jack backed away. Spencer felt his stomach turn in disgust. The man was a bigger coward than he had thought.

"If you are so familiar with the story of what happened between Dr. Saunders and my father, just remember what happens to doctors who try to cross our family," Jack hissed, keeping a safe distance.

Spencer met the challenge with an icy stare. "Oh, I'll remember. And I assure you, I won't go quite as easily. So, keep in mind what has been said here tonight, Soward. For you shall receive no other reprieve if you come near either of the Saunderses again."

Turning hard on his heel, Spencer left the room. He allowed himself a brittle smile as the unpleasant sound of Jack Soward's curses followed him out the door.

A brooding silence lay heavily upon the woods of Salem. The faint rustle of autumn leaves stirred to life by the cool night air was the only sound heard.

From the spot where she sat in the small clearing, the woman could see a storm gathering. The wind had an icy chill to it, and she longed for her warm cloak. But it lay on the ground a few feet from where she sat, neatly folded for later. Now, she had all the instruments she needed at her fingertips.

Anticipation rose as the black clouds swirled and gathered above her, obliterating the twinkle of the stars as well as the feeble light of the crescent moon. The air crackled and sparked, lifting the hairs on the back of her neck and skittering down her back like a host of spiders.

The time was nigh.

In the distance she heard a clap of thunder, followed by a new snap of lightning. The black clouds drew closer together, becoming one. As it swirled above her, tendrils writhed and squirmed from it like giant serpents.

The woman held open her arms, lifting her face to the darkness.

"O Dark One, I summon thee," she called out.

A bolt of lightning shot from the sky, slamming into the ground only a tree's length from where she sat. A deafening clap of thunder followed and the woman's ears began to ring. The calf that lay unconscious on a blanket in front of her now began to stir.

"O Powerful One," she shouted again as the wind began to roar in her ears, "the Night of the Blood Moon approaches. We, the humble descendants of the MacGow clan, come to seek your final blessing."

The wind whipped past her face, stinging her cheeks and bringing tears to her eyes. Raising her voice she began to chant, first in Scots Gaelic and then in English:

"This night the faithful wait,
By fire, fleet and bleak moonlight.
Step forward and bring us the darkness,
To vanquish the light.
Receive our souls, o Dark One.
We offer devotion sprung from the womb,
In a violent passion borne.
We await your word."

The black cloud swirled closer, the cold, wispy tendrils caressing her cheeks and neck. She closed her eyes and heard a faint whisper carried on the wind.

"Are all the MacInness gathered in Salem?"

"Aye, o Masterful One. But their powers are weak. The MacGows shall not be defeated."

"See that it is so. The Prophecy must be fulfilled."

"It will. We shall not fail you."

"Then prove to me your devotion."

Without hesitation, the woman leaned forward, pulling a knife from a sheath strapped around her waist. She grabbed the calf by the chin and pulled its head back. It bawled once as she sliced into its neck, blood and gore splattering across her face and gown.

"A sacrifice is made," she shouted, holding up the knife.

The wind screamed in answer as a jolt of bright-white lightning tore across the sky. The black cloud swirled and roiled above her in an angry and violent display. Her hair lashed like stinging whips across her cheeks and face.

"I am satisfied."

Her heart pounding, she reached up to touch the ancient amulet that hung around her neck. As her fingers closed around the sacred artifact, another bolt of lightning shot from the sky, slamming into her and knocking her to the ground.

"Naaaay!" she screamed as the heat consumed her and the blood boiled in her veins. She rolled on the cold ground, writhing and shrieking in pain.

Then, as quickly as it had come, the pain and heat disappeared. The black cloud vanished and white moonlight spilled across her body. Still gasping for air, the woman lay trembling on the ground as brooding silence once again shrouded the Salem forest.

Shaking, she finally sat up, her arms falling weakly to her side. She waited until she could breathe properly before trying to stand. Once upright, she dragged the carcass of the calf to the shallow grave she had prepared and dumped it in. Slowly and carefully, she buried it, the blood still warm on her hands.

When she was finished, she wrapped the cloak around her, pulling the hood down over her head. Although badly shaken, she also felt renewed, stronger, and empowered. She had made the required sacrifice and strengthened her clan.

The MacInness brood would never defeat them now.

ELEVEN

Gillian awoke from her nap, disoriented and hungry. Looking about the unfamiliar room, it took a moment for her to remember that she was now in Salem at the Reeves estate.

She pushed herself to a sitting position and glanced about the chamber. Someone had thoughtfully covered her with a thick wool blanket. Had it been Spencer?

Curiously, she glanced at the tilt-top table near the hearth and saw two poultices lying there, long past their usefulness. So indeed, he had been here. She wondered if he had also been responsible for the lovely dark-blue gown, clean shift, and warm woolen cloak draped over the wing-backed chair.

Throwing aside the blanket, she rose and saw only a few embers glowing in the fireplace. Just how long had she slept?

Walking over to the window and pulling the drapes aside, she was astonished to see the sun already beginning its ascent. It appeared she had slept the rest of last afternoon as well as the entire night, obviously more exhausted than she realized.

Shivering, Gillian stirred the embers in the hearth and added a few more small logs, waiting until they caught. Standing in front of the blazing warmth, she stripped naked. Dipping a strip of linen from the poultice into the water basin, she began to scrub her body, as if to wash away the ugly memories of Jack Soward's hands upon her. When finished with her ablutions, she pulled the clean shift over her head, sighing at the feel of the soft, clean material. Carefully she picked up the gown and stepped into it. After a moment of twisting and turning, she realized with alarm she would not be able to tie the gown at the back. That meant slipping into Lemuel's room and asking him do it before going downstairs. Hopefully, he'd still be there.

Now, to fix her hair. There was no comb to be found, so she used her fingers to separate the long strands, smoothing them out before winding the heavy mass into one long braid down her back. The cloak went over her shoulders to hide her unfastened gown.

She slipped out of the room and headed down the hallway to Lemuel's door and knocked softly. But there was no answer. Timidly she cracked open the door and peeked in. To her dismay, the room was empty.

Gillian closed the door, a guilty flush heating her cheeks. Was she the last one to wake this morn? Quickly she made her way to the stairs and heard a soft rustle behind her.

"You must be Miss Saunders," a woman's voice said.

Turning, Gillian saw a lovely woman with light-brown hair and a cheerful smile walking down the corridor toward her. Her resemblance to Spencer was so strong, she knew at once this must be his mother.

"I'm Rosemary Reeves," she said. "How delightful it is to finally meet you."

Gillian suddenly found herself embarrassingly tongue-tied in the presence of this elegant woman. "Please call me Gillian," she finally managed to say. "My brother and I don't know how to thank you for your kindness."

She patted Gillian's arm in a gesture that was both motherly and comforting. "Nonsense. Why, it is our family who can never repay you for your assistance to our son and his friends. We are only grateful we have the opportunity to return the kindness. I'm dreadfully sorry for your misfortune. Spencer told us what happened. Please consider our home yours for as long as you need."

"I'm certain it won't be for long," Gillian said hastily. "And we will try not be in your way. We intend to earn our keep here for as long as we stay. I'm going to help in the clinic preparing herbs, cleaning the instruments, and washing the linens. But I also have a reasonably good stitch and can cook as well. Perhaps you will need help with something in the household?"

Rosemary looked at her in surprise and then laughed, the sound coming out as a light, tinkling sound. "You truly mean that, don't you? You are indeed as delightful as both Spencer and Phineas have said. My dear child, you and your brother are our honored guests here and shall be treated as such. There is no need for you to earn your keep."

"But we can't impose ourselves," Gillian insisted. " 'Twould make us terribly uncomfortable."

Rosemary tucked her arm through Gillian's. "Oh, now I can see why Spencer is so taken with you. Charming and modest. Come, let us go down and have something to eat. You must be famished."

"I am rather hungry," Gillian admitted.

Rosemary lifted a corner of Gillian's cloak. "And chilled as well. Was there not sufficient wood in your room?"

A warm heat flushed her cheeks. "There was plenty of wood. And the room is lovely. It's just that I wear the cloak because . . ." Her cheeks warmed. ". . . because I wasn't able to fasten the gown by myself. I had hoped to have my brother aid me, but to my misfortune, he has already left his room." She felt like a simpleton. How plain and unrefined she must seem to this poised woman.

But Rosemary only chuckled. "Let me venture a supposition. Spencer chose this gown for you without giving a thought as to how you would get it fastened. God forbid that men should ever be left to handle such matters."

"I cannot say for certain it was Spencer who chose the gown," Gillian said in his defense. "It had been placed in my room over a chair while I slept."

"Oh, I assure you it was my son. He may be exasperating at times, but he is impeccably thoughtful." She drew her delicate brows together in a frown. "Yet how unusual for him to choose a gown without asking for my aid. He must have thought this color would be lovely on you." She stepped back and eyed Gillian critically. "And indeed, it is," she murmured.

"I'm certain 'tis just a loan until I can wash and repair my own gown," Gillian protested.

Rosemary shook her head. "Don't say that to Spencer unless you wish to greatly offend him," she warned. "I'd consider it a gift if I were you. Now, if you'd like, I'll help you fasten those stays."

"Oh, I wouldn't want to trouble you."

"It's no trouble at all."

Gratefully Gillian removed the cloak, and Rosemary draped it over the stair rail.

"You know, I think we are going to get on just fine," she said agreeably. "And this discussion has just given me a thought. If you are still insisting on earning your keep, I have a suggestion."

"You do?" Gillian said hopefully as Rosemary pulled the stays tight.

"I do, indeed. If you would be so willing, you can be my friend."

"Me?" Gillian said incredulously.

"Yes, you, of course," Rosemary said with a final tug, turning her around. "This surprises you?"

"Well, I . . . I don't know if Spencer told you, but my

brother and I didn't get into town much. I doubt I'll have anything of interest to offer such a friendship."

"On the contrary," Rosemary disagreed, urging Gillian to leave the cloak and descend the steps with her. "I already find you a refreshing change from most of the ladies in this town. Besides, you don't know how lovely it will be to have another woman right in the house with whom to converse. All Phineas and Spencer ever talk about is cod, ships, and medicine." She glanced sideways at Gillian and added, "Although I hear you are quite a healer yourself."

Gillian smiled, touched by the compliment. "My father was a physician. I took an interest in his profession and helped him on occasion. But I would hardly consider myself skilled."

"Well, Phineas and Spencer were quite impressed with your knowledge and skill. I assure you, they are not so easily awed."

"They are truly kind men," Gillian declared.

Rosemary smiled warmly. "Indeed, it is so. I consider myself a most fortunate woman."

She led Gillian into the dining room, where Phineas and a young girl were already seated. The girl had long golden-brown hair tied into two braids. She looked curiously at Gillian.

Phineas rose when he saw them, welcoming Gillian with a warm, beaming smile.

"How lovely to see you again, my dear, although I had no idea it would be so soon," he said, striding forward and clasping her hand between his. "I'm quite distressed to hear of the circumstances that brought you here."

"Your sympathy is much appreciated," Gillian said. "I don't know how to properly thank you for your generosity."

The young girl rose as well and Rosemary went over

to her, putting her arms on her shoulders. "This is our daughter Juliet. Juliet, this is Gillian Saunders."

"Hello," she said, giving a shy smile.

Gillian smiled back. "I'm pleased to make your acquaintance."

Juliet sat down again and Rosemary moved to one of the chairs, patting a seat next to her for Gillian to sit. She went over to her chair and Phineas gallantly pulled it out, waiting until she was seated before returning to his side of the table. Instantly, a maidservant appeared, placing a tankard of ale and a plate of bread and cheese in front of her. To her horror, Gillian heard her stomach give a loud rumble.

Phineas grinned. "Well, at least one of us shall fully enjoy the fare this morning. Eat up, dear. Not to boast, but I've heard it said that our cook, Mrs. Carlisle, makes the best bread in Salem."

Gillian picked up a piece of the bread. She took a bite and then sighed as it practically melted on her tongue.

"That is truly so. 'Tis exquisite," she said. She took a sip of her ale and then looked around at the other empty chairs. "Has anyone seen my brother this morning?"

"He ventured out early with Spencer this morning," Phineas said.

"What mischief the two boys are up to, I do not know," Rosemary offered. "Whatever it is, I'm certain they are enjoying themselves."

"I heard them laughing and whispering about something as they left this morning," Juliet offered and then blushed.

Rosemary delicately nibbled a piece of cheese. "I wouldn't be too concerned, as we are certain to hear about it shortly. Juliet, eat your porridge, please."

"Yes, mamma," Juliet answered dutifully and took a bite.

Gillian smiled at the young girl, and soon the room

was filled with the lively and entertaining sounds of their conversation. She had just finished the last piece of bread on her plate when Lemuel literally bounded into the room, in remarkably good spirits. Spencer followed, his brown hair windblown and cheeks flushed from the cold.

"Good morning, everyone," Spencer said, ruffling Juliet's hair and stopping by his mother's chair and giving her a peck on the cheek. Juliet gave her brother an openly adoring look, and Gillian understood exactly how she felt.

"And how do you fare this morning, Gillian?" Spencer asked with a grin so warm, she thought she might melt on the spot.

"Wonderfully, but I slept far too long, I fear," she replied as Lemuel slid into the empty seat next to her. "No one woke me."

"Doctor's orders," Spencer replied, reaching for the plate of bread. He took a slice and passed it on to Lemuel. "Did you all finish breakfast already?"

"We certainly did," Rosemary said. "We weren't going to wait around for you. Why, we had no idea what mischief you two were up to this morning."

"I beg your pardon for being tardy to the table, madame," Lemuel said earnestly.

Juliet hid a chuckle behind her hand, and Spencer laughed. "She's only just saying that to tease you. She wants desperately to know what we were doing but knows it would be quite unladylike to ask."

"Being unaware of such convention, I shall then be so bold to ask," Gillian said, getting a grateful glance from Rosemary. "What *were* you two doing this morning?"

Spencer grinned nonchalantly, but his eyes still twinkled. "A bit of this and a bit of that."

" 'Tisn't just so, Gillian," Lemuel said excitedly, tearing off a piece of bread. "We've been clearing out the woodshed for my workshop."

"Workshop?" Gillian repeated in surprise.

Spencer grinned. "I've just commissioned your brother for a life-sized carving to decorate our parlor. That room has long needed something to keep our patients' minds off their ills. One of your brother's remarkable creations is just what we need."

Phineas slapped his thigh in delight. "A marvelous idea, indeed. Well done, son."

Gillian felt a lump in her throat at the exuberant expression on her brother's face. "Lemuel, that's simply wonderful."

He smiled happily. "But I'm still going to do some other work around the estate as well. I've offered to work in the stables, cleaning and feeding the horses."

"I told him it wasn't necessary," Spencer protested when his father grunted in disapproval.

Lemuel raised his chin. "If the carving is to be done on commission, then I still need to earn Gillian's and my room and board here. Therefore, 'tis necessary indeed."

"And I'll be working in the clinic," Gillian inserted. "And I've offered to sew and cook as well." She looked over at Rosemary and added, "And 'twould be my honor to be a willing friend to you, if you are certain this is what you wish."

"A friend? Is that so?" Spencer said, raising an eyebrow at his mother. She lifted an eyebrow back and then patted the corner of her mouth with a cloth.

"Don't look so surprised. We women have to stay together. Especially when we are surrounded by men. But I do think it is a fine idea for Gillian to help in the clinic, if that is something she would like to do. Perhaps you'd even like to take a look at the pen where Juliet keeps a varied stock of wounded animals. And Lemuel, I'm certain you'll do a fine job with the horses. Although if word gets out that we are engaging our guests in heavy labor, I don't know what people will think."

"Someone with Gillian's skills is precisely what we

require in the clinic," Phineas said, leaning over to kiss his wife on the cheek. "Frankly, I don't care what the townsfolk think. And despite your complaints, you don't either. It's our responsibility as good hosts to see to the comfort and happiness of our guests. And that is exactly what we are doing."

"Oh, it is," Gillian assured her. "And I'd love to see the pen, Juliet. I had one just like it at my home." As she said the words, she felt a pang of loss at the memory.

"You did?" Juliet said, her eyes lighting up.

"She did indeed," Spencer said. "Somehow, I think the two of you will have a lot in common."

Phineas stood and smiled. "Well, then it is all settled. I'm especially pleased that you are willing to assist us in the clinic, Gillian. Ever since Spencer has grown into his own as a physician, we've needed a new assistant. I also wanted you both to know that I've spoken with the constable and let him know you are staying here with us. He promised to keep me informed on the progress of the investigation."

"That is very kind of you," Gillian said.

"It's the least we could do. Now, it's my great misfortune that I'm needed down at the dock for an inspection of our new vessel. I trust you will manage fine today without me in the clinic."

"I shall endeavor to do my best, Father," Spencer answered.

As he left the room, the housekeeper appeared. "Sorry to bother you, sir," she said to Spencer, "but the first patients have arrived."

Spencer stood. "Thank you, Mrs. Doyle. Well, then, I must excuse myself."

Gillian rose as well. "May I assist you?"

"Today?" Spencer said in surprise. "I thought perhaps you would rest at least another day."

"I'm fine," Gillian insisted. "Please, I'd prefer to keep

myself occupied. I promise to stay out of your way and do only as you request."

Spencer pondered her request for a moment and then nodded. "Welcome aboard, then, Mistress Gillian. Let's get to work. I hope it's an easy day for your sake."

The day had been far from easy and seemed only to be getting worse, Spencer thought in dismay.

"I'm going to cauterize the wound to keep it from bleeding," he said to Gillian, winding a linen strip tightly around the wrist of Amos Hunter, one of Salem's finest gunsmiths. "Would you heat the iron, please?"

She nodded, moving quickly and efficiently to do his bidding. She was a good worker, he thought, watching as she carefully held the instrument over the flame. Despite her skill, he hadn't been certain how she would perform under pressure when quick thinking and instantaneous decisions had to be made. But she had proved to be a quick and apt pupil.

Spencer had known in the first hour that they would work well together. She had a calming presence and soothing voice that seemed to help his patients. She had also earned his respect and trust by being able to correctly anticipate his needs.

By the third patient, they had fallen into a comfortable rhythm. She worked resourcefully and was discreet enough to disappear if she noticed any of his patients were uncomfortable with her presence.

The ailments had been fairly routine, with a steady stream of patients complaining of gout, indigestion and fever, but the afternoon had quickly progressed to a broken leg, two burned fingers, a dislocated shoulder, and now Amos's badly injured wrist.

The poor man had suffered a grievous cut, with the skin flayed clear to the bone. It was a sight that could have paled even the staunchest of assistants, but Gillian never even flinched. Instead, when Amos had been brought into the clinic, she helped lead him to a chair, holding the distraught man's hand and murmuring gentle words while Spencer took stock of the injury.

"Take another sip," Spencer said, urging the gunsmith to take a swallow of the whiskey Gillian had prepared as a sedative.

Amos's eyes widened and his face turned ashen when Gillian brought Spencer the glowing iron.

" 'Twill but hurt for a moment," Gillian said gently. "Shall I sit beside you?"

Amos swallowed hard, his Adam's apple bobbing in distress. He looked between the iron and Gillian and then nodded. She held out her hand, and he gripped it tightly.

Gillian murmured to him softly, and Amos gave an audible sigh and closed his eyes. Spencer looked at Gillian and nodded. Then he firmly brought the cauterizing iron down against the man's wrist.

Spencer braced himself for the scream that was certain to come, but to his surprise, Amos did not cry out. Instead, his face contorted in pain, and Gillian winced as the huge man squeezed her hand. Her eyes, too, had closed. For a moment, Spencer got the impression she was as in as much pain as Amos. Quickly Spencer lifted the iron and placed a soothing poultice over the wound. Gillian opened her eyes as Amos fainted dead away. She kept him from slipping out of the chair while Spencer deftly stitched the wound closed and then bound the injury. When Amos groaned, he went in search of some smelling salts to bring the big man around.

"Are you all right?" Spencer asked Gillian as he waved the salts under Amos's nose. "I thought he might have crushed your hand."

"He did not," she said, but nonetheless he noticed she was unusually pale.

"Show me your hand," he said firmly.

She obediently held it out and he took it in his own, turning it over. It looked uninjured, no bruises or redness evident.

Puzzled, he dropped it. "You have a remarkable way with people. How you managed to keep him calm is beyond me. I thought I might have to sit on him to cauterize the wound."

She smiled weakly. "That would have been difficult— getting him to the floor, I mean. He's considerably larger than you."

He grinned as Amos began to come around. "Yes, but I have you to assist me. You could have distracted him with your quick wit and beauty while I wrestled him to the floor."

She laughed, a bit of color returning to her cheeks. "Is that a common practice in your clinic?"

"I'm not above implementing it if it proved effective," he said grinning. "Some of my most effective treatments have originated from rather unorthodox techniques. I'll admit I've engaged in enough unusual approaches that, if they became common knowledge, would likely cause me considerable difficulties."

"You'll have to tell me sometime," she said, her eyes lighting up with interest.

Spencer chuckled. "Only you would reduce a physician to such confessions."

She smiled at him just as Amos came around, blinking and looking at his bandaged arm in wonder.

"Is it over?" he asked a bit groggily.

"All done," Spencer replied. "Come back tomorrow to have the dressing changed. You'll soon be fine, Amos."

The big man stood a bit shakily and shook Spencer's hand. Then he looked at Gillian.

"I don't know what I would have done without your

help, Miss Gillian. It didn't hurt nearly as much as I had thought it would with you sitting by my side."

"I'm glad I could be of assistance," Gillian said demurely.

Spencer prepared some leaves for Amos to mix with his tea to ease the pain and then saw him out the door. When he returned, Gillian was cleaning up.

"Sit down," he ordered her, sinking into a chair himself. "I think we've earned a respite."

She nodded wearily and sat down across from him. "Is this a typical day in the clinic?" she asked.

"Sometimes there are fewer patients, and yet some days there are even more. Thank God there are no more patients waiting in the parlor now. If fortune is with us, I think we are finished for the day."

"Thanks be," she agreed, taking off her kerchief. A few strands of her red hair straggled out of her braid, wisping enchantingly about her face. "And speaking of thanks, I have yet to express my gratitude for this lovely gown and the cloak I found in my chamber. Was it you who procured them for me?"

He smiled. "I hope you like them. I fear I know little of women's fashion."

She lightly fingered the material. "They are beautiful. I've never had such finery. I feel a bit overwhelmed by your kindness and generosity. I'm not certain I can ever repay you for all you've done for me and Lemuel."

"You've already repaid me," he said softly. "A hundred times over."

Gillian sighed, rubbing her forehead, and Spencer noticed with some alarm that she still looked unwell. Guiltily he realized that he had worked her hard while she had still not had time to recover fully from her own traumatic events.

Sighing, he leaned forward in his chair. "I've been selfish," he said. "You are exhausted and I've worked you far too long and hard today. Forgive me; I'm sorry."

She smiled wanly. "Nay, please, Spencer, don't apologize. 'Twas the best day of my life."

He took her hand in his, feeling the familiar jolt of heat and awareness. "You far exceeded my expectations today."

"You don't know how much that means to me," she said softly.

Their eyes locked, and without thinking he leaned toward her. His mouth just inches from hers, he abruptly came to his senses and leaned back in his chair, shoving his fingers through his hair.

"Gillian, there is something I've been meaning to tell you," he started and then exhaled heavily. "I've been a cad not to mention it earlier, but . . ."

"My, my, my . . . I do hope I'm not interrupting," a deep male voice said from the doorway.

Spencer looked up in annoyance and saw Charles, clad in a black cloak and hat and leaning casually against the jamb. He looked as dapper as ever and had an amused gleam in his eyes.

"Don't you ever knock?" Spencer said irritably. "What if I had a patient in here?"

"Cease being so disagreeable. Mrs. Doyle told me you were free. Besides, I came as soon as I heard Gillian was here." He crossed the room and took her hand, gallantly pressing a kiss on the top of it. "Gillian, my dear lady, how are you? I heard what happened to you. It's all so dreadful."

"Hello, Charles," she said. "I didn't expect to see you so soon. How is your shoulder?"

"Fine, thanks to you. I no longer require the bandage, and other than a bit of soreness, there is no evidence of an injury."

"I'm glad," she said, smiling.

Spencer pursed his lips. "And just how did you hear about Gillian's presence so quickly? Have your ear pressed to the gossip mill again?"

Charles scowled. "I'll ignore that smirch on my impeccable character and mention only that my mother ran into your father this morning. He told her what happened and it was passed on to me just minutes ago. I came as soon as I heard. You could have had the decency to tell me."

"I hadn't the opportunity," Spencer replied a bit defensively, wondering if it was really the truth. Why hadn't he immediately told his friend about Gillian's arrival?

"Are you certain you are well?" Charles asked Gillian. "You've been through a ghastly ordeal."

"I'm grateful for your concern," she replied. "I really am well. It's just that we've had an eventful day in the clinic today and . . ."

Charles looked at Spencer in horror. "My God. Tell me you are not insisting that she earn her keep here."

Spencer felt his ire grow. "I'm not insisting on anything."

"Then why is she working?"

"Because she wouldn't listen to me."

Charles gave an exaggerated scowl. "You obviously didn't try hard enough. Gillian, should you ever desire a more peaceful environment in which to recover, my estate is at your disposal."

"Now wait just a minute," Spencer said testily, moving toward Charles, when Gillian held up her hand, stepping between them.

"He's right, Charles. I did insist on working and I'm grateful to him for allowing me the opportunity to do so."

"You are far too accommodating to him, I fear," Charles replied. "Nonetheless, my offer stands."

"I appreciate your generosity."

Charles bowed gallantly. "Well, now, if that is resolved,

may I be so bold as to suggest a stroll about town for some fresh air to invigorate the senses? That is, if Spencer is through working you to near-death."

Gillian smiled demurely and Spencer felt an unexpected tug of jealousy. "Can't you see that she's weary?" he said irritably.

Gillian shook her head. "That is very kind of you to offer," she said. "Perhaps another day. But now I think I'll retire to my room for a bit of rest before supper."

With that, she bade them a good day and left the clinic. Spencer listened to her footsteps as she climbed the stairs to her room and then glared at Charles.

"What in the hell are you doing?" he snapped at his friend.

Ignoring Spencer's irritated glance, Charles seated himself comfortably in a chair. "What do you think I'm doing? She's a lovely woman. I'm quite fortunate that she is now in Salem."

Spencer narrowed his eyes. "What is that supposed to mean?"

"What it always means, of course."

Spencer scowled darkly. "Surely you are not considering her as another one of your conquests."

"*Conquest* is such an indelicate word," Charles said, waving a hand dismissively. "Gillian deserves far more than that. I was thinking more along the lines of a bit of social discourse and perhaps even romance. She saved my life, after all. I think that entitles her to a bit of special consideration."

"She's hardly the type of woman you usually pursue," Spencer grumbled.

"I know," Charles said, grinning. "And that it makes it all the more challenging. Not only is Gillian beautiful, but she's capable, intelligent, and frankly, considerably more interesting than any women I've met of late."

"Leave her be," Spencer said sharply. "She's an innocent. She doesn't know how to play your games."

Charles lifted a dark eyebrow. "Who said it would be a game?"

Spencer snorted. "I know you, Charles. You don't know any other way."

"Now I'm insulted."

Spencer stretched out his legs in front of him. "Why should you be? We both know you wouldn't suit a woman like Gillian."

"And just who do you think would suit her?" Charles asked, narrowing his eyes.

He considered it for a moment. "Someone with more, let's say, honorable intentions."

Charles burst out laughing. "Oh, that's grand, Spence," he said. "As if any man really has honorable intentions."

Spencer rolled his eyes. "You know what I mean."

"Actually, I think I do. And frankly, I'm perplexed. It's as if you wish to put some kind of claim on her yourself."

"You know that's not possible. I just don't want to see her get hurt."

"I'm hardly in a position to hurt her," Charles said pointedly. He leaned forward in his chair. "On the other hand, you are. I'm not blind, Spence, and neither are you. She *is* innocent. I've seen the adoring way she looks at you. Just what happened back at the cottage?"

Spencer exhaled a deep breath and rubbed the back of his neck where his muscles had knotted with tension. "Hell and damnation, I kissed her. I shouldn't have let it happen. I've really mucked things up, haven't I?"

"I presume that means you haven't told her yet."

Spencer gave him a wry look. "I was about to when you interrupted. But it's not as if I've had time to prepare for this," he said, resigned. "I certainly never expected her to come to Salem, and it's not a matter easily brought up in regular conversation. Besides, she's only been here a day."

Charles crossed his legs, fiddling with his boot. "Those are all wickedly poor excuses. You have to tell her."

"I know. I just need more time to determine the least awkward way to tell her."

"I'd advise you not to wait too long. It's bound to come up in conversations with your family, at the very least."

"I'm fully aware of that. In fact, I intend to warn Mother and Father that they are not to say anything until I've had a chance to do so myself."

"And Juliet?"

"She's a child. She'll do as I ask. Besides, it's only for another day or so, until the proper opportunity presents itself."

"Don't hurt her too badly," Charles said softly, and Spencer looked at him in surprise.

"You really are fond of her."

"Aren't you?"

"Yes, blast it, I am."

Charles rose from the chair and walked to the doorway, where he paused, his back still to Spencer. "Well, just so you know, if I do decide to pursue her, I will do so with honorable intentions. But you've got to tell her, Spence, or no other man will interest her. The sooner you tell her, the better."

"For whom?" Spencer muttered under his breath as Charles left the clinic without a backward glance.

TWELVE

After a bit of rest, Gillian felt much better. Her strength returned and the wicked headache finally eased. Slowly she rose from the bed, went to the window, and stared down at the busy street in front of the Reeves estate. Although physically she felt better, she was also deeply troubled. Something unusual and more than a bit frightening had happened to her today at the clinic.

Looking down at her hands, she turned them over, studying them intently. They looked like normal hands; white skin, translucent veins, and red, roughened knuckles from repeated scrubbing of linen strips. Except that when she placed them against an injured person, she seemed able to absorb pain and offer a kind of invisible healing in return.

Her mother, father, and Lemuel used to tease her that she had a healing touch when birds and stray animals miraculously recovered under her care. She had been so proud, thinking it the result of the careful tutelage and guidance of her father.

But today, when treating a large number of injured people one after another, something different had stirred to life within her. She had felt it gradually at first—a warmth, a heat, that seemed to glow from within. It flowed outward through her fingers into the patients like some kind of invisible soothing balm. In return, she'd received a portion of their pain, absorbing it into her body and becoming intimately aware of the depth and extent of their suffering.

This was a new experience for her. It had never happened before, perhaps because she had so rarely treated people.

"Who am I?" she whispered, clenching her fingers into fists. "What am I?"

She had no time to ponder further, for a light knock sounded on the door along with an announcement, relayed by one of the maidservants, that supper was ready.

Smoothing down her hair and gown, Gillian descended the stairs, meeting up with Lemuel, who was waiting for her at the bottom. He had just scrubbed his face and hands and tried to slick back his blond curls with water. He looked remarkably handsome and cheerful. Affection swelling in her heart, she gave him a peck on the cheek, and he smiled, his eyes alight with a happiness she'd never seen before.

"You should see the piece of wood that Spencer procured for me," he whispered excitedly, offering her his arm. " 'Tis utterly magnificent. The color, the texture, and the size . . . Gillian, you'll not believe it. Why, 'twill barely fit in the woodshed as it is."

"That's wonderful," she said sincerely. "I'm certain you'll create your most spectacular work ever."

He looked at her with a critical eye as they started to walk to the dining room. "You've circles under your eyes. Are you not sleeping well?"

"I feel fine," she lied, not wanting to dampen his spirits.

"Did you enjoy your work in the clinic?" he asked.

"Oh, Lemuel, it was the most exciting day of my life. But I have so much to learn."

He grinned sideways at her, pausing before they entered the room. " 'Tis almost like paradise, is it not? Da' was right when he said there is always something good that can come from bad. It's happened to us, has it not, Gillian? I'm fashioning the most important carving of my life, and you are finally among people, practicing the healing arts. What more could we ask for?"

She glanced down at her hands. "What more, indeed?" she whispered and stepped into the dining room.

Everyone was already seated, but the men rose and Spencer gallantly held out a chair. After wishing everyone a good evening, Gillian sat.

"Were you able to get some rest?" Spencer asked with concern as she settled into the chair.

"I did, thank you," she said, offering him a smile.

"Did my son work you too hard today?" Rosemary asked with a frown.

"Nay," Gillian said hastily. " 'Tis just taking me a bit of time to become accustomed to the routine here. Everything is perfect."

"She did exceptional work in the clinic today, Father," Spencer said, spearing a piece of meat with his knife. "Surpassed all of my expectations."

"Excellent," Phineas said, beaming. "I knew she would."

"Only because of the patient guidance of your son," Gillian insisted, blushing.

Spencer shrugged. "Truthfully, I did very little guiding. She's naturally adept at this sort of work, much to my great delight."

"Any difficult patients?" Phineas asked after taking a swig of his ale.

"Amos Hunter," Spencer said with a grimace. "Sliced his wrist to the bone. Gillian miraculously managed to keep him calm while I cauterized and stitched it. I've never seen anyone have such a soothing effect."

Gillian suddenly felt Lemuel's gaze intent on her face. She smiled weakly. "Beginner's fortune, that's all."

"Well, I hope it continues," Spencer said. "If word of

your healing touch and efficient manner gets out, we'll be the busiest clinic in town."

Phineas chuckled. "Oh, that would truly vex Doctor Mahoney, now, wouldn't it?"

Spencer grinned back. "I give him one week before he's nosing around, trying to get a look at Gillian."

"One day," Phineas replied. "I'll wager you three coins on it."

"Agreed," Spencer replied, and Rosemary rolled her eyes.

"Men," she said, sighing. "I would ask you to please refrain from wagering at the table, and certainly not in front of Juliet."

"I'm not a child," the girl spoke up, jutting her chin out. "And when do I get to help out in the clinic like Gillian?"

Phineas wagged a finger at her. "When you can sew a proper stitch, adequately play the pianoforte, and sing like an angel."

Juliet pouted. "But I'll never be able to do all that."

Everyone laughed and the rest of the dinner was filled with lively and interesting conversation. When everyone had eaten, Spencer rose and offered an arm to Gillian.

"I'm going to take a short stroll around the town," he said. "Would you like to accompany me?"

Gillian nodded. "I'd be delighted. Just let me fetch my cloak."

"Lemuel?" he asked with a raised eyebrow.

"Nay, but thank you just the same. I have work I need to do. Next time, perhaps."

"Can I come?" Juliet asked, standing up.

"No!" Spencer said a bit sharply and then smiled at his sister. "Another time, sweet," he said, walking over to ruffle her hair.

"But I wanted to show her my animal pen."

"You'll have plenty of time to do that later."

Juliet looked duly dejected, so Gillian smiled at her. "If you'd like, I'll look at the pen tomorrow morning. Agreed?"

Juliet nodded, brightening a bit. "Agreed."

With that, Gillian went to retrieve her cloak. When she returned, Spencer already waited for her at the bottom of the stairs, clad in his coat.

Again he offered his elbow, and she took it, thrilled to be finally able to tour the city.

"I haven't seen the town in years," she said excitedly as they walked out the front door and to the gate. Spencer unlatched it and waited until she passed through.

"You've been to Salem before?" he asked.

"Years ago. I think I was eleven. Once my father came into town for some medical supplies that an old friend of his had collected. But it was dark and I couldn't see much. We didn't really have the opportunity to visit Salem for long, and never in the day in case the Sowards were about. But I know my father missed the town dreadfully. He loved it here. It was his home."

Spencer stopped, looking intently at her. The autumn air was crisp, and his breath made small white puffs as he spoke. "I'm sorry about that." He hesitated a moment. "Gillian, I would like to ask you something quite personal. If I am too forward or it's a matter that you would prefer not to speak of, please tell me."

She gazed up at him, puzzled, wondering what he could possibly wish to discover that he didn't already know. "Certainly. What do you wish to ask?"

He blew out a breath. "Are you adopted?"

She blinked in surprise. "Why do you ask?"

"I'm just curious. Hopefully, I haven't offended you by asking."

She lifted her shoulders. "I'm not offended. And to answer your question, yes, Lemuel and I were both adopted. My mother and father were the most loving and generous people I've ever known. Lemuel and I were very fortunate."

"I agree. What do you know of your adoption?"

"Nothing. I was still a babe. But mayhap that's why I feel so comfortable in Salem. The cottage was the only home I've ever known, and yet, I know it sounds strange, but . . ." She paused, looking down the street where a few passersby strolled along, chatting happily. "Something in this town beckons to me . . . to my heart."

"I understand what you mean," Spencer said, resuming their walk. "I feel the same way about this town. I hope I didn't upset you."

"You didn't. Memories of my family may be painful, but they are also comforting. And I still have Lemuel, of course."

"As well as me and my family," he added gently. "And a host of other admirers after just one day's work at the clinic. I shudder to think of how the numbers shall grow as the days go on."

"Now you tease me," she said, tucking a strand of hair behind her ear.

"Not at all," he said, his voice sincere.

They walked past shops and piers. Gillian was delighted to see that at every turn she could catch a glimpse of the sea. Strolling arm in arm along the wharves, Gillian marveled at the majestic vessels with colorful banners, and sailors who called out cheerful greetings.

All the while, Spencer good-naturedly answered her numerous questions, stopping frequently to show her various points of interest. At one spot, she could barely hear him talk over the clang of the anchor forge, so they moved a short distance away to a wooden bench in front of a warehouse in which, Spencer told her, sail lofts were built. A large oak tree shaded the bench from the setting sun, and crisp autumn leaves crunched beneath her feet as they seated themselves.

Gillian rested, all the while taking delight in the unfamiliar but pleasant sounds of a city slowing down for the evening. A man walked by rolling a one-wheeled apple cart, while a young boy rushed past carrying a basket of cod slung down from his neck. In the distance, she could hear the clopping of horses taking their riders to various destinations.

She turned to say something to him and noticed he was deep in thought, a troubled expression on his face.

"Something worries you," she said in alarm. "It's something I've done. Did I make a mistake in the clinic that I failed to notice?"

He shook his head, but his mood didn't improve. "No, Gillian. This is not about your performance in the clinic. There is something I've been meaning to tell you since you came to Salem, but I'll be damned if I can find an adequate way to say it. Other than the fact that I've been a thoughtless and—"

He stopped as a crack and then a squeal came from the tree above them. To Gillian's horror, a young boy dropped from the tree and onto the grass behind their bench in a flailing of arms and legs.

She heard a sickening thud before Spencer leaped off the bench to the boy's side. Gillian quickly joined him, grasping the boy's hand. He was unconscious, his left leg bent at an unnatural angle.

"It's young Ben Sellers," Spencer said, sweeping the boy into his arms. "We've got to get him back to the clinic."

Gillian followed him at a run. As they burst into the house, Spencer shouted for Mrs. Doyle to send someone to fetch the boy's parents. Without even asking, Gillian dashed off to find Spencer's father.

Phineas and Rosemary were taking tea in the parlor when she appeared in the doorway, breathless and frantic. Phineas came at once to the clinic, striding over to the table where Spencer had laid out the boy and was administering smelling salts. Gillian rushed about the room, lighting candles and stirring the fire in the hearth.

"The leg is broken. We'll have to set it," Phineas said grimly.

Spencer nodded and then breathed in relief when the boy began to moan. "He's coming around, but when he does, he is going to be in a wicked amount of pain. Gillian, when I give you the word, you'll need to hold down his shoulders for me."

Gillian nodded, moving to stand by Ben's head and quickly doing her own assessment of his condition. She judged him to be about four to five years old, with a dirt-streaked face and torn shirt. He moaned again before his eyes abruptly opened and then clouded with pain. A scream ripped from his throat and he began to thrash about wildly.

"Hold him down," Phineas shouted at her while Spencer struggled to cut the boy's boot and breeches off with a knife.

Gillian closed her eyes and placed a hand on his forehead, whispering softly to him. Suddenly the boy ceased screaming and lay still.

"Mama?" he said, tears streaking down his little cheeks.

"Shush," Gillian murmured soothingly, continuing to stroke his forehead. You are going to be well. Just rest."

The boy's eyes rolled back in his head and then drifted shut. Gillian felt an agonizing rush of pain and bit back the gasp that threatened to slip from her lips.

Taking advantage of the momentary reprieve, Spencer removed the breeches and boot from the boy's leg. Phineas gave a hard yank and set the leg. He then looked worriedly at Ben.

"Did he faint?" he asked Gillian.

Ben opened his eyes, looking groggy but no longer in pain. "No," he whispered.

"Well done, my boy," Phineas declared. "You're a brave little fellow."

"I didn't faint," the boy said softly. "She made the hurt go away."

Just then the boy's parents rushed in the room, running over to his side.

"What happened to him?" the father asked.

"He fell out of a tree," Spencer answered. "Almost on top of me."

"You wicked boy," his mother chided the boy worriedly, squeezing his hand. "You're always getting into mischief." She looked apologetically at Phineas. "We've never had this much trouble with our other three children."

"Just be grateful it wasn't worse," Phineas said. "Fortunately, he'll soon be up and about, and most likely into mischief again."

"Whatever were you thinking, boy?" his father scolded.

The boy opened his eyes and smiled at Gillian. Ever so slowly his small hand crept toward her. "Thank you," he whispered.

Gillian squeezed it and then raised her gaze to Spencer. He met it for a long moment and then returned to helping his father bind the splint to the boy's leg.

When they were finished, Phineas prepared a mild sedative for Ben and then took his parents to the parlor, arranging for a carriage to take them home. When they were alone, Spencer took Gillian by the elbow.

"Are you ready to tell me what happened back there?" he asked.

"What do you mean?" she replied innocently.

"I mean, you did something or said something to that boy. By all rights, he should have been screaming in pain."

"Perhaps he just responds well to a woman's touch," she offered.

"Everyone damn well responds to your touch," Spencer said. "Gillian, there is something you aren't telling me. About you. About your touch. Just what is it you are able to do?"

To Gillian's horror, her knees buckled from exhaustion and she nearly collapsed to the floor. Spencer caught her in his arms, steadying her body against his chest. Her head fit perfectly beneath his chin.

"You soothed him," he said softly. "I saw you. If I didn't know any better, I'd say you even took the boy's pain into you. You did it with Amos Hunter, too."

"How is that possible?" she said shakily.

"I'm asking you to tell me. Is there some sort of special technique you are using?"

She shook her head. "I simply led him to believe that I could help him," Gillian said quietly. "Would you not agree that sometimes pain can be controlled by the mind?"

He surprised her by agreeing. "I do, indeed. But that boy is five years old. I don't think he yet has the mental capacity to accomplish such a feat."

Slowly he lifted one of her hands and turned it over in his, studying it intently. "You put your hand on his forehead."

" 'Twas only to provide a cool touch to a pained brow."

"A healing touch," Spencer countered. "Gillian, I know something unusual happened back there in the clinic. Not only with that boy, but with the other patients, too. Sometimes I wonder if you can actually heal . . ."

But before he could finish, a tall, slender woman with long, glossy black hair swept into the parlor unannounced. She was elegantly clad in a blood-red gown and black wool cloak, with a small, delicate pouch hanging from her left wrist. She seemed completely at ease in her surroundings, so much so that Gillian felt an alarming flutter in her stomach.

Spencer started in surprise, and Gillian realized that they still stood in each other's arms. Hastily, she pulled away from him and sat in a chair.

Spencer calmly turned his attention to the stranger. "Well, this is a surprise. What brings you here?" he asked, his voice mild.

She arched a delicate brow, and Gillian noticed with astonishment that the woman had a stunning eye color, a blue so light they were almost white. Framed by thick, black eyelashes and brows, the contrast was dramatic and dissonantly compelling.

Her perfect red mouth formed a pout. "I missed you," she said simply.

"Young Ben Sellers had a fall from a tree. He broke his leg. Father and I set it."

"How dreadful for the poor boy," the woman exclaimed, shaking her head so that gorgeous ringlets fell delicately against her cheeks and accentuated her lovely porcelain skin. Then, ever so slowly, she turned her blue eyes on Gillian.

Gillian felt an unexpected chill as the woman's gaze raked across her with an odd mixture of resentment, aloofness, and curiosity.

Spencer saw where her gaze had landed and smoothly interjected, "It's been a difficult day. Miss Saunders has been assisting me all day in the clinic and just now with Ben. She was understandably feeling a bit faint. I was just about to suggest that she sit a spell."

The woman smiled. "So I see. Well, I am glad to finally make your acquaintance," she said to Gillian. "Spencer has told me all about you."

Her voice was unfailingly polite, yet Gillian sensed a contradictory and almost predatory heat belying the woman's tone.

"You have me at a disadvantage," Gillian said, raising her chin. "With whom do I have the pleasure of speaking?"

A slow smile spread across the woman's face as Spencer looked between the women, a mixture of regret, concern, and guilt on his face.

"Gillian," he said quietly, "I'd like you to meet my fiancée, Phoebe Trask."

THIRTEEN

Why in the hell didn't I just tell her? Spencer thought with a sick twist in his gut. The stunned look on Gillian's face was his fault, the result of his infernal indecision on how best to tell her.

He'd intended to tell her about Phoebe during their stroll. He had envisioned a quiet conversation during which he would apologize for failing to reveal his engagement and for leading her possibly to draw the wrong conclusions about his feelings. But little Ben Sellers had landed in their laps just as he had been preparing to tell her. He had delayed much too long, and now the damage had been done.

Guilt rose in his throat, nearly choking him as the two women appraised each other.

"I'm pleased to make your acquaintance," Gillian finally said with a forced smile.

"As am I," Phoebe said with a delicate lift of her dark eyebrow. "Spencer told me all about your unfortunate circumstances. This must be a dreadful time for you."

Gillian sat stiffly, and an awkward silence ensued before she finally rose from the chair. "Well, if that will be all, Doctor, then I will retire to my room."

Unable to think of anything appropriate to say, Spencer simply nodded. She politely bade them both a good evening and left the room.

Feeling increasingly angry with himself, Spencer strode out of the parlor and into the clinic. Phoebe followed.

"Spencer, darling," she said, exasperation evident in her voice. "Whatever is the matter with you this evening?"

"Nothing," he said shortly. He picked up Ben's ripped breeches and boot off the floor and dropped them into a nearby basket.

Phoebe sidled up to him, wrapping her arms around his waist. "I had hoped you might call on me today." She pressed her body against his seductively, placing a light kiss on his neck.

But instead of being aroused, Spencer found himself annoyed. "I'm sorry, Phoebe. I had intended to stop by, but circumstances conspired against me."

"It's not too late," Phoebe murmured. "We could take a stroll in the garden and perhaps I'd let you steal a goodnight kiss or two."

"I'm weary," Spencer said truthfully. "Besides, I'll see you at dinner tomorrow."

"But tomorrow is such a long time away," she complained, now winding her arms around his neck. "Take pity on me."

"Tomorrow," he promised.

"Well, I should certainly hope so." She pouted, clearly disappointed. "We have a few more arrangements to settle before the wedding."

"I know," he said, moving to press a chaste kiss on her cheek. At the last moment, she turned her head so that he caught her full on the mouth. Resigned, he kissed her until she moaned deep in the back of her throat, winding her fingers in his hair. After a minute, he gently extracted himself from her embrace and urged her to the door.

"It's late. Did you bring the carriage?"

She tucked her arm into his. "Of course. Will you call it around?"

It took a few minutes for the carriage to be summoned. When it arrived, Spencer helped her into it.

"Good night," he said, pressing a kiss on the back of her hand.

She leaned down, her hair brushing against his cheek. "Until tomorrow, darling."

He waited until the carriage was out of sight before returning to the clinic and closing up for the night. Not surprisingly, he hadn't felt like being with Phoebe since his return to Salem. He felt guilty, conflicted, and even worse, unsure about his feelings for her. None of which were her fault. Loosening his neck cloth, he stopped by the kitchen. Mrs. Carlisle willingly prepared him a plate with the remainder of the evening's supper.

He finished his supper without enthusiasm and headed for his room. On impulse, he stopped by his father's library and procured a bottle of whiskey. Tonight he could use a bit of spirits to help lessen his guilt.

He took a swig straight from the bottle before leaving the library, the liquid burning a path down his throat. Carrying the open bottle with one hand, he climbed the stairs. He half hoped that Gillian's door would be ajar, so he might have an excuse to look in on her. But the door was tightly closed. For a moment he stood there, taking another swig of the whiskey and debating whether he could be so bold as to knock. Then he heard the soft sound of her weeping. Cursing under his breath, he turned away. What the hell could he say now that would make things any better?

Disgusted with himself, he strode down the hall and into his own room. He stoked the fire, added more wood, and stripped down to his shirt and breeches. Cradling the whiskey in his lap, he continued to drink straight from the bottle.

Damn it all to hell and back, he had hurt her. Badly. It pained him greatly, and yet it also caused something deeper within him to stir. It both baffled and troubled him. Why should it matter so much? He barely knew Gillian Saunders. Certainly he owed her the debt of his life, but hadn't he at least partially repaid it by taking in her and her brother?

True, they'd shared a passionate, perhaps even tender kiss. But that was all. No promises were exchanged, no binding contracts signed. It had been an unexpected action, done for the sheer pleasure of it. Except, blast it, somehow it had been so much more. Not only for her but for him as well.

Scowling, Spencer took another swig of whiskey. He grimaced as the alcohol seared his stomach. If only it could burn away the guilt now churning there. He'd made a bloody mess of things. Better to put all this behind him as quickly as possible before he made it worse. He'd have to find a way to make it up to Gillian so she'd forgive him. Then he'd rekindle his feelings for Phoebe. She was his fiancée after all. Hopefully things would return to normal.

He didn't know how long he sat there in front of the fire drinking, but when he finally fell asleep in the chair, he had almost brought himself to believe it.

Gillian awoke the next morning, her heart aching, eyes swollen from crying. She didn't know why the news of Spencer's engagement had come as such a surprise, nor could she understand why she hadn't thought of it before. Handsome, accomplished, and kind, he'd certainly be a catch for any woman. Now when she looked back, she had been woefully naive to imagine that his kiss had been more than just a passing fancy.

Sitting up in bed, she pushed the bedcovers aside. This was her problem, not Spencer's. Her hope that there had been something blossoming between them had been naught more than the simple dreams of a foolish and naive girl. Still, the fact that he had kissed her and hadn't bothered to tell her about the engagement hurt deeply.

She rose from the bed and splashed some cold water on her face, hoping to lessen the swelling of her eyes. While patting her skin dry, she vowed that from this moment on she would banish any romantic thoughts of Spencer Reeves and look at him as nothing more than a friend and benefactor. He had been kind and generous to her and Lemuel when they needed it most. He deserved her courtesy and gratitude at the very least.

Sighing, she removed her nightgown and had just pulled a shift over her head when she heard a soft knock at the door.

"Who is it?" she called out.

" 'Tis just me, mistress, Lynette. Mrs. Reeves has sent me to help you with your gown."

"Bless her thoughtful heart," Gillian murmured, opening the door a crack to let in the young, blond maidservant. She carried several gowns over her arm.

"These are for you, mistress," the woman said.

"But . . . but there are so many," she stammered.

"Mrs. Reeves insists," she said, taking them over to the wardrobe and hanging them on the wooden pegs inside. "And she says I'm also to assist you with whatever you may need."

"Me?" Gillian said in surprise. "Whatever would I need assistance with?"

"Bathing, shopping, and mending, mayhap."

Gillian blinked in amazement. "How kind of her. But I can't imagine that I would need to be waited upon."

The young woman bobbed her fair head. "As you wish." She held up a gown and Gillian stepped into it.

"What did you say your name is?" she asked curiously, slipping her arms into the silky sleeves.

"Lynette Carlisle, mistress."

Gillian glanced over her shoulder in surprise. "Is your mother the cook here?"

"She is."

"Might I mention that she makes the best bread I have ever eaten in my life, not to mention other food?"

Lynette nodded proudly. "I won't disagree with you, mistress."

Gillian sighed. "Would you mind terribly if I call you Lynette? I would very much like it if you'd call me Gillian."

She smiled shyly. "If you so wish."

"Tell me, Lynette, how long have you worked for the Reeveses?" she asked and then winced as the young woman pulled the gown closed with a yank.

"Four years—since my thirteenth birthday. The Reeveses have been good to us. They are a generous and kind family."

"To everyone they know, it seems," Gillian agreed. "How lucky you are to work here."

"Aye, 'tis so. I hear that you and your brother have also insisted on earning your keep during your stay here." She tied the last knot and then blushed when Gillian turned around. "I don't mean to pry; 'tis just that it seems rather curious to me."

"No offense taken," Gillian said kindly. "I consider it a privilege to work in the clinic."

"But why do you do it? Are you not guests here?"

"We are. But only because of an unfortunate incident that has left us without a home or means."

"Have you no other kin?"

Gillian shook her head. "Nay, and if it were not for the kindness of the Reeveses, I don't know what we would have done."

Lynette lowered her gaze. "I heard what happened. I'm sorry. I've had my own troubles with Jack Soward."

"Have you?" Gillian said in concern.

"He tried to force himself on me once when I was late coming home. 'Twas my great misfortune to run across him as he was leaving the tavern. He was under the influence of spirits and I just managed to get away. 'Twas not a pleasant experience."

Gillian shuddered. "Nay, not for me either."

"Well, I'm certain you'll like it here," Lynette said. "You've done well to make friends with the family. We all love Mr. Spencer dearly and we are thankful to you for saving his life."

" 'Twas fate, I think, that brought us together. We saved each other in more ways than one." A wave of melancholy rushed over her and she looked away, reminding herself to be thankful that while she might not have his love, at least she'd have his friendship.

"Did you happen to see my brother up and about this morning?" Gillian asked, wishing to change the subject.

To her surprise, Lynette blushed. "Aye, mistress, he's already eaten and has gone to the woodshed to work. He's an early riser like me and Mr. Spencer."

"Well, it seems I may have a duty for you after all. Perhaps you should wake me a bit earlier so I can start the day properly with the rest of the family."

She chuckled. "Trust me, mistress, you'll not be wanting to wake so early."

Even though she agreed, Gillian said, "Well, it's just that I hardly ever see my brother any more. He's either busy at work in the stables or locked in the woodshed, where he will not let me enter. Although why he insists on working in such secrecy is beyond me."

Lynette's eyes lit up. "He wants the carving to be a surprise for everyone. And indeed, it will be. You should see the beautiful piece of wood Mr. Spencer selected for the carving. 'Twas formidably expensive, and Lemuel says 'tis of the most spectacular quality he's ever seen. He's been sharpening his tools for days."

Gillian looked at her incredulously. "My brother let you into the woodshed?"

"Someone has to bring him his midday meal. Sometimes we just sit and talk a bit. I confess that at first I thought him to be a bit odd because of how he looks, but he wasn't like that at all. He knows so many things and is very clever."

"He is, indeed," Gillian murmured, both thrilled and perhaps even a little jealous at Lynette's interest in Lemuel.

"Well, if that will be all," Lynette said, turning for the door.

"Thank you," Gillian said sincerely. "I'd like it if you would come by and chat some time with me. I could use a friend."

Lynette paused at the doorway. "You know, you and your brother are not at all what I expected when you first arrived here."

"What did you expect?"

She shrugged. "I don't know. Most of the visitors here, not to mention ladies, keep me in my station, they do."

"Your station?"

"Aye, mistress. You are a lady and I am here but to serve you."

"Oh, I'm not a lady," Gillian assured her hastily.

Lynette giggled. " 'Tis exactly what I mean. There is something about you that speaks of the bearing of a true lady, and yet you seem unaware of it."

"That's kind of you to say, even if I'm not certain what you mean," Gillian replied with a sigh. "There is much for me to learn."

Lynette smiled. "Well, summon me if you need anything else."

"Thank you," she replied.

As soon as Lynette closed the door, Gillian sank into a chair, her thoughts in a whirl. So, Lemuel had made a friend, just like that. Perhaps she had been wrong all that time to insist they stay in the cottage after their parents had passed away. She had thought to protect him, but he was stronger than she had ever imagined.

Now, she wondered with a sinking heart, just who had been protecting whom?

Gillian headed down the stairs to breakfast, hoping Spencer had long ago eaten and left. She knew she'd have to face him eventually, but she wanted a bit more time to prepare herself. In the harsh light of morning, the revelation was still too painful to discuss. To her enormous relief, only Juliet sat in the dining room, nibbling on a piece of bread. She brightened as soon as she saw Gillian, and quickly bounded to her feet.

"I've been waiting for you," she said eagerly.

Gillian looked about the room. "Where are the others?"

"Spencer has likely eaten and long since gone for his daily walk. Mother and Father don't often come down right away." She tugged on Gillian's arm. "Come now. It's the perfect time to see my pen. I have an injured sandhill crane and a hawk interned there."

Gillian nodded, thankful for an excuse to escape. "I've nursed a sandhill crane or two back to health before," she said as the two fetched their cloaks and left the house. "And many hawks."

"Really?" Juliet said, her eyes lighting up. "Perhaps you can help me, then. Neither George or Skye seem to be getting well."

"George? Skye?"

Juliet smiled. "I like to name my animals. George is the crane and Skye is the hawk. Skye is a female. Her mate is always nearby, watching and waiting for her to get better."

They passed the woodshed, where Gillian could hear Lemuel whistling as he sharpened his blade. She felt another tug of jealousy that he had not permitted her to see what he was doing but had invited in a young maidservant. So much for sibling loyalty.

"Why did you name the hawk Skye?" she asked Juliet.

"I suppose it's because hawks fly so high it seems as though they are almost touching the sky. I call her mate Star."

Juliet led her to a large wooden pen surrounded by a small fence. It was twice the size of the one Gillian had had. "Spencer and Father made it for me," she said proudly, opening the pen. "Come here, George," she called out.

After a moment, a stately bird cautiously stuck its head out. Gillian smiled as the bird stretched its spindly legs and stepped out. It had a bandage wrapped around one leg.

"Broken leg?" she asked.

Juliet nodded. "Spencer seems to think it will mend, but it's been three weeks and all of her kind have already flown south. If she doesn't heal soon, she'll never survive the winter."

"Just what happened to you, George?" Gillian murmured, trying to get a better look. Not familiar with her, the bird shied away. "He'll take a few days to get used to me," she said. "Once we've established a bond of trust, I'll see if he'll let me get a closer look at that leg."

Juliet nodded and Gillian was impressed when the bird let the girl lightly touch the top of its crimson head.

"He likes you," Gillian observed.

Juliet smiled. "We've become good friends, haven't we, George?"

A fluttering noise sounded above them, and Gillian

glanced up just as a large hawk swooped down and sat on a nearby tree, watching them intently.

"Hello, Star," Juliet said.

"That is the biggest hawk I've ever seen," Gillian said in amazement.

"And very protective," Juliet said. She pulled some bits of raw meat out of an oiled cloth that hung in a pouch around her waist. "Let's give him a look at his love." She went to the open pen, holding out her hand and crooning softly. Soon a hawk cautiously appeared in the doorway, eyeing Juliet's hand hungrily.

Gillian observed that the hawk had badly injured its wing. "Have you been able to examine the wing?" she asked Juliet.

"Not yet," Juliet said, stretching her hand out farther. "She's only been here a few days." To Gillian's amazement, the hawk stepped closer, carefully taking a greedy bite of the meat right from the girl's hand.

"Extraordinary," Gillian said and then looked up as Star swooped off his branch and circled above their heads, as if daring them to try to harm his mate.

"We're not going to hurt her," Gillian called out to the hawk.

"Do you think he understands?"

"Perhaps in his own way." Impulsively, Gillian held out her hand. "Hand me a piece of the meat," she said softly.

Juliet looked at her curiously but complied. Gillian laid the meat not far from her feet, all the time staring at the hawk flying above them. He screeched and then circled a bit, not yet trusting her enough to swoop down and take it.

"Hawks mate for life," Gillian murmured. "Nonetheless, I don't ever think I've seen such devotion."

"I'm not certain it will last. Spencer doesn't think her wing will ever heal. She might not fly again."

Gillian kept her gaze on Star. "This one will wait for her until the end."

"How do you know that?"

"I just do."

At that moment, Star shot down from the sky with claws extended. In a flash, he scooped up the meat and flew to a nearby branch, where he ate it, all the while watching them suspiciously.

"Is that why you are so good with animals?" Juliet asked curiously. "Because you understand them so well?"

Gillian smoothed down her skirts. "I believe that every living thing has an aura, a sphere of well-being, if you will. You have to sense not only the physical, but the spiritual as well."

Juliet nodded thoughtfully. "Yes, I've always thought healing is much more than the physical mending."

Gillian smiled. "No wonder the animals come so willingly to you."

"I hope someday every living creature will feel free to come to me for healing," Juliet said fiercely. "I don't care if it isn't proper behavior for a young lady." She jutted out her chin stubbornly, and Gillian thought she looked surprisingly like Spencer.

"I thought the same thing as you when I was your age," Gillian replied. "I suppose I always knew healing would be my destiny. Therefore, I would encourage you to follow your dreams, whatever they may be."

Juliet smiled. "I like you, Gillian. Spencer said I would, but I wasn't certain."

At the mention of Spencer's name, Gillian felt a pang of sadness and regret. Juliet must have noticed, for a frown crossed her face. "Did I say something wrong?" she asked.

"Nay, of course, not."

" 'Tis Spencer, isn't it? What did he do?"

"Why would you think he's done anything?"

"Because you looked so sad just now when I said his name. Has he done something to trouble you?"

"Nay . . . well, mayhap. But 'twas unintentional, I think. I'm fortunate to have him as a friend."

"Friends don't make friends feel sad."

Gillian touched the young girl's shoulder lightly. "I believe that no matter how good a friend is, they're going to hurt you occasionally. 'Tis the nature of life."

"You met Phoebe, didn't you?"

Gillian pursed her lips wryly. "You are far too perceptive for a child."

"I'm not a child. And you are avoiding the question."

Gillian sighed. "Well, I did indeed meet Miss Trask last night."

Juliet put some more meat in her hand for Skye. "So what did you think of our Phoebe?"

"She's very beautiful," Gillian said, keeping a wary eye on the hawk.

"She doesn't like animals."

"Not everyone does," Gillian said with a chuckle. "Nonetheless, I'm certain she has other more important attributes."

"What's more important than showing compassion for animals?" Juliet asked.

Gillian smiled. "Respect, understanding, and love, for example."

"What about station? Mother says that is important, too."

"I daresay your mother is right. I'm afraid I don't know much about station."

"Phoebe's father is the town moderator."

"I'm certain that must be a very important post, indeed."

"The most important if one likes politics. I don't."

"I don't either," Gillian admitted. "But I'm certain the marriage will firmly establish Spencer's position in town.

It sounds as though she'll make a fine wife for your brother."

Juliet shrugged. "Mayhap." Carefully she led George and Skye back into the pen and fastened the door shut. "The wedding is one month hence. Will you come?"

Gillian felt a stab in her heart. "I don't know. I don't think I'm invited."

Juliet snorted. "Of course, you are invited. Practically all of Salem are coming."

"We'll see," Gillian replied, brushing off her skirts. "Let's go in and have some breakfast. I'm certain your mother will not approve if I keep you out here too long."

They headed back for the house when a loud series of *thwacks,* followed by a curse, came from the woodshed. Juliet glanced over at Gillian.

"Your brother certainly works hard."

"Sometimes to a fault," Gillian acknowledged.

Juliet plucked at a thread on her skirts. "May I ask you something about him? Mother said I shouldn't pry, but I wondered."

"You may ask me anything you like."

"What is wrong with him? I mean, why does his body look like . . . that? Short and stumpy, I mean."

Gillian was touched at her honest curiosity. "He was born that way. God makes all of us unique. Lemuel may look different on the outside, but on the inside he's the same as you and me, with a heart, feelings, and dreams."

Juliet fell silent, clearly considering her words. "Spencer says he's very skilled," she finally said.

"He is. Lemuel is a good man and a wonderful brother. I love him very much."

"I suppose I feel that same way about Spencer, even though he can be maddening most of the time." She hesitated for a moment. "I think I'm going to like your brother. I'm not afraid of him like some people are. I overheard someone saying he looks like he does because he was born of the devil's womb."

"That's not only unkind, it's simply not true."

"I know," Juliet replied. "I think I can sense a good heart. Besides, he's nice. He made this for me." She pulled out a small carved horse from the pouch around her waist and showed it to Gillian.

She shook her head in surprise, smiling. "Well, he certainly has been busy making friends. If he made you that, then it means he likes you, too. He doesn't make carvings like that for just anybody."

"He doesn't?"

"Nay. He must feel a special kinship with you."

Juliet beamed proudly. "I wonder if he'd make me a carving of Star and Skye."

Gillian squeezed her hand. "I think that you'd only have to ask him."

Spencer's carefully laid plans to apologize immediately to Gillian had to be abandoned when Phineas and Gillian entered the clinic together. Phineas joyfully announced that he was free for the day from any dockside duties and intended to work.

Spencer swore under his breath in frustration. He had skipped breakfast because he had hoped to be able to apologize privately the moment he saw her. Now the apology would have to wait.

Resigned, Spencer mustered a cheerful smile, but was certain it came out more as a grimace. Gillian returned the smile, but it did not quite reach her eyes. His head pounding from the spirits and lack of sleep, Spencer fiddled with some of the vials while Gillian busied herself on the opposite side of the room. When their paths crossed, she nodded or spoke to him politely. Oblivious to the tension, Phineas chattered cheerfully about the cargo that the *Steadfast* would carry to Lisbon in the spring. Wishing his father would stop being so cheerful when he felt so wretched, Spencer felt his ire grow.

"Do we have any patients yet?" he asked, his voice coming out sharper than he had intended.

His father threw him a surprised glance. "Not that I know of. Something troubling you this morning, son?"

"Nothing I can't manage."

"Would you like me to check the parlor for patients?" Gillian offered.

"No," he said, striding out the door. "I'll check myself."

He could feel his father's gaze warm on his back. He knew he was acting like an idiot, but the damn hammer in his head wouldn't quit pounding and he hated the stuffy and polite way Gillian was treating him. He didn't know what he expected after her sudden encounter with Phoebe last night, but he wished like hell that everything would just go back to normal.

To his relief, there was a patient in the parlor. At least he would have something to distract him from Gillian's new aloofness. Jonah Wilder sat patiently, his hat in his lap, waiting to have the dressing on his arm changed.

"Hello, Jonah," Spencer said as the young man rose. "How do you feel?"

"Better, Doctor" he said, twisting his hat in his hand. "But you're looking rather pale this morning. Are you unwell?"

Spencer raised an eyebrow. "Interested in taking a position as a physician's apprentice, now, are you?"

Jonah flushed. "No, sir."

"Good," Spencer said shortly. "So, do you have any more pain in your arm?"

"Not much, but it itches."

"That means it's healing."

He led Jonah to the clinic, where Phineas insisted on

changing the dressing. Spencer looked on idly while Gillian assisted him, mixing the healing balm and providing fresh linen strips. After Jonah had been treated and left, his father approached him, his hands on his hips.

"Now what is really troubling you this morning, son?" he asked quietly, his eyes glimmering with concern. "Perhaps I can help."

"You can't," he said shortly.

"I can't if you won't tell me why you're in such a black mood. Now out with it, boy."

Spencer sighed, aware that Gillian was listening even as she pretended to be overly interested in a vial of aconite. "I suppose may have partaken in a bit too much of the spirits last night," he admitted.

Phineas narrowed his eyes. "That's not like you."

Spencer shrugged. "I suppose it isn't."

His father frowned but said nothing more as Mrs. Doyle brought in the next patient. Eight-year-old Jeremy Catkins had a sty on his eye and told them that his mom had sent him over to have it drained. The boy's face was as pale as a sheet, and he looked terrified at the prospect of having his eye poked.

Phineas examined the boy and then turned to Spencer.

"Would you like to handle this one?" he said, stepping aside to let Spencer have a look.

Spencer examined the boy's eye carefully. The sty was large and on the boy's right eyelid, fairly close to the corner. Spencer glanced over his shoulder at Gillian, who was watching him intently, clearly interested to see what he would prescribe.

His spirits suddenly rose. He had just been handed the perfect way to break through Gillian's new polite facade. Cocking his head, he pretended to consider his options before shaking his head sadly.

"I'm afraid there is nothing I can do for you at this time, boy. I need at least another hour to think about it.

In the meantime, I want you to do me a favor. My horse threw a shoe yesterday and the blacksmith's apprentice, Jonah Wilder, promised to fix it. You are to take the broken shoe to him and wait while he fixes it. When you return with the shoe, I'll have a remedy ready for you."

"The b-blacksmith?" the boy stammered, confused. "You want me to take a horseshoe to the blacksmith?"

Spencer nodded, his mood improving further when he saw the appalled look on Gillian's face. "One hour," he reminded the boy. "Father, would you produce the horseshoe in question for Mr. Catkins, please?"

Phineas grinned. "I certainly will, son. And if neither of you would object, I will take this opportunity to retire to the library to do a bit of bookkeeping."

"I think Gillian and I can manage," Spencer said easily.

His father patted him on the shoulder on the way out. Smiling, Spencer began to whistle as he wound some linen strips, waiting for Gillian to speak up. To her credit, she waited nearly three minutes before she berated him.

"I can't believe you turned that boy away like that," she finally said, marching over to confront him. "It would have taken but a few minutes to drain the sty."

"Is that so?" he said in amusement.

She put her hands on her hips, her emerald eyes flashing at him angrily. "He's in pain and clearly terrified. Making him wait another hour will only make the procedure more agonizing for him."

"I see," he said, crossing his arms against his chest and regarding her thoughtfully. "And just what procedure would you have recommended?"

"A needle to the sty would have been the quickest way to relieve the pressure on the boy's eye," she said firmly. "It would be painful for a few moments, but we could have quickly covered it with a poultice soaked in white poplar."

He pretended to consider it. "How long do you think it would take for the eye to heal?"

"A few days at most. He could come in daily and we would check the progress of his condition."

After a moment he shook his head. "No, I'm afraid I don't like that prescription."

"It's certainly better than sending an injured boy off to do a task for you," she huffed. "That's no prescription at all."

She was clearly vexed, her color high, eyes flashing disapproval. Feeling a twinge of guilt, Spencer decided to end his charade. Reaching out, he took her arm, unprepared for the jolt of heat that shot through him. He abruptly released her, shaking his fingers as if he'd been burned.

"Don't touch me," she said softly. "Ever again."

"Blast it, Gillian," he swore under his breath. "This has gone too far."

"I thought you cared about your patients," she said, still bristling with indignation.

"This is not about my patients," he said, taking a step toward her and then thinking the better of it.

"It is. He's just a child," she continued. "A small child who needs your help. What reason could there be for turning him away? It's unconscionable."

Spencer held up a hand. "Truce, please. Gillian, it's only for an hour, and there is a reason behind the task I sent him on."

"Such as?" She stood in front of him, arms crossed, watching expectantly.

He leaned against the wall in a deliberately casual manner. "It's a technique my father has employed for years. Actually, it's quite effective. When children come to the clinic with a sty, we send them to the blacksmith."

"The blacksmith?" she said, confused. "Why?"

He smiled. "Because children are fascinated by the

process of repairing a horseshoe. The barn is stifling hot, and heating the hammer gives off a hissing steam. The subsequent clang of the iron hitting against iron is both terrifying and thrilling for a child."

"I don't understand how this serves as some kind of treatment."

"Imagine it. The child pushes closer to watch. Each time the hammer comes down; the child blinks hard. Within an hour, the sty will burst and weep itself away. No needle, no draining, no poultice needed. It's a natural and effective treatment. One that I thought you might actually approve of."

He saw her mouth drop open in surprise. "It's . . . it's ingenious," she finally said. "Spencer, I'm dreadfully sorry. I thought . . ."

"I know what you thought," he said, his voice softening. "You thought the worst of me. I don't blame you. I shouldn't have goaded you. I just wanted to do something to break through that horribly polite facade you've been wearing with me this morning."

"How would you wish me to behave?" she asked stiffly.

"Like yourself," he said, shoving his fingers through his hair. "Ordinary. Blast it, Gillian. I'm sorry. I should have told you about my engagement to Phoebe. I just didn't know how."

"You don't owe me an explanation."

"I damn well do. I kissed you."

He saw a flash of hurt in her eyes. " 'Twas naught but a mistake."

"It wasn't," he said and then sighed. "I don't know what it was. I want to regret kissing you, but I don't. I know I shouldn't have done it. I never meant to hurt you."

She lowered her gaze. "You thought it would be harmless. You had no idea I would come to Salem or that I would ever have the opportunity to meet Phoebe."

"That only makes me feel worse."

"Why should it?" she said evenly. "You are not responsible for my feelings."

"That doesn't justify my actions."

"You are not the only one at fault. I—I welcomed your embrace."

He frowned as her cheeks flushed scarlet. "Gillian, for God's sake, this is my fault, not yours. I'm asking for your forgiveness. I was a cad for not being honest with you from the very beginning."

"I do wish you had told me," she said softly.

"So do I. Will you forgive me now?" He held out a hand. "Please, can we be friends?"

She hesitated for just the briefest of moments before taking it. "Of course," she said softly.

The instant she clasped his hand, Spencer felt a gentle warmth sweep into him, quite unlike the fiery heat he had experienced just minutes before. His foul mood miraculously melted and the pressure in his head abated.

"How did you . . . ?" he began, when there was a knock on the door.

"Pardon me, sir," he heard Mrs. Doyle say through the door. "There are more patients waiting in the parlor. Shall I have them continue to wait?"

Spencer stared at Gillian another long moment before walking across the room and opening the door.

"Send them in," he told the housekeeper.

The afternoon wore on, the tension between them fading. Spencer was relieved when they finally once again fell into their normal working rhythm. She seemed to have genuinely forgiven him, even once daring to challenge him in private about a particular mixture he had prescribed for gout. He shook his head, puzzled and even amazed that she had taken his apology so well.

Dusk fell and he ushered out their final patient. They both collapsed into chairs, exhausted.

" 'Twas certainly a busy day," she said.

"It was," he agreed. "Thank God for your suggestion to mix lemon juice with a pinch of jalap as a fever reducer for Jacob Toomery. How did you know he's in here every week complaining of fever?"

"Just a supposition. You kept suggesting mixtures that were obviously harmless and completely ineffective. So I came to the conclusion that you were seeking a new way to provide something that would do nothing for him."

A few strands of red hair had escaped from beneath her kerchief; her nose was smudged with soot from the hearth, and her apron a mess from the day's work. Yet at that moment, he had never seen her look so beautiful. "You are remarkable," he said softly. "Utterly remarkable."

"Is something wrong?" she said, her smile fading.

He stood abruptly, walking to the door. "No. I'm just going out for a walk." Grabbing his coat from the peg by the door, he shoved his arms into it. "Mrs. Carlisle will prepare supper for you, Lemuel, and Juliet this evening. The rest of us have a dinner party to attend, so we will not be supping with you."

"Oh," she said quietly. "I wish you a pleasant evening, then."

Nodding, Spencer shoved his arms in his coat and strode out the door. His frustration level had once again grown and he had no idea why.

What in blazes was wrong with him? His apology to her had been impeccable, her acceptance gracious. They were friends once again, and the day had gone better than he had hoped for. What more could he ask for?

He pulled his jacket more tightly around him, bracing himself against the formidable chill of the wind. So, if everything had turned out so well, then why the hell did he feel so rotten?

FOURTEEN

Gillian felt oddly alone after Spencer had left. Sighing, she cleaned up the clinic and then snuffed out all the candles. She didn't feel much like sitting in her room before supper, so she decided to go out to the woodshed and see if Lemuel had a moment to speak with her.

She'd just closed the door to the clinic when Mrs. Doyle approached her, holding a basket. Inside was a large cloth-covered package tied with a piece of twine.

"This was sitting on the parlor table," she said. " 'Tis for you, mistress."

"For me?" Gillian said, looking at the basket in surprise.

Mrs. Doyle pointed to a card that sat on top. Printed across the parchment in bold letters was her name.

"How odd," Gillian murmured, taking the basket. "Who would send me something?"

Mrs. Doyle shrugged. "Perhaps a secret admirer."

Baffled, Gillian picked up the card, turning it over in her hand. As soon as Mrs. Doyle left, she sat down on the bottom stair and opened it.

A gift for you, was all it said. No one had signed it.

Completely mystified, Gillian unwound the package. To her astonishment, inside was a fresh loaf of bread, still slightly warm. She smiled, inhaling the wonderful aroma.

"Mrs. Carlisle," she murmured. How thoughtful of the

woman to wrap it up as if it were some kind of gift. She nearly tore off a piece to eat right there on the stairs but changed her mind. It would be a tantalizing reason for Lemuel to stop work and share a bite with her, and she could use a sympathetic ear.

She covered the loaf back up and slung the basket over her arm. Fetching her cloak, she walked out of the house toward the woodshed. She could hear her brother inside, whistling cheerfully.

Lifting her hand, she knocked. The whistling stopped and he cracked the door, looking out.

"Gillian," he said in surprise. "What brings you here?"

She pursed her lips in annoyance. "Must I formally request an audience with my own brother?"

He grinned and stepped out of the woodshed, carefully closing the door behind him. "Never," he said and then raised his head to sniff the air. "Do I smell bread?"

She narrowed her eyes. "And what if you do? I have it on good authority that the way to obtain your attention these days is through your stomach."

"And just whose authority might that be?"

"Lynette Carlisle."

His grin widened. "Oh, a lovely young woman, indeed."

"Lovely? Is that why you are willing to let her in the woodshed and not me?"

He leaned one arm against the doorjamb. "Partially. But also because she is willing to pay the entrance fee."

"What fee?" Gillian asked suspiciously.

"A sweet kiss."

"A kiss!" Gillian exclaimed, scandalized. "Lemuel, you didn't!"

Lemuel laughed. "Why are you so surprised?"

"It's just . . . so . . . so wonderful," Gillian said, suddenly bursting into tears.

Lemuel cursed, fumbling for his handkerchief. "Gillian, for God's sake, no tears. Besides, you don't know how it wounds me to see you so surprised that I might actually be able to command a kiss."

"I'm not shocked," she sniffed, accepting the handkerchief and wiping her eyes. "The truth be known, I'm a bit envious. I think Lynette is a wonderful girl."

He took her by the hand, leading her to a small wooden bench located near Juliet's wooden pen. "Did you really doubt I could make friends?"

Ashamed, she realized that she had been. "I'm sorry," she whispered, sitting.

He sat down beside her, putting an arm around her shoulder. "I've told you all along I didn't need coddling, Gillian. I'm a man now. I intend to take what life gives me, be it good or bad. You cannot keep protecting me, and frankly I don't look kindly on it anymore."

"I . . . I don't know how to stop."

"You have to stop worrying incessantly about me. We're both going to be fine. I'm going to see to it."

Gillian laid the basket beside her on the bench and twisted Lemuel's handkerchief worriedly in her hands. "I don't doubt you. But I'm not so certain about me."

He looked at her, concern flashing in his sky blue eyes. "What do you mean?"

"I mean . . ." she started, taking a deep breath. "I mean, Spencer is betrothed," she blurted out.

Lemuel blinked and then sighed. "Oh, Gillian, I feared this might happen. Did you fancy yourself in love with him?"

"Yes. No. I don't know."

Lemuel pressed her head onto his shoulder. "I should have warned you. You have such little experience with men. It was foolish for me to think you saw him as naught more than a benefactor. I know you've been lonely, and Spencer is quite a dashing fellow. I suppose his profession as a physician made him all the more attractive to you."

Gillian closed her eyes. "Perhaps, but truthfully, 'twas more than just that. I felt something when I touched him—something I've never felt before. It's hard to explain, but 'twas like a familiar awareness of him flowing through me. As if I already knew him somehow."

Lemuel stroked her hair softly. "I'm sorry, Gillian. I wish I could spare you the pain."

Gillian felt the tears threaten again. "He has apologized for not telling me sooner about his betrothal, and I accepted his apology. I don't blame him. Truly. It's just that he thinks everything is settled. And I suppose it is. Except I don't know how long I will be able to go on working and being near him, all the while knowing that he belongs to someone else."

"What do you want to do?"

"I don't know yet."

"We'll leave here as soon as we can, Gillian. I promise you that."

She shook her head. "It's not fair to you. You're so happy here. I'll think of something."

He nudged her chin up. "Whatever we do, we stay together. We always have."

"Now who is protecting whom?"

He grinned. " 'Tis quite heady, the power. I think I like it. Now I can see why you've done it for so long."

"You're teasing me."

"Aye, I am. Isn't that what brothers are supposed to do?" He sniffed again, poking at the basket. "Can we eat yet?"

She lifted out the bread and unwound the cloth. "Mrs. Carlisle was kind enough to make me a loaf. I think Lynette told her I am fond of her cooking."

"As am I," Lemuel said patting his stomach. "I can't remember when I so looked forward to eating."

Gillian narrowed her eyes. "Is that a disparaging comment on my cooking skills?"

Lemuel chuckled. "Of course not. You've always had a fair hand with food. But 'tis clear we were missing some of the finer ingredients to be found. Not that I'm complaining, mind you. I was always first to the table."

Pursing her lips, Gillian tore off a chunk and handed it to him. But before Lemuel could take it, a hawk appeared out of nowhere and swept down with a ferocious cry. Startled, Gillian dropped the bread. The hawk swooped down again and picked the bread up in its claws, dropping it in a clump of bushes. She and Lemuel looked on in stunned amazement.

"Where in the devil did that hawk come from?" Lemuel finally asked.

"That's Star," she said, rising from the bench. "Juliet is tending to his mate."

"Star?" Lemuel asked, raising an eyebrow.

"Juliet names her animals."

"So does someone else I know."

Gillian eyed the hawk curiously. "I wonder what he wants."

"Isn't it obvious? He's hungry."

"Then why didn't he eat the bread?"

"Mayhap you startled him."

"I suppose that could be it," Gillian said. "Let's try offering him another piece."

Carefully she broke off another piece, holding it out in the palm of her hand. "Come here, Star," she called to the hawk.

To her surprise, the hawk screeched and flew down without any hesitation, knocking the bread from her hand. It fell on the ground at her feet.

"What is it doing?" Lemuel muttered.

Gillian's frown deepened. She tore off another piece of the bread and sniffed at it. There was a faint odor of something that seemed vaguely familiar.

Shocked, she dropped the piece back into the basket. "Poison," she whispered.

"Poison?" Lemuel uttered in disbelief. "But . . . but why would Mrs. Carlisle poison the bread?"

"Because it didn't come from Mrs. Carlisle."

"But you said it did."

I *thought* it did." She pulled out the note. "This is what the card said."

Lemuel read it aloud. "A gift for you," he murmured. "No one signed it."

"I just assumed Lynette had told her mother how much I enjoyed her bread. Who else would send it?"

Lemuel grimly set his jaw. "Jack Soward."

Gillian considered it for a moment and then shook her head. "Poison bread doesn't seemed suited to his methods."

He jumped up from the bench and began pacing. "Of course it does, or perhaps that is what he wants us to think. He probably hired someone to send it to you."

"I suppose that is possible," Gillian said.

"I damn well haven't forgotten what his family has done to us. I am still planning my revenge."

"Revenge?" she said in concern. "Whatever are you talking about? The constable is handling the investigation."

"The constable isn't going to do anything and we both know it," he snapped.

"Then just what do you have in mind?"

He stopped his pacing and looked at her intently. "You have enough on your mind. You're not to worry about it."

"Not to worry about it?" Gillian said, rising from the bench. "Lemuel, this concerns me, too. I don't want to see you hurt."

"It pains me that you have so little faith in me."

"I have enormous faith in you," she said heatedly. "But you are an honorable man. Jack Soward is not."

"I'll take care of it, Gillian, in my own way. We will tell no one about the bread until we can determine what to do about it."

"And what way might your way be? We don't even know who sent it. We can't be certain it was Jack Soward."

"That's why I intend to find out for certain." He narrowed his eyes and looked up at the hawk that still circled methodically above their heads. "Just after you explain to me how in the devil that bird knew the bread was poisoned."

Gillian felt a chill creep up her spine. "I don't know," she whispered. "But he just saved our lives."

The dining room of the Trask estate was bright and cheery, illuminated by dozens of candles. The table had been elegantly set with several beautiful flower arrangements and slender, long-wicked candles in gleaming gold candlesticks. A stuffed goose sat on a huge platter, surrounded by baked apples sprinkled with cinnamon. Platters filled with sweet potatoes, artichokes, corn, and asparagus covered the table. The aroma of fresh bread filled the room as young maidservants carried in steaming loaves and scattered them about the table.

Spencer stood in the dining room, sipping a glass of fine claret and chatting with the town magistrate, Captain George Haft. Next to Phoebe's father, Haft was the second most powerful man in Salem.

"It was the damnedest thing," Haft said, shaking his head. "Benjamin Hawkes stood in front of the Reverend Goodwell's meeting house and lit the grass on fire with the most unusual contraption I'd ever seen. But he did it with such a sleight of hand that if I hadn't known better, I would have thought he'd summoned fire right out of the air."

Spencer shook his head. "I heard about it. Wasn't that what Bridget Goodwell was accused of doing?"

"A bizarre event, indeed. Add to that her broken engagement to Peter Holton and sudden wedding to Mr. Hawkes, and it is all quite mysterious indeed."

"Something odd certainly happened there," Spencer agreed. "Didn't Benjamin accompany Lydia Trask to the church picnic just a few days before all that happened?"

Haft shrugged. "Frankly, young people nowadays have me completely confounded. Present company excepted, of course. You, my boy, have a good, solid head on your shoulders. Your father should be highly commended."

"I'll be certain to tell him," Spencer said with a chuckle.

Just then Phoebe stepped up beside him, sliding her arm into his. She looked stunning in a gown of ice blue, perfectly matching her eyes. Her thick black hair had been artfully pinned up and arranged, accentuating the slender white column of her neck.

"Hello, Captain Haft," she said, giving him a dazzling smile. "I do hope you are enjoying the gathering."

"As always, my dear," he said, raising his glass of claret to her and taking a sip. "The Trasks always know how to host a good party."

Someone rang the dinner bell and Phoebe tugged on Spencer's arm, steering him toward the table. He sat near the head, with Phoebe on one side and her mother on the other. Lydia, Phoebe's younger sister by two years, sat directly across from him. He gave her a smile and she winked back at him, her tongue darting out to touch the tip of her lower lip. She'd been flirting ceaselessly with him all evening. Typically, he found it amusing that she engaged in such games with him. But tonight, for some reason, he found it increasingly tedious.

Margaret Trask said something to him and he turned to address her. She was as lovely as her daughters, with the same light-blue eyes, porcelain skin, and long black hair. Hers had started to gray at the temples, but Spencer thought it only enhanced rather than detracted from her appearance.

"Pardon me," he said politely. "You said something?"

"I asked whether you had completely recovered from your accident," she said, handing him the plate of asparagus. "You certainly look well."

Spencer skewered a few spears with his fork and placed them on his plate. "I am well, thank you."

"Phoebe told me that you and your friends were rescued by a young woman and her brother who live alone out in a cottage by the sea. How fortunate that they were there to aid you."

"We were fortunate indeed," he said, passing on the asparagus to Phoebe.

"I heard it said that the woman has some healing skills."

"She does. Has not Phoebe told you that they suffered a misfortune shortly after our departure from the cottage and are now staying with us? The young woman is assisting Father and me in the clinic."

Margaret nibbled a bite of her asparagus. "I heard and must say that it is an unusual turn of events. Isn't it a bit odd that the misfortune took place so quickly after you left? Have you considered whether it might not have been a ruse simply to take advantage of your kindness?"

Spencer felt a flare of irritation. "I assure you, it was no ruse. And regardless of whether or not it was, I would have aided them."

"Of course; you are a generous man."

"I've met her, Mother," Phoebe said, leaning toward Spencer and giving him a good view down the front of her bodice. "She looks oddly familiar."

Spencer thought for moment. "Yes," he murmured. "You are right. She reminds me a bit of Bridget Goodwell."

He saw Margaret and Phoebe exchange a meaningful

glance, and for some reason, a chill touched the back of his neck.

"Did you know Bridget wedded Benjamin Hawkes three months ago?" Phoebe asked him.

Spencer leaned back as a servant heaped several pieces of roasted goose onto his plate. "In some haste, I heard, although the circumstances surrounding the marriage are quite mysterious. She had been betrothed to Peter Holton for quite some time."

"I always thought Bridget to be peculiar," Phoebe said.

Spencer speared a piece of meat. "She is really likable despite her oddities. Her forthrightness is rather refreshing, wouldn't you agree?"

Mrs. Trask looked at him, annoyance flashing in her eyes. "I would say not," she said coldly. "Why Benjamin Hawkes chose to wed her is beyond me. She is far beneath him in position, stature, and upbringing. But apparently, he will have to lie in the bed he has made."

Spencer looked at her, surprised by the venom in her voice. "Yes, I suppose we all have to live with our choices in life," he agreed uneasily. "But personally, I wish them happiness and good fortune."

The dinner dragged on, and Spencer found his mind wandering. He tried several times to engage Phoebe in conversation about his day at the clinic, but she was clearly uninterested, wishing rather to natter on about inconsequential matters related to the wedding.

Bored with the topic, he brought up his difficulties with Tom Burke. To his chagrin, she chided him outright for being so gloomy.

"Must you ruin the supper by speaking of Tom Burke's ills?" she whispered. "Captain Haft and my father are talking about the economic feasibility of a new anchor forge. I heard your father is considering investing. Think of the significant profit you could reap if a new forge is built and turns out to be successful. Perhaps you could listen and contribute a useful suggestion."

"I don't give a damn about the anchor forge," he snapped under his breath.

She looked at him in surprise and then reached under the table to squeeze his knee. "I'm sorry, darling. No need to be so sharp with me. Now, what did you want to tell me about Mr. Burke?"

"Never mind," Spencer said, reaching for his claret. "It wasn't important anyway." He took several large gulps and then signaled a maidservant to refill it.

He gave an audible sigh of relief when dinner was finally over. Phoebe tried to talk him into a quick stroll in the garden, but he instead decided to retire to the parlor with the other men for cigars and brandy. Nonetheless, his mood had become increasingly dismal, and he wished for nothing more than to go home. Unfortunately, as the fiancé of the host's daughter, escape was out of the question. He plastered a stoic smile on his face and managed to endure the rest of the evening chatting and discussing matters in which he had absolutely no interest.

As they were finally preparing to leave, Phoebe pulled him aside, clearly worried by his mood.

"Spencer," she whispered in his ear, "is something wrong? You've been acting peculiar all evening."

"Nothing unless you count partaking a bit too much of the claret," he said grimly. "We can talk tomorrow if you'd like."

"Will you visit then?" She looked at him, her thick, dark lashes fluttering over her striking blue eyes. In spite of himself, Spencer felt his senses stir at her cool beauty and the unspoken promise held there.

He nodded. "I will." He lifted her hand and kissed it. "Good night, Phoebe."

She leaned toward him so that her breasts brushed

against his chest. "Good night, darling," she said huskily. "Dream of me, will you?"

For the first time in a long while, Spencer refused the carriage, wishing to walk home alone. He hoped the cool air and bracing wind would help him clear his mind. He felt deeply troubled and dissatisfied, yet the reason eluded him.

He felt little better by the time he reached the house. Letting himself in, he trudged slowly up the darkened stairs. He could hear his parents moving around in their room as he headed down the corridor. Passing Gillian's door, he was surprised that despite the late hour, a light shone from underneath the door. Upon closer inspection, he noticed the door was actually ajar. Without stopping to think about it, he raised his hand and knocked softly.

He heard a rustle from inside, and Gillian opened the door. Her red hair spilled loosely about her shoulders in a thick, glorious mass. She was clad in a thin bed gown and robe that she pulled tight around her when she saw him.

"Oh, I thought you might be Lemuel," she said, her eyes flashing in surprise.

"I'm sorry to disappoint you," he said, his voice suddenly husky. "It's just that I saw the light and wondered what you were doing awake at such a late hour."

She opened the door a bit wider so he could look into the room. He followed her gaze to a heavy book resting on the chair in front of the cheery fire.

"The New Physick's Guide to Common Diseases and Cures," she said. "I borrowed it from your father. It's fascinating reading, really. I couldn't put it down."

Spencer laughed, loosening his neck cloth. "Surely you jest. That book puts me to sleep within moments."

She pursed her lips. "Just because you are already familiar with all the remedies doesn't mean you have to ridicule me."

"I'm not ridiculing you. Truly. And I don't know every remedy in that book, nor would I ever claim to. It's a reference journal, Gillian. You don't have to memorize every word in there to be a good physician."

She flushed slightly. "I know. It's just that something about one of our patients today has had me baffled."

Spencer sobered immediately. "Tom Burke?"

She nodded, and he felt a flush of pleasure that they had both been thinking of the same thing.

"It just seems unusual that he is in so often complaining of stomach pains," she said. "At first glance, I would agree with your remedy of castor oil and chalk to clear the stomach. But if he is returning every week, it seems that the remedy is not curing the underlying problem."

Spencer exhaled a deep breath. "I agree, but am perplexed as to what could cause the recurring condition."

She left the doorway and went to get the book. Picking it up, she stood in front of the fire and flipped it open, looking for something. Fiery hair tumbled over her shoulder, draping across the soft swell of her breast, and her brow furrowed in concentration.

Spencer's breath caught in his throat. Standing there in clad in naught more than her thin gown and robe and illuminated by the fire, she looked stunningly ethereal. A jolt of white-hot desire shot through him, surprising him with its intensity.

A trickle of sweat formed on his brow and, uncomfortable, he muffled a curse and yanked at his cursed neck cloth, pulling it completely free.

"Here," she suddenly said, tapping a finger on the page.

Damning the impropriety of the two of them alone in her room, but knowing she probably wouldn't be aware of proper convention in the first place, he stepped toward her to see what she had discovered.

"It says here that certain foodstuffs can cause regular

indigestion in people with sensitivities to particular elements," she said.

"But which foodstuffs?" he asked, looking over her shoulder.

She nibbled on her lower lip thoughtfully. "There is a small note that says the removal of some types of grains have proved to be helpful to the digestive process of some patients. Another note indicates the removal of milk and cheese was beneficial."

Spencer was intrigued in spite of himself. "So what would you suggest? Starving the fellow?"

She looked up at him wryly. "Of course not. Anyway, it wouldn't be helpful to deprive him of all of those food items at once. But it might be useful to suggest an elimination of certain food items, one at a time, and see if his condition improves. If it does, than we will know that we are pursuing a beneficial course of action."

"An excellent suggestion, Doctor," he said, smiling, and nearly reached out to brush a strand of her hair from her cheek. Stopping himself at the last moment, he took a step back, inwardly cursing himself.

"So, is this what you do most evenings?" he asked casually, hoping she hadn't noticed what he'd almost done. "Read?"

"It is," she replied and then looked at him puzzled before smiling.

"What's so amusing?" he asked, leaning an arm on the mantle.

"It's just I don't recall ever seeing you in such finery," she said. "You look grand but a bit uncomfortable. How was your evening?"

"Tedious," he said before he could stop himself. "Long, uncomfortable, and unbearable," he added with a sigh. "Every moment was torture. I couldn't wait to get home . . . to see you." The truth slipped out before he could stop it.

Her lovely emerald eyes opened wide and she closed the book with a snap, taking a step back and hugging it to her chest as if it were a form of protection.

"I think perhaps we should bid each other a good night."

He exhaled a harsh breath, shoving his fingers through his hair. "Blast it, Gillian. I'm sorry. I shouldn't have said that. I don't know what's wrong with me."

He glanced over at her and saw her expression was one of sadness and regret. "There is something I'd like to tell you," she said softly.

"What?"

She laid the book back on the chair and folded her hands in front of her. "This afternoon, after you left the clinic, someone came by to see me."

Spencer felt his eyes narrow. "Who?"

"Dr. Mahoney."

Spencer swore under his breath. "Already? I knew it! It hasn't even been a blasted week. What did he want?"

"To meet me, I presume."

"Alone?"

"I assure you, it was all very proper. Mrs. Doyle brought us tea in the sitting room. We chatted for about an hour."

"An hour?" Spencer snapped irritably. "What in the devil did you talk about for an hour?"

"Medicine, healing, and technique. I had the distinct impression that he was testing my knowledge."

"Bloody good for him," Spencer said, his ire rising. "The sheer nerve of the fellow is astonishing."

"I like him," she said simply.

He scowled and then exhaled a harsh breath. "Curse his Irish soul, I like him, too."

She lowered her gaze. "Spencer, he made me an offer. He told me that I could come and work for him on a moment's notice."

Spencer looked at her incredulously. "Surely you jest. Are you saying he had the audacity to openly make you an offer? While you sat with him in *my* house? It's simply outrageous. I'll speak with him first thing in the morning about his impudence."

"I told him I'd consider it," she said quietly.

His jaw fell open. "You did what?"

"I told him I'd consider it," she repeated, raising her chin and looking at him squarely.

Spencer snapped his jaw shut, an unbearable mixture of anger and panic filling him. "Why?"

"You are soon to be married. Phoebe will move in here and you will be together. It might be a bit . . . awkward."

"It wouldn't," he insisted, but as soon as the words fell from his lips, he knew them to be a lie.

"I won't leave immediately," she assured him. "I'll help you find a suitable replacement."

"I don't want a damn replacement," he retorted. "I want you."

"My leaving would be for the best."

"For whom?"

She smiled at him gently. "Good night, Spencer."

He gazed at her for a long moment, his emotions in a turmoil. "This isn't over," he said curtly as he turned on his heel and left the room.

Her words followed him down the hallway. "I'm afraid it is," she said.

FIFTEEN

Changing direction, Spencer veered away from his room and stomped downstairs into his father's library. He jabbed at the embers in the fire, adding some wood until the blaze began warming the room. Once the fire was burning heartily, he started pacing back and forth in front of the hearth, trying to decide what to do about Dr. Mahoney's outrageous offer to Gillian.

He had just about convinced himself to go to the Irishman's house and pummel him into the ground when the door to the library abruptly opened and Phineas walked in. He was clad in a burgundy dressing gown with a matching cap. He looked disgruntled but not surprised to see Spencer standing there scowling at him.

"Can't a man have a moment of peace?" Spencer snapped.

"Apparently not," Phineas snapped back. "I was quite comfortable in my bed until your mother sent me down."

"What for?"

"To find out the reason for your black mood this evening—and all day, for that matter," he said, striding past him and plopping into a chair. "I'd appreciate it if you'd tell me in due haste so I may return to my bed."

Spencer's scowl deepened. "Don't be absurd. Mother is just being foolish. There is nothing to tell."

Phineas sighed. "For God's sake, boy, do you think us

all blind? You've been unbearable for days now. Just say what is on your mind."

Spencer started pacing again. "Well, where were you when Dr. Mahoney spoke with Gillian this afternoon? He came here to the house and offered her a position trying to lure her right out from under our noses. Can you believe the sheer audacity of the man?"

Phineas stretched his feet toward the warmth of the fire. "I'm not surprised. Dr. Mahoney isn't dim-witted, and it doesn't take long for news to travel in this town. Gillian is a rare gem, and he'd be a fool not to try and acquire her for himself."

"He's already got an apprentice—another one he stole out from under our noses, might I add."

Phineas shrugged. "Gillian is a far better find and we both know it."

"Of course I know it," he exploded. "Aren't you the least bit surprised or upset about this?"

"It seems you are enough of both to take care of it for the family."

Spencer narrowed his eyes. "You knew. You already knew Mahoney had been here."

"Mrs. Doyle told me."

"Then why in the hell didn't you tell me?" Anger churned in his gut.

"Why should I?"

"What kind of an answer is that? You know damn well that I'm not going to let Mahoney steal her away."

His father regarded him intently. "Would it truly be such a bad idea, son?"

Spencer looked at his father, incredulous. "Of course it would. How can you even suggest that? Gillian is the best assistant you've ever had, and that includes me. Hell, sometimes I think she'd even make a better physician than I."

"She fancies herself in love with you," he said quietly.

Spencer felt as if his father had punched him in the stomach. "What did you say?"

"She's in love with you."

"That's ridiculous," he protested heatedly. "I kissed her, yes, but I apologized and she understands. Surely she didn't draw any foolish conclusions."

"I assure you, Gillian is far from foolish. But love isn't so simple, son. She can't just stop caring about you because you apologize."

"She can't love me," he protested. "She doesn't even know me."

Phineas sighed. "You really are dense in the matters of the heart, my boy. Your mother was right. We should have spent much more time discussing it with you."

Spencer swore aloud. "I'm not going to let her go. I mean it"

His father raised a white eyebrow. "And how do you intend to stop her?"

"She'll stay if I ask her. If I insist."

"She might," Phineas agreed. "But would it be fair to her?"

"It certainly would. She likes it here, and our patients are growing increasingly fond of her. What could possibly be wrong with her staying?"

Phineas abruptly rose. "I can't answer that for you, son. I suggest you think long and hard about what it is you really want. When you have come to some sort of enlightened conclusion, we'll talk again."

With that, his father left the room. Spencer watched him go, feeling increasingly frustrated.

"What the hell is that supposed to mean?" he growled even as he feared he already knew.

Gillian awoke to an insistent knocking on her door. Sunlight spilled through a crack in the drapes, pooling on the floor like a golden puddle. Rising, she walked across the room and opened the door a crack. To her astonishment, she saw Spencer standing there. He was clad casually, his cheeks ruddy and light brown hair tousled from the wind. He'd already been out this morning.

"Has something happened?" she asked worriedly. "Is there a patient in need?"

He rested his hand against the doorjamb. "We aren't working today."

"We aren't?"

"No. It's a beautiful October morning. I'm taking you for a sail instead."

"A sail?" Gillian exclaimed in surprise. "But the clinic . . ."

"Father can manage it," he said calmly. "He has for twenty years."

"But . . . but isn't it too cold?"

"We've yet to have the first snowfall. It is still safe for a sail."

"But . . . I've never been sailing before."

"All the more reason not to wait another day," he said briskly. "Now dress warmly, and after breakfast we'll proceed down to the dock."

Without even waiting for an answer, he walked away, leaving Gillian staring at him with her mouth open, wondering what in the world had come over him.

Thus ordered, Gillian hurriedly dressed in the warmest gown she had, and wound her hair tightly into a single braid. Spencer, Lemuel, and Juliet awaited her in the dining room. When she arrived, Spencer rose and held out the chair for her. After she was seated, Juliet threw her an envious glance.

"I wish I were going sailing," she said, a small pout on her lips.

Spencer tore off a piece of bread. "The skiff is too small for the three of us," he said calmly. "Next time. I'll take you another time, too, Lemuel, if you would like."

"Aye, I'd like that," he replied and then shot a questioning glance at Gillian. She shrugged, as mystified as he as to what Spencer was about this morning.

"I thought you said the *Rosemary* was destroyed," Gillian said. "Have you another vessel?"

Spencer leaned back in his chair, and Gillian marveled at how strangely relaxed he looked. "Not yet, but Charles's father has been trying to sell me one of his. I finally decided to take a closer look at the skiff to see if I might want to purchase it. I thought you might enjoy going along."

Gillian nodded eagerly, an inexplicable excitement bubbling up inside her. It was a lovely autumn day, clear and sunny. Perfect for an outdoor excursion.

"Where will we sail?" she asked, pushing her food aside, too thrilled to eat.

"Just a bit up the coast," Spencer replied, smiling mysteriously.

Thankfully, he didn't tarry over breakfast, and when they were finished he helped her don her cloak. They bid good-bye to the others, including Phineas and Rosemary, who were just coming down the stairs to breakfast. Gillian nearly skipped as they walked down to the pier. He patiently permitted her to dawdle along the harbor, marveling at the array of assorted colorful vessels until he steered her to a dock where a small sailboat swayed gently in the water.

"Enchanted," Gillian murmured, reading the name off the skiff. "Is this the boat you shall sail?"

"It is indeed," Spencer said, pulling the vessel close and helping her aboard. "Step carefully," he said. "Sit down as soon as you are in."

She lifted her skirts and complied, unnerved by the sudden rocking movement but reassured by his steady hand under her elbow. He untied the mooring line and stepped in, readying the boat for the sail.

The wind was brisk and within minutes they were skimming across the water, the sun reflecting off the water so brightly it was almost blinding. Lifting her face to the sun's warmth, Gillian inhaled a deep breath of the crisp, fresh air, reveling in the sheer joy of the moment.

"How do you like sailing so far?" he asked her with a grin, his hair blowing about in the wind.

"It's magnificent," she replied. "I feel like I'm flying." Her eyes slowly met his. "Thank you."

His smile widened. "I had a feeling you would like it."

He maneuvered the craft out of the harbor, and Gillian took a look at the Salem countryside from a viewpoint she had never had before. The forest was thick with trees adorned in their autumn glory. Red, orange, gold, and brown leaves shimmered in a dazzling display. Stalks of tall grass intermittently hid the rocky beach, and white seagulls circled above the water, screeching and looking for food. The wind picked up, causing the waves to rock and splash vigorously against the hull. A spray of water shot up in the air, showering them with crystal droplets.

Spencer laughed and shook the water from his hair. Gillian joined him, her heart light for the first time in days. In fact, she couldn't remember the last time she had felt so blithe and carefree. At least for the time being, she would forget her worries and live in the moment.

"Sailing is magical, isn't it?" she said, spreading her hands out. "The water, the forest, the sky."

"That's why I love sailing," Spencer said, leaning back against the hull. "It reminds me to appreciate the beauty, as well as the danger, of nature."

She glanced at him, aware of his unspoken reference to the sinking of the *Rosemary*. "Nature is indeed fickle," she agreed. "She demands that one appreciate as well as respect her."

"Today I intend to do both."

Gillian looked at him, charmed and yet puzzled by his

lighthearted mood, so different from when he stalked out of her room last night.

They sailed for a while longer in companionable silence, watching the sun glitter on water and the clouds drift across the pale blue sky. The morning passed at a leisurely pace, the sun warming her face and hair. Before long afternoon arrived. To her surprise, Spencer opened a small wooden trunk at the back of the boat and pulled out a basket and flask.

"Where did that come from?" she asked in astonishment.

"I had Lynette rush down here during breakfast and store it in the boat," he said, his eyes twinkling. "We're going to have a picnic on the water today."

Gillian laughed in delight. "Why, what a wonderful idea! I'm ravenous."

"And to think I feared you might be ill. The sea is a bit rough today, and the movement can cause some people great distress to the stomach."

"I've never felt better," she said truthfully.

"Who would have guessed?" he said, shaking his head in disbelief. "You've got the stomach of a sailor."

Despite his obvious teasing, she caught a note of admiration in his voice.

He pulled out a thick slab of bread and some cheese, handing it to her. She accepted it gratefully and wolfed it down, ignoring Spencer's comments about her unladylike appetite. They ate while chatting about the finer points of sailing, and Spencer joked that at last there was something he knew more about than she.

After they ate, he poured them each a cup of wine, sloshing most of his over the side as a gentle wave nudged into the boat, ruining his aim.

They laughed and he licked the wine from his fingers before pouring some more. Gillian drank two cups of the sweet, thick wine before leaning back against the hull and closing her eyes in drowsy contentment. "This must be heaven."

"I think the clergy would be wont to say that heaven is not upon the seas but in the sky," Spencer said, chuckling.

Gillian cracked an eye, staring up at the vast blue expanse. "Well, today I feel as if I could touch the sky."

Spencer took another sip of his wine. "I won't disagree with you. The sea can make a man—or a woman, for that matter—feel invincible."

"Invincible," she murmured. " 'Tis just what I feel right now."

He was silent for a moment before he spoke again. "Gillian, there is something I've been meaning to ask you. Back in the clinic, with Amos and little Ben Sellers and many other patients, including me, you seemed able to take away the pain of an injury or discomfort with just a touch of your hand. Am I right?"

She opened her eyes and looked directly at him. "Spencer Reeves, if I didn't know any better, I would think you are suggesting I possess some sort of unnatural power."

"I suppose I am," he said, his expression deadly serious.

Her heart fluttered, but she tried to keep the mood light. "I thought you to be a man of science."

"Does that mean I should dismiss all irregular hypotheses out of hand?"

"Perhaps those that may be considered fantastic or even mystical. How could I possibly possess such a power?"

He shrugged. "I don't know," he admitted. "It sounds bizarre even to my own ears. But had I not felt it for myself, I wouldn't have believed it. There is something special about you, Gillian—even magical, perhaps. I knew it from the moment I saw you for the very first time."

She regarded him intently for a moment and then

smiled. "Is all of this—the sail, the wine, the flattery—an attempt to keep me from joining Dr. Mahoney's practice?"

He smiled, but the humor did not quite reach his eyes. "Perhaps a little. But I give you my word that if you want to leave, it will be a decision that you make entirely on your own. And, if you stay, it will be because you want to."

He spoke the words with a confidence that suddenly unsettled her. For a moment she stared at him, puzzled, hoping he might reveal the source of his mysterious new mood. Instead, he leaned forward and poured more wine into her cup.

"To friendship," he said, lifting his cup to hers.

After a moment, she raised her cup, tapping it against his. "No matter what happens, I'm glad we met," she said. "I'm grateful that our destinies crossed, even if it was to be just for a short time."

He nodded, his expression slightly wistful. "So am I, Gillian," he agreed. "So am I."

As far as Gillian was concerned, it had been a perfect day. After she and Spencer returned from their sail, they had supped with the family, and Gillian hadn't been able to stop talking about how wonderful the experience had been. Encouraged by her enthusiasm for sailing and Juliet's disappointment that she hadn't been invited, Phineas promised to procure a larger vessel and take the entire family out at his earliest convenient moment.

After supper, Spencer and Phineas decided to take a stroll about town. Lemuel retreated to the woodshed while Gillian, Juliet, and Rosemary retired to the sitting room to sew. As they sewed and chatted companionably, Gillian suddenly felt a horrid pang of loss that soon these wonderful evenings would be no more. In such a short time she had become so fond of this family. Leaving them would be the hardest thing she would ever do, yet she knew with growing certainty that it was the correct decision. Soon Phoebe Trask would take her rightful place in front of the hearth as Spencer's wife.

"You suddenly seem pensive," Rosemary said to her.

Gillian blinked, realizing she had been staring into the fire. "Just musing," she said, resuming her small stitches.

"About the sail?" Juliet inquired, jabbing her finger with a needle and sticking the wounded appendage into her mouth.

Gillian sighed dreamily. "It truly was wonderful."

"Spencer is an excellent sailor," Juliet boasted. "Except for the shipwreck, of course."

Gillian chuckled. "That wasn't his fault. Nature can pose a most formidable challenge even for the most experienced of sailors."

Rosemary nodded in agreement. "I think we can hardly blame Spencer for that unfortunate event. But I am heartened to see him go back on the water so quickly. That must have been your doing, dear."

"My doing?" Gillian said in surprise. "But he suggested it to me."

"Of course he did. It gave him a good excuse to venture out again so soon. He'd only do so with someone he trusted."

Her cheeks warmed with the praise. "Well, I'm grateful he proposed such a venture. It was probably the most exhilarating and exciting experience of my life."

Rosemary looked at her in surprise and then laughed until tears formed in her eyes. "Oh, I assure you there is at least one experience more exhilarating. But that is not a discussion for now. I'm just pleased that you had such a wonderful time."

"Oh, I did," Gillian said earnestly. "I don't know how to thank you for everything you've done for Lemuel and me. We've been so very fortunate to be the recipients of your kindness and generosity."

"Oh, but you've repaid it a hundred times over," Juliet said. "By saving Spencer and by helping me with George and Skye." She glanced over at her mother. "Did I tell you that George has already permitted Gillian to come within an arm's length? I think he might even let her touch him soon. Skye is more skittish, but I think Gillian will conquer her as well. Skye's mate is already fond of her."

"Must you name the horrid beasts?"

Gillian smiled. "Juliet is excellent with birds and animals. They trust her."

"I do worry that they may bite," Rosemary said. "Frankly, I'm not certain I'd even allow it if not for Phineas's and Spencer's insistence."

"Birds are, by in large, very gentle except when they are threatened," Gillian explained. "And they are quite intelligent. Nonetheless, it takes a certain touch to manage them. Juliet possesses such a talent."

Juliet beamed. "See, mother? I think I shall—" she began, when Mrs. Doyle abruptly rushed into the sitting room, her pudgy face drawn with worry.

"What is it?" Rosemary said in concern, setting aside her sewing and rising from the chair.

"Jacob Toomery has apparently collapsed," Mrs. Doyle said. "The family sent a young boy to fetch Mr. Reeves. He's waiting at the door now."

"Oh my, Phineas and Spencer are out on a stroll," Rosemary said, clasping a hand to her breast. "We'll have to send someone to find them at once."

"Right away, ma'am," Mrs. Doyle said and hurriedly left the room to do her bidding.

"I can go," Gillian said, standing as well. "Perhaps I can aid him until more experienced hands arrive."

"You can't go out alone at this time of night," Rosemary protested.

A glance out the window showed Gillian that dusk had already fallen on the town, and twilight was imminent.

"I'll go with her," Juliet offered.

"You certainly will not," Rosemary and Gillian said at the same time.

"I'll see if Lemuel will accompany me," Gillian said, already moving toward the door. "I'll fetch my cloak and be off."

Rosemary nodded reluctantly, and Juliet trailed her to the parlor, where a nervous young boy waited to show her the way.

"Be careful," Juliet whispered, and Gillian patted her on the hand.

"Don't worry. I'll return soon."

Throwing her cloak about her shoulders, Gillian led the boy back to the woodshed. She knocked furiously, but to her chagrin, Lemuel didn't answer.

"Lemuel," she yelled, but there was no reply.

She knocked several more times and even tried to open the door, but it was latched securely.

"Come on, mistress," the boy said, tugging on her arm. "We 'ave to go. There is little time."

With a last worried look over her shoulder at the woodshed, Gillian permitted herself to be led from the estate.

"Which way to Mr. Toomery's house?" she asked as she followed the boy down the street.

"Just follow me, mistress," the boy said. "I'll show you."

As they crossed the nearly empty streets, Gillian felt increasingly concerned. A heavy fog lay over the town, and the dampness in the air penetrated her cloak. The boy was practically running now, and she lifted her skirts to dart after him, afraid she would lose sight of him in the shroud of mist.

"This way," the boy said, suddenly taking a left turn into an alley.

She stopped, her eyes widening in concern. Despite her cloak, Gillian felt a cool chill race up her spine.

"Are you certain Mr. Toomery's house is this way?" she asked uncertainly.

" 'Tis quicker this way," the boy replied. "Come, now, we are almost there. He needs you."

Hesitantly, Gillian stepped into the alley. The boy had disappeared in the darkness and mist.

"Where are you?" she called out.

"Here," came the boy's voice.

She walked forward blindly, holding one hand out against a cold wall to guide her. Then, as if by magic, the fog abruptly parted, revealing the young boy. To her astonishment, he stood next to a tall, cloaked figure in the dimness of the alley. As she watched, the shrouded figure dropped a coin into the boy's hand. Without a word, he darted past Gillian and promptly fled down the alley.

"At last," the figure said in a woman's voice, deep, throaty, and unnaturally cold. "I've been waiting such a long time to meet you."

Gillian's brain screamed at her to run, but she seemed rooted to the spot, the hairs on her arms and the back of her neck prickling.

"Wh-who are you?" Gillian managed to say, an inexplicable feeling of dread crawling over her.

"I am your enemy."

"My enemy?" Gillian said, stunned. "But where is Mr. Toomery?"

The woman laughed, a seductive, husky sound. " 'Twas but a ruse to bring you here. 'Twas time for us to meet."

"I don't know what you mean."

"You will. Now, 'tis time to see how powerful you really are." She lifted both her arms to the sky and began to murmur a strange incantation.

> *"Morrigan, Osiris, Jackal and Kore,*
> *The cycle nears its end,*
> *Reveal to me the way, O Scurrilous One,*
> *Invoke your willful malevolence,*
> *For in the shadows,*
> *Your faithful servants wait."*

Gillian abruptly slammed backward into the cold stone wall of the alley as if a giant hand had reached down from the heavens and smashed into her. The breath in her lungs expelled in a painful rush, and her ears rang from the force of her head hitting against the wall. Gasping for air, she shook her head to clear it while clenching her hands into fists to fight off her attacker. But to her shock, there was no one near her. The cloaked woman stood motionless across the alley, where she had been all along.

"How . . . how did you do that?" Gillian stammered.

"Power," the woman said softly.

This time Gillian felt unseen hands clamp around her neck, squeezing. She dropped to her knees in the stench of the alley, twisting and clawing at the invisible fingers. Tears filled her eyes, and her vision began to swim.

"Oppono," another female voice suddenly commanded, and at once the pressure around Gillian's neck disappeared.

Gillian dropped to the ground, gasping and coughing as a second cloaked figure stepped into the alley.

"Well, well, I wondered when you would finally show your face in Salem," her attacker said to the new arrival. "Now we meet at last."

"I've been here a lot longer than you know."

"You're too late, and from this little trial I can see your offspring are woefully inadequate to the task."

"You know nothing about us."

The woman laughed coldly. "I know enough to know you are doomed forever. Watch. *Aperio,*" she commanded, raising her hand.

To Gillian's horrified amazement, an eye-searing bolt of lightning shot from the woman's fingers directly at her rescuer. Gillian stood up and opened her mouth to scream, but no sound came out.

A deafening crack of thunder sounded, and the lightning seemed to slam against an unseen wall in front of the woman and explode. White-hot shards of light sprayed across Gillian and the alley. Pain blasted into her brain and she moaned, pressing her temples between her hands.

"Seize this!" Gillian's rescuer abruptly commanded and tossed something at her.

Gillian raised her head just as a small object whistled through the air toward her. She reached out a hand and caught it. Surprised, she looked down to see a smooth stone mounted in an elaborate setting of gold and silver, hanging by a long golden chain. As if instinctively knowing what to do, Gillian slipped it around her neck.

Thwarted, Gillian's attacker shrieked an oath and summoned another bolt. This time, the lightning that shot from her fingers was as black as pitch and headed directly for Gillian. She ducked as the bolt struck the wall just above her head and erupted into a mass of writhing, licking flames.

She covered her head, fully expecting to be engulfed in the flames. After a moment, when nothing happened, she cautiously raised her head. The fire was raging around her, consuming debris and trash near her feet, but it had not touched her.

"Abyssus abyssum invocat," Gillian's rescuer abruptly commanded, and a white cloud appeared seemingly from nowhere, hovering over the alley.

Gillian's attacker screamed as the white tendrils of

smoke suddenly wound themselves around her body, slithering and writhing. Gillian squeezed her eyes shut, horrified by the unnatural images.

"This is just a dream," she whispered to herself, closing her eyes. "A horrible, dreadful dream."

"Gillian!" she heard someone shout, and snapped her eyes open.

Shocked, she looked down the alley and saw Juliet standing in the street near a lamppost, looking pitifully small in a cloak too large for her.

"Juliet!" Gillian screamed. "Leave at once. Go!"

Terrified at what might happen to the girl, Gillian tried to move but was still trapped within her space, flames dancing eagerly around her in morbid and eerie delight, as if just waiting with glee to devour her.

"Run!" she shouted again to Juliet. Her heart twisted with fear as she that realized both of the cloaked figures had now seen the girl.

But Juliet stood her ground bravely. "Father! Spencer!" Gillian heard her shout. "Over here. I've found her."

"Nay!" Gillian shouted, waving her hands frantically. "Get away from here."

To both her dread and relief, she saw Spencer dash around the corner, coming at her in a full sprint in spite of the flames and smoke engulfing the alley.

"Nay!" she screamed, waving him back. "You'll burn."

He ignored her and rushed in. To her astonishment, he darted ably through the fire, nearly colliding with her. She reached out to touch him, surprised that the barrier protecting her had somehow disappeared. They clung to each other a heartbeat before he slung her over his shoulder and ran back out of the alley.

Both of them were coughing as he set her down on the ground and slapped at the flames that were licking the shoulders of his coat. Looking down at herself, Gillian was amazed to see that she was completely unscathed.

Fearfully, she looked back into the alley but saw no one else emerge. By now, citizens were running to the spot, shouting and carrying buckets of water to extinguish the flames.

Spencer knelt beside her, drawing her into his arms without a word. With a sob, Gillian wound her arms around his neck, burying her face against his chest. He held her tightly, murmuring soft words and stroking her hair.

After a minute, he drew back, nudging her chin up with his finger until she looked directly at him.

"What in the devil just happened?" he asked, his face still blackened from the smoke.

She looked back again at the alley and then at Juliet, who stood huddled next to her father.

"I don't know," she whispered, a cold chill settling in her heart. "I simply don't know."

SIXTEEN

Gillian pulled the blanket tighter around her shoulders, sipping a glass of whiskey and trying to keep her body from trembling. The entire Reeves family and Lemuel had squeezed into the library. Now all of them stared at her and waited.

For what? Gillian thought desperately. *A rational explanation of implausible events?* How could she possibly explain what occurred in the alley without everyone thinking her raving mad?

She could hardly say that a mysterious cloaked figure had tried to strangle her without moving a muscle and had shot lightning bolts from her fingers. Or that another cloaked figure came to her rescue, spouting incomprehensible phrases and conjuring white snakelike clouds. It sounded absurd even to her own ears, and she had lived through it.

"Have another sip," Spencer urged her, sitting on the arm of her chair. "Are you ready to tell us what happened?"

Gillian sipped, coughing as the liquid burned a fiery trail down her throat. It didn't help, she thought in dismay. Everything seemed so unreal. The only tangible evidence of the night's events was the cool weight between her breasts of the odd amulet her rescuer had tossed her. For some reason, she'd hidden it even from Spencer and was still reluctant to reveal its existence.

"Spencer, fetch another blanket for Gillian," Rosemary ordered her son from her perch on a nearby chair. She stroked her daughter's hair as Juliet sat huddled on her lap. "Can't you see the poor child is still shaking?"

Gillian shook her head. "Nay, please, it's all right. I don't need another blanket—just a moment more to collect my thoughts."

"Of course you do," Rosemary said kindly. "After what you've been through, it's no wonder."

Spencer rose from the arm of her chair and then sat down again, clearly restless and troubled. "This situation is simply intolerable," he finally said with a scowl.

"I'm sorry," Gillian said softly. "You've shown us nothing but kindness and we've brought you so much misfortune."

"Nonsense," Phineas said from where he stood gazing out the window into the darkness. "Having some deranged individual trying to harm you can hardly be considered your fault."

"Nonetheless, we've placed your family in harm's way," Gillian said. "We should leave at once."

Lemuel, who had been silently pacing back and forth in front of the hearth, finally stopped. "I agree. Whatever is happening to us could put any of you in danger."

"You'll do nothing of the kind," Phineas commanded so firmly that it reminded Gillian of their own father. "This has become personal now. I fully intend to discover what is going on here."

"As do I," Spencer said, equally as firm. "But first, we need to know just what happened in that alley. For that, we need your help, Gillian."

Exhaling a deep breath, Gillian set the glass aside and pulled the blanket tighter around her shoulders.

"I have a question first," she said. "How did you find me?"

"Juliet," Spencer said, cocking his head at his sister. "She noticed as you left the estate that the boy was leading you in the wrong direction."

"I thought only to correct him, so I grabbed Mrs. Doyle's cloak and followed you," Juliet piped up. "But I couldn't catch up. And as he led you farther and farther from Mr. Toomery's house, I knew something was amiss. When you disappeared into the alley with the boy, I ran to find Father and Spencer."

"You shouldn't have followed me," Gillian chided her. "You could have been harmed."

"If I hadn't, you might not be here now," Juliet replied, lifting her chin.

"I assure you she'll face punishment for her reckless behavior," Phineas said firmly. "But for now we are simply grateful that she found you."

Gillian felt her eyes fill with tears. "I don't know how to thank you all."

"Gillian, what happened next?" Spencer asked, putting a gentle hand on her shoulder.

"I'm not certain," Gillian said truthfully. "The boy who came to the house said Mr. Toomery had collapsed. I offered to accompany the boy to Mr. Toomery's house until you and your father could be summoned. I had hoped Lemuel would accompany me, but he did not respond to my repeated knocks. I tried to enter, but the woodshed was latched."

Lemuel rubbed the back of his neck. "I couldn't answer you," he said quietly. "Someone had already hit me from behind."

Gillian gasped. "Hit you?"

"I had only been in the woodshed for a few minutes when I heard a knock. I answered it, but no one was there.

When I stepped outside to get a better look, someone clubbed me."

Gillian pressed her hand to her mouth. "Are you badly injured?"

"Fortunately, nay. But it means that someone wanted you to go into that alley alone."

"B-but how did they latch the door from inside and then manage to get out?" she whispered. "I couldn't get in."

"I don't know," Lemuel said, lifting his hands, his expression clearly troubled. "I can't explain it."

There was a moment of silence in the room before Spencer prodded her gently. "Then what happened next?" he asked.

Gillian gripped the blanket tighter around her neck. "I thought the boy was leading me to Mr. Toomery's house. He told me the alley was the quickest route to the house. Instead, a woman clad in a cloak with a hood stood in the alley waiting for me. Once she saw me, she gave the boy something and he ran off. When I asked of Mr. Toomery, she told me his collapse was but a ruse to summon me to her."

"It was a ruse indeed," Spencer said grimly. "You can imagine Father's and my surprise when we arrived at Mr. Toomery's house out of breath and nearly frantic. When he opened the door in perfect health and looked at us in surprise, my heart fairly stopped. We headed back to the house at a full run when we heard Juliet screaming."

"That took me a full ten years closer to my grave," Phineas added.

"How do you know the woman in the alley waited for you?" Spencer asked.

"She said as much," Gillian answered.

A slow frown formed on his lips. "Did you recognize her?"

She shook her head. "Nay, I couldn't see her, and her

voice wasn't familiar. Yet, somehow I had the feeling that I'd met her before."

"Why would she go to so much trouble to harm you?" Spencer asked.

"I . . . I don't know," she replied softly. "She said some strange things to me."

"Such as?" Lemuel interjected.

"I can't remember exactly. Something about her being my enemy. Then another woman came. She was cloaked as well, but she tried to help me. The two of them spoke to each other and a fire somehow started. Juliet called out to me and you came."

"That's all?" Spencer said, looking at her intently.

She felt a twinge of guilt for leaving out the parts about the searing lightning bolts and white, snakelike clouds, but decided she needed more time to consider what it all meant. "I'm afraid so," she said, lowering her gaze.

"She said she was your enemy?" Phineas mused, frowning. "What did she mean?"

"I have no idea," Gillian said honestly.

"I didn't see any cloaked women when I rushed in to get you," Spencer said. He glanced over at Juliet. "Did you see them?"

The girl shook her head. "Nay, I saw only Gillian huddled against the wall surrounded by the fire."

Gillian lifted her hands helplessly. "I assure you, they were there."

"I believe you," Spencer said, patting her shoulder. "Are you certain you are unharmed?"

"Just a bit shaken."

"Could this be the work of Jack Soward?" Phineas asked, his white brows furrowed with worry.

"I'm not certain," Gillian said. "But somehow, I don't think so."

Lemuel stepped forward. "I told them about the poisoned bread, Gillian. I thought in light of the circumstances, they should know. Not surprisingly, Mrs. Carlisle told us she did not bake it. Mrs. Doyle said simply that she found the basket sitting unattended in the parlor. No one knows from where it came."

Spencer rose from his perch on Gillian's chair, shoving his fingers through his hair. "I don't like any of this. Poisoned bread and cloaked women in an alley starting fires. I agree with Gillian. This does not sound like the methods of Jack Soward. Frankly speaking, he's not intelligent enough to plot something so dastardly. Someone took a lot of care to ensure that Lemuel would not be able to accompany her to the alley and that both Father and I were gone from the house. This required precise planning and foresight, neither of which are among Jack's finer attributes."

"I agree," Phineas said firmly. "I think there is clearly something else at work here."

"But what?" Lemuel said in frustration. "Who, other than the Soward family, would want to harm Gillian?"

"Perhaps they just wanted to frighten her," Juliet said softly. "Send a warning, mayhap."

Gillian twisted the blanket in her hands. "If so, 'twas most effective."

"Well, this occurrence has settled one thing for certain," Spencer said, standing directly in front of her. "Gillian, you are not to leave these premises without an escort. Is that understood?"

She nodded and he strode to the door. "We'll need to hire someone to watch the estate as well," he said to his father, his scowl deepening. "I'll not let someone enter the grounds and commit injurious acts at will."

"Agreed," Phineas said, nodding, his expression as grim as his son's.

"Where are you going?" Gillian asked Spencer worriedly.

"To see the constable," Spencer replied, his eyes narrowing. "I have a feeling there is something afoot in Salem that I need to know more about."

Spencer sat in the dark in his room, staring at the dying embers of the fire. He'd been sitting there for hours, ever since leaving the constable's house and returning home. After ensuring that Gillian was safely asleep in her bed, he had retired to his room to think. He hadn't bothered to draw the drapes, and now a glance out the window showed the clear twinkle of stars beneath the frosty late October half-moon.

The constable had been less than helpful, and frankly Spencer couldn't blame him. No persons had been found injured in the alley, and the story of two cloaked women— both of whom had mysteriously vanished—seemed a bit strange to his own ears. The fire had been successfully doused, Gillian was unharmed, and the constable seemed eager to forget the entire matter.

But Spencer could not. He'd never been so terrified in his life as when he heard Juliet shout that Gillian was in danger. When he rounded the corner of the alley and saw her standing there surrounded by smoke and flames, his heart had nearly stopped. Fear clawed at his throat as he rushed to her, afraid that he'd be too late and she'd burn to death right before his eyes. In the moment his arms had closed around her, he knew he never wanted to lose her—ever.

That stunning realization shook him to his very core. As he carried Gillian out of the burning alley, he faced the one truth he'd been denying from the moment he had met her.

He loved her.

Sighing, he rubbed his forehead. It was a hell of a time to come to such a realization. His wedding to another woman was set for a month hence. A wedding that had been planned and arranged for more than a year. Except he didn't love Phoebe, and now he understood that he never really had.

"I didn't even know what love was until I met you, Gillian," he murmured.

Before Gillian, love never even seemed important. But she had made him feel so gloriously alive, happy, and content that he knew he could never go back to how he was before. They seemed to have been destined for each other.

Perhaps in some way, he'd known it from the first moment they touched. From the vaguely sensuous sensation that had flowed from her fingers to his, to the unusual sense of familiarity and the fierce attraction, Gillian Saunders was definitively the woman for him.

He wasn't going to marry Phoebe.

He rubbed the back of his neck, marveling at the weight that had suddenly lifted from his heart. It pained him to know he would have to hurt and embarrass Phoebe, but it was the right thing to do for both of them. He had no wish to impose a loveless and unsuitable joining on her— one she would regret for the rest of her life.

He closed his eyes, a sense of relief flowing over him. Then, while sitting in the chair fully dressed, he slept better than he had in a week.

Gillian awoke suddenly, an odd phrase echoing in her head.

Magica tua anima tua est.

Trembling, she sat up and pressed her fingers to her temples, where a headache throbbed. Why did that phrase seem familiar when she didn't even know what it meant? What was happening to her?

Disquieted, she threw the bedcovers aside and padded to the hearth. She stirred the embers, tossing on some kindling and waiting until the fire caught before adding a few small logs. She thrust her arms into her robe and walked to the window. Drawing aside the drapes, she gazed at the spectacular Salem sunrise.

Closing her eyes, she leaned her forehead against the cool leaded glass. Something strange was happening inside her body and mind. Last night in the alley when the cloaked women had confronted her, she'd been terrified and outraged. And yet a part of her she never knew existed had come alive. There had been some kind of connection with these women, and a frightening familiarity.

"How?" Gillian whispered. "How do I know them?"

She'd gone through every bit of their conversation in her mind a hundred times over, and yet no answers presented themselves.

"She said she was my enemy," Gillian murmured.

It was possible it might be a female relative of the Sowards, but in her heart Gillian didn't believe that. There was something more to these events, something that connected her to these mysterious cloaked women on a deeper, more primitive level.

Sighing, she pushed away from the window and perched on the corner of her bed, drawing her bare feet up beneath her. Carefully she drew out the amulet that hung around her neck. It looked the same this morning as it had last night when she had examined it closely for the first time. The deep-blue sapphire stone was cool and smooth to the touch. When she turned it over in her hand, she could see a faint white light deep within its depths. It was mounted in an elaborate setting of gold and silver and hung from a long golden chain. There were no unusual markings or engravings on it. She had no idea why she wore it, except that instinctively, or perhaps intuitively, she knew that was where it belonged.

She closed her fist around the stone, wishing it could

speak. Why had her rescuer thrown it to her? What did it signify?

Magica tua anima tua est.

That haunting phrase sounded in her head again. What in God's name did it mean? What was happening to her?

Shaking her head, she slipped the amulet back beneath her bed gown and wrapped her arms around her legs, resting her chin on her knees. Ever since she'd come to Salem, she felt something shift and grow inside her—something that aided her in her efforts to heal.

She sighed. Spencer had been right. She *had* been taking on the pain of the patients—something she'd never been able to do before. The concentration and effort it required took considerably more energy than what she expended on animals, but so were the rewards. To be able to help people with just the touch of her hand was as thrilling as it was humbling. Yet it was not a gift without a price. After she touched a person in pain, she felt physically drained. She had felt something similar when the cloaked woman attacked her in the alley.

Realizing no easy answers were likely to present themselves, Gillian rose from her bed and got dressed. She was combing her hair when Lynette knocked. Glad for the distraction, she urged the young woman to come in.

"I heard what happened to you," Lynette said worriedly, taking the comb and drawing it steadily through Gillian's long locks. "Thanks be that you came out of such a horrid event uninjured."

"I was very fortunate."

"And to think someone attacked Mr. Lemuel as well, right here on the Reeves estate. He had quite a lump on the back of his head, he did. Whoever would do such a thing?"

"I wish I knew."

"He could have been killed." Her voice caught and Gillian turned around.

"You are that fond of my brother?"

Lynette nodded, tears filling her eyes. "I am. I know he's only been here a few days, but I just knew from the first time we met there was something special about him. I suppose it sounds quite foolish."

"Nay, it doesn't," Gillian said softly. "I know precisely what you mean."

The young woman blushed. "It's just that Lemuel is so clever and witty. I don't care a whit that he doesn't look like other men. He says he likes me, too, although I can't imagine why."

"I know why," Gillian said earnestly. "You are sweet, kind, and generous." Then she smiled. "Besides, you are willing to pay the entrance price to the woodshed."

Lynette blush deepened. "Mercy, he told you about that?"

Gillian touched the girl's hand. "I think you are very lucky. Lemuel has the kindest heart of any man I know."

Lynette sighed and finished combing Gillian's hair in dreamy silence. They went downstairs together, Lynette going off to the kitchen, and Gillian entering the dining room.

Spencer and Phineas were the only ones at the table, their heads bent together, deep in discussion. They rose when she entered, Spencer pulling out a chair for her. He looked breathtakingly handsome in a white shirt, tan breeches and boots, his golden brown hair loose about his shoulders. She felt a funny clutch in her heart and wondered if she would feel that way each time she saw him for the rest of her life.

"How do you fare this morning?" he asked, letting his hand linger a moment longer than usual on her shoulder.

"I'm fine, thank you," she answered. "And you?"

Still angry about what happened to you," he replied sitting down.

"Is there any word from the constable?" she asked.

"The fire was successfully doused, but there was no evidence that anyone else had been in the alley," Spencer said. "The cloaked women seemed to have simply vanished."

Gillian felt her stomach turn. "I don't know how that is possible."

"Mayhap they slipped out among those who came in to extinguish the fire," Phineas offered. "There was quite a bit of confusion and activity."

"I suppose that is possible," Gillian said but she didn't believe it.

"The constable also intends to visit Jack Soward again concerning his whereabouts last evening," Spencer added.

"He wasn't in the alley," Gillian said quietly. "It was just the three of us."

"I know," Spencer replied. "It's just a precaution. We'll get to the bottom of this. But today I want you to rest."

"Nay, please," Gillian said in dismay, pushing her plate aside. "I couldn't bear sitting in my room all day. Please permit me to assist you in the clinic. 'Twill keep my mind off my troubles."

Spencer exchanged a doubtful glance with Phineas. "I'm not certain that is a wise idea."

"I beg you to reconsider," she said, raising her chin. "I want whoever it was in that alley last night to know that I am not so easily frightened."

Phineas rose, looking at Spencer. "Frankly, I agree. If Gillian says she feels well enough to attend to her duties, then let it be so."

Spencer rose as well. "Well, it may be against my better judgment, but if you both insist, who am I to argue? Father will you be working today?"

Phineas nodded. "I'm in no mood to visit the docks today."

"Then let's begin our day," Spencer said, leading the way to the clinic.

The morning and early afternoon passed fairly quickly, with a reasonable number of patients with only mild complaints. They had just finished treating seven-year old Rebecca Simmons for a broken elbow when Spencer abruptly announced he would be gone for the rest of the afternoon.

"I'm afraid there is a matter I must attend to at once," he said, reaching for his coat. "I think the two of you can carry on without me."

"We shall try, son," Phineas said, watching him curiously.

With no further explanation, Spencer donned his coat and strode out of the clinic. Phineas glanced over at Gillian, lifting a white eyebrow. "Now, what in the devil do you think that was all about?"

Gillian shook her head, as baffled as he. "I have no idea," she said. "But whatever it is, he certainly seemed determined to do it now."

SEVENTEEN

"I'm sorry, Phoebe. I never meant to hurt you," Spencer said, dragging his fingers though his hair. The fire in the hearth in the parlor at the Trask estate blazed uncomfortably hot, so he shed his coat, draping it across the back of a nearby chair.

Phoebe's stunning blue eyes flashed with a mixture of disbelief and anger. "Never meant to hurt me? We've but a month until the wedding and you've suddenly decided we're not suited enough to wed?"

Spencer sighed. "I know it seems sudden. It's just that I've made many mistakes lately and I don't want you to suffer because of another one."

"Mistakes? Whatever are you talking about?"

"I'm talking about me . . . about you. We're not right for each other."

Her mouth fell open. "Have you gone utterly mad? There is no one more suited to you than me."

"I once thought that," he admitted, sitting in a chair across from her. "But I've been thinking."

"About what? How best to ruin my life? Your life?"

He leaned back in the chair. "When I nearly lost my life, things changed for me, Phoebe. Things that were never really that important suddenly became so."

"Such as?"

"Love, friendship, companionship. I care deeply about

you, Phoebe, but we really don't have that much in common. We don't . . . well, think alike on many issues that matter."

She looked at him in disbelief. "Do you realize how absurd you sound?"

"Why is it so absurd?" he said reasonably. "Consider for a moment. We were never really friends."

"Of course not," she retorted. "We're betrothed."

He rubbed the back of his neck. "That's just my point. It just wouldn't work. We'd make each other miserable within a month."

She leaned back in her chair and appraised him intently. "Listen to me, darling. I know you are anxious about the wedding. It's not unusual for men to feel so. But I assure you, these uncertain feelings will pass. We both know that you aren't simply going to abandon the wedding. Not after all the arrangements have been made, people invited, and coin spent."

"I'll compensate your father for all the arrangements," he said quietly. "There will be no financial loss for you."

Her eyes narrowed. "And just how do you intend to compensate me for the damage to my reputation?"

"By letting everyone know it was your decision."

He saw the surprise in her eyes before she leaned toward him, trailing a finger along his thigh.

"Spencer, I beg you to reconsider this foolhardy course of action. There is no need to be so hasty. Please give me a chance to show you just how well suited we are to each other."

"It wouldn't help."

"You owe it to me," she said, her eyes hardening.

He felt a pang of pity and regret. "I'm sorry. It wouldn't help because I don't love you," he said softly. "And I don't think you love me either. This is my fault, Phoebe. I should have never let it get this far."

Instead of hurt, he saw fury in her eyes. "Love? Friendship? What has come over you? We are right for each other in the most important aspects of any marriage: station, temperament, and ambition. I need you, Spencer, and you need me."

"To do what?" he said, spreading his hands. "I have no grand political ambitions, Phoebe. I never had. I wish only to be a doctor."

"Exactly," she countered emphatically. "What will become of you without me? Do you really wish to live your life as an insignificant physician? You could be so much more. But you need me to make you great, to bring you the power and respect you deserve."

Spencer rose from the chair, disgust rising in his throat. "My God, Phoebe, what are you talking about? I had no idea that we were so very wrong about each other."

"You're just upset, darling. Don't do this," she said. "Don't abandon me."

"I have the greatest confidence that you will do quite well, certainly even better, without me."

She rose from her chair, flipping her thick, dark hair over her shoulder. "This is all because of *her*, isn't it? Gillian Saunders has done this. She's poisoned your mind against me."

Spencer kept his gaze even. "She has done nothing of the sort. She knows nothing of my decision."

Phoebe's fingers tightened around his arm. "Oh, I assure you, she does. This has been her plan all along. What did she do? Flaunt her wares like a whore? Or did she tempt you into iniquity? If she did, Spencer, I'll forgive you."

"That's enough, Phoebe," he warned, his voice deepening with displeasure.

"You can't let her do this," Phoebe ranted. "She's bewitched you, made you believe things about me that aren't true."

"She hasn't done anything. This isn't about her. It's about you and me."

Phoebe's voice rose. "She's made you think we're somehow unsuited to each other.

"I assure you, she is completely innocent in this matter," he said, extracting his forearm from her clawlike grip.

"That's what she'd like you to believe," Phoebe said bitterly. "How little men know of women. Do I have to be the one to let you know that your precious little innocent is really a treacherous, dangerous snake? I promise you, she'll bring you to ruin."

"Good-bye, Phoebe," he said, striding to the door.

"You'll change your mind, Spencer," she said softly. "And I'll be waiting for you. I'll always be waiting for you."

He paused in the doorway, looking over his shoulder at her. "I'm not going to change my mind."

She smiled, and Spencer saw an unusual, almost unnatural light in her eyes. "You can tell me that on our wedding day," she said with a chilling assuredness.

He left the house without another word, deeply disquieted by the encounter. He started to head home and then changed his mind. He'd go by the Blue Shell Tavern. Perhaps Jonathan and Charles would be there. And, frankly, at this moment, he needed a stiff drink.

Gillian roamed about the clinic restlessly. Spencer had not returned for supper, and the meal had been a quiet and uneventful affair. Lemuel retired to his workshop, Phineas to the library to read, and Rosemary to the sitting room to oversee Juliet's practice on the pianoforte.

She'd already rearranged every vial on the shelf twice and wound and unwound all the linen strips before she decided she couldn't stand the solitude any longer. Donning her cloak, she headed around the back of the house to visit the convalescing birds. Dusk had already started to fall, but she could hear the thwack of Lemuel's ax and felt comforted that he was nearby.

Murmuring softly, she unfastened the latch on the pen. After a moment, George strutted out. She held out an empty hand to the crane, and he looked at her disdainfully because she had brought no treat. But for the first time he did not shy away. She smiled, encouraged by the progress. Soon she'd be able to touch him on his injured leg and he'd be well enough to leave.

"You'd like that, wouldn't you, George?" she crooned. "To go back to your own kind where you belong. That's what life is all about, isn't it? Belonging."

Skye sauntered out a minute later, looking warily at Gillian. A rustle sounded above her, and Gillian looked up to see Star in the sky, circling above them in a protective manner.

"Hello, Star," she called out. "You can cease your incessant worrying. I won't hurt her; I give you my word. Watch."

She held out her hand and the small female hawk approached slowly. Gillian made no move to touch her until Skye nuzzled her hand. Smiling, Gillian stroked her lightly on the back and head. Skye accepted her touch, and Gillian felt her heart swell at the trust that had just been offered her. In repayment, she gently touched the bird's injured wing, healing it quickly. For a moment, Skye stiffened and then relaxed.

"You'll need to stay until Juliet can say good-bye," she said softly. "You'll fly away from here with Star and live happily ever after."

Gillian chuckled as she carefully put Skye back in the pen and then looked up at Star, who had perched on a nearby branch and stared intently at her. "She'll be yours soon," she told him. "Don't you dare leave her now."

After a few more minutes, Gillian ushered the crane

back toward the pen. To her astonishment, Star suddenly screeched and circled frantically above her. Worriedly, Gillian looked up at him.

"Star, whatever is wrong?" she asked just as a strong arm snaked around her neck, pulling her backward against a broad chest. She opened her mouth to scream when her attacker slapped a cloth across her mouth and nose.

Gillian kicked her legs in alarm, twisting in her captor's iron grip to no avail. As she raggedly breathed in, the blackness rushed up to greet her.

"You did *what?*" Jonathan exclaimed in disbelief. "Have you lost your senses?"

Spencer took a sip of his ale. "No, in fact, I think I've finally come to them."

Even Charles looked at him in awe. "Well, I'll say this, Spence, when you do something, you do it on a grand scale. Abandoning Phoebe Trask at the altar. Who would have thought it from you?"

Spencer looked at his friend wryly. "I'm not abandoning Phoebe and we're not at the altar. I simply did her a favor by freeing her from a lifetime of misery with a dull and simple town physician."

"I always thought it a match not worthy of you," Charles said, waving at the barmaid to refill his mug. "But she certainly is beautiful and wealthy, of course."

"Why the hell didn't you two ever say anything?" Spencer said irritably. "It might have helped if you two had aided me in searching for my senses a bit earlier."

"Aided?" Jonathan interrupted. "What would we aid you with? If you were content, who were we to interfere? After all, it's a match most men only dream about."

"We aren't even friends," Spencer said, leaning his elbows on the table. "We are completely unsuited to each other, and I was simply too indifferent to care."

"Who in the devil wants to marry a friend?" Jonathan said heatedly. "And for that matter, who says you have to like your wife? She'd be good for you, Spence. She'd make something of you."

"What is that supposed to mean?" Spencer said, stiffening.

"He means you could have risen to a position of prominence in this town," Charles said in amusement, leaning back as the barmaid poured more ale. "Had you so desired, of course."

"Since when have I ever craved prominence or political influence?" Spencer growled, narrowing his eyes. "Why does everyone suddenly assume that I have some kind of grand political ambition?"

"Who wouldn't?" Jonathan said, taking a swig of his ale and setting his mug down with a thump. "Any man in his right mind would. After all, with a woman like that at your side, think of the things a man could accomplish."

"I prefer to think for myself," Spencer said. "I don't need Phoebe to do it for me."

Jonathan started to say something when Charles waved a hand, cutting him off. "He's right, Jonathan. Phoebe was never suited to Spence and we both know it."

Spencer lifted his mug in salute. "Thank you, Charles."

"But I would venture a guess that this rather shocking revelation has come about thanks to a lovely red-haired woman with a gentle touch," he added.

"No," Spencer said a little too sharply and then sighed. "Yes."

Jonathan's mouth gaped open. "Gillian? My God, Spence, you *are* mad."

Charles laughed. "No, you idiot, he's in love. And only just now realizing it."

Spencer glanced wryly at Charles. "You've been aware all along, haven't you?"

Charles nodded, amusement still glinting in his eyes.

"Of course. You've known me long enough to be certain that the rumor of my proficiency in matters of the heart is not just idle talk."

"Then that little display of interest in her back at the clinic was just a ploy?"

Charles lifted his mug to his lips and took a sip. "Not really," he said. "I would take her in a heartbeat if she would have me. But I fear a broken heart is not so easily mended. It would have taken an abominable amount of time to help her get over you. Nonetheless, it was a challenge to which I gladly would have risen, had you been the idiot I'd hoped."

"You two can't be serious," Jonathan interrupted. "Gillian has no money, no position—not even a past, for God's sake. Spence, you can't really be thinking about pursuing a relationship with her."

"I'll do whatever I damn well please," Spencer said evenly.

Charles gave an exaggerated sigh. "He doesn't want or need your advice, Jonathan. He's a man with a mind of his own, and clearly that mind is made up. Now you can see why he is so totally unsuited to Mistress Trask."

"I think you've both gone 'round the bend," Jonathan grumbled into his ale.

"You just wouldn't know a good woman if she bit you on the arse," Charles said with a chuckle.

"This coming from the man who made a spectacle of himself just to catch a glimpse of Mistress Wendall's underclothes," Jonathan retorted.

"I'll let that disparaging remark pass and say that all in all, I think at last Spence is on the right path. So, let's drink to a new future. We wish you all the best, friend." He raised his mug to Spencer.

After a moment, Jonathan reluctantly lifted his mug, and finally Spencer joined them.

"To happiness," Charles declared. "And love."

Spencer clinked his mug against his friend's. "I'll damn well drink to that."

Gillian awoke with a splitting pain in her head. Trying to sit up, she realized her arms were tightly bound behind her back and she was lying on a damp dirt floor. Her cloak had been removed and she shivered at the coldness that seeped through her gown.

She twisted to one side and saw a man sitting in a chair at a nearby table. His back was to her, but he appeared alone. A quick survey of the enormous room told her she had been taken to an abandoned warehouse of some kind. The stench of fresh cod assaulted her senses, and Gillian suspected the building was used as a storage facility. Two candles had been lit and placed on a scarred wooden table where the man sat, illuminating only a small area. Twisting, she attempted to get a more thorough look at her surroundings when her captor suddenly turned around.

"Finally awake, are you?" he said.

"Jack Soward," Gillian replied, her voice hoarse. "I should have known you were behind this."

He grinned but made no move to rise from the chair. "How do you like your little surprise, a private, intimate visit with me? I could have killed you already with just one twist of your pretty little neck, but I think this encounter is much more amusing."

Gillian brought her knees beneath her and managed to sit up. Her vision swam and she was desperately thirsty, but she tried to keep herself calm. "Unfortunately, I find your sense of humor quite lacking."

His eyes narrowed. "You won't be so haughty after I've finished with you."

"Just what do you intend to do?"

"What I failed to do the first time. Make you suffer a

slow and agonizing death. To pay you back for the humiliation and pain you've caused our family."

"Your father brought it on himself and we both know it," Gillian said evenly. "Killing me is not going to change that."

"Oh, but it will. And I intend to take great pleasure in it."

Gillian felt a cold finger of dread skitter up her spine at the certainty in his voice. "So, it has been you behind all of these attacks on my brother and me since we came to Salem."

"Attacks?" he said, and Gillian saw a flash of surprise in his eyes. "What attacks?"

"You mean you didn't send the poisoned bread?" she asked, her brows drawing together in a frown.

"Poisoned bread?" he uttered. "What the hell are you talking about? I've been trying to figure out a way to get at you and your brother since you came to town. I thought it damn near impossible with Spencer Reeves watching you and hiring someone to watch me as well. And then a miracle happened. I found myself a powerful ally."

"An ally?"

"Me," Phoebe Trask said, stepping into the room. She wore a dark cloak fastened loosely around her neck with a dazzling green emerald set in an elaborate gold design.

Her thick black hair hung loose about her shoulders, and the candlelight cast a golden glow to her nearly bloodless skin.

Gillian felt an icy gust of air brush over her, raising the gooseflesh on her arms and back.

"Phoebe," she uttered in shock. "What are you doing here?"

Phoebe's cold blue eyes narrowed. "You thought you could take him away from me. I want you to know how wrong you are. It was a grave mistake to cross me."

"Cross you? What are you talking about?"

Phoebe threw a glance at Jack. "Get out. This is between her and me. I'll summon you when you are needed."

Jack looked at Phoebe and Gillian for a time and then shrugged. Rising from his chair, he lumbered to the door and disappeared outside, closing it behind him with a thud.

After he left, Gillian felt a frosty silence fall upon the room. She tried to struggle to her feet, but with her arms bound behind her back and her skirts tangled about her legs, she was able to get only as far as her knees. She sat there waiting while Phoebe continued to stare at her.

"What do you mean I tried to take him from you?" Gillian asked, finally breaking the silence. "Are we talking about Spencer?"

"Don't act so ignorant," Phoebe said disdainfully. "This was your plan all along, wasn't it?"

"What plan?"

Phoebe took a step closer, glaring at her with such hate that Gillian felt physically ill. "Spencer came to me this afternoon and said he wasn't going to wed me."

Gillian gasped in disbelief. "He did *what?*"

Phoebe clenched her hands at her side. "You little witch whore. What did you do to him?"

"I . . . I did nothing."

"Liar!" Phoebe practically screamed. "You bewitched him, turned him against me. Mother was right. I should never have underestimated you."

"What are you talking about?"

"I'll give you one chance," Phoebe said, her voice dripping with contempt. "Remove the spell."

"S-spell?"

"You thought I didn't know about your little secret, but I do. So cease your games. We are far too alike to engage in this waste of time."

Gillian's stomach gave a horrid lurch. "Alike? You think I can do a . . . spell?"

Phoebe hissed in frustration. "I wish mother had finished you off in the alley; then none of this would have happened. Listen to me, girl. Remove the spell on Spencer or I'll kill you. Either way, I'll get what I want."

"I don't know what you mean. I didn't put a spell on him."

Phoebe stared at her intently for a long moment. "Perhaps you don't know," she murmured. "Let's just see."

She looked away from Gillian and focused on something across the room. Gillian followed her gaze, feeling a strange prickle at the back of her neck. Just as she realized what Phoebe was about to do, she felt the amulet beneath her gown begin to grow warm.

"Nay!" Gillian screamed as a thick iron pothook suddenly lifted itself from the table and flew through the air directly at her.

She had time only to close her eyes before the hook stopped a hairsbreadth from her head and clattered to the floor.

"I knew it!" Phoebe screamed. "The innocent act was just a ruse."

Horrified, Gillian watched as objects from the room began to fly at her from all directions: wooden planks, anvils, nails, rods, and hammers, each of them falling to the floor without hitting her. After a minute and having no success, Phoebe stalked across the room, grabbing Gillian by the hair and yanking her to her feet.

"You may be protected against my magic, but you can't stop me from doing this," she said between clenched teeth. She picked up a rusted blade and held it to Gillian's throat. "But that would be too swift, too easy."

Gillian didn't dare breathe as Phoebe glanced at the door. "Jack," she commanded in a loud voice. "You may enter now."

The door opened and Jack stepped in, looking about the room in surprise. The floor was strewn with hooks, tools, planks, and beams. The table and chairs were up-ended and shattered. Then his eyes focused on the blade at Gillian's throat.

"You promised me the kill," he said to her in displeasure.

"So I did," Phoebe said, abruptly dropping the blade to the floor with a clatter. "She's my gift to you. Do as you like; just make certain it's painful. Then dispose carefully of the body. I don't want her ever to be found."

"Nay," Gillian whispered, fear rising in her throat. "Please."

Without a backward glance, Phoebe walked out of the warehouse, slamming the door hard behind her. Jack smiled slowly, sauntering toward her. "This time I'm going to enjoy myself. You got away from me last time, but not again."

Gillian wet her lips, shaking her head. "I saved your life."

Jack laughed. "A foolish act. Yet I thank you." He bowed at the waist, his eyes mocking her.

"Don't do this, please."

He approached, standing nearly nose to nose with her. He shot out a beefy hand and seized her by the shoulder, twisting her back against him and hooking his arm around her neck.

"Do you know the embarrassment you've caused me?" he breathed against her cheek. "Just your presence here in Salem has started people talking again about my father's death. Some are even saying it was his own fault."

Gillian raised her chin. "It was."

Jack growled angrily and, with a sudden swipe, grabbed the front of her gown and yanked downward. Gillian heard the material give a sickening rip and felt the cool air touch her breasts. She twisted away from him as he reached out toward her chest, but he tightened his arm at her neck until she could barely breathe.

"Well, well, what do we have here?" she heard him say. She braced herself for his touch when she realized he spoke of her amulet as his cold fingers closed around it.

"Ouch!" he suddenly screamed, releasing her and staggering a few steps back. He cradled his hand against his stomach. "It's hot. What the devil . . . ?" he began just as the door to the warehouse abruptly crashed open and then smashed to the floor.

Gillian stared in shock as two hooded figures calmly stepped over the wreckage and into the warehouse. Terrified, she pressed herself back against the wall.

Jack bellowed in rage and rushed the intruders. Before he had taken two steps, his shirt inexplicably burst into flames. Shrieking, he tore the garment off and swung a fist at one of the intruders. But just as he raised his arm to strike, the figure easily stepped sideways as if already anticipating his move.

Then, to Gillian's astonishment, Jack's breeches suddenly exploded into a mass of flames. Screaming in anger and pain, he stripped until he stood naked in front of them, dancing from one foot to the other, his hair and body black from soot and smoke.

"Cease your unnatural actions," he shouted at them, a wild look in his eyes.

But instead of pursuing a more sensible course of action such as running away, he foolishly rushed them again. This time, one of the figures drew a wooden plank out from beneath its cloak and slammed it against Jack's head. The big man fell to the floor with a sickening thud and lay still.

Gillian looked up in horror as the figures stepped over Jack's body and headed for her. To her astonishment, the ropes binding her hands behind her back simply fell off.

Dazed, she looked at her hands and then clutched the remnants of her gown to her chest.

"Who . . . who are you?" she asked, her voice barely coming out as a whisper.

The two figures simultaneously pushed back their hoods, and Gillian gasped as she looked at two identical mirror images of herself—young women with red hair, warm green eyes, freckled cheeks, and the same slightly crooked nose. The slightly taller of the two women stepped forward, her eyes kind and understanding.

"We're your sisters," she said quietly. "Welcome home, Gillian."

EIGHTEEN

"Sisters?" Gillian uttered in shock. "I have sisters?"

The young woman smiled in a manner that eerily reminded Gillian of herself. "I'm Bridget and this is Alexandra. We've been looking for you."

Her mind raced. "Who . . . What are you?"

"We have a lot to talk about," Alexandra said gently. "But not here. Have you a cloak?"

Gillian glanced about the room and saw her cloak heaped in a corner. "Over there," she said, pointing.

Alexandra stepped over the debris and picked it up, shaking it out. "Quickly, now," she said, handing it to Gillian. "We mustn't tarry here."

Gillian threw it around her shoulders, still holding up the front of her gown the best she could. She walked to the door, stepping gingerly around Jack Soward.

"Is he dead?" she asked.

Bridget shook her head. "Just unconscious. We are forbidden to use our powers to kill."

Gillian stopped at the door and blinked in surprise. "Powers?"

"We shall answer all your questions in due time, I promise," Alexandra said. "But you must come with us now."

Gillian shook her head. "I cannot. Spencer, Lemuel,

and the Reeves family will be frantic about my whereabouts. I must return at once to the estate."

She watched as Bridget and Alexandra exchange a worried glance.

"I don't think that would be wise," Bridget said finally. "There might be others watching the estate. You are still in danger."

"I can't simply disappear," Gillian pleaded. "I must return to them immediately."

"If you go to them now, you will not have the answers to the questions they will be certain to ask," Alexandra said quietly.

"But Spencer should know what has happened," Gillian countered. "Phoebe Trask, his fiancée, is involved in this. She thinks I did something to him so that he no longer wants to wed her. She tried to kill me."

"We know about Phoebe," Bridget said, her voice tightening. "What are your feelings for Spencer?"

Gillian blinked at the abrupt shift in topic. "What?"

"I know it may seem strange, but 'tis important for us to know," Alexandra said gently, her eyes kind. "Do you love him?"

Gillian felt the heat sweep to her cheeks. "I can hardly see what that would have to do with any of this."

"I assure you, it has everything to do with it," Bridget interjected impatiently. "We need to know how you feel about him."

"Easy, Bridget," Alexandra warned. " 'Tis not something so easily confessed, especially to strangers."

Gillian looked from one to the other and then lowered her gaze. "I do love him," she said softly. "But until tonight, I thought his heart belonged to Phoebe."

Bridget sighed. "Well, that explains a lot. You must come with us now, Gillian. 'Tis more important than ever. I promise you that we will return you to the Reeves estate as quickly as we can. But time is of the essence now and there are many things you need to know. Please, you must trust us."

Gillian looked between the two women and then back at Jack Soward, lying motionless on the floor. Her mind warred between the need to return to the Reeveses and the gnawing curiosity as to what these women could tell her about herself and her past.

"I'll go with you," she finally acquiesced. "As long as you allow me to return as quickly as possible to the Reeveses."

Bridget nodded and opened the door. "Agreed."

Gillian stepped outside, shivering in the cool air. Like the others, she pulled the warm hood of her cloak over her head, noticing that they were at the harbor.

"How did you find me?" she asked as they started to walk down the cobblestone street.

"Your amulet," Alexandra said.

Gillian stopped beneath a lamppost. "How did you know about my amulet? Was it one of you in the alley that night?"

Bridget shook her head. "Nay, but we know about it. We each have one as well. She reached beneath her cloak and pulled out her amulet. It was a blood red ruby mounted in an elaborate gold-and-silver setting identical to Gillian's.

Gillian's mouth fell open and her hood slid off her head. "And you have one, too?" she asked turning to Alexandra.

The young woman nodded, withdrawing hers. She held it up in the lamp light. Gillian gasped as she saw that it was a clear stone, almost transparent and mounted in the same setting as the others.

"What does this mean?" Gillian whispered.

"Come," Alexandra said, taking her by the arm. "We promised you answers and you shall have them. But we are still in danger."

The three women quickly walked down the street, staying close together and keeping Gillian in the middle.

"Where are we going?" Gillian asked as they took a turn that led them in a direction away from town.

"To a cottage on the outskirts of town," Bridget explained. "There is someone there we want you to meet."

They had just passed the gunsmith shop when a dark figure stepped out of the alley. He grabbed Bridget and flung her away to the ground. Before Gillian could move, he had wrapped an arm around her middle, holding her close. She had opened her mouth to scream when her attacker dragged her into the light.

"Spencer!" she gasped.

He held a knife out toward the others, keeping her safely against his body.

"Good evening, ladies," he said grimly. "I think it's about time I'm told just what the bloody hell is going on here."

"Spencer, I'm so glad to see you," Gillian said, throwing her arms around him and nearly knocking him over. "It's all right. They saved my life."

Still wary of the situation, Spencer pushed her behind him. "Reveal yourselves," he said, narrowing his eyes.

The one he had thrown to the ground rose slowly and threw back her hood.

"Hello, Spencer," she said calmly.

"Bridget Goodwell," he uttered, stunned. "What . . . how . . . ?"

"I'm Alexandra Gables," the second woman said, pushing off her hood. "Pleased to see you again, although I wish it were under less stressful circumstances."

Spencer blinked in surprise. "Wait! I know you. I met you at a dinner at the Trasks' about a month ago. Aren't you visiting from Boston and helping to sketch a scientific collection for Joshua Williams? I heard you were engaged to his son, Pierce."

"That is true."

He looked intently at the three women. The resemblance was so strong, he suddenly had no doubt how they were connected to Gillian. He felt like an idiot for not putting it together sooner.

"You are all sisters," he said bluntly.

"Yes," Bridget said. "You can put the knife down, Spencer. We aren't going to harm her."

"Then why kidnap her from my home?" Spencer said, his voice hardening.

"They didn't," Gillian interrupted, coming out from behind him. "They saved my life. Jack Soward kidnapped me. And Spencer, I'm sorry, but Phoebe is involved in this, too. She told me you that you had stopped the wedding. She blamed me for your change of heart."

Shock and a black fury swept over him. He gripped the knife so hard, he thought he might actually crush the handle to powder. While a part of him wanted to deny it, another part believed it true.

"If what you say is true," he said through clenched teeth, "then there is much I need to do. As it is, I have just about every able-bodied man in Salem out looking for you. I'm fortunate I thought to explore this less-traveled path out of Salem." He grabbed her by the hand and started to pull her away. To his surprise, she dug in her feet.

"Not yet," she said. "Spencer, I'm sorry. I can't go home with you yet. Bridget and Alexandra have promised me answers to what is happening to me."

"I'm glad to hear that," Spencer said. "Then they can come with us to the constable."

"I'm afraid it's not so simple," Bridget said, stepping forward.

"Of course it is," Spencer replied firmly. "You simply

tell the constable what you know. See, it's not complicated at all."

"What we have to say is for Gillian's ears only," she said just as firmly. " 'Tis a family matter."

"The hell it is," Spencer snapped angrily. "Jack Soward just kidnapped Gillian from my estate and was apparently in league with my former fiancée. I'd say that makes it my matter as well."

"You'll have your answers in due time," Bridget said heatedly. "But now we need to speak with Gillian alone."

"I must go," Gillian pleaded with him. "Please."

He looked intently at her for a long moment and then crossed his arms against his chest, still lightly holding the knife. "Then you do not go alone. I'll go with you."

Alexandra stepped forward. "I understand your concern, but I'm not certain that's a wise decision."

Spencer shrugged. "It's my decision. Either she comes home with me or I come with her."

Bridget tapped her foot impatiently on the cobblestones. "This delay is intolerable. You have no idea the trouble you are causing."

"*I'm* causing?" Spencer said, looking at her incredulously. "I'm not the one trying to spirit her out of Salem in the dead of night."

Bridget threw an exasperated glance at Alexandra and then blew out a breath. "You may accompany us, then. But first we must have your word that what you are about to hear is not to be disclosed to anyone without our permission."

Spencer raised an eyebrow. "Agreed."

"Then we must make haste," she said, turning in a hurry, her cloak billowing out behind her. "We are already late."

"For what?" Spencer asked, putting Gillian's hand on his elbow. "Just where are we going?"

"Widow Bayley's cottage."

"Widow Bayley?" Spencer said in surprise. He knew of the old woman. Blind and considered eccentric by many, she lived in a small cottage on the outskirts of town. He'd seen her once or twice and she seemed harmless enough.

He had many more questions on the tip of his tongue, but for Gillian's sake he held them. As they left town, they had no light. Spencer wondered how they would ever find the small cottage. But Bridget seemed quite familiar with the path, and in a shorter time than expected, he heard her stop and open a gate. Beyond it he could make out the dim outline of a cottage and the warm light of a single candle from inside a window.

"Come on," she urged, ushering them inside and closing the gate behind her.

Spencer took a few steps forward and then jumped in surprise when he felt something brush past his legs.

Bridget turned around, making soft clucking noises. "It's just Francesca," she said, picking up a large cat and cradling it against her chest. "Say hello to your new friends, sweet girl."

The cat meowed and they continued up to the cottage, entering without knocking. Spencer blinked, letting his eyes become adjusted to the light. The cottage was small but cozy, with rough-hewn ceiling beams and walls of unpainted pinewood. Four small windows of leaded, diamond-shaped glass had been placed evenly along the walls, and a linen curtain hung from the ceiling, separating a small area where the widow likely had her bed. A square table and four chairs took up another corner of the room, and on the center of the table sat an exquisite flower arrangement, astonishing given that it was late autumn.

A giant hearth took up most of one wall and obviously provided heat for the widow and also served as her cooking fire. A black kettle bubbled with a delicious-smelling concoction, and Spencer's stomach rumbled in reaction.

Two large wing-backed chairs facing the fire were occupied by two women, their backs toward the door.

One of the women rose and turned toward them. Spencer recognized her as the Widow Bayley. Her long silver hair was unbound and fell softly about her shoulders. A warm light-blue shawl had been wrapped around her thin shoulders. Her head was cocked to the side as she listened intently, her blue eyes staring straight ahead, unseeing.

"She's here," she said softly. "At last, we have found all of you."

Everyone stood silent as if waiting for something. Spencer felt increasingly anxious as her sightless eyes turned toward him.

"There is someone else here as well," she murmured.

He cleared his throat to say something when she abruptly said, "Spencer Reeves. Well, this is certainly a surprise."

He frowned. "How did you know?"

Before she could answer, the other woman rose from the chair, turning to face them. He heard Gillian gasp and stiffen beside him.

Spencer's mouth dropped open. The mysterious woman looked remarkably like Gillian and her sisters. She had the same fiery red hair, sprinkled with a bit of gray at the temples, the identical sea green eyes, and a knowing and serene smile. Her gaze was for Gillian only.

"Hello, little one," she said softly. "My name is Hannah Bennett. I am your mother."

NINETEEN

My mother?

For a moment, Gillian could only stare at the woman in stunned disbelief, even as a part of her accepted the woman's words as truth. Not only was the resemblance strikingly obvious, there was an eerie sense of familiarity and a connection to her on a level she did not understand.

"It was you in the alley," Gillian breathed.

The woman nodded. "That is true."

"But how . . . ?" Gillian began, when the widow Bayley stepped forward.

"Please, child, I know you have many questions. Come in and sit by the fire. This will take some time."

Gillian glanced at Spencer. His face was impassive, his jaw set tightly.

"Are you certain you wish to stay, young man?" the widow asked him. "What you hear tonight may be quite disturbing. We give you our word that we will not harm Gillian and will return her to you safely. No one will think less of you should you choose to leave. But I warn you that if you stay, your fate may be inextricably tied to ours. I assure you, it is not a fate I would wish upon anyone."

Gillian swallowed hard, scarcely daring to breathe. Then, to her astonishment, Spencer stepped forward, linking his fingers with hers.

"If this concerns Gillian, then it concerns me," he said evenly. "That is, if she wishes for me to stand with her."

Gillian looked at him, her heart swelling. "I don't know what they will tell me," she said quietly. "But I have a feeling that whatever it is, it may put you in grave danger."

He squeezed her hand and gazed deeply into her eyes and soul. "Have you so little faith in me?" he chided gently. "Gillian, I didn't have a chance to tell you the reason why I decided not to wed Phoebe. It's because my heart belongs to someone else. *You.* I'm in love with you."

For a moment she couldn't breathe. Her heart gave a funny clutch and her knees went weak. She felt her eyes fill with tears. "I . . . I don't know what to say."

"Say you wish for me to stay," he said earnestly. "That whatever may be said tonight, we are going to hear it together."

She glanced around the room at the other women, who stood quietly, waiting for her answer. After a moment, she nodded. "I want that more than anything in the world."

He lifted her hand and pressed a gentle kiss on her knuckles. "Then let us have a seat and hear what is to be said."

After removing their cloaks, Alexandra and Bridget squeezed some extra chairs near the hearth, and Hannah poured everyone a cup of hot tea. Then, remembering the condition of Gillian's gown, Bridget went to fetch a spare shawl for her.

Gillian thankfully wrapped it around herself, unable to keep from shaking. She stood at the hearth, holding out her hands to the warmth of the fire until Spencer eventually led her to a chair and perched on the arm, keeping a reassuring hand on her shoulder.

"I know this is very difficult for you to accept," Bridget said softly. "Alexandra and I understand exactly how you feel. We only learned of our heritage two months ago. It was shocking, to say the least."

"Indeed, I regret the odd and dangerous circumstances that have surrounded you since your return to Salem," Hannah said, cradling the teacup on her lap. "Unfortunately, they could not be avoided. I know all of this must seem quite strange, but I am your natural mother."

Gillian took a sip of the tea, hoping the ease the tightness in her throat. "My father told me that you died years ago."

"That was what many people believed. But as you can see, it is not true."

"Then why did you abandon me? Us?" She glanced at Bridget and Alexandra and for a moment saw a flash of pain in their eyes, and knew that it was mirrored in her own.

Hannah settled back in her chair. "I think it would be prudent to start at the very beginning. You and your sisters are part of a proud and powerful Scottish legacy. The MacInness legacy."

"MacInness?" Gillian said in surprise.

"Our ancestors were once a respected clan in the Highlands, many of whom possessed a number of remarkable talents. Some could see into the future, conjure fire, and move objects with their minds. Others could communicate with animals or read unspoken thoughts. A rarer gift was the ability to heal with a touch."

Gillian pressed her lips tightly together. "That is a fascinating but farfetched tale."

Hannah sighed. "I know of your talent, Gillian. There is no need to hide it. Your power, as rare as it is, can be a wondrous as well as frightening gift. I wish I could have explained it to you years ago, to help you understand and nurture your ability to heal."

"I don't know what you are talking about," Gillian said stiffly. She looked up at Spencer, but he sat staring at Hannah, his face unreadable, his expression calm.

Bridget leaned forward. "You saw what happened to

Jack Soward's clothes. That is my talent, Gillian. I can conjure fire at will."

"And I can sometimes see into the future," Alexandra added quietly. "I assure you, it is quite an unsettling gift and one that comes of its own volition. As a woman of science, it was unnerving for me to realize I had little control over what would be revealed. Yet it is a part of me all the same."

Gillian looked at her sisters and saw the gentle understanding in their eyes. "I'm not certain I have this clear in my mind. Are you saying I was born with this ability?"

"As were we all," Hannah said.

"What of you?" Gillian asked her. "Have you a . . . talent as well?"

"I have a bit of many talents, which is both a curse and a blessing. It makes me strong because there is much I can do. But because my power is not concentrated, it also makes me weak and vulnerable."

"I'm not certain I believe any of this."

"I told you the things you would hear tonight would be difficult to accept," Hannah replied calmly. "But I am not yet done with the story. Let me tell you of a woman named Priscilla MacInness who was among the first of our ancestors to immigrate to the New World. She married a carpenter named John Gardener. She had a special talent but vowed not to use it, just as her mother before her had not. They were in a new place now, one with people who were not familiar with our customs and did not look kindly on the unnatural. Nonetheless, as I am certain you are aware, our talents can manifest themselves in ways that none of us may expect. When the witch hunts in Salem began, Priscilla fell victim to the hysteria."

"She was killed?"

"She was tried and found guilty. But before she could be hanged, her husband confessed to dabbling in the occult, stating that she was innocent. Priscilla was eventually released and the charges against her dropped."

"Did he speak the truth?" Gillian asked.

Hannah shook her head. "He did not. He loved her and he wished only to protect his unborn child. Priscilla was pregnant with their first child."

"What happened to him?" Gillian asked, her stomach turning.

"He was hanged at Gallows Hill, not far from here."

"How dreadful! What about Priscilla?"

"She had the child, but the events were not without serious repercussions. There was another clan in Salem by the name of MacGow. The MacGows also possessed remarkable talents, but they used theirs for dark purposes."

As Hannah spoke the name MacGow, the fire in the hearth flickered wildly and a rush of cool air swept across the room. Gillian felt a chill creep up her spine and leaned into Spencer, seeking his strength and warmth. He said nothing, but she felt his hand tighten on her shoulder. She wondered what he thought so far of Hannah's bizarre tale.

"What do you mean by 'dark purposes'?" she asked.

"Greed, revenge, and material wealth. The MacGow clan is an ancient enemy of the MacInnesses. For years our clans have fought, and many people on both sides have died. We thought the hostility would die out once we immigrated to Salem, but they had no intention of quitting. Even more troubling, unlike our clan, the MacGows did not abstain from their powers once they moved to Salem. Instead, they worked to make themselves even more powerful and dangerous."

"What occurred?" Gillian whispered, almost afraid to hear the answer.

"As it happened, it was a woman of the MacGow clan who accused Priscilla of witchcraft. She had long been in love with John Gardener and was furious when he chose to marry Priscilla. When the witch hysteria started, she realized she had the perfect opportunity to get rid of her competition. After Priscilla was hanged, she would be there to console John, and perhaps would eventually wed him. But when her accusations resulted in his death instead of Priscilla's, she was enraged and cast a powerful black curse on the MacInness clan."

"A black curse?" Spencer said, speaking up for the first time. "Surely you jest."

"I do not," Hannah said seriously. "According to the curse, each female in Priscilla's line would be destined to live a lonely life, as the men they chose to wed would die at age twenty-six—the same age John had been when he swung from the gallows."

Gillian gasped. "She cursed the men to death?"

Hannah nodded sadly. "It was a curse of loneliness. To have love within our grasp, but then to lose it so horribly. For many of us, it was a sentence worse than death."

"But you wedded anyway?" Gillian asked incredulously. "How could you do that, knowing what it would do to those you loved?"

"I know it sounds harsh, but we had to continue the family line," Hannah said, her eyes reflecting deep sorrow. "As it was, many of us were not told of the curse until after we wedded in order to ensure the family continued."

Spencer snorted. "That's ridiculous. Even if I were to accept this fantastic tale, why not just leave it to a male descendant to continue the family line?"

"Because there were no male descendants," Widow Bayley interjected quietly.

Spencer looked taken aback. "None?"

"None," Hannah said firmly.

The room fell silent for a minute until Gillian spoke. "You still haven't said why you left us," she said, gripping the teacup tightly in her hand. Her stomach churned so violently she thought she might be sick. "We were your children, your flesh and blood. What could possibly be more important than that?"

Hannah flinched as if Gillian had physically hit her, and then her eyes filled with tears. "I was one who didn't know of the curse until after I had wedded your father," she explained. "I loved Phillip more than anything in life. We were soulmates. He was honorable, generous, handsome, and kindhearted. When I had all three of you girls at once, I thought it was a miracle."

She tucked a stray strand of red hair behind her ear and continued. "It was the happiest time of my life. My heart was full, my life perfect. I had all but forgotten the warning my grandmama had given me on my thirteenth birthday."

"What warning?" Gillian whispered.

"She told me that it would be up to me to save the family legacy, the MacInness legacy. She said I would face the greatest trials and tribulations of my life, but that if I were not successful, the family would be cursed forever. I could not see how any of it had to do with me and my wonderfully full life. But it did. It so horribly did."

Spencer rose at this and walked over to the window, where he stood looking out at the darkness in silence. Gillian watched him for a moment and then turned back to Hannah.

"What happened next?" she asked.

Hannah set her teacup aside. "My grandmother told me of the feud between the MacInness and the MacGow clans. But she did not tell me the nature of the curse. Had I known it, I would have never wedded Phillip—never put his life in jeopardy. She knew that, of course. Only after we were safely wedded and you girls were born did she tell me of the curse that fated Phillip to death. I was horrified, but I was also determined to do whatever I could to save him, no matter how drastic. I could do no less, for I loved him with all my heart."

Gillian glanced again at Spencer. He still stared out at the darkness, his face impassive. She felt a twinge of understanding. Love was a powerful motivator, and in her heart Gillian knew she'd have done the same.

"What did you do to save him?" she asked softly.

"I divorced him," Hannah replied.

Utterly aghast, Gillian exclaimed, "Divorce?"

"Phillip begged me not to do it, but I insisted. He didn't completely believe in the curse, but he'd always known that I was different from other women. He'd seen me do things I could not explain away, and yet he loved me all the same. He agreed to the divorce because he knew I'd never accept it any other way. So we traveled to Connecticut because divorces were so rarely granted in Massachusetts. After the proceedings were completed, we returned to Salem. I thought no one need know of the divorce, and Phillip and I could go on living our lives with little being changed. How wrong I was."

Gillian squeezed the handle on her teacup so hard she thought it might shatter. "The divorce didn't lift the curse?"

Hannah shook her head. "I found out later that the divorce would not be enough. I had to remove his love for me from his heart. I knew then that I would have to make him believe I had perished. The decision meant I would have to give up both Phillip and you girls, but I could not just let him die. Only weeks earlier he had turned twenty-six. His life was in immediate danger. As handsome and charming as Phillip was, I knew he'd soon find a good woman to take care of him and you girls."

Hannah's hands began to shake and she clasped them together in her lap. "On a windy, rainy day, I staged my own drowning. Everyone in Salem thought me to be dead except Anne and Elias Bayley."

She reached out and took the widow Bayley's hand in her own and squeezed it. "Anne is my Guardian, Gillian, and she is yours as well. Centuries ago, her clan served ours. The MacInnesses were powerful in ability but vulnerable to the greedy desires of other clans. We were hunted, pursued, and much desired as captives. Imagine how useful it would be to have a fire starter at your command. Anne's clan became our protectors, and in return we aided them with their needs. We forged a special bond of trust and magic."

"What happened to my . . . my father?" she said, fearing she already knew the answer.

"He did not find another to love," Hannah whispered, her voice catching in her throat. "I should have known there would be no other for him or for me. He died at sea about six months after my invented death, at age twenty-six, just as the curse had predicted. Understandably, I did not reside in Salem at the time of his death, so by the time I learned of what had happened, you girls had already been separated and adopted."

Her expression was one of deep-seated grief and regret. "I revealed myself and my circumstances to the lawyer who handled the adoptions, and not surprisingly, he was shocked to see me. He refused to aid me and would not tell me what had happened to you girls, threatening to reveal the divorce decree if I tried to get any of you back. He assured me that no judge would return a child to my care. He was right, of course, and I could do nothing except look for you girls and wait for you to grow up so I could reveal myself to you."

She twisted her hands in her lap. "I didn't spend that time idly. Besides looking for you girls, I also spent time honing my craft, readying myself for the night of the reversal ceremony."

"Reversal ceremony?" Gillian asked.

"It is what we must do to break the curse," Hannah explained. "I'm not going to let you girls or your children suffer this horrid fate. I will not let Phillip's death or the deaths of those who came before him be in vain."

Gillian leaned back in her chair, her emotions a swirling tangle of disbelief, anger, pain, and fear. She hadn't asked for any of this; she didn't want to be a part of this bleak, unnatural future.

If she even believed any of it.

Bridget must have seen the skepticism on her face, because she leaned forward. "Gillian, please, we need your help. The spell cannot be lifted without all four of us. We must work together to do this."

Gillian lifted her hands in exasperation. "Do you really expect me to believe these things? Spells, curses, divorce, and death—it's fantastic, not to mention highly implausible. Just because some sick animals feel better after I tend to them is hardly cause to think I possess some kind of remarkable talent."

"You've seen much with your own eyes already," Hannah said evenly. "In the alley, you saw for yourself what I could do."

"It was dark and I was frightened," Gillian said, lowering her gaze, not wanting to believe. "I'm not certain what I saw."

Alexandra reached out and took her hand. "Bridget is already wedded," she said quietly. "If you do not help us, her husband will surely die. And there is a man . . . a man I love dearly and wish to wed. I do not want to spend my life without him. Please, I beg you to put aside your disbelief and trust us. We speak the truth. But we need you. We must have a circle of four."

"They speak the truth, child," the widow Bayley said softly. "Close your eyes and search your heart. You will see that it is so."

"That's quite enough," Spencer suddenly said, walking over to the chair and pulling Gillian to her feet. "You've all had your say, now let her be."

Hannah stood as well. "I'm afraid there is little time. The reversing ceremony must take place on All Hallows' Eve."

Gillian's eyes widened. "But that is but two days hence."

"It is the day, exactly one century ago, that the curse was set. It will also be the night that our powers will be at their greatest. But it will not be an easy task. Dark spells are very dangerous and volatile. There will be a great risk to all of us. Your life will also be in great peril until then. The MacGow descendants will do anything to stop us from reversing the spell, including murder. We would ask you to stay here, with us, until after the ceremony is over. We can best protect you here."

"The Trasks," Gillian breathed in sudden understanding. "Mrs. Trask and Phoebe. They are the MacGow descendants."

Hannah nodded. "As is Phoebe's younger sister, Lydia. They are very powerful, as is their magic. Black magic is unpredictable and unstable, but it is enormously potent. I assure you they will employ every ruse they know to prevent us from reversing the curse."

Gillian thought for a moment. "A reversing spell," she finally murmured. "That means if we are successful, the curse will fall back on them. Am I correct?"

Bridget nodded grimly. "Which is exactly what they deserve. A taste of their own revolting magic."

Gillian swallowed hard, looking about the room at the earnest and now familiar faces. Every fiber of her being railed against what she had been told, and yet a part of her already accepted the truth. She was as much a MacInness as Bridget, Alexandra, and Hannah.

A circle of four.

"Gillian, let's go," Spencer said, gently tugging on her arm.

Gillian inhaled a deep breath and turned to Spencer. "I can't," she said. "I have to help them."

He looked at her in surprise, a lock of brown hair falling across his forehead. "Surely you don't believe all of this. It's the most outlandish thing I've ever heard."

She nodded. "I know. A part of me agrees. But Widow Bayley was right. I have only to search my heart to know they speak the truth."

Spencer threw up his hands. "Be reasonable. This is absurd. Witches in Salem? Have we not learned anything from our lesson with this very same subject one hundred years ago? Hysteria and madness, none of it rooted in law, shook the foundations of our town, nearly destroying it. It was a shameful period of our history. Now you wish to revive it by conducting a bizarre ceremony?"

"It will have to be done in utter secrecy," Hannah interrupted. "No one in Salem other than the MacGow descendants will know."

"I *am* different, Spencer," Gillian said quietly. "As much as I'd like to deny it, there is something inside me that recognizes what has been said here tonight is the truth. You've seen it in me, too. The things I've seen since coming to Salem, and the feelings inside me, lend credence to their story. I must help them for their sake as well as mine."

She took his hand, pressing it against her cheek. Her heart stumbled then straightened. "Please understand, this is what I must do."

He looked into her eyes intently, and Gillian saw exasperation and disbelief warring with determination and concern. For a moment, she truly believed he might sling her over his shoulder and walk out with her, and to hell with what had been said. Then he blew out a breath of frustration and shoved his fingers through his hair, a gesture Gillian had come to love.

"Hell and damnation, Gillian," he finally said. "I want

you to know I'm not happy with your decision, nor do I believe even half of this outlandish tale. But if you intend to stand firm, then I'm in. What do we do next?"

Hannah stepped forward, giving him a broad smile and putting a hand on his shoulder. "Sit down and I will tell you."

"Wait," Spencer said, lifting a hand. "First tell me who these MacGow descendants are. You do know, don't you?"

Hannah nodded. "I do. And so do you."

Gillian looked at Spencer in surprise. "You do?"

Spencer stared at Hannah for a long, intense moment before swearing softly under his breath. "It's the Trasks," he said grimly. "By God, I should have known it."

TWENTY

After Hannah revealed the plan for the reversing ceremony, Spencer told her he needed to tell his parents the truth.

"Nay!" Bridget protested, jumping up from her chair, her green eyes blazing. "No one else need know."

"I'm afraid she's right," Gillian said to him. " 'Twould only serve to put them in danger."

"My parents are as concerned about your welfare as I am," Spencer replied quietly. "As fantastic and bizarre as this tale is, they are entitled to know the truth. I've never lied to them before and I have no intention of starting now, especially on a matter so important. And what about Lemuel? Doesn't he have a right to know?"

Gillian looked beseechingly at Hannah, who sighed. "Aye, they all should know," she said slowly. "The reversal ceremony will be dangerous, possibly life-threatening for everyone involved. Spencer's parents have a right to know what their son is involved in, as does Lemuel."

"Must everyone in Salem know?" Bridget said heatedly, throwing up her hands. "Why don't we just go tell the Trasks?"

"The ceremony is about doing what is right—what is good," Hannah countered firmly. "Spencer's parents need to know, as does Lemuel. We must trust them. Besides, if they are willing to aid us, then our plan will be strengthened."

"And if they won't?" Bridget challenged.

Spencer rose from the chair. "I can't say they will believe any of this, but I will be forthright. I assure you, my parents will not interfere no matter how disbelieving they may be. They respect me too much for that."

"Lemuel will help," Gillian said. "He knows about me and about my ability. He always has. 'Twill not be a great leap of faith for him. But even if he doesn't trust a word of it, he'd stand by me. He's my brother."

Hannah nodded and Bridget fell silent, both of them clearly understanding the power of family. Gillian walked over to Bridget and put a hand on her arm.

"I know you are upset because you have the most to lose," she said softly. "We are not going to fail Benjamin. We will not let the curse take your husband away from you."

Bridget's eyes filled with tears, and Spencer felt a tug on his own heart. Love was a powerful force, perhaps even stronger than magic.

He held out a hand to Gillian and she took it. Clasping tightly, he could feel her tremble. Hell, after what he'd just heard, he felt like trembling, too.

"Let's go," he said, fetching her cloak and wrapping it gently around her. "We've got a lot of explaining to do to my parents."

"Do you really expect us to believe this bizarre tale of witches, spells, and curses?" Phineas suddenly exclaimed, leaping up from his chair in front of the hearth in the library as Spencer concluded his tale.

Spencer and Gillian sat side by side while Lemuel leaned against the wall by the window and Rosemary huddled on the settee by Phineas's desk. Gillian clasped her hands tightly in her lap and looked at the floor. She had not uttered a single word since they returned. When the room fell silent, she dared a furtive glance at Rosemary out of the corner of her eye and saw the woman looked understandably faint.

"I'm not certain I believe it all myself," Spencer said calmly. "But Gillian does and that is what matters. I've pledged myself to help her. In fact, the truth of the matter is that I'm in love with her and intend to ask Lemuel for her hand, if she'll have me."

Gillian looked up at him in shock, her heart skipping a full beat. "What did you say?"

"I said I wish to wed you," he said, taking her hand. "Be my wife. I love you, Gillian."

She stopped breathing as her heart dived to her toes and bounced back up. Surely, he hadn't just said he wanted to wed her. "B-but how can you say that after what you know about me?"

"I may not be certain of all I heard tonight," Spencer said earnestly, leaning forward in his chair. "But I do know that I'm in love with you. I do believe in fate. We were destined for each other. I felt it the first time we met, the first time we touched, and when I kissed you. You are the woman for me. You always have been."

Gillian heard a sniff and saw that Rosemary was crying. Phineas swore under his breath and fumbled in his shirt for a handkerchief.

"Those had better be tears of joy," he grumbled, handing her the cloth.

"It's the most romantic thing I've ever heard," she sniffed, dabbing at her eyes with a corner of the material.

Gillian rose from her chair. "I can't do this to you, Spencer. If we fail in the reversing ceremony two days hence, I can never wed, never dare to fully love."

Spencer stood, placing a hand on her shoulder. "I don't give a damn about any curse. I'll wed you regardless."

"It may seem unfathomable and unbelievable," she said softly. "But it's not a child's tale or a game. This is life and death. Good against evil. By merely associating with me, your life is in great peril. That goes for everyone in this room."

Lemuel stepped forward and Gillian looked at him, her heart turning over in her breast. He hadn't asked a question or uttered a single word since Spencer relayed the tale of the night's events. She held her breath, not daring to move. Lemuel's opinion meant everything to her, and she had no idea what he would say.

"I'm with you, Gillian," he said quietly. "I always have been and I always will be."

With that, Gillian burst into tears and ran to him. She bent down to hug him and he held her tightly while she sobbed.

Phineas sighed. "I don't intend to back down either. But to ask us to take on the Trasks and the Sowards is indeed a formidable request even without all this talk of . . . curses."

Rosemary rose from the settee, lifting her chin determinedly. "Well then, it's settled. I shall help as well."

"You will not!" Spencer and Phineas exclaimed at the same time.

"And why not? This is a woman's fight," Rosemary said, narrowing her eyes. "And a woman, fighting for the man she loves, is a formidable opponent. And from what I understand of the plan, you'll need another woman's hand. A strong woman. That would be I."

Spencer and Phineas exchanged a worried glance, but neither said anything.

"I can't ask this of you," Gillian protested. "Any of you. Please, you have all been so good to me; I cannot repay you in this way."

"I'm afraid it's too late," Spencer said. "We all intend to stand with you, Gillian, whether you like it or not."

"So, what do we do next?" Lemuel asked quietly.

Gillian looked tearfully around the room, her heart swelling with love and terror that something might happen to them. "We'll need to help Widow Bayley set up the circle where the ceremony will take place on All Hallows' Eve. But none of us can do it. Hannah says we are being closely watched by the Trasks." She paused for a moment, thinking. "We need someone else whom we can trust."

Lemuel rubbed his chin thoughtfully and then nodded. "I have just the person in mind," he said.

The past two days had flown by faster than any of them could imagine. All Hallows' Eve had arrived, and now Spencer glanced around the candlelit room of his father's library. Gillian stood beside him, silently clutching his hand while his father paced in front of the desk, his brow drawn into furrows. Hannah and Rosemary spoke softly but intently with each other, their red and light brown heads bowed as they sat together on the settee. Lemuel stood at the window, occasionally pulling the drape aside and watching.

"There's a full moon tonight," Lemuel observed. " 'Tis a good omen for All Hallows' Eve, I would think."

Gillian lifted her shoulders, and Spencer thought she looked far too pale. " 'Twill give us light," she whispered. "Is that horrid man still there?"

Lemuel nodded. "Just as expected and tending to his mount. I fully expect him to follow us when we leave. Except now it looks as though our boy has got a hound with him."

"Good for tracking," Spencer said grimly. "Just in case he loses us."

"We must see that he doesn't," Phineas said firmly.

Spencer felt Gillian tremble beside him and squeezed her hand gently. "If it must be known, I think this plan leaves you far too vulnerable. I don't like it. And I still wish we could use our pistols."

"It's the only way, the *right* way," she replied earnestly. "Pistols cannot be used. It would alert the townsfolk, revealing us and our powers. Even the Trasks and Sowards would not risk it."

"I hope you're right," Spencer grumbled. "I damn well don't like the fact that you'll be so unprotected."

"I worry more about you," she said. "You're a healer like me. Tonight we both may be forced to betray our vows to heal and protect human life. I'm not certain I will be able to take another life."

"I will," he said without hesitation, thinking of the sturdy inch-thick iron rod fashioned by Lemuel and safely secured in his boot. "I'll kill anyone who tries to harm you. But I fear my determination will not be enough."

"Spencer, love, don't worry about me," she said. "Magic is my protector this night and the knowledge that I do this deed for our love."

She stood on her toes and placed a gentle and poignant kiss on his lips. He felt a rush of warmth and confidence sweep through him and knew this was her way of reassuring him.

He gripped her shoulders, pressing his own kiss on her lips and leaving a promise of what was to come. "I'm worried about everyone," he murmured against her cheek. "But my heart is especially with you, Gillian. Be safe."

Hannah stood, breaking the moment. "It's time," she said simply. "I'll fetch the others."

Spencer stepped back from Gillian and nodded. With a final look at her, he donned his hat and cloak and strode out of the room.

The large carriage awaited out front where he had ordered it. He climbed up to the driver's seat and took the reins. A few minutes later, Lemuel, his father and several other cloaked and hooded figures stepped into the carriage. When everyone one was settled, Spencer slapped the reins against the horses' hindquarters, starting the conveyance in motion.

As he steered the carriage out of the family's gate, he hoped the man and his hound stationed at the end of the lane would follow. He didn't dare check.

Fog hung in patches over the town, sending ominous thoughts through his mind. Gray, Hannah had told him, was the color of Samhain and the color of the cloaks they had hastily fashioned. The fog only assured him she was right. This All Hallows' Eve certainly held all the trappings of a mysterious if not dangerous night.

As planned, Spencer drove the carriage to the Williams estate, where Pierce Williams and his fiancée, Alexandra Gables, awaited his arrival. The carriage had barely rolled up to the mansion when Pierce and a hooded figure appeared like specters from the haze. Spencer assisted them into the carriage and then headed directly to Gallows Hill. There the others would soon join them.

He had told Gillian he would kill if he must in order to protect her, and he'd meant it. Still, he wasn't a foolish man. Unbeknownst to the others, he'd made a few plans of his own. And why not? A physician sought to save lives, and especially of those he loved.

The trees whispered in a sudden breeze, then quieted, leaving Lynette eerily alone on the path before a small cottage. Flickers of firelight shone through the windows, promising warmth from the bitingly cold air. Her cheeks and nose were frozen, and her heart beat so hard in her chest she thought it might burst. Determinedly she gulped back her fear.

"If Lemuel can do his part, I can certainly do mine," she whispered to herself, hoping to boost her confidence.

Summoning her courage, she knocked on the cottage door, noticing it was ajar.

"Come in, child," an aged voice called from within.

Cautiously Lynette entered and saw an elderly woman standing near the hearth. Her long silver hair hung loose, and a worn woolen shawl was wrapped around her shoulders. A few candles had been lit, but the room was largely dark and eerie.

"Widow Bayley?" she said hesitantly.

Lynette shivered as the woman turned her head and fixed her sightless eyes on her. "Come close so I can meet you. Bring me the basket now, would you?"

"How do you know I carry a basket?" Lynette asked in astonishment, looking down at her arm, where indeed a large basket hung. "I thought you were blind."

"I am," the widow Bayley said, smiling. "I only presumed Gillian sent the supplies I requested. If so, you surely required a basket to transport them."

Lynette let out a breath of relief and brought the widow the basket. She took it, examining by touch the items it held.

"You have been brave to venture here alone," she said to Lynette. "I thank you for the great service. We have little time to prepare, and I will require your help."

"Little time before what? Gillian told me only that I should aid you as needed."

"And she was wise not to divulge more. She considered you trustworthy, and that is enough for me. What I will ask you to do may seem odd, but we must make haste. To tarry could be dangerous."

Still Lynette hesitated. "Lemuel is involved, isn't he? Will he be here this night?"

The widow Bayley faced her as though she could see the concern in her soul. "I'm afraid Lemuel's destiny lies elsewhere, my child, not in this place."

A shiver ran up her spine. "How do you know that?"

"I simply do. Now, you must trust me. There is little time for questions. We must prepare the cottage."

"But Gillian told me to escort you away."

"Yes, child, but only after we have set in place all that is required. Fetch me my broom from near the hearth."

Puzzled, Lynette slipped off her cloak and hung it on a peg, readying for the work ahead. She reached for the broom by the fireplace.

"Not that one. The besom behind it."

Lynette froze, wondering how the blind woman knew which broom she reached for. She drew back her hand. "Is not a besom a . . . w-witch's broom?" she said fearfully.

"It is safe," the widow Bayley answered. "Hand it to me, please."

Swallowing her fear, Lynette reached out and took the besom in her hand. Nothing happened. No lightning bolts darted from the sky; no thundering hand smote at her from heaven. She quickly handed it to the widow, who began carefully sweeping near the hearth and around an old table that had been set before the fireplace.

She then handed the besom to Lynette. "Finish sweeping inside the circle until it is spotless. I will place the candles you brought on the windowsills."

Lynette had begun sweeping when a large white cat suddenly bounded onto the table. She stifled a scream as the widow chuckled.

"It is just Francesca. She means no harm."

"I—I know," Lynette stammered, her heart pounding. How much more bizarre would this night become? She fought the urge to run from the cottage and not look back. But Lemuel had asked her to do this, and for him she would stay.

The widow Bayley paused to give the cat a reassuring scratch between the ears. "I think Francesca knows something unusual is afoot this night. I only pray all signs are in our favor."

"S-signs?"

"Omens. Gillian and those of us who aid her will be in great peril tonight. The power of good watches over us, but our destiny is unknown."

Lynette shivered, not daring to ask for further clarification and not certain she wanted to know anyway. Better to finish these unnatural chores and leave as quickly as possible. She'd always had a healthy respect for the unknown, especially on All Hallows' Eve, but something told her more was amiss than she could ever imagine.

Sweeping hastily, she watched as the widow gathered a few of the candles and placed one in each window. On the table she put the remaining candles in a circle, leaving the largest one in the center.

"Do you wish me to light them?" Lynette asked.

"Nay, 'twill be done properly by the others."

Lynette wasn't certain what she meant by 'properly,' but she knew better than to ask further.

"Come help me with this kettle," the widow directed.

Together they set a large black cooking kettle on the floor at the end of the table. Puzzled, Lynette couldn't help but ask why the kettle had to be placed on the floor.

"It must be at the table end facing west," the widow answered.

Mystified, Lynette watched as the widow slowly poured a pitcher of water into the pot without spilling a drop.

"How can you do that so well if you cannot see?" she asked in amazement.

"Many years of practice," the widow said, smiling.

"But why put water there if it is not to cook on the fire?"

"Water is an element of earth," the widow Bayley said with a strange intonation in her voice. From a bowl on the table, she pinched salt between her fingers and gently dribbled it over the water. "Salt, an element of earth. The union of both shall be a purifying force."

"Purifying?"

"Have you ever soaked a sore finger in warm saltwater? It has a soothing, healing effect."

"Are you a . . . a witch?" Lynette asked, trembling.

The widow shook her head, clearly amused by the question. "Nay, I am not. And you have naught to fear from me."

" 'Tis strange, but somehow I know you would never harm me," Lynette said.

"Good." Obviously, the widow planned no additional explanation, and Lynette decided it best simply to cooperate without further inquiries.

The widow placed a plate of bread and cheese on the table, then told Lynette to collect a small rucksack by the door. From it, acorns, apples, and gourds were poured onto the table.

"Please, child, arrange these around the candles on the table so they appear pleasing to the eye. Then we must leave."

"Shall I also put down the fire and bank the coals?"

"There is no need. The others will be here shortly."

Lynette wanted to ask which others, but held her tongue. She quickly arranged the nuts and fruits and then swung her cloak about her shoulders. The widow had wrapped herself in her own cloak and stood by the door. Lynette placed the widow Bayley's arm on her elbow, and the widow patted her shoulder gratefully.

"Thank you. You have indeed proved trustworthy."

They stepped over the threshold, but before Lynette could close the door behind them, the widow looked back toward the hearth, where the cat sat, steadily swishing her tail.

"You are in charge, Francesca. Watch over them carefully."

As the door shut, Lynette puzzled over how the blind woman knew exactly where the cat had sat. Maybe she truly was a witch. She directed them toward the front path, but the widow tugged against her arm.

"This way, child."

"But that way is dark and I cannot see," Lynette protested.

"Do not fear. In my way, I can."

Lynette had hoped that with each step away from the cottage relief would wash over her. Instead, only questions about Spencer, Gillian, Lemuel, and the odd preparations they had just completed haunted her. Nothing held any semblance of a normal evening, and what did the widow mean, saying she could see the way?

"Widow Bayley . . ."

"Hush child." The woman suddenly pulled her to a stop, yanking her behind a tall, shadowed trunk, where they huddled close together. Footsteps sounded on the dirt road only a few feet from their position. Four cloaked figures with hoods pulled well down over their faces swooshed past them, heading toward the cabin. None of them even looked their way. When they were out of sight, the widow urged her onward.

"Who are those people, Widow Bayley? Why are they going to your cottage?"

A long sigh arose from the woman's lips. "They go to save the ones they love," she said softly. "Or die in the attempt."

TWENTY-ONE

Eerie fingers of moonlight breached the fog as Margaret Trask waited in the driver's seat of the family carriage with her daughters. A hundred feet ahead, she barely discerned the shadows of her husband and the Soward brothers mounted on horseback. They waited for direction on where the MacInness brood had headed. It would not be a difficult task. Hannah had foolishly surrounded herself with ordinary folk to provide protection. Following ordinary people would be pitifully easy.

"I still say Gillian is the most powerful sister," Phoebe hissed in a weak attempt to keep her voice low. "She survived Mother's attack as well as Jack Soward's."

"*Humph,*" Lydia scoffed. "You're simply saying that because she snatched Spencer from under your nose. Mother said the poor girl appeared oblivious as to her magic and helplessly cowered in that alley. If that is the sign of a powerful witch, then I'm shaking in my shoes. I'd say the powerful one is the science philosopher, Alexandra."

Phoebe poked Lydia on the chest. "You only say that because she used her lizard to chase you from Pierce's arms. How could you, the one supposedly able to command animals, have allowed her to overcome you? For all we know, Bridget, with her command of fire, is the one to watch."

"Cease your bickering," Margaret commanded. "The girls are but novices to magic. They have no control, no years of seasoning as you have, and no empathy with the spirits that give us our powers. The witch to be wary of is Hannah. I shall handle her while you engage the girls."

Phoebe sat back and crossed her arms. "Must I point out there are three of them and only two of us?"

"Gillian has no talent but that of healing," Margaret snapped. "If you are afraid she might succor you to death, then depart now and your sister and I shall easily handle this situation. All we must do is stop the MacInness clan from completing the reversing spell on this eve. Tomorrow it will be too late for them. Spencer will be released from Gillian's spell, and Pierce cannot have Alexandra—unless, of course, the gentleman wishes to die. I am certain they are not fools and will once again come begging to my girls."

Margaret patted Phoebe on the knee. " 'Tis time to cease this idle chatter so your sister can communicate with the hound. We must know whether they have headed to Widow Bayley's cottage or to Gallows Hill."

Lydia gave a smug toss of her shoulders before closing her eyes and becoming still. Margaret knew she concentrated on the hound accompanying the man hired by her husband. "I can sense the green of fields and grass. The carriage is headed out of town."

"But which way?" Phoebe demanded.

"Shush. Your sister must have quiet."

Lydia held up a hand as though she sensed something significant. "The hound is pausing. He smells meat. They must be at Turner's smokehouse on the road to . . ."

". . . Gallows Hill," Margaret finished triumphantly. "I knew it! A fitting location, since John was hanged there. Yet somehow, I expected Hannah to use the cottage. After all, the curse was set there."

Margaret slapped the reins, nudging the carriage forward until she reached her husband. "They go to Gallows Hill," she said. He nodded, and then he and the Sowards rode off.

Margaret followed at a distance in the carriage. Oddly, Phoebe and Lydia remained silent on the ride. She hoped it meant they were preparing themselves mentally. Fear served her purpose by keeping her daughters attuned to events and making them willing to strike without question. Strangely, she had little fear herself. Tonight she felt stronger than ever. Why shouldn't she? Only Hannah had honed her talents and presented a challenge. One witch and three novices had little chance against three witches with years of experience. Still, as past events had dictated, she had learned not to underestimate the MacInness talent any more than their luck.

Before the road's final bend, which opened to the grass-covered Gallows Hill, she halted the carriage. "Ladies, from here on we go by foot."

With mumbled undertones, the girls climbed out, tossing up their hoods against the night chill. Overhead the moon rose toward the apex, sliding behind a cloud in its path and casting the night into deeper shadows.

"The earth and grass are damp," Lydia complained as they slowly ascended the hill, out of view of anyone along the road. "It is ruining my shoes and dress."

"Enough." Margaret stopped and turned to her daughters. "If we fail to stop this reversing spell, we will lose everything. Do you understand? Everything. The curse will come back on us. Your father will die, and any man you may wed will be sentenced to death. Our wealth and position will shrivel away. There will be no more exquisite gowns, no balls, and no place in society. Need I make myself any clearer?"

As if summoned, the moon slid out from behind the cloud, illuminating the entire area with a bright golden light. The girls fell silent. Satisfied that she had made her point, Margaret scrutinized the area but saw no sign of her husband, Jack and Thomas Soward, or the hired man and the hound that followed Spencer Reeves from his home. She did see the flickering of a bonfire ahead and presumed the MacInness clan had just begun their ritual.

"Where are Father and the others?" Phoebe whispered.

"Out of sight and waiting for the signal, I presume," Margaret answered. "First I need to assess the MacInness strength."

She led them behind a mound of polished boulders from which to observe. Slightly below them she could see Hannah and her daughters, cloaked and hooded, encircling a small fire. The men stood in an outer protective ring.

"Spencer," she heard Phoebe murmur when she spotted her former fiancé. "Traitor."

"There's Pierce and Benjamin, too," Lydia hissed.

"Fools," Margaret hissed. "All of them."

The men were completely disorganized, standing yards away from the women and spread out in a weak attempt to patrol the area. Margaret could hear the chanting begin, but what she heard lacked any clarity or sense.

"The ceremony has begun," Phoebe whispered, "but I feel no magic present."

Lydia shook her head, then giggled. "And look, they circle the balefire counterclockwise."

Margaret, too, had noticed these amateurish actions. The lack of preparation to defeat a one-hundred-year-old spell spoke of utter contempt toward the spirits on this All Hallows' Eve. Did Hannah believe herself so powerful she could circumvent the necessary ceremony? The time to act had arrived.

"Lydia, give the signal, please. It is time."

Lydia closed her eyes, and moments later a dog barked

twice in the distance. She smiled up at her mother. "It is done."

"Then we shall watch for our opening. Are you prepared?"

"We are ready," the girls answered in unison.

"I will finish the job Jack Soward failed at," Phoebe hissed. "Leave Gillian Saunders to me."

"We are focused on preventing the completion of the spell, not on revenge, my dear," Margaret reminded her. "Keep your mind on the task at hand."

She held her hand up for silence as a figure approached up the hill toward the campfire.

"Here we go," she said softly.

Spencer spied the shadow in the distance and watched with concern as it came closer.

"Evenin' to you all," a man called to them. He was tall, bearded, and likely hiding something under his heavy cloak. "Is there room for another chilled soul about the fire?"

Benjamin and Spencer closed in on the man as he stepped into the area cleared for the ceremony. The women ceased chanting and stood quietly.

"Our apologies to your need for warmth," Benjamin said, "but we celebrate a family affair here. A private one, I'm afraid. Perhaps the house down the road can offer you some sustenance."

The stranger crossed his arms casually against his chest. "A bit bold, I'd say, sending off a man when you are on public property. Makes me wonder what you are about. Something I should send a constable for?"

Spencer stepped forward. "We have no quarrel with you, but we strongly suggest you move on. If you wish to fetch a constable, you have every right to do so. And if that is what you care to do, then get to it, man."

"Wait a moment," Pierce shouted from the other side of the fire. "I know that man. He's the ruffian who attacked Alexandra and me on the beach."

The stranger abruptly withdrew a sword from beneath his cloak and then put his fingers to his mouth, letting out a shrill whistle. Before Benjamin and Spencer could react, a large hound and two other men stepped out of the shadows.

"Jack and Thomas Soward," Spencer said and then moved forward to face Jack. "Haven't you had your fill of torturing young women lately? I'm afraid you're going to have to face me now."

Jack pounded a thick sticklike object against his palm, grinning as his brother faced off with Benjamin. "I think this is going to be quite enjoyable. After I finish with you, even your father won't be able to mend you."

Spencer rolled his eyes. "Are you going to talk all night, or do you actually plan on doing something threatening?"

"I plan on killing you," Jack said as Pierce stepped up beside Spencer and placed himself across from the ruffian who had once attempted to drown Alexandra. "I think that's something."

"And I thought to send the gaoler after you," Pierce drawled.

"I'm trembling in my boots," Jack sneered. "You men have no idea what you are up against. Did you know those ladies by the fire are practicing witchcraft?"

Spencer feigned surprise. "Really? Why do you say that?"

Jack thrust a finger in the women's direction. "One of those women set me afire."

"And one of those women saved your pathetic neck," Spencer said calmly. "You aren't going to stop them."

As if on cue, the women stretched their arms skyward, before circling the fire to resume their chanting.

"You shouldn't have said that," Jack growled.

Spencer felt Benjamin and Pierce stiffen beside him and knew the fight was about to begin. "Then what should I have done?" he asked, his own muscles tensing.

"This," Jack said, swinging a meaty fist at Spencer as the brawl began.

Margaret felt a tug at her cloak. "They are starting the ceremony again," a frantic Lydia whispered. "They are desperate enough to perform magic in front of those men."

"Hannah is no fool," Margaret hissed. "She knows she must complete the ceremony."

"It will take too much time for the men to reach them. We must get down there."

Although something bothered Margaret about the scene below, she nodded. "Make haste," she ordered her daughters.

The Trasks made their way carefully past flying punches, lunges, and circling opponents. Twice Hannah and her daughters were distracted, but the men urged them on. Margaret found the women's lack of concentration amazing and felt her own confidence soar. Her opponents displayed their weakness with every move they made. Hannah's daughters only hindered, not helped, their coven. How pathetically easy it would be to destroy them.

As they reached the circle, Margaret drew herself tall, raising her chin and signaling her girls to follow. She summoned a bolt of power and directed it into the balefire. The fire erupted in a hiss of steam and smoke. As the air cleared, Margaret and her daughters stood facing the hooded figures.

"What a pathetic, pitiful coven you present," Margaret said contemptuously. "You failed to seal your circle, allowing us to enter. Did you not even ask the gods and goddesses for help? Or even seek their forgiveness for undertaking a spell on the Sabbath? Fools, all of you."

Narrowing her eyes, Margaret confronted the person leading the chants. Hannah, she presumed. Oddly, no magic vibrations and no sign of power that had accompanied her on their previous meeting emanated from the witch. If anything, she sensed only fear and anger. Had they lost their powers? For the first time this evening, Margaret felt a deep uneasiness stir in the pit of her stomach. Something was amiss.

"Why do you not attack your enemy?" she commanded. She spread out her arms. "Strike out at me, woman. We are preventing you from completing your spell. Your lovers shall be doomed forever."

When the women stood silent, their faces hidden in shadow beneath their hoods, rage replaced Margaret's fear. Her hand swept out, sending a powerful gust into Hannah's face. The hood fell back off her shoulders, and a face stared at her in surprise and fear.

"Rosemary Reeves!" Margaret uttered in shock.

"Hello, Margaret," Rosemary said. Although shaking, the woman defiantly raised her chin.

"Nay!" Phoebe gasped in horror, taking a step backward.

Margaret bellowed in anger and spun around, her magic forcing the hoods back from all the women's faces. She recognized Bridget's sister, Sarabeth, old Mrs. Bisbey, who worked for Pierce Williams, and Gillian's dwarf brother, Lemuel.

Stepping forward bravely, Lemuel brandished a knife. "Stay back," he ordered, pointing the weapon at her.

Fury engulfed Margaret at the deception. She waved her hand, and the knife flew out of Lemuel's hand and into the trees. He looked at his empty hand in astonishment.

"By Osiris, we've been tricked," Margaret hissed.

"So who, Margaret Trask, is the real fool?" Rosemary said bravely.

"You!" Margaret yelled. Raising her hand sizzling with power, she pointed it in Rosemary's direction.

TWENTY-TWO

Gillian and her new family stood around the small table in the widow Bayley's cottage. The sisters wore their amulets outside their gowns, the stones glowing with an indefinable light. An aura of warmth from more than just the fire surrounded them. Deep inside grew a strength that joined each of her sisters and their mother. Tears came to Gillian's eyes as she focused on Hannah. Fortune had given her another parent. Somehow Gillian knew in her heart that her adopted mother would be happy for her.

Alexandra rose from placing a small pile of objects beneath the table and brushed her hands together. They all peered at the odd collection, which included a skillet, a large piece of pink rock, and a jar of moths.

Alexandra shrugged at their questioning looks. "I can't explain it. I just have a premonition that we will need these things."

Gillian drew a long breath. She was discovering that having sisters with unusual talents did create some curious situations. Francesca brushed against her skirt and she reached down to scratch the cat's chin.

"Courage, little one," she whispered, and the cat purred in response.

"We do not have much time," Hannah said, "but we cannot leave out a single step if we are to succeed. I shall explain the ceremony as we go along, so you will understand. Please, join hands now."

Gillian stood between Alexandra and Bridget. As her sisters took her hands, she felt a power swell between them. It both humbled and awed her.

"Tonight is All Hallows' Eve," Hannah began, "also called Samhain in the ancient days. It marks the beginning of the Celtic new year and, for us, the beginning of a new life. Our Guardian, Widow Bayley, has prepared the way by creating a place of safety for us. The circle we stand within is swept with a besom, and the ritual balefire in the hearth burns bright and steady. Within the circle, a table faces to the west, where all things begin and end and begin again. We look forward to this new beginning. No matter what happens tonight, you must remain within this circle. It is a place of safety for you and provides a united strength against any outside forces of magic." Hannah looked toward her daughters. "Do you understand?"

"I . . . I have a question," Gillian said nervously. "Are you certain the Trasks themselves will not be able to enter the circle?"

Hannah shook her head. "Physically, no. And the circle is protected to a certain extent. But they will use their magic to distract and frighten you. No matter how horrible a beast they may conjure, no matter how much pain you may feel, remember that it is only an illusion. Do not step outside the circle."

Gillian had no intention of leaving the circle, especially if Margaret Trask showed up and started casting black lightning bolts about. Nonetheless, she swallowed hard and then nodded in understanding.

"On this night the veil to the spirit world is thin," Hannah continued. "The table is set with seasonal foods to welcome them if they choose to aid us. However, we cannot anticipate their aid, as Samhain is a time to rest and celebrate, not work, as we do tonight. However, I will duly plead our case."

Gillian wanted to ask what happened if they angered the spirits or if the reversing spell did not work, but she kept quiet for fear of upsetting the ceremony. Nonetheless, she must have had a strange expression on her face, because Hannah looked at her kindly.

"Do not be afraid, Gillian. You are stronger than you think."

"I'm not afraid. Well, I am, but that's not what concerns me the most. I cannot produce fire or guess my opponent's next move. I have little to offer."

Hannah and Alexandra exchanged a glance that left a cold chill along her spine. Hannah nodded at Alexandra.

"Tell her," she said simply.

"Gillian," Alexandra said softly, "You are a critical part of the circle of four. Even though I cannot foresee how this evening will end, I know your healing talent will be necessary." She paused and appeared uncomfortable. "I'm afraid it will require a sacrifice on your part."

"What kind of sacrifice?" Gillian asked, her hands suddenly trembling.

"Not all is clear to me. I'm sorry."

"We need you to be strong," Hannah said quietly. "For the sake of us all."

Gillian nodded, raising her chin. "I'll endeavor to do my best."

Hannah gave her an encouraging smile. "The time is nigh. Bridget, please light the candles in the window to welcome all spirits."

Bridget lifted her hand, and one by one the candles flickered to life. Hannah let go of her daughters' hands and raised her arms to the ceiling.

"On this sacred night of the Blood Moon,
We call to you, O White Ones,

Forgive our impudence by intruding on a sacred night,
But allow us a chance to thwart a grave wickedness."

She took a taper from the table and asked Bridget to light it. When a flame appeared, she handed it to Alexandra.

"There is a circle of candles on the table," Hannah said. "Light one to honor Priscilla Gardener, upon whom this curse was first cast."

Alexandra did so and the light flickered small and unsteady. She then passed the taper to Gillian.

"Light the second candle for John Gardener, who died to protect a MacInness," Hannah instructed her.

Gillian wondered why Bridget could not simply light the candles on the table as she did in the window, but said nothing. Hannah must have sensed her puzzlement for she explained.

"The unlit candle in the center represents our new beginning," she said. "When the reversing spell is complete, the three of you must light it together before the hour of midnight. Bridget's magic will not suffice."

Gillian's hand shook as she held the taper to another candle in the circle. Wax dripped as the wick accepted the flame and began to glow steadily. The flame of the first candle grew still and slowly brightened. Unsure of the strange results, Gillian hastily handed the taper off to Bridget.

"Light a candle for all those loved ones that suffered under the black MacGow curse." Bridget did so and handed the candle to Hannah.

"I light the fourth candle for the generations of MacInnesses that came before us. Join us. Give us the knowledge of the ages to defeat our foe."

Hannah nudged them to move slowly around the table in clockwise fashion. She began to chant a welcome to the spirits. Gillian soon found herself repeating the words as though she had known them for years. As she walked, an occasional cool brush of air chilled her skin.

Hannah pointed to the candles. "The spirits are arriving."

The circle of candles glowed brighter and brighter. She pointed in particular at Priscilla's and John's candles. The flames had lengthened and intertwined. Gillian understood their love. Sorrow must have torn Priscilla's heart when she watched her beloved hang. Gillian couldn't help but imagine Spencer tonight on that same Gallows Hill.

"Be careful, my love," she whispered under her breath. "My heart is with you."

Jack Soward punched his stick into Spencer's stomach, and he gasped as the air escaped in a painful rush. Falling backward, he landed hard on what little padding his backside provided to cushion the fall.

"Stay on your feet, damn it, Spencer," Benjamin shouted as he landed another punch to Thomas Soward's chin.

"Easy for you to say," Spencer croaked out between gasps for air. Benjamin, having lived a much more worldly existence, was clearly having no problem taking on the younger Soward.

Spencer struggled to his feet, tightening his grip on the iron rod. He carefully approached Jack, surprised to find his attention not on him but on the women in the circle. He also dared a glance at the circle and saw his mother standing defiantly in front of an angry Margaret Trask. The woman lifted her hand menacingly.

"No!" he shouted, forgetting his fight with Jack and dashing toward the circle.

He only made it about halfway before Jack tackled him

from behind. He landed hard on his stomach, the iron rod sliding out of his grip and into the tall grass.

"Run, Mother!" he yelled.

His mother did not move. As he watched in terror, Margaret Trask summoned a black lightning bolt from the air and aimed it at Rosemary. He kicked out furiously at Jack, loosening the man's hold temporarily and sending his wooden stick flying into the trees with a crack.

At the same moment, Lemuel suddenly lunged at Margaret, grabbing her arm and causing the bolt to go astray. To Spencer's enormous relief, his mother nimbly threw herself to one side, shouting at the others to run. Screaming an oath, Margaret cast Lemuel aside with a wave of her hand, sending him face first to the ground with a hard thump.

"You made a mistake to challenge me, Rosemary," Margaret hissed, raising her arm again.

Rage and helplessness overtook Spencer. He twisted and rolled in Jack's grip, jabbing and punching. Both of them had lost their weapons and were now fighting with fists alone. Nonetheless, Spencer knew he was losing the battle. He'd never reach his mother in time to aid her, and Jack outweighed him by a good two stone.

Out of the corner of his eye, he saw Lydia grip her mother's arm just as he landed a punch square on Jack's nose. Blood spurted over them both in a spray as Jack shouted in pain and rage, clutching his nose with one hand.

" 'Twas all but a ruse, a diversion," Lydia shouted. "They meant only to delay us. We must not waste our power on them, for we will need it when we find the MacInnesses."

Margaret glared at Rosemary for a long moment and then lowered her arm. The light dissipated.

"You are right. We must go at once. They are certainly at Widow Bayley's cottage."

She whirled around, her cloak billowing in the night. Spencer felt Jack's hands fasten around his neck, squeezing. He bucked and twisted to no avail.

Then, abruptly Jack's hands loosened. Spencer gasped for air and blinked to clear the red haze from his eyes. When his vision cleared, he saw Phoebe standing above him, her hands on her hips, her icy blue eyes flashing contempt and fire.

"You made a terrible mistake by choosing her, Spencer. She was the weaker one. And now you will pay for it with your life, just as every man who chooses a MacInness does."

With that, the woman he had almost married stalked away, her long hair streaming behind her like a dark banner.

Disgust riled within him as Jack started laughing and threw himself upon Spencer again. With renewed energy, Spencer wedged a knee in Jack's chest and rolled over taking the big man with him.

It was time to get even.

Gillian chanted softly, careful to remain within the ring as they circled the table. Energy swirled about the room. The curtains fluttered, odd shimmers of light spirited about, and the sound of a thousand distant voices filled the air.

Hannah paused and raised her arms. "On this All Hallows' Eve, we invoke the descendants of the MacInness to come forth, bringing the strength of Mother Earth and the wisdom of ages. We seek to reverse a spell so wicked and ill begotten, that a lineage of men have paid with their lives for simply loving a MacInness."

She stopped, ceasing the motion around the table. Gillian watched her, holding her breath. Hannah was bathed in a golden light, her red hair shimmering and rippling like a waterfall about her shoulders.

"As was our right, a MacInness sought one hundred years ago to reverse the spell, rendering the same misery and heartache back upon the MacGows. This night marks that centennial. With the four of us here tonight, we at last have the strength and the will to complete the task. We ask for a new beginning and the right to complete a counterspell on the MacGow clan."

The flames of the candle circle glowed brightly, and a strange but welcome energy vibrated through Gillian. Her arms lightened, and she felt them lifted on each side until she held them at shoulder level with palms out and wrists bent. On each side, her palm faced only inches from one of her sisters' palms. A buzz of energy built, and soon sparks jumped between the palms of those in the circle. Fear dissipated as her curiosity and incredulity grew. She *did* have power within and discovered it blossoming with each passing moment.

Hannah began chanting a phrase over and over, encouraging her daughters to join. *"Absit omen a capite ad calcem.* Protect us against evil from head to heel."

A swirl of wind rose within their circle, moving faster and faster, accompanied by the wailing of a thousand voices. Gillian raised her voice as did they all. Amazingly, the candles flamed brighter and higher instead of being extinguished by the air movement.

Hannah broke the circle of palms by stretching her hands high. *"Ad unum omens.* So mote it be."

The wailing ceased at Hannah's words, but the energy and winds remained. She looked at her daughters.

"Quickly, we must light the candle and beseech the spirit of Priscilla to apply the counterspell against the MacGow clan."

Hannah's head jerked as though she heard some threatening sound. "Hurry, girls. The three of you must light the center candle together."

Alexandra rushed forward to grab the taper, followed

by Bridget. But Gillian's feet seemed rooted in place, suddenly overcome with a horrible feeling of dread and impending danger.

"Gillian, help us," Bridget called out urgently. With momentous effort, Gillian took one step forward as an odd pounding and beating noise commenced against the walls, roof, and windowpanes. Shaking, Gillian joined her sisters as they held the taper against a lit candle. As the taper flared to life and they reached toward the reversing candle, the windows shattered.

TWENTY-THREE

Spencer circled Jack Soward, taking a moment to quickly assess how his other friends were faring. He could see blood on Pierce's sleeves and mouth, but he seemed to be holding his own in a spectacular display of sword-play with the unknown ruffian. Benjamin appeared to be enjoying himself and was making significant headway in disabling the younger Soward, occasionally aided by Lemuel and the women, who threw stones at his opponent when they could.

Spencer's brief assessment allowed Jack Soward's fist to slam into his gut. Spencer grunted and then swung out, his bloody knuckles just grazing the big man's jaw. To his dismay, Jack didn't even appear winded.

Just splendid. I had to get the big, hulking one.

As much as Spencer hated to admit it, Jack had landed a hell of a lot more blows then he. He gulped air and felt as if every bone and muscle in his body had been battered. Sweat stung his eyes, and as he wiped it away, a swath of blood appeared on his sleeve.

Out of the corner of his eye, he saw Pierce feint to the left and then jab at his adversary with his sword. The ruffian mistook Pierce's advance and moved directly into the blade. With a scream of pain, the man sunk to the ground, clutching his side. Pierce quickly withdrew the blade and knelt at the man's side.

"Spencer," he yelled. "We could use a physician over here."

"I'm a little preoccupied at the moment," Spencer yelled back, narrowly avoiding a blow to the temple. "See if you can stop the bleeding."

At that moment he saw Benjamin swing a fist that landed directly on Thomas Soward's chin, sending the young man to the ground in a heap. When Thomas did not rise, Benjamin glanced over at Spencer.

"Need some help there?"

"Help? Me? Actually, I'm finding myself quite proficient at getting battered to death."

Benjamin had the audacity to grin as he staggered over, and the two of them faced Jack together. Jack wiped his mouth, the blood giving him a crooked and grotesque look.

"Is this the best you can do? Do you really think I fear a doctor and a shipwright?" he said.

"I'm the shipping *agent,*" Benjamin corrected him. "Pierce is the shipwright."

"It will take more than two of you to bring me down," Jack growled.

Spencer looked over at Benjamin and shrugged. "He's probably right, but I'm willing to give it a try, if you are."

"Certainly. I've always considered myself a man willing to rise to every occasion," Benjamin said in agreement.

"Spencer!" shouted Pierce. "I'm in dire need of your immediate assistance."

Spencer dared a glance and saw Pierce kneeling beside the injured man. "I hate to leave you, but can you manage Jack alone for a moment?" he asked Benjamin.

"Do I look like a woman? Of course, I can. Go attend to your duties, if you please, Doctor."

With that, Benjamin swung a fist at Jack while Spencer darted to Pierce's side. The ruffian lay unconscious, and

Pierce was trying unsuccessfully with his hands to stanch the gaping wound in the man's left side.

"He stepped right into the blade," Pierce said. "I meant only to disable him."

"He doesn't get my sympathy. He was trying to kill you." Nonetheless, he motioned to Pierce to remove his hands. He saw at once the wound was mortal. "He's not going to make it," Spencer said grimly. Still, he called for one of the women to bring a cloak, which he wrapped tightly around the man's midsection as Pierce held him up.

"Gentlemen, if you are not too busy, I could use your assistance here," Benjamin called out as Jack bellowed and charged him headfirst, sending them both tumbling to the ground in a heap of flailing and punching limbs.

Pierce and Spencer dashed over to help him. It took two of them to drag Jack from atop Benjamin, who lay gasping for breath. In the process Pierce took a hard jab to the eye, dropping to his knees and cradling his face.

"Now, that wasn't very neighborly," Spencer said to Jack, ignoring the screaming ache of his muscles.

Jack rose as well, looking a bit more tired, but clearly nowhere near the same point of exhaustion as Spencer.

"You are not leaving here alive," Jack said quietly. "I don't give a damn about the others. *You* threatened me, blackmailed me, and now you will pay."

"At least I didn't assault a young woman. Nor do I happen to consort with the blackguards that you do, with the exception of my former fiancée and her family, of course. A dreadful mistake, I now see."

"The only mistake you ever made was crossing me. And now you'll suffer the consequences."

Jack moved more quickly than a man his size should have been able to do. One fist to Spencer's left cheek dropped him to the ground like a stone. Laughing, Jack straddled him, clamping his meaty hands around Spencer's neck.

"Not this again," Spencer gasped, swinging his own fist ineffectually at Jack's face.

He heard someone scream, and for a bizarre moment he was certain he saw his mother leap onto Jack's back, clawing and scratching at his face.

Jack only laughed, squeezing harder. Spencer blinked, now seeing Lemuel, Benjamin, and Pierce all grabbing and pulling at Jack, trying to remove his hands from his neck. A red haze blurred Spencer's vision, and his sight began to dim. He focused his gaze on the sky above him, wondering if this would be his last sight of the earth.

A black dot appeared in his sight. It was strange, but he thought he saw a large hawk circling over his head, carrying something in its claws. As he watched in fascination, the hawk dropped the object not far from Spencer's hand. Mustering his last ounce of strength, Spencer stretched his hand to the side, groping in the dirt when his fingers closed around a large, cold stone. He gripped it hard, and with a final effort, he smashed the stone into Jack's temple.

The big man slid off him in a heap. Spencer rolled to his side, gasping and gagging. After a moment, he felt a cool hand on his forehead and looked up to see his mother kneeling beside him. So it had been her after all, joining in the melee to remove Jack Soward's hands from his neck. He struggled to a sitting position, massaging his neck. He looked up to see Pierce, Benjamin and the others staring at him in amazement.

"How did you do that?" Benjamin asked.

Spencer shrugged, although he still felt rather shaky. "Self-preservation, I guess. It was fortunate for me the hawk happened to drop that rock close enough for me to grab."

"What hawk?" his mother asked. "What rock?"

Spencer squinted up at the sky, which was just now starting to show the first pink and yellow rays of the dawn. "I don't know. It was up there. Didn't anyone else see it?"

Everyone was silent, and Spencer felt a queer chill snake up his spine.

"Jack Soward is dead," Pierce suddenly said. "Although I know it is not kind to speak ill of the dead, good riddance to him."

Spencer looked stunned at Jack Soward, who lay slumped on his side on the ground.

"Dead? That's impossible," he said. "A rock that small should only have disabled him." As if to prove it to himself, he crawled over to the man's body and rolled him over. Jack's eyes were open and unmoving.

"I . . . I killed him?" Spencer said, baffled. "How is this possible?"

"I don't know. I saw you wave your hand at him and then he suddenly fell off you just like that," Benjamin said. Spencer looked at his mother, who nodded in confirmation.

"Well . . . hell," Spencer said, surprised that, despite his vows as a physician to uphold and protect life, he felt so little regret.

He had little time to contemplate it, for a woman suddenly screamed. Spencer turned to see Bridget's sister Sarabeth pinned in the arms of a man who held a pistol aimed at her midriff.

"Desist from movement and drop your weapons," Edward Trask shouted.

Despite the warning, Spencer struggled to his feet. "Are you mad?" he said, short of breath, realizing how dreadfully little he knew of the family he had almost joined. "You're the moderator of this town. Discharge that weapon and you'll bring the entire population out here to Gallows Hill."

Edward smiled coldly. "I have no intention of discharging it unless I'm forced to. You all will disband and go home now. No one will speak of the events that happened this night. Your little ruse is over. Our side has triumphed."

Spencer felt a twist of fear, thinking of Gillian. "I don't think so."

"Did you really think this pathetic attempt to distract us would work? It's over. You've been vanquished."

"I beg to differ," Pierce said, stepping forward. "Together we are a formidable force. You can't possibly silence all of us."

"I don't have to. To whom will you tell this tale of witches, spells, and curses? The constable? The magistrate?" He laughed. "They all work for me. Just who do you think they'll believe?"

"You bastard," Benjamin said through clenched teeth.

Spencer stepped forward, and Edward's pistol swung out to point at him. Better to keep the pistol trained on him than on anyone else in the circle.

"One man is dead, another gravely injured," Spencer said calmly. "You can't just explain this away."

"And who will stop me? You? The fool who cast my daughter aside?"

"It was the wisest decision I ever made," Spencer said, wiping his bloody mouth with the back of his hand. "Dying would be a better fate than being trapped with her for an eternity."

"Damn your impudence," Edward said, his hand tightening on the pistol. "You should die for saying that."

"Go ahead," Spencer said, ripping his shirt open, revealing his chest. "Let's see if you have the courage."

"Nay!" Rosemary screamed.

Edward shook his head. "I have no intention of being lured into firing this weapon, as much as I would find pleasure in doing so. Despite what you may think, I am not a reckless man."

From the corner of his eye, Spencer saw Lemuel inching slowly toward Edward. Edward didn't pay the young man any attention, clearly not considering him a threat. Spencer tried to warn Lemuel away with an imperceptible shake of his head, but the young man set his jaw determinedly and narrowed his eyes.

A hundred thoughts raced through Spencer's head, but the foremost was how to keep Edward's attention focused on him. But before he could utter another word, Lemuel lunged for the pistol. Edward spun on his feet, aiming the gun directly at Gillian's brother.

Spencer saw the deadly intent in Edward's eyes and had no doubt what would happen next. Uttering a cry, he leaped forward desperately, reaching for Edward's arm.

A horrid black creature swept past Gillian's head, knocking the taper from their hands onto the table. Alexandra screamed as a bat landed on her head and another on her back. Gillian had barely turned when she felt small, sharp claws bite into the skin of her shoulder. Shrieking, she grabbed at the creature and tossed it off, only to have another take its place. The cottage door flew open and Margaret Trask boldly entered, laughing at the melee of bats and women.

The smell of singed skin filled the air as Hannah sent several creatures to the floor with bolts of magic. Bridget set afire those that closed in, but new bats entered through the window in hordes.

"No one dares to confront a MacGow," Margaret announced.

The bats and winds swirled inside the circle. Gillian and Alexandra fended them off, whacking away one after another.

"Gillian, aid me," Alexandra shouted. "Keep them off me for a few moments."

Alexandra pulled away a bat entangled in her red hair

that was whipping with the wind, and stooped under the table. Gillian stood over her, swatting away bat after bat as they tried to land on the girls.

Alexandra emerged with the large jar she had tucked under the table. As she removed the lid, a hundred moths fluttered forth and dissipated about the cottage. The bats, sensing a quick and easy meal, forgot the women and went after the tasty morsels.

Margaret's face darkened at the ease with which her opening move was defeated. However, it quickly changed into smug assurance as Phoebe and Lydia stepped into the cottage behind their mother.

"My, my, it appears we have interrupted something," Phoebe said. "Do continue. We'd love to watch as you mishandle the ceremony."

"We have already completed the reversing spell," Hannah said calmly.

"I think not," Margaret said assuredly. "Your little ruse was clever, but not clever enough. I still feel energy within this room and see you have yet to light the final candle."

As she spoke the words, a bat swooped down on the table, attempting to knock over the sacred candle. It only narrowly managed to avoid the skillet Alexandra swung at it.

"You won't be able to light the candle," Margaret said softly. "And when you fail, victory will be ours."

"We shall see," Hannah replied. "Now that we know the real battle is between you and me, I intend to triumph. Soon your ill will toward us and the citizens of Salem shall come to an end."

Bridget motioned to Gillian and she slipped next to her sisters near the candles on the table. She felt an frightening energy building between Hannah and Margaret, one that both fascinated and terrified her.

Without warning, Margaret suddenly raised her hand, and energy sizzled in the air. A bolt headed straight for

Gillian and she ducked, pulling her sisters down with her. The hair along her arms tingled at the impact, but otherwise the protection spell around the circle absorbed much of the energy.

Hannah shot an energy bolt at Margaret, who dodged adroitly, and a fiery scar etched the cottage floor.

Plates and cups shattered and suddenly flew from the hutch. A cup bounced off Gillian's arm as she ducked beneath the table to avoid the flying objects.

Phoebe madly scrounged through a sideboard, looking for knives and utensils to hurl. She launched several of them directly at Hannah, who knocked them from the air in a sizzle of light. The rest Phoebe aimed toward the candle table, sending everyone scurrying in opposite directions. Bridget shouted something and Phoebe screamed as her skirts burst into flames. Gillian felt a small victory at Bridget's spectacular handiwork, but Margaret doused the flames with a single wave of her hand.

Determined, Bridget snatched Priscilla's candle. "We've got to light the candle together," she shouted at her sisters.

A growl ripped through the air. Gillian gasped in horror as a black hound with teeth bared bounded in the door and leaped directly at Bridget, who's arm had moved outside the circle.

"Look out!" Alexandra shouted as the dog sank its teeth into Bridget's arm, trying to pull her from the circle.

Gillian grabbed Bridget's other arm as her sister screamed in pain, but the hound seemed possessed and dragged them both closer to the edge of the circle. Alexandra threw herself on top of them all, but slid off when Phoebe sent a heavy chair slamming into them, nearly knocking them all out of the circle.

A flash of white caught them by surprise as Francesca suddenly landed on the dog's back, hissing and spitting. The surprised canine released Bridget and whirled on the cat. Francesca dashed under the table and then up on the sideboard.

Phoebe shouted in anger, swinging a broom near the cat and knocking her down from the sideboard. Miraculously, Francesca landed on her feet. The two animals stared at one another before Francesca bolted for the door. The dog skidded its claws on the packed-dirt floor as it launched off in pursuit. Moments later, barking and screeching sounded in the distance.

Bridget spun toward Phoebe. "Take on someone your own size, you heartless witch," she said between clenched teeth. Phoebe's black braids burst into flames.

Phoebe screamed, clutching at her head. "Mother!"

Margaret once again extinguished the flames, and Bridget ducked a screeching bat that had been aiming for her eyes.

Alexandra grabbed the skillet and batted away knives that Lydia sent flying in rage. Gillian gasped as a flash of white appeared at the door and Francesca crept in, injured and barely able to walk. She neared the circle but collapsed a few feet away.

Margaret caught Gillian's interest in Francesca. A wicked sneer spread on her face as she pointed at Francesca. "Cold and death are partners. Shall we hasten their meeting?"

Gillian saw a rim of frost begin to appear on the floor around the cat. "Stop it!" she screamed.

Hannah raised her arms. "Gray the season, gray the night, fill the room so the candle may light." Fog swirled up from the floors, leaving only the circle untouched.

"Send what you can into the circle," Gillian heard Margaret shout to her girls.

"But I can't see," Phoebe whined. "And there is little left to throw."

"Use anything," Margaret ordered.

A shoe plopped to the ground near Gillian, and a mouse scurried past.

Safely shrouded, Gillian crouched down and crawled along the floor, feeling for Francesca. To her relief, her fingers contacted soft fur. She began to pull the cat toward the safety of the circle when a foot landed upon her arm and she yelped in pain.

"I've got one."

Gillian tried desperately to pull away, but strong fingers circled her arm as Phoebe's face became evident through the fog.

"You stole Spencer from me, you trollop," she hissed in Gillian's face. "This time you shall die by my hands."

Phoebe dug her nails into Gillian's flesh and pulled. Gillian screamed, twisting in the woman's grip, but Phoebe was too strong. As Gillian's last inch of sanctuary started to slip away, she felt a hand on each ankle.

"Put your head down," Bridget yelled as a fireball whizzed overhead and slammed into Phoebe.

Phoebe gasped but didn't let go. Moments later a wooden spindle flew out of nowhere, barely missing Bridget's shoulder but slamming into Alexandra's head. The young woman crumpled to the floor in a heap.

"Nay!" Gillian screamed, trying to squirm out of Phoebe's iron grip.

"I command you to cease all your actions!" a male voice suddenly shouted. "At once!"

Shocked, everyone paused and the fog momentarily lifted. Standing at the open door of the cottage was Phineas Reeves, holding a large knife. It was pointed directly at Margaret Trask.

"You, Madame," he said calmly, "are in a kettle-full of trouble."

Growling in annoyance that she had been interrupted, Margaret waved her hand and the knife flew from his hand. Lydia bent down to snatch it from the floor when the knife suddenly glowed red hot, burning her fingers. She dropped it, glaring at Bridget, who lifted an eyebrow at her.

At the same time, Phineas rushed Margaret with a loud bellow. Gillian shouted a warning as Margaret sent a bolt of lighting at him, sending him flying against the wall. His eyes rolled back in his head and he slid to the floor.

"Nay!" Gillian shrieked.

Mustering all her strength, Gillian yanked her arm loose from Phoebe's grasp and snatched Francesca from the floor. Bridget dragged both of them back into the circle, where they collapsed in a heap. Hannah again summoned the fog, and darkness fell over the cottage outside the circle.

"Alexandra!" Gillian sobbed, crawling to her sister and turning her over. To her relief, Alexandra opened her eyes.

"We must light the candle," she said a bit groggily.

"We don't have much time," Bridget said. " 'Tis almost midnight."

Nodding, Bridget and Gillian helped her up and to the table. Gillian glanced over at Hannah, whose brow was furrowed in deep concentration. The strain of maintaining the heavy fog was evident on her face.

"Hurry," Gillian urged.

The three sisters stood at the table, ignoring the screaming oaths and objects that whizzed blindly past them. Together they picked up the taper, lighting it from the candle of Priscilla Gardener. In unison, the three girls pressed the flame against the reversing candle and watched as it sprang to life.

A humming noise filled the cottage, so loud Gillian thought her head would burst. As the crescendo reached its height, Gillian felt a great joy encompass her. She could see that her sisters' amulets, as well as her own, had begun to glow and throb with an inner light.

"Dura lex sed lex," Hannah said. "The law is hard, but it is the law. So mote it be. The curse has been broken."

With a wave of her hand, Hannah caused the fog to dissipate.

"Nay, 'tis not possible," Margaret cried. "I forbid it!"

The swirling winds within the circle died, leaving only the soft light of the candles glowing. With renewed energy, Gillian dashed out of the circle and to Phineas's side, feeling for his pulse.

"He lives," she said in relief.

"This is not finished," Margaret said, signaling her daughters to flee the cottage. As they moved to leave, the door abruptly slammed shut, trapping them inside.

"Let us out," Lydia shouted, terror evident in her voice.

Hannah faced them. "Generations of MacGows have betrayed, deceived, and even murdered their fellow man. One hundred years ago when your wicked curse was set, a counterspell was offered, as is our right. It said that should the spell be broken within a century's time, the curse would revert to those who set it. It appears the time has come for the MacGows to accept the consequences of their actions. Are you prepared to suffer the abject misery and heartache that we have for the past one hundred years?"

"Please," Lydia begged, her eyes filling with tears. "Do not do this."

"Do not beg," Margaret ordered her daughter. "Stand proud. You are a MacGow."

Despite her order, both Trask sisters began to weep softly. After a moment, Hannah raised her hand.

"The MacGows have never given pity and thus deserve none. But because we are the MacInness, we will show you our mercy." She pointed at the large black cauldron filled with saltwater that the widow Bayley had prepared.

"The union of the elements salt and water creates a

purifying force. Behold." She swirled her hand and water rose like a cyclone above the cauldron.

Phoebe and Lydia darted close to their mother for protection. The water sailed toward them, and the women had little time to throw their hands in front of their faces before the water drenched them. They screamed, clawing at their skin and clothes as if they were being burned.

"This purification creates a partnership of magic and morals," Hannah continued. "Each time you wish to cast a spell, you and the generations who follow must first consider the moral implication."

Hannah turned back to Alexandra. "Bring me the pink rock you have brought this eve."

Alexandra retrieved it from under the table, handing it to her mother.

"It is one usually found beneath the many layers of the earth and is considered part of the earth's very foundation," Hannah said, setting it upon the table. "Return to the table, Gillian."

Gillian took another look at Phineas and then stood, doing as her mother requested. She watched in fascination as Hannah's expression softened, and she recognized many of the same physical features she shared with this woman.

Her mother. Her sisters. A new family.

Hannah closed her eyes and lifted her arms. "O spirits, your energy has served us well this night. May my children feel the renewal of their new future."

The girls' amulets grew warm, and Gillian felt hers begin to vibrate. A light streamed from the candles to each of their amulets, as if it were lightning attracted to a tree. For a moment, she felt a scorching jolt of heat shoot through her body, and she gasped both in exquisite pain and pleasure.

"I ask if the spirit of Priscilla Gardener can find it within her heart to end the malevolence that is between our clans," Hannah said softly. "If so, then I ask you to cast the curse to this rock from the foundation of Mother Earth, forever trapping it within its confines."

Priscilla's candle flickered, then brightened. Soon the light of all the candles gathered and rose in a swirl of sparks and glitters, hovering above them in the air. Gillian could feel the hot sparks lashing and stinging her cheeks, but she remained deathly still. Then, with a violent swish of wind, the light gathered and smashed into the rock with such force that it shook the table. The room fell utterly still, except for the thin swirls of smoke that now drifted from the gutted candles.

Gillian slowly released her breath.

Hannah gathered the rock and placed it in a special pocket in her petticoat. "This rock shall be placed into a river, where time shall wear it down, and the grains and their magic dispersed into the sea. Let us hold hands once again."

The MacInness women clasped hands. "Thanks to the spirits who this All Hallows' Eve have joined into our circle," Hannah said. "May your souls rest well, knowing a good deed has been done."

With those words, Hannah's head dropped to her chest, and Bridget barely caught her as she crumpled to the floor. Margaret eyed them suspiciously, her face showing surprise that they had survived untouched.

"Hurry, Mother, the door is unlatched," Phoebe called, pulling it wide. Margaret turned as if to say something, but instead fled after her daughters.

Gillian felt little sorrow for them. "I do not believe they will change their ways."

"They have no choice," Alexandra said. "Each time they attempt to use their magic for selfish or evil purposes, they will be forced to consider the consequences. So ardent and stubborn is that demand, they will find no pleasure in using black magic."

"You mean they can only do good?" Gillian asked.

"More or less."

Shaking her head, she returned to Phineas's side, relieved when he began to come around.

"What hit me?" he groaned, reaching up to touch his head.

"Margaret Trask," Gillian said grimly. "Lie still and let me help you."

He brushed aside her hand impatiently. "She hits like a man. What happened?"

Gillian looked helplessly at Bridget, who shook her head in warning. She had no idea how much Phineas had seen or heard, but it seemed better to reveal as little as possible.

Phineas must have seen the guarded expression on her face, because he shook his head. "Never mind. I don't want to know how she did it. Just tell me that our side triumphed."

Gillian nodded, taking his hand. "You were remarkably brave, but foolish. You could have been killed. Whatever possessed you to follow us here to the cottage? You were supposed to be at Gallows Hill."

"Spencer's idea," Phineas said ruefully.

Gillian reached out and impulsively kissed his hand. "Well, you saved my life and I thank you for it."

Hannah spoke up from the chair where Bridget had seated her. "You all were magnificent. Alexandra, your foresight served us well. Your preparations were flawless, the props exactly what we needed. Bridget, your gift of fire proved a formidable weapon. And Gillian, your courage was astonishing, although I can't say I approve of what you did for Francesca."

"Francesca!" Gillian exclaimed, rising from beside Phineas and scooping the cat off the floor.

"Dear Francesca, you must survive," she murmured. She gently stroked the cat's soft fur, feeling the gouges where the dog had bitten her. "You are our champion and all that Widow Bayley has." Gently she pressed her hand against the bites, feeling the pain ebb into her.

Francesca stirred in her arms, and Gillian looked over at Alexandra. "Was my rescue of Francesca the risk you said I would take?"

Alexandra bit her lower lip uncertainly. "I'm not certain. It's odd, but it seems as if there is something more to be . . ."

Before she could finish, the cottage door flew open and everyone turned in alarm. Pierce and Benjamin burst through the doorway, breathing heavily.

Gillian had but a moment to observe that they looked dreadful, with torn and bloody clothing, disheveled hair, and swollen lips and eyes.

"Gillian, you must come quickly," Benjamin said, his eyes dark with concern. "Spencer has been gravely injured, and he's asking for you."

TWENTY-FOUR

The ride to Gallows Hill seemed to take forever, even though Benjamin rode his mount as if they were being chased by the devil himself. The wind whipped Gillian's hair in her face as the countryside flew past in a blur. She clung to Benjamin's waist as if her life depended upon it, as indeed it did. A throw from a horse at this speed would likely kill her, if not injure her severely.

Pierce and Phineas followed some distance behind, unable to keep up with Benjamin's wild gallop. Gillian sobbed with relief when she finally saw the winking lights of a fire in the distance and knew they were almost there.

Benjamin thundered up to the site, sliding off the horse in one easy motion, reaching up to help Gillian down. Lifting her skirts, she ran toward Spencer, who lay on a cloak, his head cradled in his mother's lap.

"Spencer!" she breathed in horror, dropping to her knees beside him. "Oh my God, what happened?"

"Edward Trask shot him," Rosemary said, her voice shaking with anger. "That bastard shot my son."

Gillian reached for Spencer's hand, thankful when she felt the instant warmth flow between them. He was alive.

She leaned over him, smoothing the hair back from his face. His skin was deathly pale, his eyes closed. Bridget's sister Sarabeth sat on the other side of him, her eyes redrimmed from crying. She held what looked like a long strip of torn petticoat to a spot in his midsection, soaked with blood.

Sarabeth clutched her arm. "Where are Bridget and the others?" she asked, her voice choked with tears. "Are they all right?"

"Everyone is well," Gillian said. "A carriage has been sent to fetch them and will soon bring them here." She gazed back down at Spencer, fighting back tears. "I must look at the wound," she said.

Rosemary looked at her doubtfully. "Perhaps we should wait for Phineas."

"He'll be here shortly. He rides with Pierce just behind us. Please, I must see what happened to him."

Rosemary nodded reluctantly and Sarabeth lifted the cloth from Spencer's abdomen. Gillian gasped as blood oozed out of a small hole just to the left of his stomach. Quickly she pressed the cloth back down. The location of the wound was far more grave than she expected. Gillian closed her eyes, holding back a sob.

"Nay," Rosemary whispered, stricken. "Tell me my son is going to be well. Tell me."

"I . . . I don't know," Gillian said, swallowing the despair in her throat. "Why did Edward Trask shoot him?"

Lemuel stepped forward. "I tried to disarm him," he said unsteadily. "I failed. Spencer deliberately put himself between me and the ball. I owe him my life."

"Two other men are dead," Rosemary said quietly. "Pierce slew one of them, and Spencer took the life of Jack Soward. Jack was trying to kill him, Gillian. It was self-defense."

"I know," Gillian said softly. "He would never take the life of a man otherwise."

She glanced over her shoulder to where Edward Trask now lay, unconscious and tightly bound. Thomas Soward, also trussed up, had been laid out beside Edward. There was no sign of the dead men.

Rosemary's voice dripped with contempt. "I retrieved the pistol while the others subdued Edward. And I would have personally shot Edward myself had not Lemuel restrained me."

Gillian's eyes filled with tears as she tenderly smoothed back the hair on Spencer's forehead. "I do not think I could love you more," she whispered to him. "My wonderful, reckless hero."

At that moment, Pierce and Phineas rode up. Phineas quickly dismounted and rushed to his son's side, exchanging a worried glance with his wife. He lifted the cloth and then ripped the rest of Spencer's shirt off his chest and abdomen. After a quick examination, he sat back on his heels, his expression a mixture of profound disbelief and sadness.

"Nay," he whispered. "It cannot be."

Gillian leaned down and pressed her lips against Spencer's cheek. Then she grasped his hand, feeling the familiar jolt of warmth surge between them. "Hold on, love," she whispered.

To her surprise, Spencer suddenly opened his eyes. "Gillian," he said hoarsely. "Thank God you are well. Is the curse . . . broken?"

"It is," she said, her voice catching. "The ruse worked perfectly. It appears you were quite busy."

He tried to smile but winced instead. "Just another tedious day in the life of a boring physician."

"Oh, Spencer," she said, resting her cheek against his.

"Father," she heard him say, and Phineas grasped his other hand.

"We're going to get to you the clinic, son," he said, but Gillian heard his voice waver. "You're going to be fine."

"I'm not . . . and we both know it," Spencer gasped. "I'm bleeding inside. You can't stop it."

"I can stop it," Gillian said quietly. "I can try."

Spencer narrowed his eyes. "No. I won't allow it. The wound is mortal. It could kill you as well."

"It won't," she said determinedly.

"How do you know? Have you ever tried to heal this serious an injury?"

"Nay, but that will not stop me. I'm going to try."

He tried to sit up but fell back to the ground in agony. "Please, Gillian, I beg of you, don't risk it. When she shook her head, he turned to his father. "Stop her, please," he pleaded.

"He can't," Gillian said softly. "No one can. Now, I ask everyone to move back."

For a moment, Rosemary just stared at her. "Can you . . . save him?"

"I'll try."

Rosemary nodded, carefully laying Spencer's head on the ground and stepping away. Looking increasingly frightened, Sarabeth also hastened away.

"No, Father," Spencer said again, writhing in pain. "Don't let her do this."

Gillian stood, putting a hand on Phineas's arm. "You must trust me. I love him."

Phineas gazed at her intently for a long moment and then also took a few steps back. Gillian knelt by Spencer's side.

"You are my heart and soul," she whispered to him. "I'm not going to let you leave me."

He grasped her hand with surprising strength. "No matter what happens, I never will. Just promise that if you cannot save me, you'll stop before you bring injury to yourself."

"Spencer . . ."

"Promise me, Gillian."

"I don't want to believe that . . ."

"Damn it, woman, just grant me this wish," he gasped, writhing in pain.

"I . . . I promise," she said, her eyes blurring with tears.

"Then I trust you to keep your word," he said, letting his hand slip from hers and back to the ground. "Be careful, love."

"My heart is with you," she whispered back as he closed his eyes.

She bent over him, her hair framing his face. Murmuring soft words of encouragement, she carefully placed her hand on the bandage over his wound and closed her eyes.

The air had gained a bitter edge in the night, and Gillian welcomed the sensation, letting it wash over her face and heighten her mind. The cool wind blew her hair about her eyes, and every sound seemed distinct and clear: the leaves rustling, the crickets chirping, and the crackle of wood in what was left of the fire.

She concentrated hard, finding the source of his injury and taking it inside herself. She felt Spencer stiffen beneath her and knew he had felt the connection. The pain was more intense than she had expected, the wound far more complex that she'd ever imagined. He was bleeding inside, and badly.

She opened herself to him and the pain swamped her, swirling and clawing at her. Her muscles stiffened and her hands clenched into frozen fists. A knot formed in her forehead, expanding outward until she thought she would explode. Still she held firm, refusing to give up.

Again and again his pain slapped at her in icy waves. Battered, she felt her own body start to weaken. Her lungs ached and she gasped, suffocating. Panic clutched at her heart and squeezed until she felt her own consciousness dim.

At that moment, she suddenly felt as if he stood beside her. She could smell his scent and feel his presence in and around her. She could sense not only his suffering and sadness, but also an utter peacefulness, as if he had already accepted what she could not.

"Nay," she gasped, wrenching her hand from his abdomen and throwing herself atop his body. Tears streamed down her face.

"Nay, Spencer," she sobbed, her heart breaking. "Please, don't leave me."

She felt his hand rise to stroke her hair. "Courage, Gillian," he murmured softly.

"I'm not going to let you go."

"You . . . have to. You saw the truth for yourself."

"How can I?" she cried. "I love you."

"I love you, too," he said and then winced in pain. "And now . . . your future is secure."

She heard a sound and looked up through her tears to see Hannah and her sisters alight from the carriage.

"Help," she said, sobbing, and they rushed over to her side. "You must help me save him."

Hannah looked worriedly at Spencer. "We cannot," she said gently. "We do not have the skills to do so."

A fresh stream of tears ran down her face. "But you must," she pleaded. "There must be something we can do. The circle of four. I cannot do it alone."

Hannah lifted her skirts and knelt down next to Gillian. She looked at Spencer who fought bravely to hold on to his last vestiges of consciousness, still grasping Gillian's hand tightly in his own.

"Tell her to let me go," Spencer said hoarsely. "She must."

Hannah looked between them and then put her hand on Gillian's shoulder. "If you must do this, you will have to reach deep within yourself," she said softly. "You have to summon the power to heal him with every fiber of your being."

"I tried," Gillian said, swallowing a sob. "Enough so that I'd give my own life in exchange for his. But the wound is mortal. How can I save him from death?"

Hannah tucked a stray strand of hair behind Gillian's ear.

"I can only offer advice. Don't rely solely on your magic," she offered quietly. "Use also the power of your love."

For a moment Gillian gazed at Hannah, a glimmer of hope shining in the distance. "Thank you, Mother," she said softly.

"Go carefully, child," Hannah said. "Every gift has a price. Beware the abyss."

Determinedly Gillian laid her hands on Spencer's abdomen. Closing her eyes, she cleared the doubt from her mind and let the depth of her love for him wash over her. Soon she felt a heat envelop her as if she'd been securely wrapped in a warm quilt.

"Reach for the fire in your soul," she heard Hannah whisper. "Open yourself to it fully and completely. From your heart to his."

"From my heart to yours," Gillian murmured. "From my soul to yours."

Beneath her eyelids, she saw of a vivid display of colors explode into a rich and elaborate tapestry of gold, orange, pink, and red. The display was so beautiful, so breathtaking, Gillian could hardly bear the dazzling radiance.

"The color of love," she marveled in awe. "It's magnificent."

At once her senses heightened, and she could sense the purity of the air and taste the richness of the soil of Mother Earth. As if she stood in front of a mirror, she saw herself in her own destiny and recognized hers and Spencer's part in the eternal cycle of life.

"He belongs to me," she whispered. "We are as one."

This time, unlike the cold and exhaustion that had consumed her on the first try at healing him, a calm serenity filled her mind. The fire within her began to swell, flowing out from her heart to her hands and fingertips. Concentrating, she directed the heat directly toward his wound.

To her dismay, she felt a blast of freezing air in return.

A discordant melody filled her ears, buzzing uncomfortably at first and then rising to a howling, piercing shriek.

"Nay," she gasped as the cold began to penetrate her hands, forcing the warmth back.

Coldness slammed into her again and again, clawing at her and yanking her out of her warmth. She tried desperately to fight it, but something or someone was in direct violation of her will.

Death.

She faced death.

"I'm not going to let you have him," Gillian shouted. "Not without a fight."

Clenching her teeth, Gillian summoned every ounce of concentration she had, keeping the heat steadily on his injury. She swayed violently, rocked by blast after blast of freezing air. Her lungs ached and she felt nearly frozen. A monstrous echo reverberated constantly in her head, creating excruciating pain and taunting her to release him and relieve the agony.

"Release him!" she said between gritted teeth. "He's mine."

As she watched in terror, a cold, icy chasm opened. She opened her mouth to scream, but no sound issued forth. From inside its black frozen depths, a cacophony of discordant sounds rang in her head until she sobbed in anguish.

"Nay!" she screamed again.

A dark, howling wind swirled around her, pulling and tearing at her hair, face, and body. Feelings of anger, betrayal, and fury flooded over and into Gillian, weaving and tightening a mantle of pain until she could barely contain it. Dimly she could hear the worried voices of the others around her, arguing and talking, but she could no longer make out what they said.

Slowly, she felt herself slipping toward the abyss, the heat ebbing from her body. She was aware enough to know her strength was fading, even though her will was strong. Her hands were numb, and she realized that she now stood on the edge of the chasm, looking down into its dark depths. How easy it would be to fall into it and join Spencer there. If they could not be together in life, at least they could be together in death.

She teetered on the edge but was suddenly yanked back into strong, warm arms that steadied her.

Spencer.

Sobbing, she turned and threw her arms around him.

His voice whispered in her ear, "Be strong. I am with you."

Clinging to him, Gillian felt a surge of strength and recognized that there was one thing in life she believed in above all else: love. Her life, her destiny was meant to be with Spencer Reeves.

And she would not give him up. Not now, not ever.

Summoning an inner power, she cloaked herself until she was safe and buffered from the icy clutch of death. Remaining completely still, she imagined herself and Spencer growing together through life, seeing the children they would have and experiencing the moments of happiness and sadness they would share.

Heat again emanated from her body. She could feel Spencer's presence beside her, strong and solid. With a rush of joy, she knew in her heart that at last she had won.

They had won.

Lifting a hand in victory, she turned toward Spencer's presence beside her to celebrate, when a wave of blackness abruptly slammed into her and she toppled over into the darkness.

TWENTY-FIVE

Spencer came back to consciousness slowly. He had a vague recollection of being in the worst fight of his life. He tried to sit up, but every muscle, every bone in his body screamed in pain. Reaching down, he felt a thick bandage wrapped around his midsection. At once, the events at Gallows Hill came racing back to him.

"Gillian!" he cried out.

His father quickly rose from the armchair by the fire and grasped his hand tightly. "Thank God, Spencer," he said, his face etched with deep lines of worry. "I wasn't certain we'd ever get you back."

He dipped a ladle into a bowl of water and pressed it to Spencer's mouth. Spencer drank greedily and then gripped his father's hand.

"Gillian," he said hoarsely. "Where is she?"

Phineas looked at his son, lines of sadness etched deeply on his face. "She's abed," he said softly. "She's yet to awaken since . . . that night. What she did for you—I've never seen anything like it."

Spencer swore softly. "How long have I lain here? How long has it been?"

"Six days," Phineas said softly. "I'm sorry, son, but I fear her situation is quite grave. With every day, she's slipping away from us."

"I have to see her," Spencer said, trying to struggle into a sitting position. "You must take me to her."

"You are in no condition to move," his father said sternly. "You'll rip open the wound and the bleeding will start anew. Then all Gillian has done for you will have been for naught."

"And just what has she done?" he said bitterly. "Given her life for mine?"

"You offered the same for her," Phineas said quietly. "She gave no less."

"That is unacceptable."

"It is her gift to you. I'd advise you to take it."

"I don't want it. I want *her.* Let me see her. I know I can help her."

Phineas sighed. "Her mother and sisters sit with her. If there were anything that could be done, it would have been done long ago."

"But I'm a physician," Spencer argued. "Perhaps there is something they have not thought of."

"Have you forgotten that I, too, am a physician?" Phineas said, grief and despair ripping into his voice. "I assure you I have administered everything potion and treatment that I could think of except for bloodletting and leeching. Her mother would not permit it."

Spencer managed a smile. "The apple apparently does not fall far from the tree. Likely, Hannah does not subscribe to the Humoral Theory either."

Phineas looked at him in bafflement. "What are you talking about?"

"Never mind," Spencer said, sighing. "We have to save Gillian."

"But how? I am not able to help her. Her condition is . . . beyond me."

Spencer struggled to get up again. "If I could just get out of this infernal bed . . ."

His father put a hand on his arm. "I'm sorry, Spencer.

If I could, I'd give my life for her. She's given me back my son. What more could a man ask for?"

"Her," Spencer said softly. "I want her back."

Spencer waited until his father had fallen asleep in the chair before carefully moving himself into a sitting position. He'd rested all day, spoken with his mother and Juliet, eaten as much solid food as he could manage, mentally and physically preparing himself for a visit to Gillian's room. He'd even managed to convince his father to help him walk to the chamber pot on two occasions, mostly just to get the feel of his legs beneath him again.

The pain had been excruciating but bearable. He would not wait another minute to see her.

Ever so slowly, he pulled his legs to the side of the bed and stood. He paused a moment until the wave of pain passed, and then took a step forward, bracing himself with a hand on the bedpost. He made it to the door and quietly opened it, leaving it slightly ajar for his return. The walk down the hallway was a short one, but Spencer felt as though the journey took hours. When he reached her door, he was relieved to see it was not closed. With one hand he pushed it open and stepped inside.

Gillian lay still on the bed, her eyes closed, her magnificent red hair spread out on the pillow beneath her. Hannah sat beside her in a chair. She didn't look surprised to see him.

"I knew you'd come," she said softly. "Here, sit in the chair."

She rose to help him, and he accepted her assistance. He sank into the chair stiffly, suppressing a groan of pain that rose to his lips. She smiled once at him before bending down to press a kiss against Gillian's cheek. Then, to Spencer's surprise, she left the room, leaving the two of them alone.

Spencer leaned forward, taking Gillian's cold hand in his. In the flickering light of the fire, her hair looked more gold than red. Long black lashes rested against pale cheeks; the freckles he had once admired were now faded. He thought it odd that her body seemed so very small. For the first time since he had met her, he realized how very delicate she really was.

"Strength," he murmured. "You've more strength than a score of men, and yet you've the fragility of a flower. My dearest Gillian. From whence have you come?"

Reaching up, he gently pulled back the blanket that covered her body. She'd been dressed in a thin white bed gown that clung to her body. He engraved every line of her form into his memory: the perfectly proportioned legs, narrow shoulders, flat stomach, and creamy expanse of her neck. He found himself gazing intently at the graceful column of her neck, noticing the small curved indentation he'd never had a chance to kiss.

He stood, ignoring a fresh wave of pain. "Come back to me, Gillian," he whispered, bending over her and pressing his lips to hers.

"My love," he murmured against her mouth, remembering the words she had whispered to him. "My heart to yours. My soul to yours."

He took a deep breath and then closed his eyes, placing his hand over her heart. Nothing happened. No miracles, no sign from heaven.

"Concentrate," he growled. "Concentrate, damn you."

He squeezed his eyes shut, praying and willing with all his might that something would happen. To his astonishment, he soon became aware of a distant flickering of light just beyond the darkness of his eyelids.

"Come here," he muttered to the light. "I'm waiting."

He imagined himself reaching out a hand, and soon the faraway speck became brighter. As he watched with a mixture of awe and trepidation, the light suddenly exploded into flames, twisting and dancing in a myriad of colors. He threw up a hand, shielding himself from the dazzling display of purple, red, and white tendrils of fire that embraced him, caressing him and heating every pore and crevice of his body. Heat shot through him in a sensation that was exquisitely painful and bittersweet. He gasped for air as his lungs and body became one with the mysterious fire. With enormous effort, he lifted his hands above his head.

I am with you, Gillian. From my soul to yours.

The fire flared up around him, roaring to life, consuming him, yet this time without pain. Just beyond it, the most poignant melody he'd ever heard in his life filled the air. The sound brought to mind everything he'd ever held precious: the comforting arms of his mother soothing a hurt, the taste of a warm cinnamon bun, cold snowflakes on his tongue, and the memory of his first real kiss stolen behind the blacksmith's barn. He threw back his head and laughed, welcoming the heat until he was completely ablaze with it.

Come back to me, Gillian.

Beneath his hands, he felt Gillian arch her back and then gasp for breath. His eyes snapped open and he watched in fascination as her eyelashes fluttered and then lifted.

He didn't dare to breathe as astonishment and confusion flashed in her magnificent emerald eyes. Then her gaze focused on him and she gave him the most beautiful smile he'd ever seen.

"How . . . ?" she whispered weakly. "How did you do it?"

"Have you forgotten your own words?" he said softly, winding a strand of her glorious red hair around his finger. "You shared your soul with me. We are as one. For now and forever more."

* * *

One month later

Every muscle and bone in Spencer's body ached. He was fairly certain his feet would never feel the same, and even his mouth hurt from smiling. He must have shaken a thousand hands, and even his fingers screamed in agony.

Weddings were pure hell.

Except for Gillian. He had never seen her look as beautiful as she had today, clad in a stunning ivory gown edged with yards of lace and pearls. The gown had been his mother's, but he thought it suited Gillian perfectly in both its simplicity and elegance. Her magnificent red hair had been pinned up off her shoulders, accentuating her slender white neck and causing him to spend the entire day fantasizing about the different ways he was going to kiss it. Now, at last, they were finally alone.

"This has been the most wonderful day of my life," Gillian said, walking into their bedroom and sinking into an armchair in front of the hearth. A fire crackled merrily and someone had already plumped the pillows and turned back the bed. A pitcher of hot spiced wine with two goblets stood on the table, sending the sweet scent of cinnamon and cloves wafting into the air. He sighed a breath of relief to be finally released from the day's duties.

She bent forward to remove her shoes, giving him a tantalizing glimpse of her bosom and a reminder of what was yet to come. "I don't think I've ever been more exhausted," she said. "I never knew how much work it required to get wedded."

Spencer laughed, tugging at his neck cloth until it fell free. He tossed it carelessly over the back of a chair and then removed his waistcoat.

"Women don't suffer at all," he said, kicking off his boots. "It is far more agonizing for men, who must wait an interminably long time to get to the part of the day that holds the most interest for them."

"And what part might that be?" she asked innocently while rolling her stockings down one by one and sliding them off her legs. Spencer felt his blood heat and swallowed hard.

"The bedchamber," he said, tearing his gaze away and kicking off his boots. "Frankly, it's all I could think about this past month. Do you really think men give a damn what color the flowers are or what's on the menu for the wedding feast?"

"You didn't care for the roast sturgeon?" she asked, a teasing light in her eyes.

"If you must know, I swallowed without chewing in hopes that it would move the evening along quicker," he said, ripping off his stockings and casting them to the floor.

She laughed. "I must admit that sharing our wedding with two other couples did make the evening a bit longer than might have been truly representative of a conventional wedding day." She leaned back in the chair, stretching her legs out in front of her. "But it was perfect. How splendid it was to be a part of all that happiness. Did you see how Alexandra nearly cried as she exchanged vows with Pierce? It was so touching."

He leaned forward in his chair, feeling a soft tug on his heart for his sweet, sentimental wife. "You cried when Lemuel pledged his love for Lynette," he reminded her.

She sighed dreamily. "I've never seen him so happy. If only Mother and Father could have witnessed it. They would have been so proud."

Spencer stood, standing and stretching out a hand to her. "As they would of you. You were magnificent today, Gillian. Beautiful, charming, and gracious. No matter where I looked, all I could see was you."

She smiled, rising to meet him, putting her arms around his neck. "Tonight we put the past behind us and start anew."

Spencer cupped her cheek. "I admire your confidence. Yet it still troubles me that Edward Trask has come out of this a free man. And Thomas Soward has suffered no real consequences as well."

"His brother is dead," Gillian said quietly. "That is consequence enough. The spell Hannah put on him will erase any memory he had of the night at Gallows Hill. He, and everyone else in town, will believe his brother was killed in a brawl with an out-of-town ruffian. I'm confident he'll no longer be a threat to us."

"And the Trasks?"

"Edward Trask is a free man only because it would have been far more harmful than good to this town to bring up the matter of witchcraft once again. I assure you, the Trasks have far greater problems than us to face. They have been blessed with the gift of a moral conscience, something that will likely concern them for much time to come. But whatever happens, I believe that in this life we all receive our due in one way or another. I prefer to leave it in fate's hands."

He smiled at her conviction. His wife, his heart, his soul. How he loved her!

Reaching up, he tugged the pins free from her hair, letting the long red strands tumble freely about her shoulders, catching the light of the blazing fire in the hearth. Slowly his thumbs stroked the skin at her throat where he could see her pulse beating. He bent over, pressing a kiss on that pulse, and felt his loins tighten when he heard her catch her breath.

"Tonight we will think of nothing else but each other," he murmured. "No curses, no witches, no spells. Only you and me sharing our first night together as husband and wife."

She nodded, her emerald eyes luminous. "Agreed."

He moved his mouth against her cheek and ear, his teeth grazing the delicate skin. Just holding her, he felt the day's exhaustion fall from him. He breathed deeply, drawing both the scent and strength of her into his lungs. Gently turning her around, he unfastened the ties at the back of her gown and pushed the material off her shoulders to her waist. She wore a thin white chemise beneath, the square neck edged with a delicate muslin frill. Carefully she stepped out of the gown and then her petticoats. He gently laid the voluminous material over the chair.

"Your mother was kind to lend her gown to me," Gillian said softly, fingering the soft material. He had never seen her look so lovely, enchanting, and serene. "You once told me she was a good woman, and now I know that for myself. I am now fortunate enough to have two new mothers."

He smiled, running a hand over her shoulder and watching her shiver with awareness. "My mother knows me well," he agreed. "She said I'd find you irresistible in this gown, and she was right. It's taken every ounce of self-will to keep myself from removing it from you until now."

"Then what's next?"

With a growl, he scooped her off the floor and into his arms. She protested, but he ignored her, carrying her to the bed and gently depositing her upon it. Then he returned to the table by the hearth, where he poured them both a goblet of the thickly spiced wine. He sat on the bed and handed her a cup. She took a sip, regarding him over the rim.

"I know what you're thinking," she said softly.

He raised an eyebrow. "You do?"

"You're thinking I'm afraid. Afraid of what will happen in this bed between the two of us."

He sipped the wine thoughtfully. "Are you?"

She smiled. "A little, perhaps. Mostly because the idea of joining is still so unfamiliar to me. But you are not. That's why I know that as long as we are together, I am safe. I want to join with you, Spencer. I have since the first moment I met you. 'Twas my destiny all along. I just had to find my way, just as you had to find yours."

Spencer placed his goblet on the bedside table and reached out, taking back the cup he had just given her. She leaned back against the pillows as he bent forward, lowering his mouth to hers in a warm, possessive kiss. A hot jolt of desire shot through him as she reached up to touch his face, her fingers brushing against the newly formed whiskers on his cheeks. She felt so soft against his muscle, so fragile against his bulk. But he knew she was so much more inside, stronger than anyone he'd ever met.

Mine.

He moved his mouth over hers, hungry for the taste of her, eager to claim what at last was his. His lips devoured her softness, explored the silky caverns of her mouth, and stroked the sweet velvet of her tongue.

Wishing to see all of her, he tugged on her chemise, pulling it up and over her head. At last she lay naked on the bed, trying modestly to cover her breasts with her hands. Her cheeks were flushed a delightful pink as he bent down to press a kiss to the secret hollow in her neck that he'd come to have a fondness for.

"When will you remove your garments?" she asked, trying to hide her discomfort.

Without a word, Spencer yanked his shirt over his head with one hand and then pulled off his wedding trousers, kicking them to the floor in a heap. He laughed when Gillian gasped in disapproval.

" 'Tis no way to treat such fine garments," she scolded him.

He reached for her. "I'll buy another damn pair," he murmured, a jolt of heat shooting through him as their bare bodies met.

She shivered either with desire or cold, so he rolled over on top of her, pulling the bedcovers over them. He smiled as she snuggled against him, unaware that the motion caused an unbearable need to take her at once. He kissed her again, coaxing her mouth and then her tongue into hot sensual foreplay.

She twisted in his arms, arching her back and molding the soft contours of her body against him. Reluctantly he pulled back, reminding himself to take it slowly.

Grinning, he reached over to the bedside table and dipped his finger into the cup of wine.

She watched him, her eyes wide. "What are you doing?"

He traced his wet finger around her nipple. "Tasting you," he said.

He lowered his mouth to take the nipple between his lips and was rewarded by a sharp gasp as she fell back against the pillow.

"It feels magnificent," she sighed and then moaned as his tongue circled again and again. His hands explored the soft lines of her waist and hips, and she wound her fingers in his hair, squirming beneath him. Spencer felt his own breathing become shallow and more difficult as she became bolder with desire, running her hands across the muscles in his shoulders and chest and then dipping ever lower toward his abdomen.

He kissed her again, his lips burning, his heart racing. His arousal became more intense, pounding through him like the steady beat of a drum. A hot tide of passion roared through him, his blood boiling as if it had turned to liquid fire.

"Gillian," he said softly, trying to quiet the thunder of his heart, "let me love you now."

She opened her eyes, the look in them so trusting that he felt a hot ache in his throat. "Please, Spencer," she said, her eyes half closed. "Love me."

He stroked the silk of her inner thigh and brushed against the soft curls of her womanhood. He touched her, marveling at the moisture he met and knowing she was ready for him. Gently he parted her legs and leaned between them, his hands cradling her hips. Slowly he inched forward until he pressed against her opening and then paused.

"I fear this may hurt a bit at first," he started to say and then stopped in surprise when she grasped his hips and pulled him forward.

"I'm not afraid anymore. I want you to show me how to love you."

His restraint thus shattered, he plunged into her, feeling only a brief moment of resistance. He paused guiltily when she inhaled sharply.

"I'm sorry, love," he said, between gritted teeth.

She opened her eyes. "Does it hurt you, too?" she asked innocently.

He didn't dare breathe. She sheathed him so perfectly, so tight and wet, he felt ready to explode. He felt a groan escape his lips. Sweat beaded his forehead as he fought to remain perfectly still.

"Not in the same way," he managed to get out. "It's just that you are so damn beautiful, it is hard for me to contain myself."

He saw her eyes flash with wonder. "You think I'm beautiful?" she asked.

"Gillian," he groaned, "are you begging for compliments? At a time like this?"

A bright flare of desire sprang into her eyes, nearly driving him mad. Slowly she ran her fingertips across his back and buttocks until he thought he'd simply die from need.

"I've never felt this way," she whispered. "Teach me how to love you."

Groaning, Spencer lowered his mouth to capture hers, moving his hips. He'd made love before, but she made it feel like his first time. There was something in the air, something deeper, more passionate, more magical than anything he'd ever experienced before.

It took her only a minute to capture his rhythm and meet him thrust for thrust. The warmth of her soft skin, her body arching up for him, was intoxicating. A dim part of his mind reminded him that she was untouched before him, but something more primal and needy had overtaken him. He slid his hands into her hair, winding the silky strands about his fingers, gripping the softness in his fists. He could feel her essence, smell her unique scent, and taste the salt on her skin.

My witch. My wife.

She was magical, alluring, gentle, and kind. And so much more.

A primal need burned inside him, flaring up and scorching his heart. His thrusts became harder and harder, more determined and fierce. He couldn't control his need, his desire any longer. He shuddered as she wrapped her legs around him, squeezing him as hard as she could. Her fingers dug into the muscles in his shoulders, but he barely felt it. Her breathing now came in rapid, shallow gasps, matching his own. Not willing to share even that, his mouth reached down to claim hers, stealing her very breath.

"I . . . love . . . you," he heard her murmur, her mouth against his ear. Then she moaned in ecstasy and he felt her body tremble uncontrollably. Moments later, he soared to his own astounding, shuddering climax.

"Gillian," he cried, spilling his seed into her with a fiery explosion of heat. Spent, he collapsed upon her chest, not daring to breathe for fear it might be his last.

It was Gillian who moved first, wiggling and squirming until he rolled off. Just the same, he kept her tight in his arms, refusing to release her.

"I fear I have not provided a suitable first lesson," he said wryly when he could speak at last.

She reached up to touch his cheek, looking at him with such awe and admiration that he would have laughed if he hadn't been so damned exhausted.

"I fear I might not survive a second joining," she said happily. "Spencer, it was the most wonderful, extraordinary experience I've ever had. I thought I might explode into a thousand tiny pieces."

He chuckled, letting his hand trail lightly across her back. "I assure you, I can do better."

Her emerald eyes lit up. "Really?"

Growling, he rolled over, pinning her beneath him. "You've truly bewitched me, woman. Ever since we met, I could think of nothing else but you. And now that you're mine, I'm never, ever letting you go."

She lifted her lips to press a kiss on his chin. "You have naught to worry about because I'll never go. We're together forever. Remember?"

She gave him a smile so dazzling, so beautiful, that he felt his body stir again. She was a witch, indeed. *His* witch.

For a moment, he lay back on the pillow, staring at the ceiling, astonished at the sense of fulfillment he felt. He no longer wondered why she was different, or whether she was a witch, or even why he had been chosen for her. He no longer had a need to know. Whatever the reason, they were together, bound for all eternity by a force greater than he. Love.

For him, that was magic enough.

Contemporary Romance by
Kasey Michaels